*A Novel*

# SAINTWOOD:

# REVELATIONS

## JOHANNA DELACRUZ

# DISCLAIMER

# CHAPTER 1

## CARRINGTON

**Carrington**

"I'm going to beat him with every inch of his life!" Christine said.

"You will do no such thing," Kate told her.

"Kate! He put food dye in my shampoo." Christine pointed at her green hair.

"It will eventually wash out." Kate shrugged.

"Ugh." Christine stomped to her bedroom.

In case you're wondering, Kate and Christine are my two older sisters. Yeah, I added food dye in Christine's shampoo and chose a green this time. I enjoy riling her because it keeps things interesting. Hell, I love riling all my siblings.

"Carri!" Mason said.

I strolled out of my bedroom and over to the second-floor railing. "Yeah, Mas."

Mason beckoned me with his finger as I sighed and came downstairs. Mason is the oldest and in charge of all of us since our parents' death. He deals with all of us, including Kate, Charles, Theresa, Joseph, Christine, me, and Elliot. There's at least one- or two-years' difference in our ages. We all live with Mason and his wife Luciana, who we refer to as Luci.

I reached the main floor and strolled over to Mason.

"I received word from the school that they suspended you again. Would you care to explain why?"

"They need to chill out." I shrugged.

"Putting super glue on a teacher's seat or causing mass destruction with pies is not chilling out."

"What's wrong with pies? Everyone likes pie, especially coconut cream."

My answer didn't amuse Mason because he needs a sense of humor.

"Get your shit together, or I'll send you to military school."

I gave Mason a look as he walked away from me. Mason wouldn't play with us. If we did something wrong, he would manage it.

"I see you're at it again," Charles said from the living room.

I swiveled to face him and walked towards Charles sitting on the couch. I sat down on the couch's arm. "People are too serious at that damn school."

"Carri, you have a few months left before you graduate from Saintwood."

"Then I'll grow up to be a boring-ass adult. Oh, joy." I rolled my eyes.

Charles gave me a sympathetic expression. "It's not the first time Saintwood will survive a Jones and won't be the last."

"That is doubtful." I sighed.

"Hang in there. Now excuse me, I must meet Greg, Frank, and Maurice." Charles got up and left.

Charles hung out with Greg Hartley, Frank Shaw, and Maurice Frazier while growing up. They seemed like decent guys, but

each had issues. Greg enjoys gambling, Maurice drinks, and Frank likes the girls.

Maurice belongs to the Frazier family. Our family does business with the Fraziers from time to time. I didn't care for the Fraziers because their deals bordered on the underhanded.

"Off the arm of the couch. Were you born in the wild?" Luci entered the room.

"That is Joseph." I moved off the couch's arm.

Luci looked at me with that face I knew too well. I walked over to her.

"Carri, your brother wants the best for all of you."

"Mason wants us to live a boring ass life as he does. I'm not into boring and prefer fun. Life is to live, not to exist."

"Such a free spirit you are. I admire that quality about you."

I smiled. Yep, I'm a free spirit, while my siblings had distinct personalities to them. I walked away from Luci and came out back to find Joseph talking to animals. Welcome to the animal kingdom and the animal whisperer.

"Are you speaking to your woodland creatures? The last time I checked, you're not Snow White or Cinderella," I told Joseph.

Joseph gave me an annoyed glance. "Carri, you would do well to spend time in nature. It clears the mind and the soul."

"Yo, Grizzly Adams, I'm not into your hippy ways or hugging any damn tree."

Joseph rolled his eyes.

I will never understand how my brother turned out to be a hippy. He missed the sixties since he wasn't born yet.

A knife whizzed past my head and landed into a bird.

Joseph swiveled his head. "Listen, you psychopath. No one has time for your bullshit!"

Elliot walked over, yanked his knife out of a bird, and wiped it on the grass. "Joseph, birds carry diseases like most of our family's business associates." Elliot stood up.

"That is the problem with this family. They don't value human life," Joseph said.

"Only because you believe there's good in people when there isn't. I'm the youngest, and I even realized this."

"Fine, then you can deal with Christine."

Elliot glared at Joseph.

Did I mention my brothers were insane? You have Mason, the head of the family, and Charles, who did some shady shit. Joseph is the resident hippy. And Elliot is the psycho. Then you have me who prefers fun.

I left my brothers to bicker. Theresa walked into the kitchen as I entered the house.

"I see you're at it again," Theresa said.

I shrugged.

"Carri, one day, you'll realize that not everything is fun and games." Theresa poured a cup of coffee.

"Theresa, Dad enjoyed a good joke next to anyone. This family is too serious."

"You're like Dad." Theresa smiled.

That made me feel good. I'm the most like our father, which irked the others.

"Remember, one day, you'll meet someone, and they may not enjoy your pranks."

"I doubt it."

Most girls worried too much about insignificant things and didn't enjoy themselves. Unless I found someone that understood me, I prefer the single lifestyle.

# CHAPTER 2

## THERE'S MORE TO LIVING THAN TRICKS, OR IS THERE?

**Carrington**

After the school lifted my suspension, Mason threatened me with military school if I didn't get my shit together. Yeah, okay. I'll go to college and wreak havoc. Joseph, Theresa, and Christine will be there to keep an eye on things. Kate was moving closer to the college to open a bakery. Charles was getting married at summer's end.

Charles sees Maggie while Theresa dates Grant. Christine is dating Troy, and Joseph is with Mary. My siblings will marry after they graduate from college. Kate had gotten engaged to a fellow, but he died while serving in the military. She refused to date anyone after the guy, and I didn't blame her.

I finished by the grace of God, and Saintwood College accepted me. It's because my family owns the damn school. Our parents helped build it, considering they were wealthy. Mason invested, as did Kate. All of us would become partners in the school. The idea was ridiculous to me.

I pranked my siblings that summer, which earned their wrath and a knife thrown at my head. Thanks, Elliot. Mason punished me and made me endure brutal training with a former drill instructor. I swear my family has no sense of humor.

Why couldn't I have fun? Was that too much to ask?

"Carri!" Charles said.

I groaned and strolled into the living room with my hands shoved in my pockets.

"Maurice tells me you're fighting with his brother."

"Maurice's brother is an idiot, as are the rest of his damn family. He deserved to get his ass beat. How the hell are you friends with him? Better yet, how the hell is Mason doing business with Marty Frazier?"

Mason entered the living room. "That is none of your business."

"The Fraziers are scum, and you know it," I told Mason.

Mason gave me a disapproving expression. "Carri, there are things you don't understand. When you get into the business, you will learn them. Now excuse me, I have a meeting with Edward Morgan." Mason left.

That was the problem with this family. They had their hands in shit they shouldn't. Our parents would turn over in their graves if they knew what my brothers were doing. Mason is brilliant and understands the game, but Charles made the wrong choices.

"I understand you don't care for Fraziers, but Maurice is my best friend, and he's not into what his family is doing," Charles said.

I had my doubts. The rotten apple doesn't fall too far from the corrupt apple tree. Maurice's crooked, as was Frank Shaw. "You need better friends."

Charles walked away as I shook my head. Charles forgets I went to school with his acquaintances. They're not squeaky

clean. Greg had a gambling problem, Maurice had a temper and a drinking issue, and Frank enjoyed little girls. Yeah, those were great friends. God help them if they ever have kids.

I went to bother Joseph, who was communing with nature. I found him sitting in the backyard with his eyes closed, making an ohm sound. What's wrong with my family?

I grabbed an empty pail, filled it with ice-cold water from the outside spigot, and dumped it on Joseph.

"Carri!" Joseph stood up.

I held the empty pail in my hand.

"What the hell is wrong with you?"

"This place bores me."

That's all it took as we duked it out in the backyard. Joseph received a fat lip while I received a bloody nose out of the deal.

We sat there. I handed Joseph a handkerchief while holding a cloth to my nose.

"Must you start shit to cure your boredom?" Joseph asked me.

"I have to do something. I pissed off Charles, going after one of the Frazier brothers."

"Why did you do that?"

"Because he's an idiot, and I hate that family."

"Yeah, well, Mason is meeting with Edward Morgan. The Fraziers reneged on a deal and pulled some shit."

"Then Mason should speak to the big brother because he's into some shady shit."

"What did Charles do?"

"I don't know the details, but Marco Frazier let something slip about Charles negotiating a deal, and it's bad."

"Christ."

I wanted nothing to do with my brother's business dealings. I knew I would go into the family business after I graduated, but whatever they were doing was on them.

"Stay out of it, Carri. I'll talk to Mason."

I raised my hands in defeat. You didn't have to tell me twice since I had enough on my plate without getting involved with shady dealings.

*****

Joseph talked to Mason. I don't know what was said, but Mason warned Charles about his deal. Does my brother listen? No, he's an idiot.

Charles will do what he wants, dragging his idiot friends into the mix. God help us if he and his buddies have children one day, and I'm sure the kids will have the idiot gene passed down to them.

Most of the summer, I harassed my siblings, who threatened to beat my ass. Mason forced me into hard labor to straighten my ass out before attending college. My family was the fun police. Was it my fault I put a cherry bomb in one of Mason's billion bathrooms in the house? No, it's not. However, I got yelled at for doing it while Christine was using one bathroom.

Theresa had to separate us because Christine wanted to hurt me. She tried to destroy Elliot the most when he flung a knife at her, and she beat the hell out of him. Kate played a mediator

between us. It's excellent that she didn't run off, get married, and have kids. We needed her to play peacemaker.

*****

The summer ended, and I was going to college with Theresa, Joseph, and Christine. We would return home around Christmas for Charles's wedding.

We arrived at the campus, and Joseph drove us to the house that we were staying in while we attended college. It made me happy not to live in a dorm since I can't deal with a stuffy roommate. I'm lucky to remain with my siblings, and they're stuffy enough for me.

Joseph pulled into a driveway, and we exited the car.

"Carri." Joseph got my attention.

I looked at him.

"This isn't high school, and the school won't tolerate your obnoxious behavior."

"I'm surprised they tolerate your pompous behavior."

Theresa snickered, and Christine rolled her eyes.

"Lighten up, Joseph. Our family is far from exhibiting good behavior."

"Don't make me call Mason."

"Call him. Mason doesn't scare me, and neither does anyone else." I shrugged.

Christine walked over to me. "Carri, one day, you'll understand why you must conduct yourself properly."

"Well, until then, I'm okay with having fun. The rest of you can worry about yourselves." I grabbed my bags.

That was the problem with my family. They worry too much about people's perceptions of us. People will think what they want. Let them. One day, societies will fear us, making us powerful in our own right.

Now, I intend to enjoy myself. But my life would take an unexpected turn.

# CHAPTER 3

## LIFE IS TO ENJOY

**Carrington**

I settled into school. The courses were okay if you consider your basic classes such as English, math, science, and history fun, which they aren't. The people here were stodgy, so I livened things up a scant.

When I say a scant, I meant a lot by putting cherry bombs in the lavatories. The toilets exploded, causing the school to shut down, so they could fix the plumbing. It earned a trip to the dean's office, and it also won a visit from Mason. Oh, joy.

"What were you thinking?" Mason asked me.

I sat on the couch. "This place needed fun."

Mason didn't like my answer. Mason never enjoyed my answers because Mason wasn't fun.

"Carri, life isn't always about fun and games."

"No, because why should anyone have fun?" I stood up. "People reach a certain age and become old, then wonder why they die early."

Mason gave me his infamous expression. It's the one that says straighten up and fly right, or you're doing hard time. That's the face I got now.

"You have a lot to learn about life. There's more to it than pranks and jokes."

"And you need to lighten up. Not even Dad was serious like you, and he knew how to balance life."

Mason furrowed his brows. "It's amazing how much you're like, Dad. You even resemble him, including his emerald-green eyes."

Out of the eight of us, I'm Dad's mini version, even with our personalities. It's what kept Mason from throttling me.

"Stay out of trouble, and I will handle the school." Mason left. I sat down on the couch.

"Mason should have punished you," Christine said.

"Do you know what your problem is?"

"What?"

"You stick your nose in other's business."

Christine frowned, then stormed out of the room. My sister would be likable if it weren't for her personality, and Troy might help her with it. I'm still wondering how those two were together, considering I like Troy.

Theresa walked into the house with Grant. "How did it go with Mason?"

"It's the same as always. I got a lecture. Then, I mentioned Dad, and that shut Mason up and made him back off from me."

Theresa laughed because she knew Mason's weakness was Dad. Dad and Mason were close. When our parents died, Mason took it hard. Plus, it tasked Mason with raising some of us since we were still in high school.

"I'll visit Kate." I got up and left. I walked to Kate's bakery and entered the building as she directed the workers. I strolled over to her.

She turned to face me. "I hear you're causing trouble."

"Pft, I'm having fun."

Kate gave me an uh-huh look.

"I can't help it if people are boring and need to lighten up." I shrugged.

"Carri, it's okay to have fun, but there's a time and place."

"That is debatable."

"You have four years to get through here, then join Mason in the family business. We must get you there. Now behave." Kate returned to directing workers.

Kate's right, but I'm doubtful. That's one reason I didn't date since most girls didn't understand me or my sense of humor. All they cared about was money.

My family conducted business that I didn't want in my life and told Mason this when he mentioned bringing me into the family business. I'll let him deal with the shady shit.

I walked out of the bakery and ran into someone. I recognized Edward Morgan's kid, Brian Morgan. "What are you doing here?"

"I came to see Kate."

I spoke little to him as he entered the bakery. Mason does business with Brian Morgan's father, a crime boss, and Brian is around Joseph's age. I didn't know him well, but the Morgans were nothing like the Fraziers. The Fraziers were as corrupt as they came. There are six kids in the family, and Maurice was the third brother.

Then you had the Santiagos, who are horrible. Don't get me started on them since I can't stand either family.

As I walked, I heard a familiar, annoying voice.

"Well, well, well. Look, what we have here."

I turned to see Marco with his idiot cronies. "I see they let you out of your cage."

Marco glared at me.

"Didn't anyone tell you that getting your ass kicked over and over makes you a loser?"

"Let's see if that's true." Marco marched towards me.

"Marco!" Someone said.

Marco stopped and cursed to himself. Marty walked towards him. Ooh, big brother was in town. That should be interesting.

Marty and Marco argued as I stood there, bored. Then Marty escorted Marco away. Well, if you consider getting jerked away, we'll go with that.

I strolled down the street, whistling without a care in the world. Let's see. I had four years to survive this shithole, Marco Frazier, my family on my back, and have fun. What could go wrong?

*****

Over the next year, I found out how wrong I was about that question. Not only did I deal with the stodgy school officials who threatened to expel me many times, but Marco Frazier and I fought. I hate that family.

It tasked my family with keeping me in line at school, which they weren't happy about except for Theresa, who agreed with me. She's my favorite sibling, and the others not so much.

Kate opened her bakery, and Charles got married, moving into an enormous house. Why does anyone need such a vast house when there are only two of them? Charles tried to compete with Mason, but I prefer a decent size house myself.

I wonder about my family sometimes. Who was I kidding? I wonder about them all the time.

\*\*\*\*\*

While I dealt with my family and other issues, Maurice, Frank, and Greg married women. My brother Charles attended the weddings, and we didn't because they're not our friends.

\*\*\*\*\*

**Charles**

I had a get-together with everyone at my new house. "Here you go, boys." I handed my friends a glass.

"So, when is this deal going down?" Frank asked.

"In due time, Frankie. I'm working out the final details."

"What if it falls through? I have debts to pay back before my wife finds out," Greg said.

"I told you to stay away from the bookies. How much do you need?"

"A hundred grand," Greg said.

"Fine, I'll lend you the money, but stop gambling."

"I can't wait to tell my wife that we'll be living on easy street, and I won't have to deal with my family." Maurice gulped down his drink and got another one.

"Slow down."

"Charles, I'm enjoying myself. You need to chill." Maurice poured another drink.

*****

**Carrington**

The problem with my brother was he agreed with the Santiagos, whom you couldn't trust. Mason dealt with the Santiagos and the Morgan family, who didn't appreciate secret deals or reneging. It earned you a dirt nap, considering Edward Morgan is a mob boss.

Mason recommended that Charles drop the arrangement, but my idiot brother chose not to listen. It would set in motion what's to come, causing lies upon lies. I would make the mistake of falling in love with someone, resulting in a greater love than I ever imagined.

That's when you'll realize how powerful our family was.

# CHAPTER 4

## ISSUES THAT AREN'T MINE

**Gloria**

Maurice and I exited Charles's house, and I drove us home since Maurice was drunk again. It was a bone of contention between us.

I pulled into the driveway of the tiny house, got out, and helped Maurice inside as he stumbled.

"Baby, we will be on easy street," Maurice slurred.

I shook my head. "Come on. You need to sleep it off." I helped Maurice into the house and upstairs. When he was half in the bag, I learned not to fight with him. It never ended well.

Once we got upstairs, I put him to bed, then left the bedroom. I came downstairs to see the empty beer cans and sighed. I disagreed with Maurice's drunken stupor when I married him. He couldn't hold a job, and I had to work several hours to support us, putting a strain on our marriage.

The front door opened, and Maurice's brother strolled into the house. "Where's my brother?"

"He's upstairs sleeping off his booze-induced night."

I didn't like Maurice's family.

"Tell him that when he sobers up tomorrow, we got a job for him." Maurice's brother tossed cash onto the coffee table. "That is the advancement for the job. If he fucks this up, he can deal with Marty." With that said, he left.

I learned not to touch the money even though the bills were late. I finished tidying up and retired to bed. When a spouse doesn't help, and the other spouse lacks attention, you seek attention elsewhere.

*****

The next day, Maurice woke up, groaning. He came downstairs, found the cash on the table, and came into the kitchen as I made a cup of coffee.

"Did Mateo come by?"

"Yes." I drank my coffee.

"What did he say?"

"They have a job for you. That is the advancement."

"Gloria, about last night...."

"It's fine. I have to leave for work." I placed my cup in the sink. "I'm working a double." I stepped past Maurice, grabbed my purse, and left. Our marriage was rocky, and Maurice's drinking didn't help the situation.

*****

**Carrington**

Joseph and I came out of class and headed to a coffee shop. He wanted coffee, but I didn't enjoy the taste or smell.

We entered, and the place bustled with customers. Both of us stood in line and waited for Joseph to receive his coffee, and I swear my brother was a caffeine addict.

We reached the counter as a woman waited on us. Joseph placed his order as I gazed at the woman, finding her breathtaking.

"Did you want to order something?" The woman asked me.

I read Gloria on her name badge. "Yes, Gloria, I would. I'll have a black coffee."

She beamed. "Two coffees are coming up."

I spotted her dimples. Joseph gave me a weird look as Gloria got our coffees.

"Carri?" Joseph asked, breaking me from my infatuation.

"What?"

"Coffee?"

"Well, we're in a coffee shop." I shrugged.

"You don't consume coffee."

"There's always a first time for everything."

Gloria returned with our coffees. Joseph was going to pay her, but I paid her instead, handing her a twenty. She gave my change to me.

"Keep it," I responded.

Gloria's brows lifted. "That is over seventeen dollars."

"You offered excellent service." I nodded.

We turned and walked away. Gloria didn't know what to think, but I appreciated her dimples.

We exited the coffee shop. I sipped my coffee and spat it out, then dumped the rest of the container.

"You bought coffee, then discard it. Carri, you're a confusing man."

"I prefer dimples." I strode away.

That alerted Joseph to one thing. The woman in the coffee shop attracted me to her.

I knew nothing about Gloria but became smitten with her. With all the girls on campus, there was something about her. My mission was to learn more about her, even if I had to buy a coffee and dispose of it.

Later, I took a stroll by myself and arrived at the coffee shop. It was empty except for Gloria. I opened the door and strode into the place as she was tidying up.

"Oh, I'm sorry. We're closed."

"Oh."

"I should have bolted the door." She hurried to the door and locked it.

"You shouldn't be here alone. It's unsafe."

"It happens when you work a double. I'm usually alone at closing time, so no one bothers me, and that makes me thankful."

"I can stick around until you leave. Then, no one will bother you."

She knitted her eyebrows.

"I'm Carri."

"Oh, I don't know."

"I won't hurt you. I'll keep you company until you leave."

Gloria relaxed. "Okay."

I smiled and watched her go about her business.

"Are you a student?"

"Yeah, I started my second year. My sister graduated, so that leaves my brother and my other sister here until our baby brother arrives."

"Wow, you have a big family."

"You don't know the half of it," I muttered.

"What was that?"

"Nothing." I beamed. "So, do you care if I stay?"

"No, I don't mind. It's nice to speak to someone." Gloria gave me a slight smile.

Something told me that Gloria had few friends or not many people to talk to in her life. She seemed lonely.

"So, how did you end up working in this place?"

She cleaned up. "I didn't have many options. The owner was hiring, and I accepted the job since bills don't pay themselves. It's a decent job."

"What about school?"

"School wasn't for me. It never held my interest."

"I hear you. My family insists I attend so I can join the family business, but I prefer fun."

Gloria had a gorgeous smile that lit up her face. "We all make choices in our lives. Some good, some bad, but they're ours to make." She finished cleaning.

I walked her out. Gloria locked up, and I escorted her to her automobile. When she was safely inside, I lingered until she sped away. I found her intriguing and friendly. She wasn't like the other girls that attended here. I craved to learn more about her, then ask her out.

I wandered home and entered the house.

Joseph greeted me. "Where were you?"

"I took a stroll." I nodded my head, then walked past Joseph and upstairs. I didn't want to discuss Gloria with anyone. It was bad enough that my family knew every aspect of my life, and it was one part that I demanded to keep private.

*****

## Gloria

I arrived home and met a drunk, Maurice.

"Where were you?"

"I was working until closing."

"I better not catch you with any guy, or you'll pay."

"How about you lay off the booze?"

I felt a palm connect across my face. I seized my cheek.

Maurice furrowed his brows. "Gloria...."

I spoke nothing except ran upstairs. It was the first time Maurice had hit me, but it wouldn't be the last time. I would find this out soon enough.

*****

## Carrington

My life was simple until I met Gloria. I didn't realize who she was or what would happen. I enjoyed life, not grasping the idea that meeting her would change events and my perception of life.

The problem was I didn't plan on falling in love with someone who's forbidden, culminating in deceit. The truth would smack

me in the face later. As for now, it made me happy to keep my blissful ignorance, and it would prove a wrong move on my part.

# CHAPTER 5

## FALLING

**Carrington**

I got ready and headed to class. I planned on stopping by the coffee shop after class to visit Gloria. After class was over, I trekked to the coffeehouse, whistling. I was in a good mood, but that's nothing new there. After entering and approaching the counter, I saw Gloria.

"I'll be right with you."

I waited there, smiling.

"What can I get you?" She turned to face me.

That's when I saw the bruise on her cheek. My brows furrowed.

"Hi, Carri." She beamed.

"Hi, Gloria." I studied the bruise but said nothing. I didn't need to draw attention to it, but I'll ask her about it later. "A coffee, please."

"One coffee coming up." She grabbed my coffee.

I wondered about that bruise. It wasn't there yesterday.

Gloria returned with the coffee. I paid for it and offered a genuine smile, which she returned. She needed that smile today. I left the coffee shop, and when I was out of view, I dumped my coffee. Later, I'll return and speak to her.

I had two more classes. Afterward, I returned to the coffee shop to discover Gloria tidying up, and I tapped on the window.

She walked over and let me in, then bolted the door. "Did you need something?"

"I don't want to sound intrusive, but I couldn't help but notice the bruise on your cheek." I pointed to her cheek.

She put her hand on her cheek. "Oh, it's nothing. I'm such a klutz, running into a door in the middle of the night."

It was a lie. But I didn't press Gloria about it. "So, are you closing up?"

"Yep, then I can go home. My feet are killing me, but the bills won't pay themselves." Gloria smiled.

"Would you mind if I kept you company?"

She tilted her head.

"Sometimes, it's nice to talk to someone when you're alone."

She showed me a slight smile. "Okay, you can talk while I finish my work."

I sat at a table as Gloria worked while I chatted about things that caused her to laugh. Gloria had a splendid laugh. Every time she grinned, her dimples showed.

I spent most of the time speaking while she worked. Gloria answered briefly, but I didn't mind. She was busy and wanted to go home. Gloria finished up, and I walked her to her car. I waited until she drove away as an ache entered my chest.

I met Gloria yesterday, but her personality captivated me. I didn't care if I dumped out my coffee. If it meant I continued to see her, I would continue to dump it.

*****

Over the next few months, I would visit the coffeehouse, order a coffee, and ditch it. I would return later and kill time with Gloria while she worked. She told me about herself, and I spoke about myself.

We would joke and laugh, which was terrific. I didn't care if Gloria worked in a coffeehouse because I loved spending time with her. The conversations were natural and genuine. I didn't have to pretend to be someone I'm not, and I didn't judge her.

We hadn't had a date yet. But I was falling in love with her. How can you fall for someone you have known for a brief time? I didn't know. But Gloria made me happy.

I loved spending time with her at her work and helping her clean. One night, I took a chance and showed her how I felt. Hopefully, it didn't blow up in my face.

Gloria was sweeping the floor. I played music from the jukebox in the coffeehouse's corner. I chose a song she would like, then strode over to her. I held my hand out to her.

She stopped sweeping. "What are you doing?"

"I'd like to dance with you if you don't mind."

"I need to finish…."

"One dance is all I want. Dance with me."

Gloria nodded, then leaned the broom against the counter, walked over to me, and placed her hand in mine.

I pulled Gloria to me and held her in my arms as we danced. I never felt this way about anyone, how I felt about Gloria. I held her close to me as we floated around the floor. She laid her head on my shoulder as I rested my palm on her lower back.

Something told me that no one held Gloria this way, as I did now. As we swayed back and forth, my emerald-green eyes met her chocolate brown eyes. I seized a chance, leaned down, and pressed my lips to hers.

The kiss started softly. Then I deepened it. I released Gloria's hand and wrapped my arms around her waist. I pressed her body to mine as she wrapped her arms around my neck. I poured everything into that kiss as she kissed me back.

Gloria broke from the kiss and me. I remained there, confused as she twisted her back at me. "Gloria."

She spun to face me. "I can't do this, Carri."

"What?"

"I'm married."

I stared at her, speechless.

"I assumed nothing would happen between us until you kissed me."

"But you kissed me back."

Gloria furrowed her eyebrows.

I crept towards her. "Does your husband make you happy?"

"It doesn't matter. I can be your friend, but nothing more. I'm sorry."

I nodded in agreement.

"If you don't wish to be friends, I understand." Her eyes held hope.

"Okay, we'll be friends." I gave her a reassuring smile.

"We'll forget about the kiss."

I nodded. Gloria waltzed over to the counter and grabbed the broom, and I stayed as she finished her work.

After she concluded, I escorted her to her car. She got inside and sped off into the distance. I laid my fingertips on my lips and smiled.

I didn't care about Gloria being married because I craved to be a part of her existence and to remain in her world. Something told me there would be interference from others.

# CHAPTER 6

## FRIENDSHIP?

**Carrington**

Gloria could only offer friendship, but I didn't want friendship since I craved more from her. I had to lie to myself and her, claiming friendship was okay with me, but it wasn't.

I spent time with Gloria, trying to fight the urge to pursue her. It was so damn hard. The more time we spent together, the harder I was falling. How can a woman make this happen? She's married, for crying out loud.

Gloria talked about different things, and I focused on her. I don't think many people listened to her.

"What do you think?" Gloria asked me.

"It's a fantastic idea." I grinned.

Gloria's face lit up. "It's a dream, but one day, I'll own a coffee shop. I love people and won't deal with home." Gloria sighed.

"Is it that bad?"

"When my husband isn't drinking, it's okay, which isn't often. He wasn't always that way. When we met, he was a sweet guy. Then, after dating for six months, he would have a casual drink."

"And now, he drinks all the time?"

"Yeah, but what can you do?" She shrugged.

Gloria finished cleaning the floor as I crumpled my eyebrows. How can someone like Gloria live with a man that drinks all the time? I didn't understand it.

"Are you hungry?"

Gloria glanced at me. "I could go for a bite."

I beamed. Gloria locked up, and we escaped the coffee shop.

We walked to her automobile, got in, and drove to get some food. We pulled through a drive-thru, placing an order of burger, fries, and two pops, and I paid for the food and drinks. Then we drove to a secluded spot to eat.

"This is nice," Gloria mentioned.

"What is?" I sipped my pop.

"Being able to eat a hot meal. Working doesn't give me much time to cook, and my husband prefers the bottle over making dinner." Gloria bit into her burger.

"Why do you deal with that?" I ate some fries.

"Where will I go? I don't have family or friends except for you."

"Don't you have any female friends?"

"The females that I speak with, and that's iffy, are my husband's friend's wives. It's difficult to connect with folks who didn't grow up as I did."

I regarded her.

"One had money. Another came from the middle class. And the third was from the working class. I grew up in poverty. My father drank himself to death, and my mom checked out mentally, landing in the psych ward. I have worked since the age of fourteen." Gloria shrugged.

I pondered what she had told me. Even though my parents died when we were young, we never wanted for anything. We

had money, thanks to our parents and Mason. Gloria's family subjected her to the life she lives now.

"For what it's worth, I ignore where you come from because I enjoy your company. You're not stuffy like the individuals at school." I mocked my schoolmates.

Gloria laughed. "I take it that you don't like rich people?"

"It's not that. I hate the pretentious nature. Plus, those people need to get the stick out of their asses. I enjoy life. Who prefers to be miserable? I don't." I ate my burger.

"You have a unique way of looking at life."

"You don't understand the half of it."

"Then, tell me."

I told Gloria about my exploits and pranks. She laughed a lot. Most girls would get annoyed by my childish behavior, but she enjoyed hearing about it. I can kid with her, and she gets it. That's what differentiates Gloria from anyone that I have met. If it weren't for her marriage, I would make her mine.

I wanted Gloria and could make her happy. She would want for nothing. This husband of hers didn't deserve her. How can someone discard a woman like her? It made little sense to me.

We finished our meal, then Gloria dropped me off by the coffee shop before heading home. I strolled to the rental house.

When I entered, Joseph met me. "Where were you?"

"I was hanging out with a friend." I grinned.

"When did you make a friend?"

My grin faded. "Hey, I can make friends."

"Is that before or after you get arrested?"

I rolled my eyes. "That was one time, and Mason made me do a hard time for it."

"It wasn't one time. Try ten times. You forget I was with you."

"I didn't forget. I ignored the fact that you perched in the jail cell while chanting."

Joseph shook his head. "Carri, you don't hang out with people for the sake of friendship."

"I don't have a choice." I shrugged.

"Why?"

"Because I'm hanging out with a married person."

"Huh?"

"It's a woman, and she's married."

"You can't be fucking serious?"

Okay, Joseph's zen nature flew right out the door.

"Mason will kill you if he finds out you're wasting time with someone who's married."

"Then, don't tell him."

"Carri, he will find out. Someone will snitch, and it won't end well."

"I don't care. I like Gloria." I didn't care what he or anyone else thought. Spending time with Gloria made me happy.

But someone would toss a monkey wrench into my plans in the form of my sister, Christine. She was looking for anything to cause me grief, and I didn't realize she listened to our conversation. She dashed to her room and called Mason to snitch on me.

Christine couldn't reach Mason because he was dealing with Charles. It seems there was trouble back home.

*****

### 3rd person

Maggie and Charles had almost made it a year of marriage. Then, he took it upon himself to dally with some girl from work. The woman flirted with Charles. And Charles being Charles, took an interest in the flirtation.

Charles collected a room key in the casino and met the girl in the hotel room. It got heated between Charles and the girl. He was enjoying himself until the staff informed Maggie a key was missing. She thought someone lifted a key to stay free and grabbed the master key.

Maggie opened the room door and caught Charles fucking the girl repeatedly. Yeah, Charles wasn't the sharpest tool in the shed, and Maggie almost cut off his dick.

Chaos ensued, and someone placed a call to Mason. He showed up to find Charles partially naked and the girl in her underwear. Yeah, Charles' actions pissed off Mason.

"Get dressed," Mason ordered Charles and the girl.

Maggie stood there as both dressed.

"Your services are no longer required," Mason informed the woman.

The woman scratched her eyebrows. Two men entered the room and dragged her away.

Charles glanced at his wife and Mason, saying nothing. Maggie left the hotel room.

"Maggie!" Charles started after her, but Mason stopped him. "I have to catch Maggie!"

"No, you don't."

"I can't lose her."

"Then, you shouldn't have fucked another girl who wasn't your wife. I will fix this mess, along with your so-called deal that you made involving your friends."

"What?"

"I froze your assets, dumbass. Your part of the arrangement is over."

"You can't do that!"

"I can because you're using the family's money. I warned you against doing work with the Santiagos, and you didn't listen. I refuse to lose everything because of it. You'll be fortuitous if you earn Maggie's forgiveness." Mason left the hotel room.

*****

**Carrington**

I told you my brother was an idiot. I'll find this information out later. Charles would toss everything away with poor decisions, and I wasn't too far behind him.

My situation would escalate, culminating in a hard truth. My stubbornness will be my downfall.

# CHAPTER 7

## ALL HELL BREAKS LOOSE

**Carrington**

I spent time with Gloria even though Joseph recommended against it. Troy kept Christine busy. She tried to call Mason without any luck.

Mason was busy dealing with Charles's situation. Maggie kicked him out of the mansion, angry with Charles, which sent him running back to Mason's. With the help of Edward Morgan, Mason killed the arrangement with the Santiagos. That pissed off Luis Santiago, but Edward was good at persuading people to listen.

*****

**Mason**

"You'll pay for this," Luis told me.

"I would advise against idle threats." Edward sat in a chair, staying calm.

Luis glared at him.

"I'm a reasonable man with business, but I'm not reasonable with finding your family intercepting merchandise intended for me."

"You won't always be around, old man."

"No, but my son will. He'll conduct the business accordingly. Unlike Mason Jones, I have no issue giving you a dirt nap." It was a threat from Edward Morgan. You heed warnings from a boss, or you sleep with the fishes. "Conduct your business with the others, but Charles Jones is out since he currently has no viable assets."

With that final word, Edward stood up and left with me. We walked out to the car, and Edward turned to me. "I have cleared my debt with your father for the many times he saved my ass, and I am no longer indebted to the Jones family. We will conduct business but avoid the Santiagos because they don't play fair."

It was a warning.

"Understood. My father would roll over in his grave if he knew the bullshit Charles pulled. This arrangement would ruin the family."

"Because he craves to play with the big dogs when you should cage him. You're a smart man, Mason, and I trust you. Your brother has a lot to learn. I'm retiring soon, and Brian will take over the organization. I will remain as a consigliere to my boy. Any business conducted at that point will go through him."

I nodded as we got into the car and left. It wouldn't be the last time we dealt with the Santiagos. Our family would have run-ins with them later, and the Morgans would become our greatest allies.

I returned home, entered my house, and confronted Charles. It wasn't pretty.

"I swear all I was going to do was make enough money, then get out," Charles said.

"You don't get it. The Santiagos don't care. They will take your money, then rat you out and bring the family to its knees. Dad made friends with people along the way. He knew who to trust and who to distrust. He never trusted the Santiagos, and for good reasons. Your faulty business deal is the least of your concerns. I must smooth over the waters with the Cascade family since we're partners in the casinos. You'll be fortuitous if she forgives you!"

"Mason?" Someone asked.

I rounded to catch my pregnant wife standing there with a concerned expression. I sauntered over to Luci and kissed her.

"Is everything okay?"

"Everything is fine. I don't need you to worry. The stress isn't good for the baby, and it's a family matter." I smiled.

Luci smiled, having faith in me. She knew I would handle things, allowing her to relax. It was a promise I kept when we met, unlike our idiot brother, who couldn't seem to make the right decisions, which included keeping his dick in his pants.

Someone rang the doorbell, and Luci answered it. Maggie entered the house, and Charles and I paused there.

"I invited Maggie over to fix things. She didn't want to come, but I insisted. So, fix it." Luci gestured with her hand.

"Luci," I replied.

Luci looked at me, then spoke Italian with her spitting afterward.

*****

**Carrington**

I don't understand why Italian's spit, and it's the same with their food. Leave it to my brother to marry a woman from Italy.

Theresa married a man from Mexico. My family has a fetish for marrying people from another country. She was expecting as well, and both babies were due around the same time. My family wastes no time with getting hitched and popping out kids, except for Charles. The way he's going, he'll be lucky to keep his manhood.

*****

**Charles**

Mason and Luci left Maggie and me alone.

"Maggie, I'm so…."

"Put a sock in it." Maggie stepped towards me. "You humiliated me, and you're an idiot. I should divorce you, but I won't."

I raised my eyebrows.

"I will conclude that you're a dumbass. Since you felt sticking your dick in someone was crucial, you will listen to me. As of now, it finishes you with your so-called friends. You will not associate with any woman besides your sisters, sisters-in-law, and me. I own you if you want to save this marriage, or I will destroy you."

I furrowed my eyebrows.

"Take it or leave it."

I accepted the deal, agreeing to Maggie's terms.

### Carrington

So, my brother takes Maggie's deal, turns around, and makes a deal that would include people he shouldn't. Did I mention my brother was an idiot?

The arrangement would include innocent people used as a pawn to compensate for a terrible deal and keep the Fraziers at bay. While two friends would benefit from this, one would not, creating hatred and setting up a revenge game.

This arrangement would also blow up in their faces in the end. My brother would drag me into the mess, setting the stage for what's to come later.

While my brother dealt with Maggie's terms, Maurice, Frank, and Greg invested the money they shouldn't have. They thought the arrangement was good, then found out the hard way.

Edward Morgan was correct when he said not to trust the Santiagos. Luis set up the other three to take the dive for Charles, reneging on the deal. Maurice, Frank, and Greg met at the location, not understanding they were dealing with an undercover fed.

Luis made an anonymous call, setting everyone up to take the dive. While the three intercepted the merchandise, the feds busted Greg, Maurice, and Frank for drugs and guns.

Marty Frazier got Maurice out by paying off the district attorney. Greg took a plea deal to avoid jail time, and they left Frank holding the bag. Frank spent two years in prison when Greg rolled over on him, claiming it was Frank's idea. With friends like them, who the hell needs enemies?

Part of Greg's plea deal was he had to give up his bookie, which caused him to skip town. Maurice owed his brother a profound debt that his drinking became excessive, as did his violent nature. He turned his anger onto his wife.

It would be the catalyst to send Gloria into my arms, along with a visit from Mason. Yeah, Christine reached big brother finally. It wouldn't end well and would result in deception from both Gloria and me.

Mason called and told Joseph. Joseph informed me. Yeah, so much for secrets with this family.

# CHAPTER 8

## HAVE YOU LOST YOUR DAMN MIND?

**Carrington**

After speaking to Christine, Mason and Charles paid me a visit, which I wasn't aware of their impending visit.

\*\*\*\*\*

**Mason**

Charles and I arrived in town and stopped at the coffeehouse to buy a coffee. When we reached the counter, it surprised Charles to see the woman.

"Gloria?" Charles asked.

"Hello, Charles."

"I didn't realize you worked here."

"It helps to pay the bills."

"You both know each other." I gestured between the two.

"Gloria is Maurice's wife," Charles said.

I studied Gloria, wondering how she married one of the Frazier boys. She had a warmth to her, and the Fraziers didn't.

"What can I get you?" Gloria asked.

"Two black coffees," Charles replied.

Gloria giggled.

"Is something amusing?" I asked.

Gloria got our coffees. "My friend Carri orders a black coffee when he comes into the coffeehouse, but most customers get cream and sugar in their coffee."

Gloria's mention of Carrington's name alerted Charles and me.

"Would this friend have chestnut brown hair, five foot eleven, and emerald-green eyes?" Charles asked.

Gloria turned to the counter with our coffees. "Yes, he does. Do you know Carri?"

Charles and I gave each other a knowing look.

"Yeah, we know, Carri," I responded.

"He's a sweet guy and a great friend. He'll stop by tonight if you wish to say hi."

Gloria wasn't aware Carrington wouldn't be stopping by after we visited him.

"Sure," Charles replied.

Gloria grinned, and I paid her. Then we left the coffeehouse.

"It seems little brother has been messing with the wrong damn woman, and it ends today. I refused to embroil this family in another scandal," I told Charles.

Charles sighed.

We approached the rental home to speak to Carrington about Gloria. It wouldn't be a pleasant visit, but one we needed to handle with Carri.

I knocked on the door, and Joseph answered it with brows raised.

"Where's Carri?" I asked.

Charles and I stepped inside and past Joseph.

"Upstairs," Joseph said.

"Get him. We have a matter to discuss," I replied.

Joseph knew why I was visiting. It doesn't take a great genius to understand why I'm here.

*****

**Carrington**

Joseph got me. I followed him downstairs to discover Mason and Charles. Mason gestured to me, then to the couch. "Sit."

"Do I look like a hound?"

I earned an irritated look from Mason, rolled my eyes, strode to the couch, and sat down. Christine came down a few minutes later to enjoy the show. My sister has a lot to learn about meddling in people's business.

Mason undid his overcoat and sat down in a chair. "I hear you're enjoying company with someone's wife."

"Who informed you of that?" I noticed Christine, who smirked. "Never mind, I can guess." I shot her a glare.

"Carri, this stops now. I refused to have you embroiled in a scandal like our idiot brother." Mason thumbed at Charles.

Joseph and I glanced at Charles.

"What did you do?" Joseph asked Charles.

"Maggie caught Charles fucking another female employee in a room at the casino hotel." Well, Mason outed Charles.

Christine, Joseph, and I gawked at Charles. Charles didn't respond.

"I won't allow you to continue with a married woman," Mason told me.

"We're friends."

"You're not friends, and you don't stay friends. Your so-called friendship will lead to more, and it ends now."

I rose. "You can't tell me what to do, Mason! I'm not fifteen!"

Mason stood up. "Like hell, I can't! I can, and I will! You might be an adult, but this is unwelcome news! Use your brain!"

"Because our family reputation is more important than me!"

It became heated between Mason and me.

"Carri," Charles replied.

I peered at Charles.

"Gloria is Maurice Frazier's wife."

"What?"

"What?" Someone else asked.

We turned to find Kate standing there, stunned.

"What are you doing here?" Mason asked Kate.

"I called her because we needed a mediator." Joseph shrugged.

I rolled my eyes.

Kate stepped in. "I notice you all were busy. You with your stupidity." Kate pointed at Charles.

Charles sighed.

"You with your shady business dealings," she told Mason.

Mason gave her an annoyed face.

"You with your snitching," Kate told Christine.

Christine averted her eyes.

"And you with your lack of judgment and hiding Carri's secret."

Joseph cringed.

I remained there.

Kate stepped over to me. "And you, who understand better than anyone that married people are off-limits even as friends. Carri, what are you doing?"

"Kate, Gloria is sweet and has no one. We talk and laugh."

"And she's wed to someone whose family you despise. Do you think the Fraziers will understand your closeness with Gloria? They will shoot you like a dog and not think twice about it. I understand everyone's point, but I agree with Mason."

Kate wasn't unjust, but I hated giving up my closeness with Gloria.

"That's it? I can't believe this!" Christine said.

"You put a sock in it! No one likes snitches. Why would you rat out your brother?" Kate asked Christine.

"Because what Carri is doing is wrong."

"But that's none of your concern." Kate stepped over to her. "We're family, and we protect each other. We don't rat them out. One day, you'll have a child and protect that child as we have protected you."

Christine frowned at her.

Kate glanced at her unamused. "Never bite the hand that feeds you, Christine. One day, you will need help. And God forbid if anyone turns their back on you."

Christine failed to realize one detail. While she snitched me out, she would need me later when she found herself in a

precarious situation of her own, and it would alter everything between us.

I hated the Fraziers, but I cherished Gloria and fell in love with her. I didn't wish to turn my back on her.

"Don't I have a say in my life? I meet someone interesting, sweet, fun, and has no one, and you come in here ordering me to stop seeing her. I'm not Charles!"

Charles furrowed his brows and peered at me with annoyance.

I ambled over to Charles. "Maggie is a good person, and you're lucky she's allowing you to stay. You might be older, but you're an idiot."

"Carri, be careful. Your mouth will bring you trouble."

"Big brother, I learned a long time ago that you beat me to the punch."

Charles scowled at me.

"Enough, Carri!" Mason walked towards me and stared me in the eyes. "You may assume this is about the family reputation. But it goes deeper than a reputation. A scandal will destroy you in a heartbeat. People will use your faults against you, and no one will trust you. It isn't about the family. What if you pursue this relationship, and it doesn't work out? Do you think a woman will tolerate a man who cheated with a married woman?"

My siblings weren't irrational, but my heart was leading me in a different direction. We can't help who we fall for, whether it's good or bad.

"Fine." I strode past my siblings and ran upstairs.

Even though I agreed with my siblings, my heart wouldn't listen. It would lead me into a situation, proving Mason correct, resulting in a greater love I never imagined.

Sometimes, love isn't romantic but a different love that shows us what's important.

# CHAPTER 9

## STUBBORNNESS AT ITS BEST

**Carrington**

I considered what Mason and the others said and stayed away from Gloria, but it didn't mean I didn't check on her. I worried about her, and my heart ached for her. I longed to be with her, and my family didn't understand that.

A month passed, and I figured whatever feelings I had would dissolve, but they didn't. It wasn't right to disappear from someone like Gloria without an explanation. I visited her one night at closing time.

I tapped on the window. Gloria saw me, strode to the door, and unlocked it. I entered, and she locked the door again.

"Carri."

"Hi, Gloria."

"Is everything okay? I haven't seen you in a month and figured you got busy with classes."

"I wasn't busy with classes."

"Oh." She crumpled her eyebrows.

"I came to visit you and explained that we can't spend time together anymore."

Gloria's expression changed to sadness.

"I thought that if I stayed away, it'd be easier."

"I understand." She tried not to cry.

"I don't wish to cause issues between you and your spouse. Plus, the more I'm with you, the more difficult it is for me to resist wanting more from you." I struggled to keep my composure.

"I understand. It's that I don't have anyone in my life that cares about me."

I glanced at her with empathy.

"You're the first person who offered genuine friendship to me. It was nice, but I understand." She brushed a tear away. "Thank you for telling me. I have to get back to work." Gloria walked over to the broom and swept the floor as her body shook.

I shifted and stepped to the door but stopped. If I leave now, I may lose a chance, but it can be disastrous if I stay.

Gloria sniffled.

I twisted around. "I don't want to go."

She stopped and faced me with tear-streaked cheeks.

"But I don't crave to be your friend either." I strolled towards her. "I can't be your friend anymore because it's too difficult."

Gloria furrowed her eyebrows.

I crept towards her, rested my palm on her cheek, and caressed it with my thumb. "I don't want to be friends, but more from you, and I don't care if you're married."

"Carri...."

"Gloria, if I felt nothing for you, friendship would be okay, but I can't with how my heart aches for you. I hate that you leave here and return to a man that doesn't deserve you. I can love you the way you need it if you allow me. Please." I was pouring my heart out to her, hoping she would accept.

Gloria stared at me with a longing. At that moment, I took my chance and leaned in and kissed her, and she didn't resist my kiss and kissed me back. I withdrew my hand from her cheek and wrapped my arms around her as she draped her arms around my neck and kissed me.

I didn't care if she was married or what my family thought. I can't refute my emotions any longer, and neither could she.

\*\*\*\*\*

Gloria locked the coffeehouse door. We got into her car. I drove to a motel outside of town and entered the office. I paid for a room, returned to the car, and pulled around, and we got out, entering the motel room.

Once inside, I pulled Gloria into a kiss as we removed each other's clothes. I carried her to the bed, laid her down, placed protection on, and found my way inside of her. Our lips never left each other as I made love to her.

I took my time with her as my hand glided along her body, caressing every inch of her. My lips captured her skin as I planted soft kisses along her jawline and down her neck.

We became lost in our passion as we made love to each other. I didn't care if this was unacceptable since I craved to make love to Gloria as we found our release. Then I peeked at her with love.

\*\*\*\*\*

After a few hours, we got dressed. I sat on the bed and tied my shoe as Gloria smiled at me. I couldn't help but smile back. I stopped dressing, rose from my seat, strolled towards her, and tugged her to me.

"What happens now?"

"I want to be with you. If we must keep it quiet, then so be it."

"My husband will suspect."

"I don't care what Maurice thinks."

That revelation shocked her.

"I know Maurice is your husband, and I don't care. I hate the Frazier family."

"You don't understand what they'll do if someone crosses them."

"Yeah, I do."

"How so?"

"Because my brother Charles was friends with Maurice."

Gloria's eyes swelled.

"You're Carrington Jones?"

I nodded as she pulled away from me. She turned her back to me, placed her hand on her forehead, and ran her palm through her hair.

"I didn't know Maurice was your spouse, but it doesn't change my feelings about you."

She spun around. "Carri, you don't understand. The minute Maurice's family finds out about you, it will be trouble for your family, and I don't want you to get hurt."

I cupped her face with my palms. "We won't tell anybody about us. Gloria, I don't want to lose you or regret what happened tonight. We can do this, and when the moment is right, we will break you free from that rotten family."

Gloria knitted her eyebrows.

"I love you."

Gloria looked at me in awe.

"It's hard not to love you."

"I love you, too. Spending time with you made me fall for you. But if I kept you at arm's length, I could refute it, but I can't anymore."

I dragged her into a kiss. Every time I kissed Gloria, I fell deeper for her, and it relieved me that she felt the same way about me.

We left the motel, and she dropped me off in town, then drove home. I didn't know what would happen. But I would do everything in my power to stay with her.

*****

**Gloria**

I returned home and rested in the car, reflecting on tonight. It was wrong for Carri and me to have sex, but I didn't care. Maurice prefers the bottle over me.

I headed into the house to discover Maurice passed out on the couch again. Beer cans covered the floor and furniture, along with empty liquor bottles. Maurice drinks himself into a stupor until he passes out. Since I close at work, he passes out before I

come home. Maurice wouldn't realize whether I was with Carri or not, and it's not as if he cares.

I climbed the stairs and showered to rid the smell of Carri's cologne. I didn't need Maurice suspecting.

After I got ready for bed, I settled in bed alone, pondering tonight. It was the first time that I received love from someone. Carri cared about me, and it was lovely. It has been a long time since I experienced that from someone.

People assume when you get married, you never fret about loneliness. But that isn't true. My dad drank himself to death, and my mom ended up in a mental institution. I had a few friends while growing up until I met Maurice.

Maurice was smooth and persuaded me to go out with him. Little by little, he started showing his controlling personality and alienated me from people. After we wed, it got worse, and so did his drinking. He was watching my every move, especially around Charles's friends and their wives.

People wonder why I stay. It's easy when someone threatens your life. Maurice's family wouldn't hesitate to harm Carri or me if they found out what happened tonight. If I had to hide my indiscretion, I would. For once, someone loved me, and I refused to give that up for anyone.

# CHAPTER 10

## A SECRET AFFAIR

**Carrington**

I didn't tell anybody about my night with Gloria because it wasn't any of their business. I kept up pretenses concerning Gloria since Joseph and Christine would become suspicious, so I created an excuse that I was studying for my courses. I made sure I left the house every night with my books.

I strolled to the coffeehouse, and we would leave and drive to the same motel. I paid cash for the room. The minute we arrived at the room, we stripped off our clothes and had incredible sex.

I sat in the bed as Gloria straddled me and rocked her hips backward and forth. I thrust inside of her repeatedly. We were like jackrabbits and couldn't get enough of each other. As the bed squeaked and our moans increased, we moved faster until we found our release.

We collapsed onto the bed, breathing hard. I laid on my back as Gloria moved over to me and kissed my chest. I removed the protection and tossed it into the trash can.

She settled on my chest as I ran my fingers through her hair.

"It's nice," Gloria said.

"What is?"

"Being here with you and not dealing with anyone."

I grinned. "I'm considering taking summer courses and staying here while my siblings return home. Joseph is

graduating, and Christine is going home for the summer. It would leave me alone in the rental house and give us a place to be together and not go to a motel."

Gloria grinned. "Maurice is working with his brothers more, and they send him away constantly. I'll say I picked up hours at the coffeehouse."

"I don't feel guilty about what we're doing."

"Neither do I."

I flipped Gloria onto her stomach, crawled behind her, replaced the protection, and knelt behind her. I yanked her hips to me and entered her, then thrust. I pinned Gloria to the bed and showed her that she belonged to me as I claimed her.

As I thrust, I spoke in a husky voice. "You belong to me. You're mine."

She moaned as I continued to claim her and her body.

"Say you're mine," I growled.

"I'm yours." She groaned.

I continued until we both exploded. I pulled out of Gloria and sat back on my knees as Gloria struggled to catch her breath. She rolled over and studied me.

"You're mine, Gloria. Your body is mine. Only I can have sex with you. I don't want anyone to touch you how I do." I grazed her body. I didn't want anyone to touch Gloria, not even Maurice, because he didn't deserve her.

She sat up and draped her arms around my neck. "Carri, you're the one I prefer to touch me. When I'm with you, you cherish me. Since we started this, I refused to let Maurice touch

me. Knowing Maurice, he's screwing some poor unsuspecting girl."

"That doesn't bother you?"

"No, then he leaves me alone, and I can be with you."

I laughed, yanked her to me, and made love to her again.

While I was doing unholy things to Gloria, she was right. Maurice wasn't the Boy Scout or faithful husband he claimed to be.

*****

**3rd person**

Maurice had a woman bent over the office desk at his brother's company and fucked her. The Fraziers, Santiagos, Morgans, and even the Jones were less than faithful to their women. The families were also less than honest with business. You must wonder how many of them were loyal to someone. Mason was a prime example of faithfulness, as was Joseph. Charles and Carrington, not so much.

Charles cheated on his wife, and Carrington was cheating with someone's wife. When you're having sex with someone, logic flies out the window.

Maurice finished and fixed his pants as the woman yanked down her skirt and buttoned up her blouse. She fled the office as Mateo showed up, looking annoyed.

"If you want to fuck a woman, take them to your house," Mateo said.

"A guy has needs."

"Then fuck your wife. Or do you spend too much time as a drunk?"

If anyone knew the Frazier family, Mateo had the shortest fuse, and Marty was the oldest. Then you had Mateo, Maurice, Marco, Maximilian, and Mickey. They're equally a pain in the ass and all idiots. I'm confident they will pass the idiot gene onto their offspring, considering they can't keep their dicks in their pants. Some brothers had bastard kids with the women they screwed.

If the wives mentioned the kids, their wives got met with a hand. Violence ran rampant in their household, and the Fraziers were certifiably insane.

"Why don't you go have another bastard child, Mateo?" Maurice asked.

Mateo glared at his brother.

Marty stepped into the office, smacked Maurice, and squatted down at the desk. "Shut the fuck up, Maurice. It's not like you don't have a couple of bastard children running loose. If I find you screwing another one of your whores in my office, I'll cut off your dick." Marty made some calls.

Can't you feel the love with these assholes?

"Mateo, take dipshit here and meet with the Garza family. Here's the payment for the merchandise they have for us." Marty tossed Mateo a bag. "If they fuck us over, kill them."

Mateo said nothing but left the office with Maurice. They would be away on business for a month, and that would allow Gloria and Carrington to spend quality time together.

*****

**Gloria**

I arrived home to find Maurice packing, and I remained there, playing the dutiful wife. "Where are you going?"

"Mateo and I are going on a business trip. We'll be away for a month."

"Should the trip worry me?"

He stepped towards me and smiled. "No, baby. It'll be okay."

"As long as you stay safe."

"Always. When I return, we should start a family."

I cringed inside with the thought of him touching me. "Sure."

Maurice gave me a quick peck on the mouth before grabbing his bag and leaving. I waited, hearing the door close. Relief washed over me since I was free for a month to be with Carri.

Marty kept his brothers busy, so I didn't fret about any of them snitching me out to Maurice. Carri was more of a man than Maurice. When I was with Carri, love captured me. With Maurice, disgust engulfed me. The minute I had a chance, I would leave Maurice and this godforsaken family.

I wanted happiness, and Carri could provide that. I got tired of dealing with the drinking and the threats. Maurice hit me that one time, but it was a matter of time before it escalated.

When the time was perfect, I would leave and be happy. Something would alter that, but I didn't realize what it was.

# CHAPTER 11

## FREEDOM

**Carrington**

My relationship with Gloria was going well, and I couldn't be happier. When Joseph and Christine questioned my upbeat mood, I informed them that I'm always jovial. They were suspicious, but I ignored them. My siblings need to get a life and stay out of mine.

Most people disagree with my choices in life, but it's not their life. That's the problem with people. They have opinions about everything, including my family. Opinions are like assholes, and everyone has one.

The best part was Maurice left for a month, which gave Gloria and me time alone. I couldn't wait for summer to devote time to her without prying eyes, namely Joseph and Christine.

I prepared plans for a weekend getaway with Gloria where no one recognized either of us. I appreciated the freedom of not hiding our relationship.

We drove to the UP, where I rented a small cottage, and we could see the sights. I wasn't planning on a freaking blizzard to hit—freaking Michigan weather. Mother Nature needs to take her meds and stop her nonsense.

We trudged through the snow with zero visibility and made it inside the cottage. Gloria glanced at me and laughed, considering I resembled the abominable snowman.

"Cute." I rolled my eyes and shook off the snow.

Gloria giggled.

"I'll start a fire if you want to make us something to eat."

"Okay." She snickered and removed her coat and boots, then strolled into the kitchen.

While Gloria cooked, I started the fire. Thanks to Joseph, the hippy that he was, he took us camping and taught us the basics. Once the fire was roaring, I shuffled into the kitchen to help Gloria.

"Where did you learn how to make a fire?" She stirred the hamburger on the stove.

"My hippy brother loves to commune with nature. Joseph was always dragging Elliot and me camping, and Elliot enjoys hunting, considering he prefers to throw knives at us."

Her eyes widened.

"I'm positive that my baby brother inherited the psycho gene from some distant family member."

Once the meat browned, she added spaghetti sauce. I placed a pan of water on the burner and cranked the heat.

"What are your siblings like?"

"Well, Mason is the oldest and father figure, trying to keep us in line. Kate is reasonable and no-nonsense. Charles, who you met, makes poor life choices and is an idiot. Theresa is down-to-earth and enjoys humor. Joseph is the resident hippy and loves to commune with nature, while Christine is uptight and loves to snitch on people. Then, you have Elliot, who's psychotic and hates stupid people."

The water boiled, and I added some oil, then the pasta to the pot.

"It must be interesting to grow up with so many brothers and sisters."

"It has its moments, but they're my family."

Gloria smiled at me. I loved this time with her because it wasn't about sex with her but more. I connected with her in a way that I didn't with anyone.

After the timer dinged, I drained the pasta, and Gloria turned off the stove. We dished out the food onto plates, then sat down at the table. It felt normal to eat dinner with her, and we talked about everything and anything. Then she dropped a bomb on me. "Maurice wants to start a family when he returns."

I stopped eating and peered at her. "And what did you say?"

"I said sure."

My anger started to build.

"But it won't happen. Maurice drinks and will pass out before he can do anything."

I started eating. "Good, because you're mine."

Gloria looked at me as I ate, saying nothing else. People can say I'm a dick, but I don't care. My love for Gloria was vaster than the ocean.

After a few minutes of silence, I said something. "Look, I'm sorry. I don't mean to be a dick, but imagining him touching you, pisses me off. He doesn't deserve you."

"I know, but Carri, I'm still married, and you're still in school. If we ran off together, your family and Maurice's family would

hunt us down like dogs. I don't prefer that but to leave that family and cut ties with them so that we can be happy together."

"I prefer that, too. I want to marry you, have a family with you, and give you the life you deserve."

Gloria smiled at me. "You want a family?"

"Yeah, I do."

"Maybe one day, we'll have a family."

That idea made me happy.

We finished dinner, then cuddled in front of the fire and discussed the future. We agreed to wait until I completed school. Then, Gloria would file for divorce from Maurice and leave town together.

Plans have a way of altering as time goes along. We would find this out.

That night, I settled behind her as we made love. Our bodies rocked backward and forth as I drifted in and out of Gloria.

"Oh, God, Carri!"

I went faster until we both burst. Our breathing became labored, and we took a break until we started again. All night we went at it like jackrabbits, and I couldn't get enough of Gloria. We finally collapsed into a peaceful slumber after wearing ourselves out. I could get used to this.

\*\*\*\*\*

**Gloria**

I was sleeping until someone woke me up in his way. I moaned as Carri enjoyed dessert before breakfast. I loved it

when he woke me up like this because it was better than waking up to the foul stench of day-old beer.

Carri continued until I groaned and released. Then he moved up and made his way between my legs. He placed on protection, slid into me, and made love to me until we exploded.

"Good morning, baby." Carrie pressed his lips to mine.

"Morning, babe."

"Did you enjoy your morning delight?"

I beamed as he grinned. "You're something else. Don't you ever get tired?"

"I haven't had sex in a long time. It's so much better with someone you love."

"I agree."

He strutted to the bathroom naked as I admired the view. Then his phone rang with his brother was calling.

"Carri, your phone is ringing."

He finished in the bathroom, came out, climbed into bed, and answered the phone. "Hi, Joseph."

*Where are you, Carri?*

"I informed you that I was taking off for an assignment for school."

I got on my knees and placed kisses on him.

*It's wintertime, and I doubt teachers assign anyone out-of-town homework.*

"It's for a business class. I'm checking out different stores. Be glad I'm not putting dye in your shampoo."

*Thanks to you, I looked like freaking Lucky Charms!*

Carri laughed.

*That wasn't funny!*

"Oh, it was hilarious, but I gotta go. I'm meeting with some classmates." Carri hung up the phone, then twisted and studied me. "Now, where were we?" Carri laid me down and made love to me again.

It was sinful to lie to people and carry on a forbidden affair. But I didn't care. I craved to be with Carri. He made me feel things I never did with anyone. I basked in the love and affection from a man that knew how to treat a woman. I couldn't get enough.

The trouble was it caused me to crave his attention, making bad decisions. We continued with a forbidden affair, knowing it was dangerous. When you play with fire, you will get burned.

I would find that out, and it would alter everything.

They say a romance can start innocently enough. Most people fall in love, expecting to live happily forever after with one person. When a friendship begins, you never expect a romance to enter the picture until one day it does. You fall in love, hoping for that happily forever after. Then you wake up and realize you're living in a fantasy world.

That was my and Carri's problem. We lived in a fantasy world, expecting to have blissful happiness. But reality would kick us in the teeth, setting in motion the events that would affect others. It would take one person to show us our mistakes.

# CHAPTER 12

## LITTLE ARRIVALS

**Carrington**

The preceding month, Gloria and I spent as much time together as we could together. We kept our affair a secret from everyone and met at the motel for our rendezvous.

I imagined the day when Gloria was free from Maurice, and we began our life together. I couldn't wait for the day when we left, married, and had a family.

The weather warmed, and Mason welcomed his son, Cole. We arrived home to welcome the new addition to the family. I cradled my nephew, and he was a mixture of Luci and Mason with Mason's blue eyes. As I held Cole, I imagined Gloria and me welcoming a little one, and that thought made me beam.

"Well, Mason, he's the spitting image of you," Charles mentioned while holding Cole.

"That means Cole will be devilishly handsome when he's older," Mason said.

We chuckled.

"What about you, Charles? When are you expanding your family?" Joseph inquired.

"Not for a while. Maggie and I are working through our difficulties." Charles handed Cole to Luci. "Maggie doesn't trust me to start a family, and it's my fault for destroying her trust."

I could hear the disappointment in Charles's voice. My brother was an idiot, but family was essential to him.

"I'll enjoy my nephew and Theresa's child when it arrives," Charles said.

A regret will hinder you and make you stagnant. I understand Maggie's viewpoint, but Charles hung around the wrong people, and his buddies weren't squeaky clean.

I left the hospital and visited Maggie. I'm not sure how helpful my visit will be, but I hope it is. I arrived at Charles and Maggie's home and knocked on the front door, and someone answered it. I entered. Maggie closed the door as I settled there. "Hi, Carri." Maggie's tone held a coldness.

"Hi, Maggie."

"What can I do for you?"

"I came to speak to you about Charles."

Maggie pursed her lips and crossed her arms.

Well, this visit will be fun. "My brother is a fool, and you have a right to your anger. But the longer you punish Charles, the more distance you will place between you and him."

"Carri, you weren't there. Charles humiliated me at my parent's hotel. People assume it's because of his friends, but Charles decided of his own accord."

"I understand, but we aren't perfect. We do things we aren't proud of, but it doesn't mean you keep rubbing the person's nose in it. Charles humiliated and angered you, Maggie, but he made one mistake."

Maggie furrowed her eyebrows. "Do you understand how it felt when I discovered Charles with that woman? I questioned

myself about what I did wrong for Charles to cheat, then questioned everything. It was the first time I didn't consider myself sufficient for anyone."

I recognized something about her anger. It was the same way as Gloria. A man promises to love and honor her, and then they do the complete opposite.

"You did nothing wrong, and Charles realizes that. I can't excuse his behavior, but tonight, my brother regretted his decision. When he held Mason's son Cole, he assumed he wouldn't have a family."

Maggie's expression shifted.

"When we lost our parents, it was difficult for all of us. Mason did his best, but it would have been different if they had lived."

Maggie peered at me with empathy. I didn't show up here to persuade her to forgive my brother but help her understand Charles better.

What Maggie said next surprised me. "People say you should leave when a man cheats on you. But how do you give up when it involves your heart? You don't. You deal with the anger and hope you move past it. As angry as I am with your brother, my heart won't allow me to leave because he can become the man it destined him."

It was at that moment I realized Charles and Maggie would overcome this difficulty between them. I headed to Mason's. Tomorrow I was returning to school and Gloria.

*****

Two months later, we received a call informing us that Theresa delivered a baby boy, Dean. We traveled to meet our new nephew.

Dean was a mini version of Grant, who's Mexican. Dean's skin tone was darker than Cole's since Cole has an olive skin tone because of Luciana. Girls would favor the boys when they were older.

Theresa cradled her son. It made me yearn for a family of my own one day. I imagined having a son who would take after me but inherit Gloria's heart, and that notion made me smile.

We stayed, visited Theresa and her family, then spent the night at Mason's house. The next day, we were returning to school.

I rested on the couch at Mason's, reflecting on Gloria.

"It's lovely to have little ones in the family," Christine replied.

"Yes, it is. You can spoil the kids, then give them back to their parents," Joseph said.

Christine rolled her eyes as Elliot walked into the room. "Elliot, you missed seeing our nephew."

"What's there to see? Babies cry, mess their pants, and demand attention. I don't get the fuss," Elliot replied.

We all stared at him, annoyed.

"You're young. One day, you will have children." Luci rocked Cole.

"That is debatable. Women cause you grief, and children cause you headaches, and I have no need for either in my life," Elliot said.

I shook my head. Our baby brother thinks he knows everything but knows nothing.

"What about you, Joseph?" Christine asked.

"Kids are wonderful when they belong to someone else. Mary and I decided we don't want children but will enjoy spoiling our nephews," Joseph said.

"We don't have to worry about Carri since he isn't dating anyone," Mason said.

I shrugged. I didn't tell my family about Gloria and our plans because they would react to our affair.

Later, I retired to bed. The following day, I'll return to school. Soon, Gloria will have freedom from Maurice, and we will be together.

*****

**Gloria**

I wondered how Carri's visit had gone with his family. Two babies in two months were terrific news, and it made me think of what it would be like to have a child with Carri, and that idea made me beam.

"Gloria!"

I strode out of the kitchen to see Maurice swaying back and forth.

"I ordered you to clean up this place. I'm not living in a shit hole."

"It's your mess, so you clean it up. I'm not your maid!"

"Watch your tone!"

I swayed my head, walked past Maurice, and mumbled, "Why don't you order your whore?"

"What did you say?"

I rounded him. "I said talk to your whore that you're fucking." That's all it took as Maurice punched me, causing me to stumble backward. He didn't stop at one time as he struck me several times, unleashing his drunken state on me.

Maurice finished, then spit on me. "You're pathetic. Now get your ass up and clean this damn house!"

I rose to my feet, touched my face, and discovered blood. Maurice didn't flinch, stumbled past me, and went upstairs.

I stumbled into the downstairs bathroom, flicked on the light, and stared into the mirror. My reflection horrified me. My nose and lip were bloody, and bruises started forming on my face. My eye swelled.

Maurice hit me before but hadn't touched me since that day until now. I cleaned up, hearing a knock at the door. Now what?

I finished, then answered the door to find Mateo standing there. He strolled into the house as if he owned the damn place.

"Did you need something?" I asked.

"I'm delivering a message. I'm aware of your extracurricular activities."

I stood there, emotionless.

"I won't tell Maurice what you're doing, but if you think about leaving, I will tell him. Then, enjoy the show." Mateo smirked.

I glared at him.

"The Fraziers don't need embarrassment." He stepped towards me. "You will not ruin my baby brother with your ways. If you do, I'll kill you."

I furrowed my brows.

He looked around the living room. "Clean up this mess. You're a disgrace as a wife." With those words, Mateo left.

I stood there, thinking about the day I would leave with Carri. That day couldn't come soon enough.

# CHAPTER 13

## CHOICES

**Gloria**

We all make choices in our lives. Some decisions are good, and some are bad. I didn't need Maurice knowing about Carri or Mateo telling him, even though Mateo didn't know about Carri.

Carri was returning today, but I couldn't let him see me in my current state. I wrote a note, dropping it off at his place before returning. Maurice would still be passed out from last night, and I returned before he woke.

I stood at the stove and cooked breakfast, feeling numb. My face swelled, and I wasn't sure if Maurice had broken my nose. I stared at the pan on the stove, hearing that familiar sound.

"Morning, Gloria." Maurice groaned and lumbered towards me. He kissed my cheek as I stood there, emotionless. "Baby, I don't like getting angry with you."

I said nothing.

"I expect you to clean the house before I return."

I turned off the stove, dished food onto a plate, and handed it to him. Maurice took the plate from me, then sat down at the table. I refused to cry, giving him the satisfaction of my tears because he didn't deserve my tears.

I stared out of the kitchen window as Maurice ate his breakfast and rambled. I said a few words here and there, but I

didn't bother to engage in a discussion. He got up, put his empty plate in the sink, then took a shower.

I cleaned up the kitchen, hearing Maurice's footsteps, then the front door. Once it closed, I cried. I wanted Carri to hold me and tell me everything would be okay, and one day, he would.

*****

**Carrington**

We returned, and I found an envelope attached to the front door with my name on it. I took it and shoved it into my pocket.

"What's that?" Joseph asked.

"It's probably a note from a classmate about an assignment I missed while we were away. I'll read it later."

We entered the house, and I hurried upstairs. After setting my bag down, I opened the envelope.

*Carri*

*Let's cool it for a while. I realize you were hoping to see me tonight, but there are some things I need to take care of here, and I don't want to drag you into any issues.*

*Once I handle things, we will meet. Please understand.*

*Love*

*Gloria*

I looked at the note, perplexed. I didn't know where Gloria lived to speak to her, so I'll visit her at work tomorrow. I folded the letter and packed it away.

Hopefully, everything is okay.

$$*****$$

**Gloria**

I phoned work, explaining I was sick. My boss told me to call when I was better. I couldn't let anyone see me until the swelling subsided and the bruises faded because I didn't need the questions.

I cleaned the house from top to bottom as my face throbbed. It took me all day, but I finished. I waited for Maurice to come home, and he did, drunk.

He stumbled to the recliner, plopped down, and passed out. I climbed the stairs to take a bath. After filling the tub, I climbed in and laid back. I thought about everything.

People say if you're not happy, don't cheat, leave. If your spouse hits you, go. Everyone thinks it's simple when it's not when someone threatens your life.

Out of the Frazier family, Mateo frightened me the most. Maurice has a temper, but Mateo is the type to keep his word. He has the personality of a rattlesnake.

Tears fell down my cheeks as my happiness slipped from my grasp. Carri made me happy, and someone wanted to rip it from me. When I was with him, I felt alive. I laughed more. Now it was disappearing.

I got out of the tub, dried off, and put on some clothes. I walked into the bedroom, crawled into bed, curled into a fetal position, and cried myself to sleep.

$$*****$$

**Carrington**

After class the next day, I visited the coffee shop to see Gloria. I walked in, not seeing her, and I stood in line until I reached the counter.

"Can I help you?" An employee asked.

"Is Gloria working?"

"No, Gloria called and said she was sick."

"Do you know how long she'll be out?"

The person shrugged. I asked no more questions and ordered a beverage so that I didn't draw attention to myself.

As I stood there, someone asked, "What do we have here?"

My left eye twitched, hearing that voice. The employee handed my drink to me, and I paid for it, then turned to see Marco and his idiot cronies standing there. They walked over to me.

"It's surprising to see you here since you don't drink coffee," Marco said.

"Because it's hot cocoa, considering this place serves many beverages." I took a sip of my drink.

"Do you expect me to believe that?"

"I don't give a shit what you believe and don't answer to your stupid ass."

Marco glared at me.

"Typical Frazier boy, who doesn't use his brain. Oh, wait, you don't have one."

Marco got into my face as I looked at him. I could easily wipe the floor with him, as I have done so many times.

"Well, well, well. Marco Frazier." Brian Morgan entered the coffeehouse with two people that I didn't recognize.

Marco looked at Brian as they walked towards us. "Morgan, this has nothing to do with you."

"That's where you're wrong. It has everything to do with me, considering your family intercepted goods belonging to my family. My old man sent me to collect what belonged to us. You remember him?" Brian leaned into Marco. "A boss that your family pissed off." Brian leaned back and smiled.

Marco hightailed it out of the coffeehouse. I find it hilarious to watch a Frazier boy trip over himself. I chuckled and looked at Brian.

"I'm sure that it will interest Mason about this new development," I said.

"It would be if there were a new development, but there isn't one. I enjoy watching the Frazier family squirm." Brian chuckled.

I shook my head as we left the coffeehouse.

"I'm guessing you didn't come here for the coffee."

I gave him a suspicious expression.

"Relax, Carri. I'm not getting in the middle of a family business since it's not my place. But I will warn you these things never end well for anyone."

Brian and I were close to the same age, and Brian wasn't the poster child for good behavior.

"Be careful. The truth has a way of rearing its ugly head."
Brian walked away with his friends or associates. You can never
tell with that family who the people were to them.

People think I should end my relationship with Gloria, but I
love her. When I got a chance, I would talk to her because
something was going on with her, and I would find out what it
was.

# CHAPTER 14

Time

**Carrington**

I haven't seen Gloria during the past two weeks. She didn't work any of those days. I didn't understand what was going on with her, but it had something to do with Maurice. I prayed I was wrong.

I minded my business, attending classes, but I won't lie. I missed Gloria terribly, and it was like a piece of me was missing.

I was leaving a bookstore one day, flicking through a book, and not paying attention.

"Carri?"

I lifted my head to see Gloria standing there. It was a pleasant surprise, making my heart flutter. "Gloria."

She smiled.

"How are you feeling?"

"I'm feeling better. You understand how pesky colds can be."

Then I remembered what her note said. "I got your note."

"I'm sorry it was short, but things were a little crazy."

"I'm guessing this has to do with Maurice."

When Gloria's expression changed, it confirmed my suspicions.

"I understand you have to deal with Maurice, and I don't want to pressure you into making a choice."

Gloria furrowed her brows. "It's not that."

"I can ask, but you won't tell me. You wanted to cool it, so we'll put the brakes on."

Gloria knitted her brows. I didn't know what else to say, so I walked away from her. My heart wanted her, but my head said it wasn't worth the hassle.

I returned to the house to read. It'll keep my mind off Gloria. What else will I do with my time? Do you have to ask?

Joseph came home to find me watching American Pie and laughing hysterically when the apple pie part appeared on the screen.

"What in God's name is that guy doing to that poor pie?" Joseph sat down.

"He's assessing the waters." I chuckled.

Christine walked into the house with Troy.

"What in the world are you watching?" Christine asked me.

"American Pie," Troy said.

Christine gave Troy an incredulous face as he sat down and watched the movie. We sat there rolling as we watched. Christine rolled her eyes.

My sister has no sense of humor. She continued upstairs, screamed, and came flying down the stairs. Troy and Joseph looked at her in confusion.

"Spider," Christine said.

Troy stood up and rushed to her side like a dutiful boyfriend. I'm messing with you. He sat in the chair, as most guys do. What guy comforts his significant other when the person screams like a raging lunatic? Plus, Christine was acting overdramatic.

"Aren't you going to do something?" She asked Troy.

Troy sighed and walked upstairs.

Wham!

He came downstairs and sat down in the chair. "Spider is dead." Troy continued watching the movie.

Christine groaned and stomped up the stairs.

"Shouldn't you deal with your girl?" Joseph asked Troy.

"Christine is fine." Troy shrugged while watching the movie.

Let me explain about Troy. He wasn't that guy that catered to a girl as most guys do. He found humor in the most obscure things. Christine is melodramatic, where Troy isn't. Things don't bother this guy. I like him better than the other guys that Christine dated who jumped to her beck and call.

Christine should marry Troy because I can tolerate him, and I can't stand most people, including the Fraziers.

*****

It has been a couple of months since I saw Gloria. She wanted to cool it, so we cooled it. It sucked ass. I saw her and had the need to jump her but had to refrain.

I don't understand why she doesn't leave that idiot. Hell, I don't see why any woman would want to wrap themselves up with a Frazier boy. Have you met them? The Fraziers are the definition that their mom should have swallowed them. I don't understand how Charles was friends with Maurice, and Mason did business with Marty.

Mason was brilliant at stopping business with those boobs. Charles married an intelligent woman who killed his friendship

with his idiotic friends. My brother is an idiot for cheating on her. Hell, I was an idiot for having a relationship with Gloria. Damn, I missed her.

After class, I wandered through campus without a care in the world and found myself at the coffeehouse. Yeah, I learned nothing with my time apart from Gloria. You think the distance would kill any romantic urges lingering, but it doesn't. It makes the heart grow fonder, but in my case, stupider.

My brain said to run, and my heart told my legs to go to your woman. These two things conflicted a lot with each other, putting me in a situation that I didn't need. I looked at Gloria after walking into the coffeehouse. Even though I don't need it, I want it.

I stood in line and waited until I reached the counter. Gloria looked at me, surprised.

"Yeah, give me a coffee and," I leaned in, "you."

Gloria bit her bottom lip as I leaned back. I'm playing with fire, but I didn't care. I wanted Gloria in so many ways.

She grabbed my coffee and returned with it. I paid for it, then left. Once I was out of view, I dumped the coffee out. I should have ordered hot cocoa and stopped wasting my money.

Later, I returned to the coffeehouse to find her cleaning up and tapped on the window. Gloria noticed me standing there, and I smiled and waved as she walked to the door and unlocked it. After stepping inside, she locked the door.

"Did you take care of your issues?" I asked.

"In a manner of speaking." Gloria returned to cleaning.

I followed her. "Does it have anything to do with Maurice?"

Gloria wouldn't look at me as she cleaned. "When doesn't it have to do with Maurice?"

That answer bothered me.

"Maurice and his family can do whatever the hell they want, and nothing happens."

"You don't have to stay with Maurice."

Her head snapped up. "It's easy for people to say that. Leave your husband if you're unhappy. Find a new place if things aren't working. It's easy to say but harder to do."

"What about our plans?"

"Carri, you still have another year of school to finish. Do you think when you graduate that you will wait for me?"

"I will wait forever."

Gloria's expression changed to surprise.

"I meant what I said. After I graduate, I want us to leave, and I'll take care of the legalities of your marriage. We'll start over, and you'll never deal with the Frazier family again."

"I'm not sure." Gloria shook her head.

I know she was unsure of us. "I don't perceive what is going on at home. But we can be together when Maurice leaves."

Gloria gave me a doubtful glance.

I walked towards her and took her hands in mine. "Trust me."

Gloria sighed. She had doubts, but it was time to call in a favor. Someone owes me for saving their ass. I smiled as Gloria furrowed her brows.

*****

I borrowed Joseph's car, waited in an empty parking lot, and leaned against it. A few minutes later, a car pulled up next to me and stopped.

Brian Morgan appeared, along with two guys. They walked over to me.

"Carrington, this is Chance Bradley and Shep Holliday," Brian said.

I shook Chance and Shep's hands.

"Now, what did you need?"

"I need you to keep Maurice and his brothers busy."

Brian gave me a sideways glance.

"I'm cashing in a favor that I did for you." I shrugged.

Brian gave me an annoyed glance.

"Or should I tell your dad about your deal with the Mendoza crew that flew south?" I was playing with fire.

The Mendoza family was a cartel in Mexico that did business with the Santiagos. Both families were into guns and drugs. The Morgan family received their supply of weapons from both families, making the guns untraceable.

Charles made a deal with Santiagos, dealing with drugs and enlisting Charles's idiot friends. It was a lousy deal and pissed off Mason. Our family moved money through a business front, and drugs were a dangerous game. The feds referred to it as racketeering.

All families have skeletons in their closets, and we hid ours well.

Brian thought about it, then agreed to help me. We shook on the deal, and it would prove to be the wrong decision on my part with what was to come.

Love makes us do dumb things and make bad decisions, but someone will show me that love comes from a different source. That person will give me the unconditional love that I thought I had found with Gloria.

# CHAPTER 15

## DIRTY LITTLE SECRET

**3rd person**

Brian kept his end of the deal and made sure Maurice and his brothers stayed busy. He orchestrated deals with several families in Florida, New York, Michigan, Mexico, and other territories that his family controlled.

The problem with this scenario is that it brought Carrington's family to the forefront, with Mason transferring an obscene amount of money. It made everyone targets because of Carrington's dirty little secret.

When you're moving a vast amount of cash, it'll keep the feds busy, which it did with the families. Some families fled the country while others hid. The Fraziers landed in jail for their part while Mason and the Morgan family eluded jail time. It helps to have someone in your pocket.

That gave Gloria the freedom to be with Carrington without scrutiny from Maurice and his family. If you knew anything about Maurice, his drinking was excessive. Jail doesn't help because you have no choice but to dry out. It's not rehab where they help you. Prison is worse because you suffer through the DTs, which he did.

"Help me!" Maurice's body reacted to the lack of alcohol in his system. "Please!" He gripped the bars of his cell.

A guard walked over after hearing his cries radiate from the cell.

"Please give me a drink."

"You know the rules about alcohol, inmate."

"I need one little drink."

"I said no. Now, shut the hell up before I throw you into solitary confinement!"

Maurice whimpered. For a feared family, he was making his family look like a joke. Jail has a way of making or breaking you, and it was breaking Maurice.

While Maurice dealt with his withdrawals, two of his brothers talked, namely Marty and Mateo. The other three were in a different prison section because of their age and degree of the offense. Marty and Mateo sat at a table in the central area.

"Our suit is getting us an early release," Marty told Mateo.

Mateo gave his brother an unamused glance. You could never tell with Mateo. He's the person who would slit your throat in a heartbeat. The one thing that kept him from losing his shit was his kids. That is irony in a nutshell.

"I'll believe it when I see it." Mateo wasn't a pessimist, but he knew the game, and that's what made him calculating and dangerous.

"How's Maurice?"

"A little bitch. Damn drunk, can't go a day without the sauce."

"Maurice will dry out and return to his old self."

"That is doubtful." Mateo didn't care if he pissed off his brother.

The village idiots made their way to Marty and Mateo.

"Who let you out of your cages?" Mateo asked his brothers.

Maximilian sat down as Marco and Mickey joined him. "I need to get out of here. My old lady is pissy about me doing business. Plus, it doesn't help that she's ready to pop out my kid."

"I told you to take your old lady in hand. The problem with you idiots is that you let your women shackle your dick," Mateo said.

His brothers glared at him. He shrugged because he didn't care.

"Enough, Mateo," Marty said.

Yeah, Mateo was a real prick. How he ever got a woman was beyond anyone?

"When are we getting sprung?" Mickey asked.

"Soon, and I have a bone to pick with a certain family," Marty told his brothers.

"What about Maurice?" Marco asked.

"Jail should dry out, Maurice. Those excuses he had for so-called friends got him messed up, and I'm not happy," Marty said.

"You're never happy. That isn't news," Mateo said, earning a glare from Marty.

"I heard Shaw is doing time," Mickey said.

"Who cares? I want out of this joint, and I want that family to pay for us being here," Mateo said.

That was the thing about Mateo. While his brothers were clueless, he wasn't. He knew who was behind it all, and that was Carrington's family. The rift between the families was growing.

The Frazier family planned how they would make the Jones family suffer, and it would involve kids.

They were terrible people. Does this surprise you?

*****

While the Frazier boys were plotting against the Jones family, another person was seeking revenge in the form of Frank Shaw.

A man close to Frank's age sat down across from Frank. "Hey, Frankie."

"Henry."

Henry leaned in. "You got yourself into a mess. I told you that Charles would screw you, along with Maurice and Greg."

"Thanks for the reminder, brother."

"Chill, Frankie boy, I got plans." Henry smiled.

"Is my old lady behaving?"

"Yep, I got tabs on your wife. She knows not to screw you over. Plus, she's madly in love with you." Henry rolled his eyes.

"Get the girls young, and they can't do enough for you. I figure when the time's right, I'll trade her in for a newer model." Frank smirked, along with his brother.

Yep, they were sick bastards. They enjoyed the young girls.

The Feds tried to nail Frank sleeping with underage girls, but his wife refused to roll over on Frank. Young and dumb is the assumption.

"I'm getting out of this joint and leaving town. I got plans for the others, especially Charles. He wants to fuck me over, then he'll suffer," Frank told Henry.

"What do you have planned?" Henry arched an eyebrow.

"Payment for what Charles took from me. He convinced us to invest in this deal and left us holding the bag. Greg ran off like the weasel he is, turning me over to the cops. Maurice turned his back on me. Now, it's my turn to make them all fucking pay." Frank slammed his fists on the tabletop.

Henry looked at his brother, and a smile curled upon his lips. The thing the Shaw brothers liked more than young girls was money. Frank was hell-bent on revenge with everyone who got involved in that deal Charles orchestrated. He didn't plan on one person throwing a monkey wrench into his plans.

The Fraziers, Shaws, Hartleys, and Jones' families forgot that certain people would form a formidable friendship when they met. It's a friendship that differs from Charles's friendship, proving loyalty is everything.

Carrington would play an intricate part in that friendship unbeknownst to himself or anyone else. What was coming would piss off Mason entirely. When doesn't Carrington piss off Mason?

# CHAPTER 16

## A SUMMER FLING

**Carrington**

I stayed at the rental house and took summer courses with the Frazier boys preoccupied and school letting out for the summer. It also gave me a chance to spend time alone with Gloria.

I awoke to the shower running and got out of bed. I strutted into the bathroom, opened the shower curtain, stepped into the tub, and closed the curtain. I wrapped my arms around Gloria, pulled her to me, and kissed her neck.

A soft moan escaped her lips as I moved my lips along her neckline, roaming my hands over Gloria's body, feeling the soft, delicate features of her. I maneuvered between her legs and slid into her as a moan escaped her lips.

Gloria held onto me as I thrust into her, enjoying her. I waited until she found her release before I pulled out and released it into the tub. I hated finishing this way because it was anticlimactic to me, but I didn't bring protection.

Gloria washed up and turned to me as I washed my body. "When we agreed to this, I didn't think we would stay in."

"There's nothing wrong with staying in." I gave her a mischievous glance.

Gloria rolled her eyes and shook her head as I chuckled. I rinsed off, wrapped my arms around her, and pulled her to me.

"I know you want to go out, but if anyone sees us together, it won't bode well for us."

"I know." Gloria sighed.

I leaned in and kissed her before getting out of the shower. I dried off and strolled into the bedroom to dress. Gloria wanted to go out like any couple, but people enjoy gossiping. The people here are worse than a gossip columnist.

Couldn't they find other things to do than poke around in other people's affairs? It was as if I had several Christines around me. The one quality I disliked about my sister would make her more enjoyable if she dropped that characteristic.

Gloria walked into the bedroom and dressed as I admired her body. Damn, she had a beautiful body.

We finished dressing, then left. Gloria had to work, and I had class. I figured we could play cards tonight.

After class, I visited Kate since Gloria was at work. I strolled to the bakery to find it bustling with customers. It was nice that the business was doing well, and customers kept Kate busy, providing her enjoyment out of it. That made me happy.

I sat at a table, waiting until customers cleared out of the bakery. Someone placed a glass of iced tea in front of me, then joined me. Kate smiled.

"Busy?" I smirked.

Kate arched a brow at me, then shook her head as I chuckled. "It's good when you find your passion, and people enjoy it."

That's what I noticed about my sister. It contented Kate with doing what she loves. Kate enjoyed baking and had no use for

the family business, preferring to speak to people, and this business provided it.

"I'm surprised you stayed this summer."

I shrugged.

Kate gave me a knowing glance. My sister is astute to situations, and she is in tune with mine. "Carri, I won't lecture you, but if you play with fire, you will get burned."

Lying to my sister is the worst thing you can do. She sees through bullshit quickly, and it never ends well if you do. It's best to be honest, and suffer the consequences rather than lie.

"It's fine, Kate. I'm happy." I sipped my drink.

"There comes a time when you realize that happiness doesn't come from another person but yourself."

I didn't understand what she meant, but I would find out later. "What about you?"

"What about me?"

"You can't tell me that you're happy alone." I arched my brow.

Kate rolled her eyes. "I don't need a man to make me happy. I'm happy with the bakery because it keeps me busy, and I meet people."

"It devastated you when William died, but I doubt he would like you to close yourself off to love."

Kate shook her head and sighed. "I didn't close myself off to love, but I don't need to find someone else. That is the difference between others and myself. I enjoyed my time with William, but sometimes things work out as they should."

There was no somber tone or disappointment. Kate wasn't like most people who gave up on love when something didn't

work with another person or died. My sister was secure with being alone because she wasn't lonely.

"William died."

"Because William wanted to serve in the military and died doing what he loved. I don't fault William for his choice, supporting it. Carri, we make decisions that affect us, and it's whether we can live with that choice."

My sister wasn't an unreasonable person, but she knew our actions could have consequences.

"Don't wake up one day and realize you lost the moon while counting the stars."

I didn't understand what she meant. Gloria was my moon, and I wasn't looking for the stars.

I finished my visit with Kate, then left. I strolled to the coffeehouse as Kate's words plagued my mind. I didn't understand what she meant because I was missing the concept. It wouldn't be until years later that Kate's advice would make sense to me.

Sometimes, it's not the person who you think is the moon, but someone different. That person will show why things work out for the best.

*****

After we got back to the house, we ate, then played cards. What did we play? A game of Old Maid, and I kept sticking Gloria with the Old Maid and pissed her off.

"Knock it off, Carri!"

I chuckled. "I can't help it if you're terrible at this game."

Gloria glared at me.

"It's a kid's game, which you should know how to play it."

"Yeah, if you didn't cheat."

I feigned offense to her accusation. "I don't cheat."

Gloria gave me a strange face.

I contemplated it. "Ignore that."

She giggled.

That's ironic if I ever heard it.

I set the cards down and crawled over to Gloria, then captured her lips with mine. Our kissing turned passionate as we lost our clothes. I put on protection and made love to her on the living room floor. Most people don't consider that romantic, but when in Rome.

Any time I can make love to Gloria, I did. We were like two jackrabbits going at it everywhere. We couldn't get enough of each other, and it showed. One day, we would return to our rendezvous at the motel when Christine and Elliot showed up.

Joseph graduated this year, so he wasn't returning. He got a computer degree and began doing things with computers that he shouldn't do. My family's crimes didn't stay in one area as they expanded. If Joseph didn't end up in prison for his dirty deeds, it would surprise me.

My family wasn't innocent at all, and I fell into that category, along with them. The big problem was my crime resulted in the most significant way, leaving me with a present. I wouldn't find out until later what that gift was. But it would change everything.

# CHAPTER 17

## THIS SHOULD BE FUN

**Carrington**

Fall came with the arrival of Christine and Elliot, and it also ended my time at the house with Gloria, which I had enjoyed.

The prison also released the Frazier boys. Their slime of an attorney got the Frazier boys out on a technicality. That was my luck. Brian couldn't help me since he had more significant issues with his family business.

I called the Mendoza, Garza, and Santiago families and put a bug in their ear about shipments regarding the Frazier family. I figure that would keep the Frazier boys busy.

*****

**Gloria**

I got ready for work and thought about Carri. This summer was excellent, and it was nice not to worry about Maurice or his brothers. Then the front door opened and closed.

I walked out of the bedroom and to the top of the stairs, coming face to face with Maurice.

"Hey, Gloria." Maurice smiled.

Words eluded me. I gulped. "I didn't know you had gotten out."

"Yeah, our suit found a technicality, and the judge released us."

"Oh."

"I had time to think. It happens when you're in the clink and drying out. I was terrible to you. But I want to make it up to you if you let me."

I didn't trust Maurice after what he put me through before he went to jail. He moved closer as I stepped back, and he stopped. "Gloria, I won't hurt you."

I gave him a disbelief expression.

"That was the issue. Drinking caused me to become a terrible person. I'm sober now."

I wish I could believe him, but I couldn't. That's how it started.

"I'm attending my meetings, and my brothers warned me that if I touch another drop, they'll kill me."

"I wish I could believe you, but I can't. Excuse me." I walked past Maurice.

He stood there, crestfallen, but I didn't care. I endured abuse from Maurice. He can claim that he's sober, but it's a matter of time before he falls off the wagon.

It didn't matter. When Carri graduates, I was leaving with him. But something would change my decision, and I didn't know it yet.

\*\*\*\*\*

**Carrington**

Christine and Elliot settled in. Christine visited Troy, leaving me with Elliot. Let me rephrase that. She ordered me to watch Elliot. He enjoys creating issues.

I walked out back to find Elliot to show him the campus. A knife flew by my head and landed in the back of the house. I looked at Elliot, annoyed.

Elliot walked over and yanked the knife out of the house. "Do you mind? You distracted me from my target."

I noticed a picture of Christine tacked to the house behind me and took the film down. "Flinging a knife at a picture of our sister isn't a target." I rolled my eyes.

Elliot shrugged.

"Be nice. Christine helped change your diapers."

"That doesn't matter. Everyone changed my diapers."

"Christine also beat your ass several times."

"Semantics, Carri."

I sighed. Christine terrified Elliot, and he refused to admit it. Our sister took Elliot in hand many times, and it wasn't pretty. Even when he got older, he didn't scare her. It didn't matter if he could chuck a knife up a hill fifty feet into a tree. Yeah, my siblings were crazy.

"Let's go."

"Where?"

"I'm showing you the campus today." I turned to walk away.

"And to check on that woman that you're seeing."

I stopped and turned to him. "I'm not seeing anyone."

Elliot walked towards me. "Well, you're a cheat and a liar, and your deception will make Mason proud." Elliot walked past me.

I'm sure if Christine doesn't beat Elliot into oblivion, I will.

We left the house and traveled to the campus. I showed Elliot everything, taking him to Kate's bakery when we encountered Marco.

"Look, who it is," Marco said to his cronies, who snickered.

"Who let the dog out of his cage?" Elliot asked.

Macro and his cronies stopped laughing. Elliot didn't smile.

"Be careful, boy."

A pocket knife landed at the tip of Marco's shoe. I did a double-take. Elliot stood there, unamused. Marco reached down, yanked the knife out of his shoe, and screamed as blood pooled. Elliot took the knife from Marco and wiped the blade on Marco's shirt before replacing it in his pocket.

"You aren't the most intelligent one in the bunch, are you?" Elliot asked.

Marco hopped around, holding his leg. "I'll kill you," Marco spoke through gritted teeth.

"Challenge accepted." Elliot walked away.

I sighed and followed Elliot, leaving Marco to cry like a little bitch. I caught up with Elliot. "Was that necessary?"

"Yes."

"Why?"

"Because while you worry about sticking your dick into someone you shouldn't, that family is planning."

"The Fraziers are idiots."

"Never underestimate an opponent, brother. It will cost you."

We walked to Kate's bakery.

Elliot might be the youngest of us, but he read people better than anyone. He didn't bother with romantic entanglements because he didn't have the patience for them. If he met a woman, it would be a miracle.

We entered the bakery, and Kate noticed us. She walked over and hugged us. Then Kate looked at Elliot. "I understand you're starting trouble."

"That's doubtful," Elliot replied.

Kate pointed at the door as Maximilian and Mickey entered the bakery.

"It seems big brother called crazy one and two," I said.

Maximillian and Mickey strolled over to us.

"Maxie and Mickey Mouse. It's been a while. I guess Marty let you out to play," I said.

"We got a message for you," Max said.

"Dare we ask what that message is?" Elliot asked.

Kate shushed him.

"Watch your back," Mickey said.

They turned and left. There wasn't anything cryptic about that message.

Kate rubbed her chin. She did this when she was thinking about something. Elliot was stoic, not reacting to the situation, which made him dangerous.

"Those boys are planning something. I'll call Mason." Kate went into the back.

"I don't think we have to worry," I said.

"What did you do?" Elliot inquired.

"Nothing yet." I walked away to make a phone call.

If the Frazier boys were out, I needed to keep them busy, especially Maurice. I made an anonymous phone call to the Santiago, Mendoza, and Garza families about the Fraziers and shipments. That would keep the Frazier boys busy, but other deals got made that I would find out about later.

Why couldn't I have a normal family?

# CHAPTER 18

## A TEMPORARY TRUCE

**Carrington**

With the Frazier boys running amuck, that made it difficult for Gloria and me to get together. We could be together if Maurice and the others left town, and that depended on the other families keeping the Frazier family busy. I didn't have high hopes.

While I was trying to figure things out with Gloria, Mason and Brian met with Hector Santiago, who became a liaison between the Santiago family and other families. Brian became a boss when his father retired. Edward's health took a significant turn, resulting in the lateral movement and changes in how his family conducts business.

Brian wanted a truce between the Santiago, Morgan, and Jones families. The ceasefire would help our family the most, leaving the others to fend for themselves. I would learn this after entering the family business.

\*\*\*\*\*

**3rd person**

Brian and Mason arrived at a meeting spot with Hector at the Moretti compound. It was a neutral meeting place in Florida. The Moretti family didn't tolerate bullshit and will shoot you dead

instead of dealing with you. They had a loyalty like no other, and Carrington wouldn't experience this loyalty until later.

Cassius Moretti was sitting at a table when Brian, Mason, and Hector walked up. "Sit." Cassius pointed at empty chairs.

They sat down at the table. A woman walked up with drinks, placed them on the table, and left.

"I hear you want a truce between your families."

"That's correct," Hector said.

"What about the other families?"

"The other families are out since they fight amongst themselves and have proven untrustworthy."

"And like your family is trustworthy?" Cassius saw through the bullshit Hector spewed. "Don't lie to me, Hector. Your family will backstab faster than anyone. Luis is untrustworthy, along with the rest of your family."

"We want to change things," Brian said.

"How so?"

"Mason agreed to keep his business out of troubled territories, conducting business between my family and the Moretti family without issue. That will allow the Santiago family to control the cartels, leaving Michigan and Florida out. If Luis makes a move, he dies, along with his family. The Feds are watching the Mendoza family, along with the Garzas."

Cassius rubbed his chin. The only person who conducted this business move was Edward Morgan since Cassius had done business with him. "Your father advised you on this decision."

"My father has been my consigliere since he retired." Brian left out the part of Edward's health, taking a turn. Until Brian

fully rose to power, Edward was his protection. If Edward dies before that happens, families will go after Brian. This truce would provide Brian with what he needed while offering protection for the Jones family.

It's a move that helped them.

"Your father was a loyal man and protected people who needed it. He saved many families' parents from harm, earning their loyalty in return. Too bad, their children don't have the same loyalty," Cassius told Mason.

Mason knew loyalty was vital to Cassius and disapproved of the shit his family was pulling. If Mason wanted this truce, things had to change in his family.

"My father raised us with the same loyalty, and I will continue his legacy," Mason replied, taking a gamble.

"Then I suggest you get your family to fall in line with that concept. I have received word that your brothers don't understand the concept."

Here's what people had to understand about these deals. If you plan on making a truce, don't pick a person who dislikes shady shit. Cassius hated disloyalty in all forms, including cheating in relationships since it proved you untrustworthy.

"My brothers will fall in line when I return."

Okay, Carrington's big brother lost his damn mind. Who the hell agrees to keep someone's dick in their pants? Mason does, and it's not his dick he agrees with here.

"Cassius, I understand you expect loyalty, but we aren't here to police our family's relationships. We came here today to conduct a truce between our families with the intention neither

of us will attack the other and keep others at bay. We'll offer protection if that happens," Brian told Cassius.

Cassius tapped his fingertips on the tabletop, deciding how to conduct this truce. His territory was neutral, which meant he had no say with family matters of other families. When you conduct a respite, a Moretti member will arrive to eliminate the person if one member violates it. It was a guarantee.

"Fine, the truce shall state that the Jones and Morgan family conducts business without incident, staying out territories except for Michigan. The Santiago family stays out of Michigan and Florida. If a violation of this truce happens, I will send Salvatore to clean it up." Cassius waved his finger to a man close to him.

The man walked over and stood there.

"This is Salvatore Moretti, my right-hand man and brother. He cleans up violations for me. We're neutral territory, but that doesn't mean I won't end a threat. I suggest you get your affairs in order."

It wasn't a threat or warning but a promise.

Cassius made a call, then a few minutes later, a woman walked out with a piece of paper and handed it to Cassius, along with a pen. Cassius slid the paper and pen across the tabletop as Mason, Brian, and Hector signed the truce.

There's a problem with this truce. It doesn't prevent family members from violating the ceasefire terms, which they knew the Santiagos would do. The Morgan family would break the ceasefire, invading the Florida territories when a member of the Moretti crew attacked one of Brian's own and invaded the Michigan territory. That would come later.

Carrington had a more significant issue trying to see Gloria and keeping the Frazier family busy. That kept him busy, while Elliot thought he was an idiot for this idea.

You throw in Christine living with them, and it makes for an exciting dynamic. The problem was while Carrington dealt with his relationship with Gloria and planned, Christine, will get hit with unsettling news of her own.

Let's say that Carrington's sister wasn't as pure as the driven snow. While Christine enjoys throwing her family under the bus, especially Carrington, she will find herself in a predicament, dragging Carrington into the mess. Unlike his sister, he'll help Christine and not out her to Mason.

# CHAPTER 19

## HOUSTON, WE HAVE ONE HELL OF A PROBLEM

**Carrington**

Attempting to see Gloria was impossible with the Frazier boys lurking around. Then I discovered that dear old brother Mason made a damn ceasefire with the Santiagos, shooting my plan in the ass.

I had to wait to meet with Gloria when Maurice left town, and that wasn't often. It turns out Maurice saw the light and got sober in prison. Now, he's the doting husband. Note the sarcasm because he's as attentive as my dick is.

The good thing was I took some courses over the summer, which meant I'd graduate earlier than expected, like around Christmas next year. Gloria and I could leave and not look back. Now, I had to settle for senseless comedies, junk food, and my damn hand.

I rented some movies, then headed to a corner store and picked up snacks. Chips, pop, candy, and anything else I could fill my arms. The clerk gave me a strange expression as I rolled my eyes. There's no need for judgment.

The clerk rang me up. I paid for my junk food, then left the store. One day, you will understand my pain, buddy.

I returned and set the bags down, along with the movies. I started with Miss Congeniality. Who doesn't like a good Sandra Bullock movie?

I settle in with my snacks on the couch, cracking open a Coke. I watched the movie and laughed my ass off with the beauty pageant scene. Now, that's how all beauty pageants should be in real life. Did you ever watch one? They're boring as shit. Everyone wants to save the world and the children. Then after the pageant, both seem to fall by the wayside. Those sad children will grow up in a forgotten world.

After the movie, I headed upstairs to use the bathroom, not realizing Christine was here. I opened the door, and Christine's head snapped in my direction as she looked in shock. Then I noticed something in her hands.

I walked over to Christine as she held a pregnancy test. The best part was it was positive, and Christine had the look of a deer caught in headlights.

"I'm guessing that was a pleasant surprise." I pointed at the pregnancy test.

Christine's face contorted in horror.

"Or not."

Here's where Christine and I differed from each other. While she will rat me out to Mason, I wouldn't do that. She's a big girl and understands the consequences.

"I guess you'll call Mason and inform him that I'm pregnant." Christine stared at the test. "I deserve it for telling him about your dalliances, and Mason will make me get rid of it. A child out of wedlock is a scandal." Christine sniffled.

I furrowed my brows.

"Troy doesn't want a baby since we haven't discussed a family or marriage. If Mason cuts me off, I'll ask Kate for a job. I can finish school and raise a baby alone since many single parents do it every day." Christine looked at me with tear-streaked cheeks.

My sister had a terrified expression. So, I hugged her. She wrapped her arms around me and buried her head into me as she sobbed. I offered her comfort. No matter our differences, Christine is still my sister.

"How do you know Troy doesn't want the baby? Did you talk to him?"

"We never discussed kids or marriage."

I pulled back from Christine. "Now, you should decide together. If it were Gloria, I would want to know." I didn't realize what I said until the words left my mouth.

Christine stared at me, shocked. I cursed myself. I let go of her as she gave me an incredulous expression. Yeah, that wasn't good.

I pursed my lips, avoiding eye contact.

"Do you love Gloria?"

I nodded. Christine gave me a compassionate expression.

"It's not something I planned on happening, but it did. Most people would consider it a fling, but I don't."

"It's because it involves the heart. Carri, carrying on a relationship with a married woman doesn't end well. A married person rarely leaves their spouse, and you'll get your heart broken."

"It's the chance I'm willing to take because I love her."

I know people don't understand, but when you fall in love with someone, you can't help it. There's an issue with that scenario. When you should listen to people, your heart doesn't. It would be a hard truth that I would learn for myself.

Later, Christine called Troy over to tell him the news while Elliot and I spied on them. Yeah, we have no shame.

"This is utterly ridiculous," Elliot whispered.

"Shh, I can't hear." I shushed him, peering through an opening through the kitchen door. I told you that we had no shame.

Troy quietly sat there as Christine told him about the pregnancy.

"Now, if you don't want the baby, I understand. I can raise the baby alone. I'll get a job, find a daycare, and finish school. I won't ask for any financial help, and you won't have to see us. I'll tell Mason, and he'll cut me off financially."

I shook my head. Leave it to our sister to ramble, although Troy didn't help with sitting there and not saying anything. Say something, you idiot. Our sister is dying right now.

"So, that is it. You're off the hook."

I facepalmed myself.

"Are you finished?" Troy stood up. "I resent that you let me off the hook when it's my baby, too."

Wait. What? That is a new development.

"What?"

"It's my baby, too, and we'll get married and raise the baby together."

"But we didn't discuss marriage or kids."

"What's there to discuss? I planned to marry you when we graduate and have kids." Troy shrugged. "It'll happen sooner than expected. If Mason disowns you, then so be it. I'll support us."

Well, Troy has balls. He didn't even argue or throw a hissy fit, making me like him more and more every day.

"Tell the two eavesdroppers that we're getting married."

Elliot and I fell through the kitchen door and landed on the floor. We looked up to find Christine and Troy looking at us.

"What are you doing?" Christine asked us.

"We're trying to be stealth, like ninjas, but we suck at it," I said.

Elliot stood up and left me on the floor. "This idiot on the floor wanted to eavesdrop and dragged me along for the ride."

I stood up. "No one said you had to agree. That was your choice."

Elliot glared at me. Nice try, little brother. But if I'm going down, so are you.

*****

The next day, we traveled to City Hall, and Christine and Troy got married. The ceremony was short and sweet because Troy barely said anything. Out of my sisters' boyfriends, both said a few words. How did they manage a relationship for years? You talk to your significant other, except for Grant and Troy, because they're monks.

Elliot and I were witnesses to the union, signing the marriage license. After the quickie wedding, Christine called Mason, and his response was less than favorable. Mason yelled the word fuck more times than I could count, and he wasn't on speakerphone.

After Mason's tirade, he didn't disown Christine, which was a plus. Christine was moving out and moving in with Troy, leaving me alone with Elliot, which wasn't a plus.

How did I get stuck with my psycho brother? Pure dumb luck, I guess. Now I had to contend with Elliot while waiting to meet Gloria, and the Frazier boys had to leave town soon before I lost my shit.

# CHAPTER 20

## A CRAZY THING CALLED LUST

**Carrington**

I finally got to spend time with Gloria. It had been a while. As soon as we hit the motel room, we lost our clothes. I made love to her repeatedly, making up for a lost time. It had been too damn long.

We took a breather and laid in bed. Gloria laid on my chest as I held her.

"I missed you, Carri."

"Thanks to my brother Mason, my plans flew out the door like a bird." I made a fluttering sound with my mouth.

Gloria propped herself up and looked at me.

"Mason signed a truce with the Morgan and Santiago families, so I can't ask them for help to keep Maurice and his brothers busy." I sighed.

"It doesn't matter, Carri. I don't plan on staying with Maurice."

I ran my fingers through her hair.

"Maurice thinks because he's sober that it erases everything that happened between us. He broke his promises to me, and I get tired of listening to him constantly."

"Then we stick to the plan. When I graduate, we'll leave and never look back."

Gloria nodded. I pressed my lips to hers and rolled Gloria onto her back. Then I slid back into her, thrusting inside of her repeatedly. I would make love to her all night long. I couldn't wait until we left, then we would make love every day. I would show Gloria so much love.

The problem is what we think, and the reality of a situation are two distinct things. You make plans, then they fall apart, leaving you dumbfounded. I will find this out later.

*****

**Gloria**

I couldn't get enough of Carri when we met at the motel room. With Maurice at home and sober, it made seeing Carri difficult. I could meet Carri before when Maurice got drunk or was screwing some whore.

I knew about Maurice's extracurricular activities, along with the drinking. I thought I would stay in a terrible marriage until I met Carri. The day I met Carri, I knew he differed from Maurice. Carri didn't drink, smoke, or drink coffee. I chuckled, knowing he bought coffee and dumped it out. I never told Carri. I didn't want him to feel ashamed.

Even when we were apart, Carri wasn't looking at another woman. I can tell with the way he makes love to me. Plus, he says how horny he is, and his hand gets tired. That thought made me giggle.

The sex with Carri was unbelievable. He does things to me that no guy has ever done. Plus, Carri makes me scream his

name every single time. With Maurice, I would find excuses not to have sex. Then I would take care of my needs. People would disagree with my choices, but I didn't care because I was happy.

The minute Maurice announced that he was leaving for business, I played my part. I functioned as the dutiful wife, sad to see him go. I waited an hour after Maurice left to meet Carri.

Sometimes, we didn't make it to the motel and parked in a secluded area. Our bodies craved each other, and the sex was phenomenal. I was ready to leave with Carri and start a life together.

One day, I came home from the grocery store, and I walked into the kitchen and almost dropped my bags of food. I planned to meet Carri later but didn't realize Maurice had come home early from his trip.

"Did I surprise you?" Maurice held a bouquet in front of him.
"Yes."

Maurice's presence didn't surprise me but shocked me. Maurice walked towards me. "I wanted to come home to my girl. I hate leaving constantly. I don't want you to feel lonely." Maurice stood in front of me.

Trust me. I'm not lonely. You can leave anytime now.

Maurice leaned and whispered into my ear. "A little birdie mentioned you have been staying busy while I leave. We need to fix that."

My eyes widened.

Maurice leaned back. "I didn't get sober so that my wife won't have sex with me. I should remind you of your duties."

I looked at Maurice, horrified. I didn't care if he got sober, and I didn't want him to touch me. I made a mistake by refusing Maurice, and he unleashed his anger on me. I endured a severe beating from Maurice.

Maurice finished his punishment with a warning. "If I find out you let another man touch you, I'll kill you, you fucking whore." Then he spat on me, and Mateo must have told Maurice.

That moment made me determined to leave and never look back. The problem was someone would stop me.

*****

**Carrington**

I was getting ready to meet Gloria and left the house. On my way to the motel, I stopped, noticing Marco with Maximilian. Shit. If they're here, so is Maurice, and that means Gloria couldn't meet me.

I changed course and walked to Kate's bakery as both followed me. Where the hell was Elliot when I needed his psychotic ass?

I reached the bakery when the idiot brothers stopped me.

"Oh, look, who it is," Maximilian told Marco.

"Well, if it isn't Maxi pad and Marco Polo. Shouldn't you idiots be doing time?" I asked.

Max and Marco glared at me. What? It was an honest question.

"I would be careful if I were you," Marco said.

"Do you want to do this? Because it would thrill me to oblige and provide you with a beat down?" I smirked.

While the idiot brothers kept me busy, the third idiot brother hit me from behind, catching me off guard. Three against one wasn't a fair fight. I defended myself the best that I could, but it didn't work. Then someone screamed.

I spat out blood as Mickey dropped with a knife sticking out of his leg. Another blade flew past me and landed on Max's shoulder as Marco ran off like a chicken shit that he is.

I grabbed my side, rising to my feet. Elliot walked over and yanked a knife out of Mickey, then out of Max. They screamed like little bitches as Elliot wiped off his blades on them. He helped me back to the house.

"I almost had the idiot brothers."

Elliot arched an eyebrow. "You didn't have shit. You were busy getting your ass beat."

"Semantics."

He rolled his eyes. My brother might be a psycho, but he had my back. No one matched Elliot's loyalty, and it will come in handy later in life.

After that night, I healed and didn't see Gloria for a while, but it wouldn't be the last time I would see her. We played with fire, and it will burn us, resulting in a secret I'll find out about later.

No matter how hard you hide a secret, they don't remain a secret. Our indiscretion will cause a more significant issue that wouldn't prepare either of us, causing a deadly altercation, and someone will take the blame.

# CHAPTER 21

## A NEW ADDITION TO THE FAMILY

**Carrington**

As the months passed, I longed for Gloria. While I pined for my love, Christine and Troy welcomed a daughter and named the baby Sarah. We visited Christine and her new family in the hospital. My siblings came, bringing Cole and Dean, who were over a year old.

I cradled the baby in my arms. Sarah was sleeping. I became eager to start a family with Gloria. First, I needed to extract her from Maurice. One day, I will give her the world, along with a family.

While we welcomed Sarah into the family, the Frazier boys had kids, namely Mateo and Maximilian. Max had a child named Max, and he was around the same age as Cole and Dean. Mateo had a child, calling the kid Mario. Leave it to an idiot brother to name his kid after a plumber in a video game.

The Frazier boys having kids and bastard kids are their idiot gene and family increases. God, save us all.

Charles held Sarah, then handed the baby back to Christine. He withdrew from the hospital room. What was up with him?

I stepped out of the hospital room while the family visited with the baby, including Maggie, Luci, and Mary. Charles was looking out of a window in the hallway.

"Are things not better between you and Maggie?" I asked.

"Our relationship is better, and I'm on the straight and narrow, keeping myself in check with other women. I'm lucky that Maggie forgave me and gave me a second chance." Charles continued to look out the window.

"But…"

"I don't think I will have kids."

I glanced at my brother with concern.

"When I mention the possibility of kids, Maggie changes the subject. I wrecked any chance of having a family since I broke Maggie's trust. Who wants children with a liar and a cheater?"

That question bothered me.

"I'll spend time with our niece and nephews, and that will help me with wanting a family of my own."

It doesn't matter how much we persuade ourselves to forgo a dream. It still nags at us. It did with me. I wanted to graduate and leave with Gloria. I paused there with Charles as he stared out of the window. I struggled to tell my brother it'll be okay, but not sure if it would be.

"Can I chat with my husband?" Maggie asked.

"Yeah, sure." I turned, walked towards the room, then reached it.

"Are you positive?" Charles asked.

I noticed Maggie nodding.

"You're pregnant?"

"Well, I took a pregnancy test, and it showed a positive result. I will confirm with the physician."

I peeked at my brother's face. Charles wanted to show excitement, but he's afraid he'll lose his chance at parenthood if he does.

"Aren't you happy?"

"I am, but I'm afraid of losing a chance at parenthood."

Maggie noticed Charles's expression.

His brows furrowed as he fidgeted with his fingers and stared at the floor. "I'm afraid that you'll leave and take the baby. I won't blame you if you do. You have every right to leave. I did a terrible thing and hurt you. If you never forgive me, I understand, but I hope you allow me to be a father."

My brother was an idiot for what he did to Maggie and proved foolish in every way, but he longed for a family. Our parents' deaths devastated us, and we all wanted an opportunity to continue their legacy.

Maggie took Charles's hands into hers. "Charles Ryan Jones, you look at me. Yes, you made a foolish mistake, and it hurt me, but no one is flawless. I offered you a second chance because I received brilliant advice from someone. The person told me that people make mistakes. That's what makes us human, and no one is flawless, but you have a big heart." Maggie pressed her fingertips on Charles's heart. "I pray if we have a boy, he has your heart."

Charles smiled. "Whether we have a boy or girl, I beseech the baby has your intelligence because I married a brilliant woman."

"Yes, you did."

They laughed.

I beamed as Charles and Maggie embraced. My brother will be a terrific father one day. Fatherhood changes things because it did with Mason, and Mason mellowed with Cole, unlike with us.

*****

**3rd person**

While Charles celebrated his news with Maggie, other issues were popping up, namely Frank Shaw. The prison released Frank, and he wasted no time knocking up his old lady, but his wife wasn't the only one.

Frank's wife was two months pregnant with their child when he headed to the bar to celebrate. After many rounds of alcohol, he hooked up with a girl in his car. Frank ignored the woman's identity and didn't bother to ask. When you're drunk, you're not exchanging information with each other.

Frank remained in the back seat as the girl moved back and forth while he thrust inside her. With loyalty, all bets were off with Frank Shaw. The guy couldn't stay loyal if you paid him, and he enjoyed the young girls. The girl was willing and able with Frank, taking full advantage of it.

It wouldn't be until later that Frank would recognize the girl from the bar as Henry's wife. Henry's wife kept a secret from Frank and Henry because of Frank's drunken escapade. That secret was disturbing, and Carrington would learn this information many years later.

Here is the problem with people's secrets. They never stay a secret. No matter what you do, that information rears its ugly

head at the worst times. It would be for Carrington when he least expected it.

*****

## Gloria

Carri wanted to leave. I had planned on going with him, but Maurice watched me like a hawk. Maurice dragged me to meet his nephews, which I didn't wish to do. He warned me to behave, or I'd receive a punishment. Mateo was worse and threatened me. I complied.

I watched the brothers with their families, and it disgusted me. Maurice's brothers didn't discipline the kids, and Maurice's brothers taught the children poor behavior. That made me not want any kids with Maurice because I didn't prefer my child to misbehave.

It didn't matter. The minute I had the opportunity, I was leaving with Carri. I can't live this life anymore. Carri and I would begin a life together and enjoy happiness, except a situation will prevent that from happening. Someone will come before my pleasure, and it will be the ultimate sacrifice in my life.

# CHAPTER 22

## A SITUATION

**Gloria**

A few months passed, and I met Carri to talk to him about leaving sooner. We met at the motel, giving into our passion as we made love. I craved to be with Carri, and wasn't aware that it would be the last chance I would see him.

Carri made passionate love to me as I gave in to him. After we finished, we talked.

"Are you sure?" Carri asked me.

"I can't remain there any longer. I hate that family, and I'm miserable. You make me happy."

We lay in bed.

"Okay, yeah, let's do it."

I grinned.

"Once we get settled, I'll finish classes and earn my degree. It won't make Mason happy, but it doesn't matter. I love you, Gloria."

"I love you, Carri."

Carri smiled at me, then tugged me to him and made love to me once more. We dressed, and I drove home.

I arrived home and showered so that Maurice wouldn't suspect. Maurice was waiting when I finished bathing and appeared from the bathroom in a towel.

I glimpsed at Maurice, then grabbed clothes from the dresser to wear.

"Gloria, I've been hard on you, but I'm trying. It seems like you don't care."

I closed the dresser drawer and dressed.

"Gloria, talk to me."

I snapped my head towards him. "What do you want me to say, Maurice? You tell me that you changed, then beat the hell out of me every chance you get. You have people watching me like a hawk, which is no way to live."

He walked towards me as I backed away until my back hit the wall. Maurice cornered me against the wall.

"Get away from me, Maurice," I spoke through gritted teeth.

"No, you'll act like my wife." Maurice pinned me to the wall.

I furrowed my brows, knowing what was coming.

"Even if it means taking it."

I became horrified as Maurice held me against the wall, undid his pants, and made his way inside me. I tried pushing Maurice off me, but his strength was more significant than mine.

As Maurice thrust inside me, he growled. "You're mine and no one else." I closed my eyes as Maurice continued until he finished. He removed himself from me as I remained there, numb. Maurice fixed his pants. "I'm tired of you denying me sex, so now I will take it."

I leaned against the wall as Maurice left the bedroom. How will I tell Carri? It wouldn't matter because tonight will change everything.

After that night, trying to meet Carri was impossible. It didn't help that Maurice would force me to have sex with him. I laid there and faked enjoyment most of the time since it was the only thing I could manage.

Two months after that night with Carri and Maurice, I was late. I picked up a pregnancy test. Maurice wouldn't be home, so it'd give me a chance to discover if I was pregnant.

I followed the instructions and waited. If it was positive, I was packing my shit and leaving. I waited until the test revealed a positive result. I held the test in my hand, not realizing Maurice had come home early.

"Is that a pregnancy test?" Maurice entered the bathroom and peeked at it, then at me. "You're pregnant?"

I nodded since I had no words.

Maurice walked over to me. "I'm going to be a dad!"

I gulped, nodding my head.

"I can't believe it!" Maurice pulled me into a hug and spoke about fatherhood.

But I didn't know whether the baby was Carri's or Maurice's.

"I can't wait to inform the family." Maurice left before I added anything.

Tears dripped down my cheeks.

Maurice called his family, and they showed up at our house. I acted happily, so no one suspected except for one person. I was in the kitchen, preparing beverages, when Mateo walked over to me.

Mateo didn't look at me but out of the kitchen window. "I find it interesting that my brother will be a father when his whore wife lays with another man."

I peeked at Mateo, horrified.

"I will make it simple. If you plan to take off, knowing it will destroy my brother's happiness, I'll slaughter you and that bastard child."

I gawked at him as he glanced at me. "Are you threatening me?" I crumpled my eyebrows.

"Consider it a promise, whore." Mateo smiled.

He left the kitchen as I paused there, shocked. I placed my hand on my stomach. I'll sacrifice my happiness to save my baby.

I'm sorry, Carri.

*****

**Carrington**

The last time I saw Gloria, we planned to leave after this semester, picking a date and a meeting place. The semester ended, and I packed my bags, then loaded the suitcases into the trunk.

"Carri? Where are you going?" Elliot asked me.

I twisted to face my brother. "I'm leaving. I met a woman, and we're going to be together."

"What about school?"

"Once we settle, I'll finish school. Elliot, no one understands, but what provides us happiness doesn't come from a book."

"What if this woman disappoints you?"

I beamed. "I love her." I got into the car and left Elliot standing there. I drove to the destination, which was an hour from town, and waited. I remained outside of the vehicle and lingered. I'll wait forever for Gloria.

I glanced at my watch and checked the time, expecting Gloria to turn up. Hours passed as a car pulled behind my car, and the headlights turned off. Someone stepped over to me.

"Gloria's not coming, is she?" I noticed Joseph standing there.

Joseph glanced at me with empathy.

I looked down at my shoes and sighed. "How did you find me?"

"Elliot called me. It took little to figure out where you were."

I blew air past my lips and kicked the ground with my foot.

"You expected to run off with Gloria. But it never ends well with a married woman."

"Will you tell me, 'I told you so?'" I expected the boom to drop.

"No."

I peered at the ground.

"I'll offer comfort." Joseph wrapped his arm around me as my heart broke.

My family recommended that I not get involved with Gloria, but I didn't listen. What do you do when it involves your heart? Do you risk the chance of breaking it, or do you hope the other person catches you?

When you fall for someone, you hope they catch you, not letting you fall. That is trust. When you open yourself up to someone, you pray the person loves you how you love them.

That is faith. You risk happiness for someone else and protecting them from harm, knowing you'll suffer. That is love.

You have faith, trusting the person to love you when there's a chance it won't work out. That is sacrifice. We all sacrifice something in our life for someone else, and I didn't grasp it now, but Gloria sacrificed us for someone more significant. When I discover the truth, my anger will disperse, and happiness will replace it.

It will take one person for me to understand Gloria's sacrifice.

# CHAPTER 23

## STARTING OVER

**Carrington**

After that night, I came back to Mason's house. I said nothing after arriving and expected a lecture from Mason. I entered the house as Mason met me at the door. I glanced at him as he studied me.

No lecture came as I hiked upstairs to my bedroom. Over the summer, I stayed to myself. I vowed not to fall in love again. Elliot was right that love was nothing but trouble. I wouldn't report to Saintwood College in the fall since I took correspondence courses to finish my degree during the summer. It's better this way.

Gloria made her decision, leaving me upset and angry. As I focused on moving on, Cole toddled into my room and touched my leg. I peeked at Cole as he held onto my leg and steadied himself. He stared at me with his blue eyes as I smiled at him. I spoke nothing as Luci walked in and picked him up.

"Cole, you shouldn't bother Carri. He's busy moping."

I peeked at her unamused. "I'm not moping but focusing on school and preparing to work with Mason."

That was a lie, and I was moping.

"That is bull. You can fool everyone else, but you can't fool me."

I offered her a knowing look.

"Before I met Mason, I assumed I loved a man. I planned to run away with the man, thinking it would make me happy. The man left me standing at the train station, waiting, and never appeared. I cried, thinking love won't happen, then I met this man who taught me why it was better that it didn't work out with the other man."

"You met Mason."

"Heck, no! I met a man named Antoine Pizzo."

What was the point of this conversation?

"We dated, then Antoine took me to a dinner party where I met Mason."

I still didn't understand the point of this conversation.

"Mason stole me from Antoine, and I disliked your brother for dragging me away from someone I love. That was until Mason showed me why he's the better man." Luci smirked.

I groaned. I didn't want to hear about my brother's sex life or anyone's sex life.

"One day, mark my words. You will meet a woman for you." Luci left the bedroom with Cole.

I had my doubts and wasn't looking, not caring to meet anyone. My family's right that I should have ended things with Gloria, but I didn't listen because I didn't care what my family said.

*****

I concluded my schooling, earned my degree and started working with Mason and Joseph. I parked in an office, crunching

numbers when Mason walked in and sat down in a chair. I continued working, saying nothing.

"I'm sending you to Russia."

My head snapped up. "Why?"

"I need you to take care of a deal for me."

I scratched my eyebrows.

"When you get home, pack a suitcase. You'll have a ticket and passport waiting for you, along with money."

"Do I have a vote?"

"No, you don't."

"I didn't think so."

That was Mason's punishment for not listening to him about Gloria. My brother has a way of punishing us when we disobey him. I hated traveling, and he knew it, so he dispatched me to other countries.

Mason punished Charles for his activities and froze his money. Joseph had to endure Mason when Mason destroyed nature for Joseph's cyber crimes. Mason made Christine's life difficult for her snitching. My brother could be a real prick.

Theresa and Kate stayed out of the line of fire with Mason. They were brilliant, but not the rest of us.

When I got home, I packed. Then one of Mason's men drove me to the airport, and I boarded a jet and flew to Russia. When I arrived, I exited the plane and sighed. I studied my itinerary, left the airport, and checked into a hotel.

After settling in, I met with the people who Mason sent me to meet. The business meeting was going well until a schmuck

pulled a gun on me. He fired and shot me, and I got the hell out of there. I'll kill Mason when I see him.

I held my arm and stumbled to a hospital. The worst part was I learned little Russian and was losing blood. I passed out on the floor with blood pooling around me. Well, I'll kill Mason if I survive.

*****

My eyes fluttered open, and I scanned the room to find myself in a hospital bed. I shifted and winced. My shoulder hurt like a bitch.

"I see you're waking up," someone spoke with a thick accent.

I blinked, trying to focus. Whatever the hospital gave me was one hell of a drug. I laid there in a daze as someone checked the machines and my shoulder.

"Everything looks good. I'll be back later." The person left the room.

My eyelids closed as I drifted off to sleep. Okay, so I'm not dead. That's a good sign, but it's not great when I see Mason. Asshole.

*****

After three days, I remained awake. What the hell did they give me? I spent more time sleeping than anything. Someone brought me food, and I ate it. It was nasty but would do until I got the hell out of here.

I rested there as a woman entered the room in a white lab coat. Great, they're locking me up in the looney bin.

The woman checked my chart. "You're awake."

I didn't reply but lay there.

The woman shuffled over, lifted my bandage, and examined my wound. "It's good. No infection."

"Who are you?"

"Your doctor, Dr. Nikita Petrova." The woman smiled.

I gawked at her with a blank expression.

"I check you later. Rest now." The doctor left the room as I remained there in bed. I didn't come to Russia to land in the hospital.

I heard from Mason. I returned his concern with a few choice words. I instructed him to suck a dick. Asshole. I swear to God, I'll kill him when I return.

After a week, the hospital released me. I had gotten dressed when the doctor came into the hospital room.

"You up."

"Yeah, they're springing me from this joint." I struggled to pull on my coat.

"Let me help." The doctor helped me with my coat.

I glanced at her, and she offered a smile. I had to admit that the physician was attractive.

"There, you can leave now." She beamed.

It was something about the doctor's smile that drew me to her. It seemed kind. I shook the thought from my mind since I didn't need any issues, namely women issues.

I fled the hospital room and returned to my hotel. I remained there until I was well enough to travel home. I called Joseph and informed him. I wasn't speaking to Mason since it was his fault for sending me here.

Something nagged at me that this trip would change my life.

*****

I remained in Russia, learning the language and conducting business. Mason and I patched up our issues. He sent some men to deal with the asshole who double-crossed us, and I didn't ask.

I stopped in a cafe to get hot cocoa and ran into someone I wasn't expecting.

"I see you better," the physician said.

"My shoulder is a little stiff, but I'll survive."

The doctor chuckled.

"No coffee?" She pointed to my hot cocoa.

"I'm not a fan, but I enjoy a warm beverage."

"Hot cocoa is delicious. Coffee, not so much, and it's bitter." She formed a face and stuck out her tongue.

I chuckled. "I don't see a doctor's coat on you." I checked out her attire.

"I go later."

"Do you work a lot?"

"Yes, less time for personal life. I love caring for people." That statement affected me, not understanding why.

"Yeah, I work a lot."

"I have time. Will you have hot cocoa with me?"

"Lead the way."

She ordered hot cocoa. Then we parked at a table and talked. Nikita told me about herself, and I mentioned myself, leaving out Gloria. I didn't need to ruin our conversation, recanting my affair. I didn't know what would happen with Nikita. But I didn't want to think about Gloria.

Gloria made her choice, and I moved on from her. But something would bring me face to face with Gloria, and it would involve someone significant.

# CHAPTER 24

## A NEW LOVE

**Gloria**

I had no clue about the baby's paternity and acted like Maurice was the father. I knew Carri waited for me, but I didn't meet him to save the baby. I accepted my fate with Maurice, knowing I'd have someone who would love me.

I ran my hands over my growing belly as the baby kicked. Maurice left for extended periods, leaving me alone to fend for myself. I assembled the crib and set up the nursery, and I was having a boy, which excited me.

"Okay, little one, we'll work together to discover our happiness." I used my paycheck to buy the baby items since Maurice didn't bother, and his family didn't throw me a baby shower as I purchased items for the baby.

"So, when you arrive, it'll be us against the world. I hope you'll love me, and I won't disappoint you." I struggled not to cry, but the baby kicked, reassuring me. That was my boy.

"Yep, it's you and me against the world." I finished, then ate.

Maurice thinks I'm naming the baby after him, but I chose the baby's name, calling the baby Dylan Michael Frazier. The only name Dylan would get from Maurice was Frazier, and he didn't deserve to have a baby named after him.

*****

**Carrington**

I tapped on the door and waited as the door opened, revealing Nikita. She grinned as I beamed. She came out of her apartment as we left for dinner.

We found a quaint place, had dinner, and chatted about everything. I joked, making Nikita laugh. She told me some corny jokes, and I chuckled. I didn't expect someone like Nikita to have a sense of humor, but she surprised me. Nikita's personality endured me to her.

I enjoyed spending time with Nikita. We went to dinner, the theater, museums and spent time together. It helps that she didn't have a man in her life, which was an issue when the woman wasn't single.

I even visited Nikita at the hospital. I showed up with a bouquet, and she smiled when she saw me. She strolled over to me, kissed me, and took the flowers from me. She inhaled the flower's scent. "Lovely bouquet, thank you."

"Lovely flowers for a lovely woman."

Nikita smiled. "Carrington, you charm me."

"Is that a good thing?"

"Yes." Nikita grinned. "I report to work, but we meet later."

"We will."

Nikita walked away from me. I was falling deeper for Nikita. So considerable that I craved to marry her, but I would have to confess my past to her. I hope she understands.

Later, I headed to Nikita's apartment. She let me in, and I removed my coat. I kissed her as we waited for the food to arrive.

"I need to speak with you."

We sat down on the couch.

"Okay."

I pondered what I needed to say. I wasn't sure how Nikita would react.

"Carrington, you worry me."

I turned to face her. "I wish to be straightforward with you."

She furrowed her brows.

"Before you, I met a woman. We became involved, but she had a spouse."

Nikita's eyes expanded.

"I didn't realize that she had a spouse. But when I found out, I continued the affair. I'm not proud of my actions, and I understand if you prefer to stop seeing me. I wish to be virtuous with you if I want a future with you."

Nikita said nothing, which worried me.

"Are you speaking with the woman now?"

"No, it ended months ago. I don't have any idea where Gloria is."

"So, we have no issues?"

"You're not upset about this revelation?"

"It's past, and I'm future." A smile curled on her lips.

Relief washed over me.

"But if I'm future, no cheating or lies. I inform my family, and they chop you into pieces."

That shocked me.

Someone tapped on the door.

"Food is here. We eat, now you understand." Nikita answered the door.

Well, I chose an exciting woman to fall in love with now. I'm sure if I fuck up, Nikita will follow through with her warning.

We ate. I stuck around and watched comedies with Nikita, then left. We haven't had sex yet. Nikita informed she was waiting for marriage to have sex. It wasn't a casual thing for her, and she refused to engage in it until marriage. I respect her decision since I planned on marrying her. I didn't inform my family about my plans with Nikita. I didn't even tell them that I had met someone.

*****

**Gloria**

I progressed with my pregnancy. When Maurice came home, I didn't have a say with sex. He expected sex, and I gave it to him. He arrived home long enough to fulfill his needs, then left.

I dealt with pregnancy alone. When we were around Maurice's family, he put on a show for everyone, acting like the dutiful husband and father. It's complete bullshit because Maurice wanted bragging rights.

One day, I was getting baby items together, and Maurice came home announcing we were moving. He wanted the baby to grow up with his family, and I didn't. I preferred to raise Dylan right

and knew that wouldn't happen if we stayed around Maurice's family, but I didn't have a say.

We moved, and it wasn't easy. I spotted twice but made sure I didn't lose the baby. Life was difficult, but I managed. Mateo would have found the baby and me if I had left with Carri and killed us both, and I refuse to let that happen.

They say a mother's greatest gift is sacrificing her needs for the baby's needs, but I beg to differ. The greatest gift you can give is to safeguard the baby from harm, and I protected my child even if it cost me my happiness.

I vowed to raise Dylan with love and kindness and didn't want him to turn out like Maurice's family. The kids were terrible, unruly, mean, and nasty. Max even kicked me while Mario slapped me. The brothers did nothing. Maurice told me I couldn't touch the kids since they weren't ours. That angered me.

More kids arrived, and they were the same way. I shook my head, knowing the kids would be worse when they grow up.

One night, I rubbed my belly, talking to Dylan. "I promise to love you if you promise never to turn out like Maurice's family."

*Kick!*

"I will protect you, no matter what. I wish I could identify your father."

*Kick!*

"I pray it's not Maurice. I met a man, and he was incredible. He was kind, thoughtful, caring, and funny. He made me laugh a lot." I snickered, remembering Carri.

*Kick!*

"He had the prettiest emerald-green eyes." I sighed.

*Kick!*

"My luck, Maurice, will be your dad." I didn't feel a kick. "Maybe you'll be Carri's son."

*Kick!*

Something told me after Dylan arrived, I would discover who his dad was. When I mentioned Maurice's name, Dylan didn't kick. When I said Carri, the baby kicked up a storm. The truth would unleash a rage from Maurice and cause me to shield Dylan, and it will cause someone to appear when Dylan and I need help.

All I could do was accept the brunt and defend my son.

# CHAPTER 25

## A SPECIAL ROMANCE

**Carrington**

I collected Nikita from her apartment and planned an extraordinary evening for us. It took some digging, but I discovered a game room. Cultural activities are pleasant, but I prefer fun.

We were going to a place that had a giant ball pit, except the balls were all white. I haven't been in a ball pit since the eighties. I made sure Nikita wore comfortable clothes.

We arrived at the place, and I paid rubles for us. An employee showed us to a room that had an enormous ball pit. After kicking off our shoes, I helped her by pushing her into the ball pit. I realize it's not romantic.

"Carri!" Nikita tried to get up but kept falling.

I laughed and pissed off Nikita. She found her balance and yanked me into the pit. After that, all bets were off. We chased each other, falling. I tossed her with her landing into the white balls. Nikita jumped on my back, causing us to fall into the pit. I hadn't had this much fun in a long time, and we giggled a lot.

After an hour, we took a pause and rested in the ball pit as I tossed balls around it.

"I like this," Nikita replied.

"What? Getting tossed around in a gigantic pit with plastic balls?" I threw a ball.

"No, fun. I study for doctor, and the family disapproves of dating and goofy behavior. Is that correct? Goofy?"

"If you mean fun, yes, that's correct. My family hates when I pull pranks, but they miss the point."

"What are pranks?"

"Pranks are jokes you play on people for fun, and they're never harmful. When the prank is, it's selfish behavior."

"Show me prank."

A smile curled on my lips.

We finished our time at the ball pit and left. I showed Nikita how to prank people, making her laugh. The people chased us, and we holed up in a cramped area as people ran past us.

Once the coast was clear, we roared. I took Nikita's hand, leading her to food. The thing about fun is it creates an appetite.

We discovered a place with treats. I ordered hot cocoa and donuts for us, and we sat down at a booth.

"Is nice." Nikita bit into a donut.

"What is?" I sipped my cocoa.

"Fun and pranks. I laugh." Nikita smiled.

"I'm glad because life is dull as it is. I prefer enjoyment over boring." I dug into a donut.

"I enjoy you."

That provoked me to smile. It's been a while since I beamed. Never in a million years, I figured I would meet someone who would provide me happiness. I thought it was Gloria, but it wasn't.

*****

The next day, I was sleeping, not realizing someone had come into my hotel room. Someone sprayed whipped cream all over my face, and I popped up to find Nikita holding a can of whipped cream and laughing.

"You're right. This fun." Nikita giggled.

I stared at her with brows lifted and whipped cream covering my face. "Oh, you think so?"

"Yes." She laughed and nodded.

I scrambled out of bed and chased Nikita around the room as she climbed on the bed, and I chased after her. Nikita turned and sprayed more whipped cream at me, and I caught her and tossed her onto the bed.

Nikita giggled.

I wavered over her, covered in whipped cream. "I love you."

Nikita stopped giggling. "You love me?"

"Yeah." I gazed at her. It can go two ways. Nikita declares her love for me, or I made a fool out of myself. I was hoping for the first part because the second part sucked.

"I love you, Carri."

I grinned, then captured her lips with mine and gave her a whipped cream-induced kiss.

Nikita pushed me off as she got up to wash off the whipped cream. I waited until she finished and showered.

After dressing, I came out to Nikita sitting on the lounge. "Thanks for the stickiness, which is like cleaning cement off you."

Nikita giggled. I prepared us some hot cocoa and joined her on the lounge. "So, I want to talk to you about something."

Nikita sipped her cocoa.

"I'm returning to the States, and I wish to bring you with me."

"I have a responsibility and no visa."

"Well, how about if I get you employment and a visa?"

Nikita contemplated me.

"As in, we wed, which will take care of your visa, until you become a US citizen. The hospitals need doctors, and Mason can help with the paperwork."

"Marry?"

"It seems sudden, but I don't want to leave without you." I shrugged.

"We marry with big ceremony. The family attends. I put on dress. You wear suit. We celebrate."

"I was thinking of a modest wedding as in you and me."

I received a face from Nikita. You recognize the expression, which says you're insane if you expect this wedding to be small.

"Okay, no small wedding."

Nikita laughed.

"What's so funny?"

"I joke. You so serious." Nikita pinched my cheeks. "We have small wedding."

Note to self. I need to learn Nikita's sense of playfulness because I can't tell whether she's joking or serious. Nikita's personality was like mine.

*****

**3rd person**

While Carrington and Nikita planned their elopement, Charles was dealing with impending parenthood. To say Charles was a nervous wreck was an understatement.

Charles hovered over Maggie, attending to her.

"Relax, Charles. I'm not due for a few more months." Maggie sat on the couch and caressed her swollen belly.

Charles paced the living room. "What if I mess up? What if I make the wrong choices? Our baby needs a dad who doesn't have his head up his ass."

Yeah, Charles was still beating himself up over his indiscretion.

"We will learn together. Charles, you screwed up once, and it hasn't happened again. I forgave you, and it's time that you forgive yourself."

You got to love a woman that forgives you for being a dumbass. If you find that woman, keep her because they're one in a million.

Charles sat down on the couch next to Maggie. "I understand, but I didn't think I deserve fatherhood or your forgiveness. I accepted that you would walk away from me, and I don't want our child to make the same mistakes that I did."

"Teach our child loyalty and love. Show the child the error of their ways when they do something wrong. A baby loves you unconditionally, and you love them the same way."

Charles smiled. "I married a brilliant woman."

"Yes, you did."

Charles chuckled.

Charles could be an idiot, but he had a big heart. Fatherhood will shape his thought process, especially when Charles and Maggie discover a surprise when she gives birth.

While Charles awaited impending fatherhood, Frank's old lady gave birth to a boy named Jordan Elijah Shaw. Frank showed up to see the baby, acting like the doting father, which was bullshit because Frank couldn't care less whether he had a kid or not.

He had bigger plans involving the Jones family. While his wife recovered from childbirth, Frank was busy with the Frazier family. He knew the Fraziers hated Carrington's family because of obvious reasons. Frank's alignment with the Frazier boys would draw in Charles and Greg Hartley. It would cause a plan so significant that it will affect the upcoming generation.

Hell, hath no fury like someone wanting revenge for landing in prison. There's an issue with this alignment. Frank and the Fraziers didn't expect an alliance between other people, and these people will prove what loyalty means to each other.

Secrets will emerge, causing issues amongst the Jones family, and it would start with a death. This death was the catalyst for what's to come later.

# CHAPTER 26

## MARRIAGE AND BIRTH

**Carrington**

Nikita and I eloped since I refused to leave Russia without her. I called Mason to ask for help with Nikita's paperwork and explained what I had done. The word fuck flew from Mason's mouth many times. Yeah, I pissed off, Mason.

Mason didn't enjoy hearing that I ran off and married when he sent me here for business. Mason needs to chill, or he will have a stroke. It should make him happy that I eloped since it's less money to spend.

My elopement disappointed my siblings, and Christine asked if Nikita was pregnant. Leave it to Christine to question marrying someone because you love the person. No, Nikita wasn't pregnant.

After marrying, we had dinner. Dinner was fun until Nikita's brother showed up and started quarreling with Nikita in Russian. Did you ever listen to Russians argue? It's interesting because they're so serious with threats. Since I knew some Russian, I understood bits and pieces of what the argument entailed.

Long story short, Nikita's family disowned her. Schmucks. This news upset her because her face showed it. I refuse to let my wife deal with disappointment.

We cut dinner short and retired to the hotel. I comforted Nikita, assuring her that it was us against the world. She doubted me, but I didn't have any doubts.

"I have no family." Nikita sniffled.

I brought over two cups of hot cocoa. "You have family." I sat down and handed her a mug.

She looked at me with furrowed brows.

"I'm your family, and I promise to care for you. When we have a family, I'll care for them, too."

Nikita furrowed her eyebrows even more. "I can't have babies." Nikita set her cup down and rushed out of the living room.

I got up and walked into the bedroom to find Nikita facing the window. I strolled over to her.

"My birth bore me without ovaries. Doctors give me pills to help with menstruation. The doctor told my parents I never have babies." Nikita cried.

It broke my heart to discover her anguish. I pulled Nikita to me. "Okay, so no children."

She glimpsed me. "You want child."

I gave her a reassuring glance. "But I want you more."

Nikita's eyes held hope. I never thought of not having children, but sometimes you give up a dream when you love someone. I will sacrifice my dream for my love of Nikita.

Mason situated the paperwork so that I could return with Nikita. It was that, or I stayed in Russia because I wasn't leaving without my wife. It set us to arrive around when Charles

welcomed his child, but we didn't perceive it would be on Christmas.

*****

### 3rd person

"Charles, wake up." Maggie shook Charles.

"Mmm."

"Charles, the baby is coming."

Charles continued sleeping.

"Charles?" Maggie's water broke, waking Charles from his slumber.

"What in the world?"

Maggie slid out of bed. "My water broke, you idiot!" A contraction hit Maggie.

Charles jumped out of bed. "Why didn't you wake me?"

Maggie glared at him. Yep, Charles was an idiot, and let's hope his child was more brilliant.

"Would you like me to drop the baby here? Get me to the hospital, dumbass!"

Another contraction hit.

"There's no need for name-calling."

After that, I can't repeat what Maggie said because I'm confident she used every curse word out there.

Charles got Maggie to the hospital, albeit with a lot of yelling. With all the ranting on the drive to the hospital, I'm sure that youngster will become anxious.

*****

## Carrington

Nikita and I were in the middle of landing when the delivery was going down at the hospital. Mason came to the airport to retrieve us when we landed. My big brother wanted to make sure we made it to the hospital and lecture me about my life's decisions.

While I was busy, Charles dealt with Maggie giving birth.

*****

## 3rd person

"You did this to me, you asshole!" Maggie shook Charles.

"I'm sorry, but you enjoyed our moment of insanity! Now, let go of me!"

"Get this baby out of me!" Maggie turned into the exorcist.

"Then let go!"

Maggie released Charles and shoved him away, then reached for the family jewels. "If you ever cheat on me again, I'll rip off your nuts!"

"Mother of God!"

Yeah, Maggie forgave Charles, but it didn't mean she wouldn't use this information against him in the delivery room. I don't know if Charles will have any more kids after this time.

"I swear to God that I'll never glance at another woman!"

"Maggie, can you release your husband's manhood so that you can push?" The doctor asked.

Maggie released Charles and pushed. Charles cringed while helping Maggie, trying not to cry. Getting the death grip on your manhood sucks, but a cup helps. No offense, but Charles deserved it.

Maggie delivered the baby, which was a boy. The nurse took the baby to clean it up.

"Okay, I need you to push for the second baby," the doctor said.

"Second baby?" Maggie and Charles asked.

"Yes, now push."

A second baby appeared. Maggie pushed, and the second baby arrived, which was a girl. The nurse took the baby to clean her up. The doctor tended to Maggie before taking her to a private hospital room.

*****

**Carrington**

Nikita and I arrived to find out my brother- and sister-in-law had twins, shocking Mason and us. We walked into the hospital room to see Charles and Maggie holding the babies, along with my siblings visiting, and everyone stared at us.

"Long time no see, family. Meet my wife, Nikita," I said.

"Wife?" Everyone asked.

The babies cried.

I smiled. Nikita didn't know what to say.

*****

After explaining about Nikita, my family understood, well, somewhat. Geez, you thought that I killed someone when I got married. Why does this surprise people?

"So, how did you not realize you were having twins?" I asked.

We only knew about the one baby, and I'm not sure how the second one fits into the equation.

"Beats me," Charles said, holding his son.

"Who cares? What are the baby's names?" Nikita asked.

Everyone glanced at her.

"Sorry, my wife is a little outspoken." I nodded.

"Not outspoken. Anxious." Nikita's response revealed her accent.

"Well, meet Ryan Matthew Jones and Elena Margaret Jones," Charles said.

"You gave the baby Mom's name?" Mason asked.

Charles nodded. Elena was our mother's name, and that made us smile.

"Can I?" Elliot motioned to Elena.

That shocked me.

"Sure." Maggie handed Elena to Elliot.

He cradled the baby as we discovered sniffling. "Mom would be proud because she loved babies." Then Elliot spoke to the baby. "You're special, Elena."

Elliot took our parent's death hard. He wouldn't cry at the funeral or talk to anyone afterward, and it took months for Elliot to talk about anything. He refused to discuss our parents. It was a moment that changed everything with all of us. We didn't

realize it, but the twins will change how we conduct ourselves, especially Ryan.

I pray the kid doesn't develop the idiot genes from my brother in the future.

# CHAPTER 27

## A SPECIAL DELIVERY

**Gloria**

Maurice left for a couple of months. It was the end of February, and I awoke to cramps and used the bathroom. My water broke, and I called people to help me, and no one bothered, so I called an ambulance.

The paramedics arrived and took me to the hospital. The labor was difficult, but I delivered a boy. The doctor placed my son in my arms, and I cried, and he was beautiful.

I stayed in my hospital room for two days without visitors. I spent time with Dylan. I finally had someone that loved me, and I wasn't alone anymore.

The hospital released me, and I called a cab to take Dylan and me home. Since I didn't bring a car seat with me, I held Dylan in my arms. The cab driver dropped us off at my house, and I took Dylan inside and got situated.

Maurice came home to find us waiting. He looked at the baby and shrugged. I didn't expect more from Maurice and took care of Dylan alone since Maurice didn't help me. The only time Maurice acted like the doting father was around his family, and it didn't matter because Dylan was vital to me.

I picked Dylan up and rocked him in the rocking chair as I fed him.

"It doesn't seem as if anyone cares about you, but I do. You're important to me, and I don't want you to turn out like Maurice's family. I will raise you properly and have a kind heart."

Dylan drank his bottle.

"See, we have choices in life, and those choices can be good or bad. I made poor decisions, but you aren't one of them. One day, I hope you understand my decision. I love you, Dylan." I cradled Dylan.

Something told me that I would understand why Dylan was significant in my life. No matter what, I will love him until my final breath.

*****

Since Dylan's birth, my son grew and did things early. He reached his milestones earlier than most kids. I read books and kept track of each thing Dylan did. Not even Maurice's family's kids hit their milestones when it happened. It boggles my mind.

I noticed while taking care of Dylan, Maurice started drinking again. Maurice would come home drunk and pass out in a chair as Dylan played amongst empty cans. I kept making sure I picked the house up to keep Dylan from getting a hold of the empty beer cans.

All I could do was watch out for Dylan even when Maurice went on his rampage. Dylan started teething, making him fussy. Maurice got irritated and tried to go after Dylan. I stepped in front of Dylan, taking the abuse because no one was touching Dylan if I could help it.

When Maurice sobered up, he apologized profusely. I didn't want his apologies and had to protect Dylan because he didn't deserve Maurice's drunken tirade.

I endured the hits and protected Dylan, even if it killed me. One day, Maurice came home, flying into a rage and going after Dylan. I stepped in, enduring his wrath and hiding Dylan. Maurice finished his assault and left.

I laid on the floor, bloody, as Dylan came out of his hiding place and shuffled over to me.

"Mama." Dylan shook me.

I groaned and propped myself up.

"Booboo." Dylan pointed at me.

"I'm okay." I sat up, pulled Dylan into my lap, and hugged him.

Dylan hugged me back.

"Any time this happens, you go to your hiding spot."

Dylan nodded as I held him.

If I left, Mateo would find us and kill us. I didn't want to think about it. I looked at Dylan as he looked at me, then I noticed his eyes. That's when I realized who Dylan's father was.

*****

**Carrington**

Nikita and I settled into marriage. She got a job at the hospital while I worked with my brothers, and we bought a house close to my brothers. It wasn't fancy, but it suited us.

We visited Charles's twins since Nikita adored children. Even though we couldn't have kids, we settled with the nieces and nephews.

My family has grown fond of Nikita since we got together. She played with the kids, giving the parents a break.

"I must admit, we thought you lost your mind when you got married," Theresa said.

"Why?" I asked.

"Because who would marry your stupid ass?" Christine asked

I gave her an annoyed expression. The others laughed. My family was something else.

"Let's play a game," Nikita said.

The kids screamed. Great, there goes my eardrums.

"Nikita was great with the children. One day, she'll make a fantastic mother," Christine said.

I turned and walked away. My family glanced at each other.

I leaned my backside against the counter in the kitchen and rubbed my eyes.

"Carri?" Mason asked. "Are you okay?"

I lowered my hand and leaned on the countertop. "Yeah." I looked down.

Mason walked over to me and stood next to me.

"Nikita can't have children. I won't go into detail, but she informed me the night we got married. I always wanted a family, but sometimes loving someone means sacrificing other things."

"And sometimes, it doesn't always destine us to have children."

Something touched my leg. I looked down to see Ryan grabbing my pant leg. He reached up, and I didn't hesitate to pick him up. Ryan looked at me with his chocolate brown eyes and was the spitting image of Charles, while Elena favored Maggie.

"I'm learning that. If I can't have kids with Nikita, I'm okay with that. Plus, I understand how hard it is on Nikita. Nikita thinks she disappointed me, not giving me a child, but she didn't." I held Ryan.

"Perhaps, one day, you will have a child." Mason gave me an empathetic look.

The weird part of our conversation was a nagging feeling I had for months. I didn't tell anyone I had this feeling, not even Nikita, figuring it was nothing. One day, I will find out how wrong I was to ignore my gut feeling.

*****

**Gloria**

I cleaned up and looked in the mirror. I looked like hell and felt like it, then felt a tug on my pant leg. I looked down to see Dylan holding onto me.

I picked up Dylan and looked at him. God, he looked like his father in every way. I didn't need a paternity test to recognize Dylan's father. I set Dylan on the countertop in the bathroom.

"You don't understand what I will tell you, but I hope you will later. Maurice isn't your father, but people think he is. To protect you, I must pretend. Forgive me, Dylan."

Dylan held out his arms. I hugged him as he hugged me back.

One day, this life will end, and Dylan will be safe. All I could do was to make that happen. I will discover something devastating and leaving me to stay in my situation, and it'll be news that will seal my fate.

# CHAPTER 28

## HERE COMES FRAZIER

**Gloria**

I kept my promise to Dylan, shielding him from Maurice, but it's proving difficult. I left one night with Dylan, hoping someone understood, but that decision would prove futile.

I packed two bags with Maurice, passed out from another binge. I left with Dylan, drove until I found a diner, and pulled into the parking lot. I unbuckled Dylan and carried him into the restaurant.

I sat down in a booth with Dylan. A server brought me something to drink, and I grabbed some cereal for Dylan. I sat there, figuring what I would say to Carri. While I pondered, Dylan grabbed a newspaper on the table.

I took the newspaper from Dylan as something caught my eye. I opened it to see a marriage announcement of Carrington Jones and Nikita Petrova. I stared at the paper as my heart sank.

I set the paper down and sat there as Dylan ate his cereal. Carri got married? I looked at Dylan while he ate and realized my idea wouldn't work. I made a choice, and I can't blame Carri for finding happiness.

"It looks like it's you and me, Dylan. I'm sorry."

Dylan smiled. He even had his father's smile. I finished my drink, paid, and left the diner. I drove home with Dylan as he fell asleep in his car seat.

It doesn't matter what happened to me now. The only thing that mattered was protecting Dylan. I returned to find Maurice waiting for us.

"Gloria."

"Maurice, it's over unless you quit drinking. You lay one hand on Dylan, and I will kill you." It's stupid, but I had nothing to lose now.

Maurice furrowed his brows at me.

"I mean it, Maurice. You will not harm Dylan." I went upstairs to put Dylan to bed. It's time to fight back, but it won't last. With someone like Maurice, he changes his way briefly, then slips back to his old ways.

I would find this out as Dylan grew up. I didn't realize it, but Dylan will carry my burden. All I could do was to protect him.

*****

As Dylan got older, I saw things in him that I couldn't imagine. He turned out to be kind and loving. Dylan enjoyed a good prank, pitting him against his cousins.

We attended a barbecue at Maurice's family's house, and Dylan pulled a prank on the other boys. It turned ugly as the other boys pounced on Dylan. I came out of the house, seeing Maurice not intervening as his brothers egged on their children.

"Stop it!" I ran over and pulled the boys off my boy.

"Gloria!" Maurice said.

My head snapped in Maurice's direction. "No! Dylan is smaller, and you did nothing!"

Maurice took a step towards us.

"Don't! You come near Dylan, and I will hit you with something!"

Everyone stopped.

I didn't care if it pissed off his family. I refused to let Maurice hurt Dylan and turned to Dylan. "Let's take you home."

Dylan nodded as I wrapped my arm around him. I walked him to the car as Maurice glared at me. Glare all you want, but it doesn't matter. I took Dylan home, cleaned him up, and put a bandage over his eye.

"Dylan...."

"Mom, I hate my cousins." Dylan furrowed his brows as his emerald-green eyes gazed at me.

"Hunny, I understand, but we don't have a choice."

"They're boring and would rather fight. I don't like my cousins because they don't have a sense of humor."

I couldn't disagree. "Promise me that you won't instigate issues."

"I make no promises, Mom." Dylan put up his hand.

I don't know what I'll do with this child. I'll deal with Maurice later.

\*\*\*\*\*

**Frazier**

Mom patched me up because my cousins were jerks. Every time I go around my cousins, they jump me. So, I got even with

them. I swear the idiots don't have a sense of humor. As always, my dad did nothing, and I hated him.

I'm only six, but one day, I will protect my mom. She deserves it.

The door slammed as my parents started arguing. Great, Dad's home. I heard footsteps, followed by noise, and hid in the spot that Mom showed me. I sat there, hearing my bedroom door open.

"Where is that little shit?"

"You're not touching Dylan!"

I placed my hands over my ears and closed my eyes. There were crashing sounds and stuff breaking. Mom and Dad fought as I hid. Then it became silent.

I opened my door to Mom on the floor and rushed to her. "Mom!"

"It's okay, Dylan. Get me a washcloth, Hunny."

I did as she said. The water ran in the bathroom as I gave her the washcloth, and she took it and cleaned off the blood.

"Everything will be okay."

I furrowed my brows. "Dad hurt you."

Mom set the washcloth down and crouched in front of me. "I know, baby, but I promise to protect you. And that's what I'm doing."

"But he's hurting you."

"Because it's what happens when you protect someone you love. I love you unconditionally, Dylan. It's you and me against the world. If we must fight, we fight, but only to protect the ones that we love. Promise me that you will hurt no one intentionally."

"I promise."

"Never pick up your hand to a woman or hurt someone weaker than you. No matter what the person does, never let them make you mean. You're too good for that."

Even though I was only six, I understood my mom. "One day, you won't have to protect me because I will protect you."

She raised her brows.

"It's us against the world." I gave Mom a cheeky grin.

Mom smiled. "Yes, it's us against the world."

I might not have friends, but I have my first friend, and I call her Mom. I hugged her because she needed a hug. I also decided that I hated the name Dylan since it reminds me of bad times, and I preferred Frazier because it sounded cooler.

"Can I ask one favor?"

"What's that?"

"Can you call me Frazier?"

"But I like the name, Dylan."

"I don't." I got a glance from Mom and shrugged.

"I'll make you a deal. I will call you Dylan when it's serious. But other times, I'll call you Frazier."

"Deal." I grinned.

Mom chuckled. It was even better that I got her to laugh. Humor makes everything better, even with the tough times. My father's a jerk who didn't have a sense of humor — no wonder he's miserable.

Something told me this was the beginning of what was to come for me. I didn't realize that the truth would come out, setting events into motion. It'll escalate my hatred for my dad.

# CHAPTER 29

## AN UNHOLY ALLIANCE

**3rd person**

While Carrington enjoyed wedded bliss with Nikita, the Frazier boys were up to their old tricks, allying with none other than Frank Shaw. Frank held a vendetta towards the Jones family for a terrible deal that landed him in jail.

The Frazier boys had an ax to grind with the Jones family because the Jones family had gotten them sent up the river. You add that Marco and Carrington hated each other, and it gives the Fraziers motive.

Maurice met with his brothers.

"I'm surprised Gloria let you off your leash," Marty spoke. Yeah, Marty wasn't happy with Maurice.

"Gloria doesn't control me," Maurice replied.

"Are you sure?" Marco raised an eyebrow.

"I could turn that brat into a man if Gloria didn't protect him."

"It shouldn't matter. Fraziers don't allow people to walk on them," Maximilian told Maurice.

The brothers argued, except for Mateo. "Considering it's a bastard child, the situation needs handling," Mateo said.

His brothers stopped.

"What are you talking about, Mateo?" Maurice asked.

"That kid doesn't have either of your eye colors."

Maurice furrowed his brows.

Mateo stepped towards his brother. "I warned Gloria. You handle it, or I will."

Maurice understood what Mateo meant with handling it since Mateo didn't give idle threats.

"We'll deal with this bullshit later. We have another business to address," Marty replied.

Someone walked towards them.

"Frank?" Maurice asked.

"Thanks for leaving me to hold the bag, you asshole. I spent two damn years in the clink!" Frank said.

"Hey, I got jail time, myself!"

"And you got out of it because of your brothers."

"Enough!" Marty spoke.

Everyone peered at Marty.

"Mason Jones and his family allied with the Morgan family and the Santiago family."

The news shocked everyone except for Mateo, and he realized this would happen and warned his brother against conducting business with Mason.

"Now, the Jones family owes us, and we're collecting. Frank receives a cut from our share as we take down that damn family," Marty told his brothers.

"How are we supposed to do that? It's not like we have access to that family," Mickey said.

Ah, yes, that was an interesting point. How does one gain entry to a well-protected family? It's not like they can waltz through the front door and announce their presence. Have you

seen the compound Mason has and the many men guarding him and his family?

"Because we have something they want. Our brother here," Mateo pointed at Maurice, "has their blood. We also have another snitch with the last name Hartley."

"It'll never happen. I haven't spoken to Charles in years," Maurice replied.

Mateo stepped towards Maurice until they were face-to-face. "It'll happen, and you'll make it happen."

Maurice gawked at his brother.

"You'll create an arrangement with Charles in exchange for that brat. Frank will put his kid in place to watch, and Greg will follow because there's a bookie who's dying to visit him. We can't let this situation slide any longer."

Now, this plan seems reasonable, but you have the Frazier boys and Frank Shaw planning it. Nothing goes according to plan when it includes other people, especially kids.

Since Greg is a runner and keeps moving his family, contacting Charles wasn't the issue, but Greg. Don't gamble, kids, because it pisses off the wrong people.

Now, Maurice chooses not to listen to his brothers because he thinks he's more brilliant, and he's not. Have you met Maurice? He cut a deal with Charles. Yeah, that situation will escalate.

When you disobey your brothers, it causes you to rethink your living arrangements. Then you throw in Frank Shaw wanting revenge, and you have a massive mess on your hands. Frank will resort to dirty deeds of his own.

But Maurice had learned that Gloria kept a dirty little secret hidden from him, which pissed him off. He had plans of his own for Gloria and the boy.

*****

### Frazier

I was sitting at the table, drawing a picture for my mom, when my dad came home. I didn't bother to look at him and continued drawing.

"Clean up this mess."

I stopped drawing, slid out of my chair, strode over to my toys, and plucked them up.

Then Dad grabbed my arm and jerked me to him. "You and I will talk about disrespect."

I furrowed my brows. My dad dragged me out of the living room as I screamed. Then he pulled me outside, removed his belt, and smacked me.

"Stop!"

"No! You'll learn not to embarrass me in front of my family!"

The leather connected with my skin as I cried while enduring every smack.

Dad finished as I trembled with tears falling down my cheeks. "If you tell your mother, you'll get worse."

I stared at him. My hatred for my dad grew that day.

"Frazier!"

Dad shook his head. I remained as he shuffled away.

A few minutes later, Mom came outside into the backyard. "Hunny, what's wrong?"

"I ran into a door handle."

"Let's get you some ice."

I nodded. We shuffled into the house, and Dad stood there, smirking. The sadistic jerk enjoyed my punishment. One day, I will be bigger, and he won't hurt me again. But I had to survive first.

*****

After that day, Dad waited until we were alone and unleashed his torture on me. He waited until Mom wasn't around to beat me, and it didn't matter what I did or how I acted. He made sure I suffered and cried until I stopped and refused to give him satisfaction.

Mom found out, and all hell broke loose. Dad went after Mom, and I protected Mom. I remembered what she told me. You never hit a woman. If I had to endure the beatings, then so be it. I refuse to let Dad hit Mom.

When Dad left for his business trips, we could relax and have fun. I learned to use humor to mask the pain. It was better that way. So, I became the class clown at school. No way was I letting anyone learn about my home life. I didn't seek their pity or crave it, although it would be nice to have a friend.

Those people were the type you could hang out with, harass, and tell your secrets. I didn't need a billion friends, but only one. If I make a friend, they'll become my bestie, and I need a bestie.

**Ryan**

I perched in an armchair, reading when Elena bounded into the living room.

"Play with me, Ryan."

"No, I'm busy."

"I'll tell Mom."

I tossed my book aside and stood up. "You're a tattletale."

"Mom! Ryan called me a tattletale!" Elena crossed her arms and stuck her tongue out at me.

I frowned at her.

Mom walked into the living room. "Can't you two get along for two-seconds?"

"She started it!" I pointed at Elena.

"Nuh-uh, you're a meanie."

Mom sighed as we fought.

Dad walked into the room. "Hey! What's going on here?" Dad placed his hands on his hips.

"Ryan's a meanie!"

"Elena's a tattletale!"

"Enough!" Dad responded.

We stopped, and Dad gave us a glimpse. Then we started again, and dad glanced at Mom. "Our children need friends."

"I agree." Mom nodded while Elena and I argued.

When you have a twin, you share everything. The dilemma with a twin is you share everything. Elena needs a friend, so she can leave me alone because my sister was annoying.

# CHAPTER 30

## A STUPID DEAL

**Carrington**

While I endured the wonders of marriage, such as a frying pan getting thrown at me, Charles was negotiating with a particular Frazier boy. We'll get to Charles in a minute.

"Nikita!"

The frying pan flew past my skull and struck the wall.

"That's not funny, Carri!"

"Well, neither is someone throwing a frying pan at you."

"Then don't put ice down my back!"

"Come on! I always wanted to say Ice, Ice, Baby!" Yeah, that earned a glare. "Okay, you win." I held up my hands in defeat and strolled into the living room.

After sitting down and picking up my hot cocoa, along with a newspaper, something landed in my lap. It caused me to flip out, scream, and scramble to my feet. I spilled my hot cocoa, which burned, and noticed what landed on me.

I picked up a counterfeit spider and noticed Nikita laughing. "Oh, you think this is funny?"

"Well, you toss ice down my back. I throw fake spider at you." Nikita shrugged.

I tossed the spider and chased Nikita as she laughed. "Let's see if you're laughing after I spank you."

"You'll have to catch me first." Nikita laughed.

Nikita ran, and I caught her. I flung her over my shoulder, swatted her ass, and carried her to the bedroom. From there, I delivered Nikita's punishment over and over. Yeah, we were unholy.

After we finished with our sinful behavior, we laid there and cuddled together.

"Does it disappoint you that I can't have children?"

"I'd lie if I said not having children weren't disappointing, but you accept it when you love the other person." I didn't want to lie to Nikita but didn't want her to feel terrible, either. "Nikita, I fell in love with you, not because of having kids. Joseph and Mary choose not to have kids. It's a personal decision with everyone."

"I love you."

"I love you more." I leaned in and kissed Nikita.

Yes, kids are great to have, but it's not the end-all, be-all with me. Sometimes, you accept situations because you love the other person more than yourself.

Later, Nikita and I would face a brutal truth, and it'll make or break our marriage as my past rears its ugly head.

*****

**3rd person**

While Carrington was busy with Nikita, Charles was handling other issues, such as Maurice Frazier. Now, Charles promised his wife that he cut ties with his former friends. Why he meets with one is beyond anyone? It also brought Greg Hartley into the mix.

Charles showed up at a secluded place outside town to meet Maurice, not realizing Greg was there. Charles exited his car and strolled towards Maurice and Greg.

"Charles," Maurice said.

"Maurice," Charles replied.

Charles noticed Greg standing there and didn't understand why. "What do you want, Maurice?"

"My brothers are plotting, and it involves Greg and you."

"Your brothers are always scheming."

"It also involves Frank Shaw."

The mere mention of Frank's name got Charles and Greg's attention.

"What does Frank have to do with this meeting?" Greg asked.

"Frank's pissed because he took a dive for Charles's bad deal. The same one when Charles didn't show up," Maurice said.

They both glanced at Charles.

"That wasn't my fault because Mason discovered the agreement and froze my assets," Charles responded.

"Yeah, thanks to you, I had to leave town, so my bookie wouldn't locate me," Greg said.

"The deal cost my brothers money and pissed them off," Maurice replied.

Charles sighed.

"I came to you because I distrust my brothers and also to get the hell out of town."

"What do you suggest?" Greg asked.

"I suggest that Charles compensate us."

"I won't give you money," Charles responded.

"That's a shame because I have something that your family wants."

"What's that?"

"I have someone that belongs to your family."

Charles thought about it, then understood what Maurice meant. Yeah, it took Charles a minute because he's slow on the uptake.

"Fine, I'll wire you the cash," Charles replied.

Here's the issue when you agree to an arrangement with Maurice Frazier. You can't trust the idiot as far as you can throw him. That's not the stupid deal Charles makes. It comes after Maurice leaves.

Satisfied with the agreement, Maurice left. The complication was Maurice had double-crossed his brothers, sending him running and settling smack in Saintwood, especially when Mason got involved.

After Maurice left, Greg remained. Charles rubbed his chin.

"That's fine, and all that Maurice will get what he wants, but it sticks me. If Frank and Maurice's brothers find me, I'm a dead man." Greg sighed.

Charles glanced at Greg.

"I have a wife and kid who don't deserve my mistakes."

Charles contemplated it, then made a decision that would affect everything. "What if I can guarantee protection for your daughter?"

"What do you mean?"

"Maurice and Gloria have a son. Maurice will hand over the boy for money. When I receive the boy, we will arrange for your

daughter and the boy to marry, and it will protect your daughter."

Greg cocked his head and wrinkled his forehead.

"The boy is my blood."

Greg realized what Charles meant. "You promise?"

"Yes."

"Okay, then deal." Greg shook hands with Charles. After the handshake, Greg left.

That is the trouble with Charles. He makes stupid deals. Who the hell arranges a marriage between two kids? He does, forgetting things have a way of working out differently.

Charles headed home. When he entered the house, the twins greeted him.

"Hey, Dad," Elena said.

"Hey, sweetheart." Charles studied Ryan, who had a black eye. "Do I want to know?"

"What do you think?" Ryan asked.

"Christ, Ryan. Isn't there a time that you're not fighting?"

"Don't be harsh with Ryan. A guy at school made an inappropriate comment about me," Elena replied.

Charles altered his tone. "Okay, but cool it with the fighting."

Ryan shrugged.

"Now, I have to talk to your mom." Charles walked away.

"Why did you lie to Dad?" Ryan asked.

"Because Dad will blow his lid if he finds out you're fighting."

"I don't need you mothering me."

"Well, you need your head examined."

Ryan and Elena bickered. Ah, you must love the teenage years. The twins are fifteen now.

*****

Charles strode into the kitchen to find Maggie cooking. He shuffled over and pecked her cheek.

"What did Maurice want?"

"To make a trade."

Maggie gave him a glimpse.

"It's complicated."

"How so?"

"It involves someone, and I need to speak with Mason."

Maggie furrowed her brows.

"You were right all those years ago. I didn't understand it then, but I do now. Distancing myself from Maurice, Greg, and Frank was a good decision but wasn't great regarding their kids. I made poor decisions, but I think about our kids and how it would feel if someone played with their lives."

Maggie turned to Charles. "Then do what you have to do because no child deserves the sin of their parents."

Charles married an intelligent woman. It's the one thing that didn't make him a complete idiot. Charles will make a decision that affects more than one person when he visits Mason. The truth will emerge that no one was expecting, especially Carrington.

# CHAPTER 31

## RUTHLESS

**3rd person**

It didn't take long for Maurice's brothers to discover Maurice's arrangement with Charles. How did they find out? Charles kept his word and visited Mason, explaining the meeting, leaving Greg Hartley out of the conversation.

Hearing this information didn't make Mason happy. "Sonofabitch!" Mason cussed more and tossed around the word fuck when he got pissed.

Charles let Mason rant and rave like the lunatic he was and rested in a chair, waiting for Mason to finish. Mason finished his ranting and squatted in his desk chair.

"Mason, I came to you because I don't trust Maurice. If he'll double-cross his brothers, who are to say he won't double-cross me."

"Oh, Maurice would double-cross you and start a war. I quit doing business with Marty and his family because of their bullshit. I have an agreement with the Morgans and Santiagos, but I distrust the Santiagos."

"It doesn't help that Frank aligned himself with Maurice's family."

"Does this surprise you? The Shaw brothers are worse. Rumors circulated about them, and it sickened me. Frank is the

least of our concerns now since I must deal with the Frazier family first."

Over the years, Mason became powerful, aligning himself with the Morgan family. The Jones name became synonymous with the underground world, making people terrified of them. Mason spent years building an empire that made his family ruthless and powerful. Did I mention they took matters into their hands with people? I must have left out that piece of information.

\*\*\*\*\*

**Carrington**

While Mason figured out his next move, Joseph and I took care of a business deal that had gone wrong.

"I promise I'll get you the money!" A guy begged on his knees as we looked at him.

"Why does Mason keep sending us on business trips with pleading people?" I asked Joseph.

"Mason gets tired of whiny people."

"That sounds reasonable." I shrugged, lifted my gun, shot the guy twice, and killed him. The guy's body fell to the floor.

"That was quick."

"I got bored with the guy's whining. Oh, please. I promise. Blah, blah, blah." I blew a raspberry.

Joseph chuckled as we left. The cleaners will arrive to clean up the mess. Mason had hired men to clean, dispose of bodies,

and leave no traces behind, including the person's identity. It's as if the person never existed.

It tasked Joseph and me with dealing with people domestically while Elliot traveled abroad. Mason's reasoning was Elliot didn't have a wife or kids, and Joseph and I had spouses. My sisters stayed out of the family business, helping when we needed it.

We grabbed a bite since Nikita was working late tonight at the hospital. Before we ate, I brought Nikita dinner. I walked into the hospital, found her at the nurse's station, and strolled over to her.

Nikita turned to me and smiled.

I kissed her and held up the bag. "I figure you'd be hungry."

Nikita took the pouch. "I'm starved. The hospital was so hectic that I didn't have time to eat."

"Joseph and I finished working and are grabbing a bite. I wanted to bring you dinner first."

"You're so thoughtful. Thank you." Nikita kissed me, then checked on a patient.

I met Joseph at a restaurant. Nikita's loyalty earned my respect, and I never had to worry about her cheating on me. I got lucky, considering my past. All it takes is meeting the right person to become faithful.

I strolled into the restaurant, joined Joseph at a table, ordered, and we talked.

"How's Nikita?"

"Starved. The hospital keeps Nikita hopping so much that she doesn't have time to eat."

"You surprised me, Carri."

"How so?"

"You grew up and stopped disregarding people." Joseph referred to Gloria.

"Because everyone was right, and I didn't want to see it." I hated discussing the past because I wasn't proud of it or my reckless behavior.

"We all learn from the past, or we're doomed to repeat it."

"Well, it's over, and I moved on in my life." I wanted to drop the subject.

My past will smack me in the face when I come face-to-face with it.

*****

**3rd person**

While Joseph and Carrington enjoyed dinner, Mason paid a visit to Marty Frazier. Two armed men had gone with Mason because he didn't take chances with anyone, including the Frazier boys.

Mason entered Marty's office and sat down as his men stood by the door.

Marty looked at Mason, unenthused. "What do I owe to this visit?"

"It seems your brother is making deals with my family, and you have your hand in it."

"I don't know what you're talking about, Mason."

"Cut the bullshit, Marty. Your family is planning something against mine, but it's too bad that your brother altered your plans."

Marty's expression changed.

"Yeah, I figured you didn't know."

Marty's jaw clenched as his lips pressed together.

"You touch my family, and I'll put you down like the dog that you are. Consider that a warning." Mason stood up and left the office.

Mason needed to rattle Marty enough to do what he had planned. He wanted the boy since he's blood but didn't know who the boy belonged to for sure. Mason suspected but needed confirmation. That put in motion bringing particular people to Saintwood, including Greg Hartley and Frank Shaw.

How do you draw out your enemy? You keep the enemy close enough to watch them.

Mason left the building and got into the backseat of a car as Charles sat there.

"Well?" Charles asked.

"Marty took the bait. Now, we wait."

"What about Frank and Greg?"

"Frank's careless and will follow. I'll take care of Greg."

Mason was bright and had plans of his own. He knew no matter what you planned, plans changed. Charles had become more concerned about Greg Hartley than Frank Shaw, and that made Mason wonder why.

What did Charles do that involved Greg Hartley? The family would find out when Greg arrived in town.

Mason and Charles left with Hunter driving. "Hunter, contact my brothers when we return."

"Yes, Mr. Mason."

Hunter Michaels was a kid that Mason found on the streets. Mason saw potential and took Hunter in thanks to Luci, who ordered Mason to take Hunter. You must love an Italian woman who yells at you in Italian, and Mason didn't want a scolding from Luci.

Mason trained Hunter. Hunter, in return, trained Cole and Dean and oversaw things for Mason. Hunter's loyalty was like no other. When a person rescues you from the streets, they will earn your loyalty.

While Mason and Charles returned to Mason's house, Marty and Mateo visited Maurice, except Maurice wasn't home since he and Gloria were out, leaving their son alone.

\*\*\*\*\*

### Frazier

I came downstairs to see my uncles standing in my living room.

"Where is your old man?" Marty asked.

"Dad and Mom are out." I shrugged.

"When will they be back?" Mateo asked.

"Beats me." My answer pissed off, Mateo. Yeah, I loathed my uncles because they're assholes, and I also despised their kids, especially Mario.

Mateo walked over to me, pulled a revolver, and placed the end of the barrel against my forehead. "Watch your tone, you disrespectful shit. Your dad isn't high on my priority."

I didn't flinch.

Mom and Dad came home and found my uncles with me. Mateo lowered his pistol and put it away.

"What are you doing here?" Dad asked.

"We came to have a word with you," Marty responded.

"Take the boy into the kitchen, Gloria."

Mom escorted me out of the room. It didn't matter because my old man never called me by my name but always called me, boy. Yeah, I hated my dad.

"Mason visited me and told me that you made a deal with his brother," Marty said.

"Bad move," Mateo said.

"Since you enjoy betraying us, you will bring the boy to me tomorrow, or I'll kill you." Marty and Mateo walked past Dad.

"Don't fuck this up, Maurice." Mateo and Marty left.

Mom and I came out of the kitchen as the car left.

"Get packed. We're leaving," Dad said.

"And go where?" Mom asked.

"Saintwood. It's time to cash in on an offer." Dad headed upstairs.

What offer, and why Saintwood? I didn't understand any of it. Great, it's another school with assholes. It's not like I didn't have them at my current school, along with my sperm donor. FML. Plus, I didn't tell my mom that the school was getting ready to

expel me for breaking into my school records. Yeah, I didn't need more lies.

# CHAPTER 32

## ARRIVING IN SAINTWOOD

**Frazier**

We packed and left last night, turning up in a city called Saintwood. Dad found a shack and paid cash for it. It had your standard rooms with two bedrooms. I settled into my bedroom and looked around at it.

"Dylan!" Mom said.

"I'm in my bedroom!"

Mom came into the bedroom and stood close to me. "It's not fancy. But we can make do, right?"

I exhaled. I didn't blame my mom for coming here. She did what she could for me.

"Hopefully, you'll make friends at this school."

"Eh, it doesn't matter. If people don't want to be my friend, then they lack taste."

Mom gave me a strange glance.

"Gloria!"

Mom sighed. I knew what was coming. She left the room, and I followed. The minute she reached the bottom step, Dad hauled off and swung, except that he hit me instead of Mom.

"Dylan!" Mom said.

I gripped my nose as blood dripped from it. "I'm okay."

Mom took care of me. Dad glared at me, but I didn't care. One day, the asshole will pay.

Mom cleaned me up and placed an ice pack on my nose. I held it, trying to stop the blood. It didn't matter. As soon as Mom left the house, I endured punishment from Dad, especially when he drank. I didn't understand why he hated me so much, but the feeling was mutual.

Mom had me go upstairs and lay down. I ascended the steps but didn't lie down but threw open my window, climbed out, and shimmied my butt until my feet hit the ground. If my parents wanted to stick me in an unfamiliar place, they had another thing coming.

I explored Saintwood, finding it your typical suburban city where people had beautiful yards and houses and saying hi to their neighbors. I strolled through the neighborhood, whistling. Okay, so Saintwood wasn't terrible, and it's better than the last city, which was the lower class.

I checked out some stores and restaurants, coming across a group of girls. Okay, it's getting better here. The girls were hot, and I used my charm. "Ladies," I told the girls.

They stopped and looked at me.

"Did anyone tell you that you're a gift from heaven?" I placed one arm around one girl and another arm around a different girl. "I have a philosophy that all girls are beautiful and a present. Guys are lucky if you pay attention to them."

"Who are you?" One girl asked.

"Who I am isn't important. Who you are is. Girls are a gift, and you treat them as such. When you cherish a girl, the girl will cherish you. It's a solution where everyone benefits." I winked.

That caught the girls' attention as I charmed them. These girls ate up this bullshit. Okay, note to self. The girls in Saintwood were a little dumb and reminded me of the girls back home.

I dated a couple of girls and had a girlfriend for a brief period, got my cherry popped, and it ended. I told no one because Mom would flip out. She thinks I'm sweet and innocent, and I prefer to let her believe it. My mom was everything to me, and I didn't want to disappoint her.

Out of the group of girls, I hooked up with one. The girl was a little older, and we made out in her car. That escalated with us having a lot of fun. The girl wasn't the only one. I found many girls here willing to drop their panties.

Do these girls not have any dignity or self-respect? Ah, who cares? I'm fifteen and a horny teenage boy. If a girl wants to ride the Frazier train, then so be it. She has excellent taste.

The problem with this idea, you never knew who had a boyfriend. It's not like you do a lot of talking while a girl is going down on you. Protection is vital, though. No offense, but I don't want any visitors.

I found out that one girl I hooked up with had a boyfriend. The dude wanted to kick my ass. Does he realize I deal with a douche at home? You learn to fight back. I might be smaller, but it didn't mean I stood there and took it.

"Get back here, you piece of shit!" A guy and his buddies chased me down the street.

I stopped and turned. "Well, if you didn't have a one-inch dick, you could satisfy your girl!"

That pissed off the douche. "I'm going to break you in half, asshole!"

"You sound like a chick! Damn, dude, grow a pair, will you?"

The guys chased me, and I scaled a wall faster than your neighborhood Spider-Man. That reminds me that I need to get the latest comic book edition to add to my collection.

A visit to a local comic book store after it closed was in order. Since the idiots were too big, they had an issue climbing the wall. I jumped down and strolled down an alleyway, whistling.

Yep, I'm going to like Saintwood.

*****

Later, I snuck out of the house while my parents fought because I needed a break from the yelling. Plus, before passing out, my dad ties one on and beats the crap out of me. Yeah, no thanks.

Most businesses had closed, so I strolled to the comic bookstore. I walked around back, noticed a door, and picked the lock. People call it breaking and entering, which is criminal, but I call it using your brain.

I disabled the alarm, found the Spider-Man comic book, and searched through them until I found one and hid it in my clothes. I got the hell out of there, reset the alarm, and relocked the door.

Once the coast was clear, I flipped through the pages carefully. I placed it back into its clear sleeve as I walked.

"Well, well, well, what do we have here?" A voice asked.

I stopped and twisted to encounter Mario and his cronies. I hid the comic in the back of my waistband.

Mario stalked towards me. "It's interesting that I find you here, and it will interest my dad that you're in Saintwood."

"Who cares? Your dad's a douche, and so are you."

Mario took a swing at me, and I ducked, punched him in the dick, and dropped his stupid ass, then took off running.

"You wait, you little shit! Your ass is mine!"

"Why don't you suck your boy's dick since that's all you're good for?"

"You're dead, Dylan! You hear me!"

I shook my head. Mario can fuck himself, along with my dad and his family. Stupid dicks. I hate that family.

I got home and snuck into my bedroom as my light clicked on and revealed my dad. I climbed through the window, and all hell broke loose. Well, when Dad was sober, he didn't go after me, and it was nice while it lasted.

After Dad finished doling out his punishment, I made my way to the bathroom and grabbed the first aid kit. It's pathetic that I must administer first aid to myself. I got good with sewing needles, and it didn't faze me when I stitched myself. Now to hide the bruises because it's not like anyone cares besides my mom.

As Mom said, it's us against the world. Perhaps the universe will give me a freaking break.

# CHAPTER 33

## OH, SH*T

**Carrington**

Have you ever learned a truth, not expecting to learn it? Well, I found out the fact, and it wasn't how I expected to learn it.

I returned from a business trip to speak to Charles about a business associate of Mason's. The guy was a certifiable idiot, and I didn't understand why we associated with him.

I strolled into Charles's office to discuss the situation. While we spoke, Ryan came home with someone. We finished our meeting and came out of the office to find Ryan with a kid. Ryan talked to his dad while I stared at the kid. Then I noticed the eye color and studied the kid.

Charles introduced Ryan's friend as Dylan Frazier. The kid told me it was nice to meet me as he shook my hand, and I informed him likewise. Ryan and Dylan left the foyer, and Charles walked me to the door.

That's when I asked Charles to do some digging on Ryan's friend. "Find out anything you can on that kid."

"Carri, why is Frazier so important to you?"

"Charles, I'm not proud of some things from my past. But I need to confirm my suspicion."

"What's that?"

"To figure out if Dylan's my child." I walked away, leaving Charles stunned. My dirty little secret would bite me in the ass, but I didn't care.

I left Charles's house and had to talk to Nikita. If this kid turns out to be my child, I have to figure out my next move. I arrived home, and Nikita greeted me with a Nerf gun, shooting foam pellets at me.

"Nikita!"

"Welcome home, Carri." Nikita smiled, then blew across the tip of the Nerf gun.

I shook my head and walked over to Nikita.

"How was the trip?"

"The trip was okay, but I have a bigger issue now." I walked into the kitchen.

"What issue?"

I opened a kitchen cabinet, pulled out a bottle of vodka, grabbed a tumbler, and poured a drink. I don't drink, but I needed something to calm my nerves. I gulped the contents and cringed. Okay, that was nasty.

"Carri, you're worrying me."

I stared at the countertop with my palms resting on it. "Remember when I told you about a woman from my past?"

"Yes, you said it was over."

"The affair is over, but something might have resulted from it."

"What?"

I lifted my head. "A child."

Nikita's eyes expanded. I wasn't confident what would happen between us.

"Are you positive?" Nikita asked.

"No, but I asked Charles to find out information about Ryan's friend." I stepped towards Nikita. "The boy resembles me, including his eye color. I need the truth whether he is my child."

Nikita knitted her brows.

"We agreed about not having kids, but if this boy is mine, I can't turn my back on him. The worst part was that I didn't know." I leaned against the counter, wondering why. If Ryan's friend was my child, why didn't Gloria tell me?

Nikita put her hands on my cheeks. "Carri, I understand you want the truth. But if the boy turns out to be your child, then what?"

"I don't know." I furrowed my brows. I had an affair with a married woman. A child might have resulted from the affair, which I knew nothing about for years. I didn't plan on any of this happening, but it did. I wasn't proud of my behavior.

"I do."

I glanced at her.

"If he's your child, then spend time with him. Carri, we can't have children, but that doesn't mean you don't deserve a chance to become a father."

I couldn't love Nikita more than I do now. Most women wouldn't understand if a kid came from your past, but Nikita wanted me to spend time with this kid. That's if he is my son, and I prayed the boy was. If he were, then I would visit Gloria since she's in Saintwood.

*****

**3rd person**

While Nikita and Carrington discussed the possibility of him having a child, Joseph showed up at Charles's place. Charles handed Joseph a freezer bag with two plastic bottles in it, and Joseph took the bag.

"Those are water bottles that Dylan Frazier and Carri used today."

"Who's Dylan Frazier?"

"Does Gloria Frazier ring a bell?"

Joseph did a double-take. "No!"

Charles gave Joseph a knowing glance as Joseph sighed. "What?"

"Remember when Carri returned home and took correspondence courses to finish his degree?"

"Yes."

"Before Carri came home, he planned to leave town with Gloria. She didn't show, and now we realize why." Joseph held up the bag. "This DNA test will confirm the truth."

"It doesn't matter because Maurice mentioned he had something belonging to us. It's not something, but someone."

That's all it took, and Joseph left to dig. Joseph sent the bottles to a lab to have a DNA test run three times. He also conducted an illegal activity and scoured for information on Dylan Frazier. It would take time to hack through firewalls to confirm their suspicions.

If Dylan Frazier were Carrington's son, Carrington would confront Gloria for keeping Dylan from him. Carrington wanted to learn why she didn't tell him. He would have done anything for his child. The worst part was Maurice Frazier had his hands on the boy, and Carrington hated that family. His hatred would escalate into an unfortunate event and set issues in motion for the kids.

While Charles and Joseph were trying to find out about Dylan Frazier, the Frazier boys turned on Frank Shaw, ending their alliance with Frank. Did you ever poke a rattlesnake? The snake attacks and kills its prey with its deadly venom. Frank was the rattlesnake, and everyone had poked him.

Frank made his old lady disappear because he had other plans involving his niece and sons. No one knew what happened between Henry's kid and Frank, but everyone would discover that later. The other issue was Frank needed to put his plan in motion and enlisted his oldest son Jordan to help him. The problem with this scenario was Jordan hated his dad, and the kid had a good reason.

Jordan came home from school with his brother Josh to discover his dad packing. "What's going on?"

"We're moving," Frank said.

Jordan furrowed his brows. "Where?"

"Saintwood."

Jordan and Josh glanced at each other.

"Saintwood has better opportunities for us, boys." Frank pretended to care, but he didn't.

Jordan shook his head and walked away. "Good, then I won't have to play sports."

With Frank Shaw heading to Saintwood with his boys, it set in motion with events to come. Jordan will prove he's not his father's son, and it's an alliance that no one will see coming.

# CHAPTER 34

## RESULTS

**Carrington**

Joseph found out the information about Dylan Frazier. He met with Mason and Charles to talk to them, who was with Elliot. I arrived thirty minutes later to yelling.

"Are you fucking kidding me?" Mason asked.

"Do I sound like I'm kidding?" Joseph asked.

Charles put his face in his palm, and Elliot rolled his eyes.

"I told Carri to stop seeing the woman!"

"Well, little brother didn't listen."

"No, shit! I'm not fucking stupid!"

"Are you sure? Even you didn't notice what Carri was doing," Elliot told Mason.

Mason's head snapped towards Elliot. "This isn't the time for your condescending bullshit."

Now, while my brothers were discussing an urgent matter about me, they forgot I was arriving.

"Mason, there's nothing we can do to change the fact that Dylan Frazier is Carri's son," Joseph said.

I strolled into the house and stood there. "Dylan's my son?"

My brothers turned to see me standing there.

"Christ," Mason said.

I suspected it when I saw the kid but didn't think it was possible. Now it all made sense. I ambled over to my brothers. "So, it's true? I have a son?"

"Yes." Joseph handed me a file.

I took the file from Joseph, opened it, and started reading the information. I shuffled over to the couch and sat down. Joseph found everything he could on Dylan Frazier, including his birthday, blood type, and other vital information. It included his school record and test scores.

I stared at the information. This kid was my kid, all right. I'm surprised Dylan didn't get expelled for half the shit he did. Then something caught my attention, making my anger boil.

"Maurice has been putting his hands on my kid." I seethed.

"Carri, I'm managing that situation," Charles said.

I stood up and glowered at Charles. "You're managing it? Did you know that Dylan was my son?"

"No, not until today. I had suspected. The only thing I learned was Dylan's father was hurting him and offered him a haven."

"That wasn't your decision, Charles! You knew Dylan belonged to Gloria yet didn't tell me! What the fuck?"

"You want to go there? Okay, let's go there!"

"Charles," Mason said.

"No, Mason, our little brother is forgetting the shit he did behind our backs and hiding an affair after you told Carri to stop. Now, his actions are biting him in the ass!" Charles walked over to me. "Do you understand what you and Gloria did? You produced a child who knows nothing about your extracurricular

activities and suffered from it. All for what? So that you can disregard everyone else?"

"You forget that you're not as innocent as you claim." I didn't care if Charles was angry. Gloria kept my son from me.

"Watch your tone, Carri."

"Enough!" Mason walked towards me. "You disobeyed me when I told you to end the relationship. I warned you, Carri, but you chose not to listen. Now, there's a kid involved from you ignoring us."

"I need to talk to Gloria." I started for the front door.

Elliot stopped me and shook his head.

"Let go, Elliot!"

"No, Carri. If you show up at her house to confront her, it will make things worse."

"What are you talking about, Elliot? I have a right to confront Gloria."

"Not when it involves a situation we are dealing with now," Mason said.

I glanced at my brothers.

"I'm overseeing particular situations and don't need you going there with guns a-blazing."

That pissed me off. My brothers wanted to stop me from confronting Gloria about Dylan to further their agenda. I stormed out of the house, not saying a word. I had a right to find out answers, yet they tried to block me.

Joseph stopped me as I reached the car. "Carri, you don't want to do this."

I looked at Joseph with furrowed brows. "That's my son, and Gloria kept him from me!" My voice cracked as tears rolled down my cheeks. "A son, I didn't have for years! Do you understand what it's like to have something ripped from you? You would do anything for a child but not given a choice!"

Everyone was keeping me from my blood.

"Carri, you're angry, but there are issues with the Fraziers. If you go to see Gloria now, it will cause Maurice and Gloria to flee, taking the boy with them. Since Ryan is friends with Dylan, we can keep an eye on Dylan."

"I don't care. Dylan is my son, and I will take him. Maurice won't stop me!"

"No, but Maurice will kill Gloria, then Dylan because Dylan refuses to leave her. No matter how angry you are with Gloria doesn't compare to how that boy adores her. Dylan hasn't learned that you're his father, but he knows Gloria is his mother. If you get his mother killed, he will never forgive you."

I hated to admit Joseph was right, but I wanted my son. "Fine, but you tell our brothers to figure it out before I take control of the situation. If I find out Maurice laid another hand on my boy, I'll kill him." I got into the car and left.

My brothers were on borrow time. I knew the Frazier boys' tempers.

I drove home and entered to have Nikita jump out at me, wearing a hideous-looking mask. She lifted the mask. "Carri, you're supposed to scream like a little girl."

"I'm not in the mood for jokes." I walked by Nikita.

Nikita removed the mask and followed me. "Carri, what's wrong?"

I strolled into the bedroom and parked on the bed. "I found out Dylan Frazier is my son. For sixteen years, I had no clue until I visited Charles. Then I see this kid that looks like me. How do you keep that secret?"

Nikita sat down next to me on the bed. "Maybe the mother had a reason. I'm not saying it's right, but neither is what you did. We all have our reasons for what we do, Carri."

"I always said if I had kids, I would protect them. But I failed Dylan."

Nikita took my hand in hers. "But you didn't. Now, give Dylan what he needs."

"What's that?"

"A father." Nikita smiled.

I looked at my wife with wonderment. Most women wouldn't tolerate a child showing up in your life, but Nikita understands me, which helps a lot.

*****

After my talk with Nikita, I kept my eye on Dylan. I didn't care what my brothers said. I wanted my son.

I watched Dylan with Ryan. Ryan towered over Dylan but protected Dylan as Dylan clung to Ryan. Even though Ryan showed annoyance with Dylan, I studied his actions with my son. At least, Dylan had someone looking out for him.

As I kept an eye on Dylan, another boy hung out with them. The boy seemed familiar. Until one day, I noticed Frank Shaw in the school parking lot. The boy argued with Frank, then flipped Frank off.

"You get your ass home now, Jordan!"

"Screw you, Dad!" Jordan walked over to Ryan's car.

If Maurice and Frank were in town, Greg wasn't too far behind them. Something told me that when Greg arrived, all hell would break loose.

Our past has a way of biting us in the ass, and our children's paths will directly result from our past decisions. These boys would be a force of nature with loyalty like no other.

# CHAPTER 35

## CONFRONTATION

**Carrington**

I grew impatient with my brothers. While they sat on their asses doing nothing, I visited Gloria to confront her about Dylan to get answers. I pulled in front of the house and got out of the car. There were crashing sounds and screams coming from inside.

"What are you doing? Put the gun away, Maurice!"

I ran to the front door, opened it, and stepped inside. Maurice was pointing a pistol at Gloria. Gloria was bloody and bruised as Maurice made her beg.

Then I heard a click. Before Gloria reacted, I tackled Maurice, and we fought as the pistol got knocked out of his hands.

"You piece of shit!" I slammed my fist into his face.

"Carri!" Gloria yelling distracted me.

Maurice knocked me off balance.

"Run, Gloria!"

We fought and crashed into furniture. No way was I letting this asshole go this time. Maurice and I fought, and he reached for the pistol.

Maurice seized the pistol as I charged him. We struggled with the weapon as it discharged, making Gloria jump. Maurice stared at me as I faced him, and he dropped to the floor. The door

opened as Dylan entered to see me holding the revolver. Maurice laid in a puddle of blood.

Gloria grabbed the pistol from me and wiped it with her shirt. "Go, Carri."

I left the room and hid. Dylan walked over, took the gun from his mom, and held it.

The door opened as Ryan entered, along with Jordan. They paused there, shocked as I laid the back of my head against the wall.

*****

I remained there until I heard Charles's voice, along with the police. I was ready to turn myself in for shooting Maurice and turned to confess but came face-to-face with Charles, and he shook his head and put his finger to his lips.

Charles returned to the other room as I stayed there, waited until the police left, and then met Gloria. She looked like hell.

"Gloria."

"Thank you." Gloria started crying.

I pulled her and held her as she buried her head into me and cried. My anger dispersed when I saw Gloria in this state, and it made me wonder how long she dealt with the abuse.

When the coast was clear, I came out of hiding. Gloria entered with Dylan, and I looked at my son.

"Dylan, this is your father," Gloria said.

Dylan's eyes expanded, but he turned and walked away. It broke my heart that my son had rejected me.

"Give Dylan time."

"Time? That's all I had, Gloria. Not having time to know my son. Why didn't you tell me?"

"Because it wasn't that simple."

"Then explain it to me. For fifteen years, I never knew I had a son, and then one day, I met him at my brother's house. So, explain to me how it's not simple!"

"Because Mateo threatened to kill us!"

"What?"

"The last night we were together, I came home, and Maurice forced me to have sex with him. Then I took a pregnancy test, and it turned out to be positive. Maurice saw it and assumed the baby was his, but I wasn't sure whose baby it was. Maurice told his family, and Mateo cornered me in the kitchen and threatened me. He said if I revealed the truth about my affair, he would kill Dylan and me."

"But I would have protected you."

"I wanted to wait until I could leave, and one night I did. Dylan was about two years old. We left to find you. Then I found out you got married in a newspaper announcement. I couldn't show up at your door, announcing you're a father and ruining your happiness. I hurt you enough."

"Nikita knows about you because I told her. Even though it's over between us, I wouldn't turn my back on Dylan. I sure as hell would have protected him against that asshole."

Charles entered the kitchen. "Gloria, it's time."

"Time for what?" I asked.

Gloria looked at me. "To protect Dylan and you. I'm signing over my rights to Charles so that he can adopt Dylan. Since your name isn't on the birth certificate and Maurice is dead, there won't be any dispute. Please don't fight this, Carri. Our son needs peace." Gloria turned and left.

I was losing my son again. How fair was this?

Charles walked over to me. "Just because I'm adopting Frazier doesn't mean that you aren't his father."

"What?"

Charles smiled. "Carri, you can see Frazier anytime. It's a cover to keep Maurice's brothers away from Frazier and protect him. You deserve to get to know your son, and you might find out he's more interesting than you realize."

"That's if Dylan lets me. He's angry, and I don't blame him. I want my son, Charles."

Charles nodded.

Now, the ball was in Frazier's court. I hope that Frazier gives me a chance. If he doesn't, then that's my punishment for having an affair with his mother. I had wondered why Gloria never showed that night, and now I have my answer. I loved her at one point, but that love faded. Another love replaced it, and the person was a child.

How do you love someone you recently met? One day, I hope to find out.

# CHAPTER 36

## WHAT DO I DO NOW?

**Frazier**

I sat on my bedroom floor with my back against the bed and my arms wrapped around my knees. I thought about everything that had happened, learning that Ryan's Uncle Carrington was my father. Not only would I be Ryan's brother, but I'm his cousin. It was surreal and confusing.

I ran my hand through my hair, wondering how this was possible. It made sense since I never formed a bond with my so-called sperm donor and didn't resemble that family.

"Fraz," Ryan said.

"What?" I snapped

"Are you okay?"

"Gee, I don't know. I find out your uncle is my father, and an asshole raised me. I'm peachy." I got to my feet.

Ryan and Jordan entered the room.

"It's not like I get a say in all this. Oh, hey, Dylan. I slept with a guy who's your father but passed a dick off as your daddy! Or here's the truth, I'm sorry." I was so angry that I started trashing my room. I got tired of bottling up my anger and hiding my frustration.

Ryan and Jordan restrained me as I fought them until I broke and cried. Ryan held me as I sobbed.

"Why, Ryan? Why did my parents let me suffer? What did I do? Why did they hate me?"

"I don't think your parents did it intentionally. It sounds like your mom found love at the wrong time, not able to escape a dire situation," Ryan replied.

I cried. All I wanted was people to love me. The abuse and yelling made me miserable.

"Frazier, you grew up in a shitty situation, but consider how you turned out," Jordan said. "You could have easily turned out like that asshole, but you didn't. You have the biggest heart and tenderest feelings out of anyone, which speaks volumes."

I looked at Jordan with glassy eyes.

"We got your back. Whatever you decide, we'll back you," Ryan responded.

I nodded as my best friends comforted me. After I calmed down, Ryan released me. The three of us sat around and talked.

"Sorry, I called your sister hot," I told Ryan.

"Don't worry about it. That makes you an idiot," Ryan replied. We chuckled.

"So, what are you going to do?" Jordan asked.

I squatted, thinking about the situation. "What if Carrington doesn't like me? What if I annoy him?"

"You annoy everyone, and you're worried about that?" Ryan arched his brow.

I rolled my eyes. "I meant annoying Carrington so much that he wants nothing to do with me. My mom left, and I'm with a new family." I furrowed my brows.

"Then take a chance," Jordan said.

I looked at him.

"Think about it. It's not like Carrington knows anything about you."

I had my doubts. Who would want a kid that's an adult? Carrington has a wife and a life. Hey, that rhymed. Stop it, Frazier. You need to focus on the current situation.

"Frazier, Uncle Carrington is the most laid-back person you will ever meet. He enjoys kidding around with people and loves pranks," Ryan said.

I raised my brows. Ryan gave me a knowing glance.

"Okay, I guess I can meet Carrington. But I still have my doubts." I sighed and shook my head.

After talking to Ryan and Jordan, I came downstairs and walked to Charles's office, and he was sitting at his desk working.

I knocked on the door, making Charles peek up at me. I entered the office. "You're busy taking care of things and dealing with Ryan's love crises, but I was wondering…." I trailed off. Man, this was hard.

"Frazier?"

"I was thinking of talking to Carrington. But I'm not sure what to say to him. Mom claims he's my father, but it's tough to believe when people lie to you your entire life."

"Do you want to talk to Carri?"

"Maybe. Never mind. It's a terrible idea. Forget I said anything." I retreated.

"Dylan."

I stopped in my tracks. Damn it. I was this close to leaving. I turned around to face Charles.

"That is an excellent idea." Charles smiled.

"You're not saying that to placate me, are you?"

"No, because you should talk to your father."

"Is Carrington my real father, or are you messing with me?"

"DNA doesn't lie, Frazier."

That surprised me. Well, okay, then.

*****

**Carrington**

Someone knocked on my front door. I opened it, revealing Charles. "Charles? Is Dylan okay? Does he need anything? Let me get my checkbook." I walked over to a desk drawer and pulled out my checkbook.

"Frazier is fine, and no, he needs nothing."

I set my checkbook down. "Oh." Charles was here to inform me that my son wants nothing to do with me. "If Dylan needs anything, you inform me."

Nikita walked into the room and greeted Charles. "What's going on?"

"Charles stopped over to update me on Dylan. It's nice to discover he's okay. One day, Dylan and I can talk." I tried to keep my composure.

Nikita knitted her brows.

"It's my punishment for falling in love with his mom and not giving a shit about anyone but myself. I deserve my son to keep

his distance." I turned around and wiped my eyes because I didn't want them to see me cry. I regained my composure, then turned to face my brother and wife. "So, tell Dylan when he's ready to meet; I'll be waiting. If he needs anything, you tell me, and I'll make sure he has it. My kid deserves everything."

"That's a good theory, but Frazier deserves a dad," Charles said.

I looked at him.

"I came here to inform you that Frazier wants to speak to you. The problem is that he's uncertain how you will accept him."

My expression changed to shock. "Accept Dylan? I will do anything if he lets me be his father. When can we meet?"

Charles smiled.

Today I became excited. My son wanted to meet with me, and I couldn't wait. I hope Dylan likes me because it would suck monkey balls if he didn't.

# CHAPTER 37

## MEETING

**Carrington**

I stood by the railing near the water on the boardwalk and waited. I wasn't sure how Dylan would receive me. I missed so much time with him. Will he like me? Will he hate me? Will he tell me to get bent?

I waited as I did with Gloria that night, but my gut said Dylan wouldn't show. That thought depressed me. I'll give it another thirty minutes. I tapped my watch, hoping it was working. As the minutes ticked, I started losing hope. Dylan wasn't coming. When the time ended, I turned, coming face to face with my son.

"Sorry, I'm late, but Ryan and Jordan had to pry me away from Call of Duty. I was this close to beating a level, and they're always ruining my fun."

"Yeah, I hate when that happens, especially when you're to the end."

"Do you play video games?"

"Video games, board games, Old Maid."

"Oh, Old Maid is the shit. Jordan hates when I beat him, but you move your card slightly, and the person picks it."

"I know what you mean."

Damn, Dylan was so much like me.

"So, you're my father."

I nodded.

"I'm not sure how this works. The last douche I called Dad beat the hell out of me, and that makes you distrust people."

"That isn't a dad. The funny thing is I wanted someone to call me Dad, but my wife can't have kids. I thought it would be great to hear." I tried not to overstep my bounds.

We stood there for a few minutes.

"You can't be any worse than what I dealt with while growing up."

"Oh, God, no. I hate that family. The Fraziers are assholes."

"Yeah, I do, too, especially the cousins because they're pricks."

I chuckled as Dylan gave me a cheeky grin.

"I wanted to talk to you, but you were angry. I called Charles to ask about you and told Charles if you needed anything to tell me. I want to take care of my son properly since I didn't get a chance for almost eighteen years. It doesn't make up for you growing up without me, but I'm hoping...."

Dylan walked towards me and hugged me, which surprised me. I wrapped my arms around Dylan.

"I don't need anything, except for you, Dad."

Hearing Dylan called me Dad meant everything to me.

I gripped him. "I love hearing that."

Dylan lifted his head.

"I love hearing you call me Dad." I smiled.

Dylan smiled and continued to hug me.

How do you love someone you just met? It's easy when the person calls you Dad. I might have fallen in love with Gloria. But it didn't compare to the love I had for our son.

Dylan and I talked, joking with each other. We have the same personality, which was scary. While we spoke, my brothers watched us.

"Now that's a sight," Mason said.

"It seems Carri found the love he wanted," Joseph said.

"Nothing beats the love of a child," Charles said.

"Great, you're becoming soft because of a child. I told you women and children were a nuisance," Elliot said.

Mason, Charles, and Joseph glanced at Elliot as he stared at them, unamused. Yeah, Elliot still wasn't fond of women and children. I will never understand my baby brother.

*****

**Frazier**

Okay, Carrington turned out to be a cool dude, unlike the other family members. They're too uptight, but I'll let Alex deal with Ryan's family. Well, my family, too.

"So, do you care if I call you Dad because calling you Carrington is weird?"

"I prefer you to call me Dad."

"Cool, then can you call me Frazier?"

Dad stopped. "What's wrong with Dylan?"

"I hate it. It's lame."

"Dylan was my father's name."

"Good for him, but I don't prefer it." That earned a look. I shrugged.

"How about Michael?"

"Meh."

"Michael is my middle name."

"Good for you. Call me Frazier." I walked away, whistling.

"Yep, this is so, my child." Dad chased me.

I ran as he picked me up. We played fought with each other.

"You ugly," I told Dad.

"You look like me."

"I'm the better version." I smirked.

"Oh, it's on." Dad chased me. For an old dude, he sure could keep up with me.

We hung out and made plans to hang out more. Yeah, I'm glad Ryan made me meet Carrington.

Carrington left, and I walked towards a car as Ryan and Jordan got out of Ryan's car.

Ryan leaned against the car. "How did it go?"

"Okay, you were right. Carrington is okay." I rolled my eyes.

Ryan smirked.

"So, will you spend more time with your dad?" Jordan asked.

I thought about it and smiled. "Yeah, I want to learn about the man that made me a love child."

Ryan and Jordan gave me a strange look. I started laughing as they laughed.

"Frazier, you're an idiot," Ryan responded.

"Yeah, but this idiot finally has a father."

Ryan nodded.

We got into the car and headed home, and I sat in the backseat, smiling. I haven't learned my parents' entire story. One day, they might tell me, but now, it delights me that they wanted

me. That's the best feeling in the world when you realize that your parents wanted you no matter what.

# CHAPTER 38

## ARE YOU FREAKING KIDDING ME?

**Carrington**

Frazier and I learned about each other slowly. Oh, who was I kidding? Pft, we dove headfirst with our father-son relationship, which became a problem when we pelted Nikita with water balloons when she came into the house.

"Oops." I snickered.

"You're so dead!" Frazier said.

Nikita rolled her eyes. "That's not cool that you start without me." Nikita put up her hand.

"It's not my fault you worked later than usual." I shrugged.

Nikita rolled her eyes as she went upstairs. Frazier and I laughed. We stopped laughing when Nikita changed and pelted us with her water balloons.

"They got me!" Frazier acted dramatically. "Tell Ryan to buy a new toothbrush." He faked cough.

"I don't want to know what you did to Ryan's current toothbrush," I replied.

Frazier opened an eye. "You're supposed to mourn me, not worry about Ryan's hygiene."

"Oh, right. Oh, God! It's so terrible!"

"You both suck at this," Nikita said.

We looked at her, then gave her a devilish smile, and Nikita's eyes widened. We grabbed water balloons and chased her around the house, and we ended up soaked.

That's how our weekends were. Frazier spent time with us, and I got to spend time with my son. I even taught him some pranks. He taught me how to pick a lock. We needed to work on his timing.

When Frazier didn't hang out with his friends, he hung out with me. One night, I came downstairs to find Frazier on the couch, and I shook him.

"Sorry." Frazier yawned and sat up.

"Frazier, what's going on?"

"Living at Charles's house is okay, but I miss my mom."

I furrowed my brows.

"It was us against the world. Now, it's one against the world." Frazier sighed.

I squatted next to Frazier. "It's time you knew how I met your mom."

Frazier looked at me.

"When I started college, my brother Joseph dragged me to this coffeehouse. I met your mom and ordered a coffee, but I don't like coffee."

Frazier chuckled.

"We started as friends. Then I changed things one night. Your mom told me no, as did my brothers. I didn't listen and pursued her, not knowing she had a spouse, but I didn't stop when I found out. I fell in love with your mom and planned on having a life together with her, but I'll spare you the sordid details."

"Thank God."

I rolled my eyes.

"Anyway, the last time I saw your mom, we spent a passionate night together and created you. I wasn't aware that night resulted in a child. I hadn't seen your mother in a couple of months because of Maurice. We set a date to run off together, but she never showed."

"I understand I resulted from an affair. It's harder to deal with people despising you."

"Your mom and I don't. I'm not proud of my actions or behavior, but I don't regret it. Our relationship gave us you." I wrapped my arm around Frazier and held him.

He needed comfort that only a parent could give.

"No matter what, we wanted you."

That made him feel better as we talked. It's a lot to deal with when you find out the truth. I might have regrets, but Frazier wasn't one of them.

I don't want Frazier to hate his mother. She did what she had to do to protect him, and I can't fault her for sacrificing her happiness for our son because I would've done the same thing.

*****

I was in the kitchen cleaning up when I heard the TV. What in the hell? I know I shut it off. I wandered into the living room to see someone sitting there, watching a movie. "Are you freaking kidding me?"

Frazier turned to face me with a shit-eating grin on his face. "You need to beef up your security system since I disabled that bitch in two-seconds flat." He snapped his fingers.

I shuffled over, snatched the remote controller from Frazier, and clicked off the TV.

"Oh, come on! It was getting to the good part!"

"Breaking into my house doesn't give you privileges. What are you? Ten?"

"No, seventeen."

"I don't need to bail you out of the clink again!"

"Oh, come on! It's not my fault those assholes can't take a joke!"

"You stole a horse and yelled hi-ho Silver. I have to find Tonto now."

"Yeah, that pissed off Ryan and Jordan."

I rolled my eyes. "I'm trying to get you to graduate, but you make it difficult when you do stupid shit."

"You sound like Mason."

"Oh, hell, no! You did not go there!"

"Oh, I went there, all right." Frazier smirked.

"That's it! Get a controller. I'm taking you down in Call of Duty."

"Bring it on, old man!"

We grabbed two controllers and turned on the video console, then played Call of Duty. No way was I turning into Mason, that grumpy bastard. We played, accusing each other of cheating, like father, like son.

They say our father's sins mess with our future. I don't believe that's true. It's the choices we make that shape us to be who we are later. Meeting Gloria was fate, and falling in love was a chance. But producing a child was destiny.

I never thought I could love someone more than I did. Then one day, I met a fifteen-year-old kid with emerald-green eyes. That kid called me Dad.

The person I ended up loving the most was my son, Dylan Michael Frazier. Sometimes, love comes from unexpected people, and that person offers you, unconditional love. Who would have thought it would be a child? I didn't, but I'm thrilled that it did. Thank you, Gloria, for protecting our son.

While I bonded with Frazier, others were plotting. It will escalate and bring our kids into the mix, making the boys the most feared boys of Saintwood and the original bad boys. God have mercy on their soul because the boys won't.

# CHAPTER 39

## SAINTWOOD: THE ORIGINAL BAD BOYS

**Ryan**

I strolled into this hell hole again, knowing I'd get detention again for tardiness, but I didn't care since it was all bullshit anyway. It's the end of sophomore year, and next year, I'll be a Junior, then a Senior.

Every year was the same. The school had little recourse with their threats of expelling me. My grades were stellar, and I did nothing except beat the hell of guys that deserved it.

"Ryan!"

Christ. Now what?

"Mom and Dad will kill you if you get suspended again." Elena was my fraternal twin. We had the same IQ and similar problems, but she tried to keep me on the straight and narrow.

"Like I care. It's not like our parents are always around."

It was true. My mom's family had a chain of casinos, and my dad was always away on business. We were rich and had this huge ass house, but it didn't matter. None of it did.

Elena gave me the same frustrated expression that she always did. "You do care, but heaven forbid if you show it."

I rolled my eyes and patted my gaping mouth because Elena bored me with her mothering. I hated this school and the fucking people here. Pretentious snobs. They always caused trouble for someone. Mostly, they left me alone. I was six foot two, brown

hair with brown eyes. For a sophomore, I towered over the majority of the kids here.

"Fine, be that way, but don't say I didn't warn you." She walked away. Whatever, primadonna.

I scoffed, shook my head, started walking, and made my way to the boy's bathroom. I rounded the corner as a kid bolted out of the restroom and pressed his back against the door.

He was short, wiry, and had brown hair with blonde highlights. His emerald, green eyes held a mischievous expression to them. *What the hell was he doing?* I thought to myself.

He spun and noticed me staring at him. He straightened up and walked towards me. "Oh, hey. If anyone asks, you never saw me, and I was never here." He strolled past me, whistling.

What the hell was that?

As he rounded the corner, I heard a loud boom, and the bathroom door flew open. I walked in to find the toilet gushing water, inhaled, and ran my hand through my hair. Within minutes, a teacher rushed into the restroom. He saw me, saw the toilet, and narrowed his eyes.

"What?"

"Detention, Mr. Jones."

"I didn't do it."

"Yeah, and I'm the pope. Now get to class, and I'll meet you in detention." He shoved me out of the restroom.

"Blow me, Cassen!"

Hell, if I'm going down for something I didn't do, I might as well go all the way.

Fuck school and all the assholes that attend here. Every class was the same, with the teacher whining about something that no one cared about while most kids figured out their social life.

Here I was in advanced classes, and even those classes bored me, along with the people. The guys were ridiculous, and the girls yammered about insignificant topics. Only a few were good for one thing.

That reminds me. I need to get a hold of one of those girls.

"Mr. Jones, are you listening to me?"

"Nope."

"Okay, smartass. What's the answer to X?"

"Twenty-five. Any more questions, teach." I chomped my teeth together.

"I'll be so glad when you graduate."

You and me both.

A few more weeks and two more years, and I'll finally get done with this hell hole. Let the countdown begin.

# CHAPTER 40

## FRAZIER

**Ryan**

After my fourth period, I strolled toward the lunchroom only to see the same kid from an earlier run through the lunchroom as a couple of guys chased him. He climbed onto the tables, doing a little dance, picking up someone's pie, throwing it at one guy, and hitting him in the face.

"I'll kill you, you little weasel!" One guy said.

"Well, first, you have to catch me, but not before I fuck your mother. Tell her that Frazier says hi." He gave the guy a raspberry and pissed him off.

Who the hell was this kid, and did he have a death wish? What he did next surprised me. He ran towards the guys, slid between the guy's legs, jabbed him in the dick, and dropped him. Then he did a foot sweep on the other guy and decked him in the face.

I got to hand it to him. The kid had moves, and he leaned over the guys. "You guys fight like girls. Up your game, dicklicker!"

"Dylan Frazier!"

"Oh, hey, teach." He smirked.

"Detention, Dylan!"

"It was worth it." He laughed.

Okay, so this kid had a few loose screws, but hell if he can't fight.

He walked by me and grinned, then walked away. Yep, he was a few tools short of a toolbox.

*****

I strutted into detention and took a seat in the back. As I sat there, the door flew open with a bang. "Have no fear! Frazier is here! Huh. Huh." He pointed to himself.

Cassen said, "Frazier, sit."

"Aww, Cassen. You're no fun. Are you still miffed I blew up a frog in biology? Yea? No? Aw, never mind." He waved his hand dismissively. He strolled over, whistled, and took a seat next to me. Then he angled and stared at me.

I twisted my head and looked at him. "What?"

"How old are you? Like thirty?"

"I'm sixteen."

"You're big for sixteen."

"Aren't you ten?"

"Nope. Sixteen. I'm short for my size, and my mom said I haven't hit my growth spurt yet." He gave me a cheeky grin.

"Whatever." I rolled my eyes.

"Ooh, big man. Whatever. Pft, hahahahaha."

I glared at him.

"No offense, but you don't scare me."

"Oh? I bet I could beat your ass, right here, right now."

"Go ahead. I'd like to see you try."

I waited until Cassen stepped out. With quickness, I was out of my seat, grabbed him, and yanked him up by one hand. I cocked my arm back and was about to let it rip.

"Go ahead! It's not like I haven't had worse!" He struggled in my grip.

That's when I discovered the bruises on his stomach.

"Why are you waiting? Do it already! Put me out of my damn misery!" Tears streamed down his cheeks as I stared at him. Then I made a decision that would affect us. I set him down and let him go.

He stood five foot four and was a skinny little thing.

"Take your shirt off."

"Nah, man. I don't swing that way."

I sighed. "Take it off."

He reached down to the hem of his long sleeve shirt and dragged it off over his head. Bruises covered his body, and some had faded to a yellowish color, while others looked fresh.

"Where did you get those?" I pointed at the marks.

He sniffled. "The sperm donor tied one on and needed a punching bag."

"What?"

"It was my mom or me, and I choose to throw myself in the pathway of his fist. Can I put on my shirt now?"

"Yeah."

He pulled on his shirt and dragged it down before Cassen returned. "I'm not a charity case, and I can handle myself."

"I noticed how you took those two guys down in the cafeteria. What did you do?"

"Put itching powder in their jockstraps." He grinned.

"Why?"

"Because they're a bunch of douches. They think they can push me around because I'm smaller than them. I'm small, but it doesn't mean I'm less of a person."

"I suppose not."

"I'm Dylan Frazier, but I prefer Frazier." He extended his hand to me. "I hate the name, Dylan."

"Ryan Jones." I took his hand and shook it.

"Well, Ryan, I guess this makes us besties now." He grinned.

I swayed my head and rolled my eyes. "I guess it does." God, I hope I made the right decision with befriending this kid.

*****

I strolled out of detention. When my parents found out about my stint, I would endure a lecture, which was nothing new. Then something, or should I say someone grabbed my arm.

That wiry kid yanked my arm. "Wait!" He was leaning over, trying to catch his breath. He held up a finger. "Give me a minute." Then he popped up. "Whew, you walk fast!"

"I walk like normal people. It's not my fault that you're short."

"And you're an ass, but we all must be something, now, don't we?" He flashed me a cheesy grin. I would lay out most guys right here, but there was something different about this kid.

I rolled my eyes and shook my head. "I suppose."

"Oh, lighten up." He smacked my arm with his palm.

I glanced at my arm and back at him. Does this kid have a death wish?

"You're so uptight. I'm sure if someone put a piece of coal up your butt, you could squeeze out a diamond."

Yep, this kid had a death wish.

I shook my head. He was like a lost puppy needing a home. He had his hands in his pockets, rocking back and forth on his heels and whistling. I was debating if I should invite him to my house since I didn't bring people home.

"So, will we stand here all day, or will we hang out?"

"Do I have a choice?"

"No, but if you want to feel as if you have a choice, then, by all means, think that way." He smirked.

What was wrong with this kid? Seriously, there was something wrong with him.

I studied him for a minute. "Were you dropped on your head as a baby?"

He furrowed his eyebrows and tapped his lips with his finger as he crossed his arms. "No, I don't think so. But then again, how the hell should I know? I was a baby, so it's not like you remember anything from that period."

"An idiot?"

He gave me a weird face. "Ah, no."

"Did the milkman leave you on your parent's doorstep?" I leaned in and touched the tip of his nose with my index finger.

He was like a cat when you did that. His eyes crossed, and he swatted his hands around, trying to bat away stuff from his face. "Stop that!"

Ooh, I hit a nerve with him.

"We could stand here, having a weird debate, which you suck at or hang out. Either way, I'm not leaving, and you're stuck with me. So, deal." He stuck out his tongue at me, then strode past me.

I took a deep breath and walked after him. There was no getting out of this one. Let's hope I don't regret this decision.

# CHAPTER 41

## DAMN, SON, YOU GOT SOME BALLS ON YOU

**Ryan**

We walked into the house, and Frazier let out a low whistle. "Damn. I didn't peg you for a rich kid."

"I'm not rich, and my parents are." I tossed my bag aside and strolled towards the kitchen.

He ran after me. "I'll need one of those motorized scooters for your house. You wouldn't happen to have a map, would you?"

"Why would I need a map? I live here."

"Well, not all of us have the luxury of knowing our way around in a fortress."

"Kitchen, living room, bathroom, and front door." I pointed to each area which was all this kid needed to know.

"Ryan Matthew Jones!" Shit. My dad was home and must have found out about me getting detention again.

"Stay here and touch nothing."

He touched the counter and grinned. Smartass.

*****

**Frazier**

While Ryan dealt with his dad, a girl walked into the kitchen. She noticed me as she opened the fridge. "Who are you?"

"I'm Frazier, and you 're hot." I grinned.

"You must be Ryan's friend." She rolled her eyes.

"We're besties. I blew up the toilet, and Ryan got detention. Then I punched some prick in the nuts and got detention, and we bonded. And now we're besties."

"Okay. Want some water?"

"Ryan said not to touch anything. I touched the counter. I don't think it amused him." I shook my finger at her.

"Because my brother doesn't have a sense of humor." She smiled.

"Yeah, he's a dud." I shrugged.

"That is putting it lightly."

*****

**Ryan**

Dad and I walked into the kitchen.

He looked at Frazier. "Who are you?"

Frazier turned to Dad. "I think the question is, not who am I, but who are you?" He pointed his finger at Dad.

"I"m Ryan's father, Charles Jones"

"I'm Ryan's bestie, Frazier."

"Did you say bestie?"

"Yep, sure did." He grinned.

What is with this kid grinning?

"Nice pad you got here, Charles, although a bit much for my taste."

"What do you mean?"

"Well, if I'm not mistaken, there's you, your wife, and two kids. Twins. You have a million bedrooms and bathrooms, and there are no maids, and the place is spotless. Correct me if I'm wrong, but how the hell do you clean this place?"

This kid compliments our house, insinuates things, then asks how we clean our house. That's his question.

"We work together to clean it."

"Well, at least you aren't lazy. I can't have lazy besties." He grinned.

I swear someone dropped this kid on his head at least once, twice, ten times.

He turned and walked away as we followed him. He started to intrigue me. We found him sitting on the couch alone.

"Who is this kid?" Dad asked me.

"I already told you. My name is Frazier, Charles."

"Does he have super hearing or something?" Elena asked.

"That is Superman. Do I look like a freaking alien that wears a cape and tights?" He waved his hand around erratically.

We stared at him.

He turned to face us. "My name is Dylan Michael Frazier. I'm sixteen, five foot four, with an IQ over 200. I must deal with a sperm donor that likes to get drunk and use me as a punching bag when he's not punching on my mother. Any more questions?" His smile disappeared.

"You're quite honest, aren't you?" Dad asked him.

"Lying gets you nowhere, and people see right through that bullshit. I'd rather be truthful and have no one around me than a million people lie to me. It's a simple truth." He shrugged.

Something about this kid threw me. I didn't know him, but he was honest about everything. He made no sense but made sense. That was scary.

I took a seat on the coffee table in front of him. "Okay, Frazier. You got my attention. What do you want?"

"I already told you. I want to be your bestie."

"No money?"

"No. Plus, what would I do with it? If I wanted money, all I would have to do is hack an ATM."

"What?"

"Insert a card, type a few numbers, and wah-la, instant money. But then I would go to jail, and stripes look hideous on me. And I'm not gay, so I don't feel like being anyone's bitch." He rubbed the side of his face and leaned towards me.

"You're strange."

"And you're an asshole."

"Damn, son, you got some balls on you," Elena said.

"Eh, at least I have them." He shrugged.

From what I could tell, this kid had some mood swings. One minute, he's happy-go-lucky, and the next minute, he's a little angry.

"Frazier?"

"Yeah?"

"You don't want money, have no problem taking down guys twice your size, and have mood swings. How is your loyalty?"

This is where it will make him or break him. Loyalty was everything to me.

He tapped his finger against his lips while Dad and Elena waited for a response. "My loyalty is everything to me. You be my friend, and I be yours. You got my back, and I got yours. Without loyalty, you got nothing."

This time, he looked at me and didn't smile. That's when I knew he was serious.

Frazier might be a little goofy, but he's the guy who you want in your corner, even if he could be a pain in the ass.

My dad walked over and sat down next to me. "You say your father uses you as a punching bag."

He lifted his shirt to reveal the bruises, and Elena walked over to us.

"What do you think?" He lowered his shirt.

Elena took a seat next to him. "Why?"

He turned and looked at her. "Why what?"

"Why would he do that?"

"I'm a reminder that I was a mistake."

"What do you mean mistake?"

"How the hell should I know why the douche comes home drunk and beats the shit out of my mom and me? He does."

I looked at him, then at them as we all sighed.

"Would you like me to talk to your father?" Dad asked him.

"Nope."

"Okay, if you don't want me to talk to him, then how about another solution. Whenever things get rough at home, you come here."

"Now you're talking, Charles." He smiled.

That was it. Frazier was looking for a haven from the abuse. I couldn't help but wonder how a kid could deal with something like that for years and say nothing. He must be hurting, and he's angry for sure.

"Charles, I'm home!"

We all turned our heads to discover Mom standing there.

She noticed us, then walked towards us. "Oh, hello."

He let out a whistle. "Damn, Ryan. You got a hot sister and mother."

What the hell?

"Well, aren't you an interesting boy," Mom said.

"Boy? I see no boy here! I see a man!"

Dad shook his head. "Maggie, this is Frazier." He turned and looked at Frazier. "Did I get it right?"

"You got it, dude."

"Did you quote Full House?" Elena asked him.

He shrugged. "I like tv."

"Anyway, Ryan met Frazier at school," Dad told her.

"Good. Perhaps, Ryan won't be so damn moody." She smirked.

I wasn't moody and had no time for bullshit which school produced an abundance.

"I'm going to make dinner. Frazier, are you staying?"

He got up and walked over to her. "Do you need any help?"

"Oh, okay."

They both went into the kitchen.

Dad looked at me. "I like him because he's interesting."

"He's an idiot."

"Still, I like him. But if he has any more issues, you inform me. No kid needs to deal with that." Dad got up and went into the kitchen.

I ran my hand through my hair.

"Ryan, I understand that you're feeling anxious, but this might be a good thing for you."

"Elena, you understand how I get around new people. Then someone bursts in like it's a normal thing, and this situation isn't normal because he's not normal."

"Yeah, but normal is a dryer setting. Frazier is the friend you need. Think about it. Both of you need each other, whether you both want to admit it." She got up and walked out of the room.

Did I need a kid like this in my life? Time will tell.

# CHAPTER 42

## NORMAL IS A DRYER SETTING

**Ryan**

Over the next two weeks, Frazier clung to me like Saran Wrap. Everywhere I turned, he was there. At first, it annoyed me, but after a while, I got used to him. Until one day, I hadn't seen him during the last day of school.

As I made my way home, some noises came from behind the school. I walked towards the noise to find Mario and a couple of his cronies attacking Frazier. Fucking Mario.

"Hey! Leave him alone!"

"Stay out of it, Jones! It has nothing to do with you!" Mario slammed his fist into Frazier again. "This is between my dear old cousin and me."

Cousin?

"Your mother is like a ride where everyone gets a turn." Frazier spat out blood.

***Crack!***

I got tempted to leave but realized this kid had been through enough. Mario never knew what hit him when I slammed my fist into his face.

Mario was your typical bully and went after weaker people. I couldn't stand him. The only reason he stayed away from me was because of Elena. He had a thing for her, but I preferred him to pick another girl.

Elena would never tolerate this behavior. She hated caveman behavior and considered that a bully's mentality. She was also stubborn as hell, so telling her that Mario was a bully would make her think the opposite. Women.

I threw a couple of punches at him with my fist connecting every single time. I lifted him and glared at him. "Touch him again, and I'll beat the shit out of you."

"Why is this kid so important to you?" He glared at me.

"Because he is my friend." I dropped him on the ground, stood up straight, and looked at the other two guys. "Beat it." They ran off. And Mario, well, he scrambled to his feet and stumbled away.

Frazier was sitting with his back against the dumpster and wiping the blood from his nose. "I had them."

"You're so full of shit. All you had was their first connecting with your nose." I walked over to him and held out my hand as he took it, and I yanked him to his feet.

"Yeah, well, I got in a few good shots."

I pulled out a handkerchief from my pocket and handed it to him. "I didn't realize you're related to Mario."

"It's not something I like to mention. Mario is a dick. He always picked on me when we were little because I didn't resemble the rest of them. I don't know who's worse, him or my dad." He spat out blood.

"I never asked you. Why did you come so late in the school year?"

"Beats me." He shrugged. "Came home one day, and my parents said we were moving to this place called Saintwood. It didn't matter, anyway."

"Why's that?"

"Because they were going to expel me at my last school."

"For what?"

"The school frowns upon hacking into the school files." He grinned.

I stared at him. "Why would you want to hack into those? Grades I could understand, but student files?"

"I wanted to see my school file, and no one would show it to me. Said it was confidential. Confidential, my ass. They're my files, and I have a right to them. If they are putting things in there, I want to know what they are."

"So did you?"

"Yeah."

"And?"

"It was your typical stuff. Grades, behavior, tests, the usual except something caught my eye."

"What's that?"

"I'm not normal." He gave me a cheeky grin.

"No shit."

"Well, when you're nothing like your parents and don't resemble your father, you wonder why." He walked away.

Wait. What?

I ran towards him. "What do you mean?"

"Someone is lying, and I plan to find out why."

"Wouldn't it be better to ask your mother?"

"My mother won't tell me shit, and my father hates me. So, no."

"Okay, then."

If Frazier learned the truth, it would be his undoing. The kid was ready to snap, and what would happen when he did?

I walked with him to his house. Two reasons. One, to make sure no one jumped him, and two, to find out where he lived. We walked up to a small house.

"Welp, here is my stop."

I walked towards the house.

"Where are you going?"

"Inside." I opened the door, entered, and noticed the empty beer cans, and the house was a mess.

"Welcome to my humble abode. Here you have our living room and many beer cans, where the sperm donor likes to get hammered. Through there, you have the kitchen, and upstairs you have the bedrooms and bathroom." He pointed in each direction.

How can anyone live this way? Frazier walked into the kitchen and returned with a garbage bag. He cleaned up, and I think the scene embarrassed him more than anything.

I helped him.

"Sorry, it's a mess. Haven't had time to clean up before having company."

I don't think many people come over much, or he wanted company.

"I take it your friends don't come over often."

"Funny thing. I don't have any friends." He continued cleaning.

"What do you mean?"

"What part didn't you understand? Me, no friends."

I could hear the irritation in his voice. Frazier wasn't a bad guy. A little off his rocker, but other than that, he wasn't terrible.

"I don't have any friends, my family hates me, my sperm donor uses me as a punching bag, and I'm stuck in hell for school." He shoved trash and empty cans into the garbage bag.

"What about your mom?"

"She refuses to leave, so it's her or me. I would rather take the punch than for her to get hurt."

The situation stuck him between a rock and a hard place. Frazier would do anything for his mom, even if that meant taking a punch for her. If that wasn't loyalty, then I don't know what was.

"Okay."

"Okay, what?" He looked at me. "If you want to give me pity, don't. I don't need pity."

I shook my head. "Okay, I will be your best friend." I gave him a look, and he returned a blank stare. I think he thought I was joking.

Then he dropped the bag, ran over, and threw his arms around me. "You're the best person in the whole wide world! You won't regret it!"

"Okay, but stop hugging me." I pushed his head from me.

"Oh, right." He dropped his arms. "That is gay." Then he flung his arms around me again.

I gave up, sighed, and patted the top of his head.

The door opened and closed. Frazier let go of me, and I turned to see a man and woman standing there. They must be his parents.

"What did I tell you about bringing people here, boy?" The guy asked.

I don't like this guy. I shoved my hands in my pockets to keep from hitting him. "He didn't bring me here since I followed him." I shrugged.

"Is this a fag thing? Because I ain't raising a fag."

The dude was pissing me off.

"First, you shouldn't use the word ain't. Use proper grammar. Second, fag is a derogatory term, and Homosexuality is the proper terminology. Third, I don't like you because you're uncouth."

Frazier whined, and I shot him a glimpse.

"Who the hell do you think you are?"

I walked over to him and stared him dead in the face. "Ryan Jones."

Frazier's mom dropped her bag of groceries, causing the glass to break and her eyes to widen.

"You enjoy putting your hands-on kids and women. Bad move. If I find any more bruises on him." I thumbed at Frazier. "I'll put my hands on you."

"Is that a threat?"

"No, that is a promise." I might be sixteen, but I could fight. Hunter taught me how a couple of years ago before I hit my

growth spurt. I turned to Frazier. "Come on, Fraz. We're going to my house."

He followed behind me as I left. "Thanks."

"What are friends for?" I shrugged.

With that, he smiled, and I chuckled.

I wasn't sure where this friendship would lead, but Frazier needed a friend, and I was that person that would watch out for him. Even the little guy needed friends and protection.

# CHAPTER 43

## THE BEGINNING OF A BEAUTIFUL FRIENDSHIP

**Ryan**

Frazier turned out to be cool when he's not freaking annoying. We hung out during the summer, especially at my house. When things got bad at home, I found him at my door at ungodly hours of the night.

I didn't care if it kept him safe. Also, he put on some height over the summer, like six inches, hitting five foot ten, and Hunter helped him increase muscle mass.

He had changed a lot since the first time we met. His scrawniness vanished, and his fighting became more precise. He kept the same hair with those mischievous emerald eyes, along with his sense of humor.

People who suffer the most tragedy in their lives hide behind the biggest smile, which was true for Frazier.

Then I found him crying alone. He sat on the top of a picnic table in the park, and I walked over and sat down next to him.

"I'm not crying. The sun is making my eyes water." He rubbed his eyes.

It was getting dark.

"If you say so."

"I say so." He sniffled.

"Fraz, it's okay. I won't think less of you for crying."

He wiped his eyes and let out a deep breath. "It's hard pretending everything is okay. Until I stepped through that door, and it's not."

"Has he laid a hand on you?"

"Not since I fought back, but he still hits my mom. He waits until I'm not there. I don't even understand why he is the way he is. Mom told me that he wasn't like this years ago. Then one day, he changed."

"She won't tell you why."

"No. My mom refuses."

I ran my hand through my hair and rubbed the back of my neck. Parents keep things from their kids because they think it protects them. But in the end, it hurts them. Whatever Frazier's mom didn't tell him, she had her reasons.

After meeting his parents, Frazier didn't look like either of them. Sure, he had a few of his mom's features. But his dad? Not even close. They didn't have the same eye color. She had blue, and his "sperm donor" had brown eyes. So, where the hell did he get green eyes?

I would find out, and we wouldn't like the answer.

We walked back to my house. I had gotten my license at the start of summer but took a walk tonight to clear my head. In a couple of days, we would start our junior year. I'm that much closer to getting out of this hell hole.

I fucking hated this school and everyone in it. Well, except for Frazier. We became best friends and would taunt Mario whenever we could. Now that Frazier's bigger and taller, Mario couldn't jump him as he did. It's great watching him get his ass

beat. Now, it would be even better if he would stay away from my sister.

We walked into the house to hear voices. Then Dad came out of the kitchen with Uncle Carrington, who must be here on business.

"A bit late, isn't it, boys?" Dad asked.

"We still have a couple of days left of summer vacation." I shrugged.

"Next time, take the car."

I shrugged. Whatever.

Carrington studied Frazier.

"Oh, Carri, this is Ryan's friend, Frazier," Dad said.

Frazier held out his hand, and Carrington shook it.

"Nice to meet you." Frazier grinned.

"Likewise," Carrington replied.

"We're going to my room to hang. Is it okay if Frazier stays over?"

"Why must you always ask me that? Of course. He knows where his room is when he needs to stay," Dad said.

"I thought I'd check."

We headed up to my room. My parents gave Frazier his room when he needed to stay. They also said he could crash any time he wanted. He had one bad habit. He liked to jump on me in the morning when I was sleeping. One time, I punched him. Idiot.

\*\*\*\*\*

**3rd person**

Charles walked Carrington out, and Carrington stopped. "Charles, who is this kid, Frazier?"

"He is Maurice and Gloria's son."

"And he's friends with Ryan?"

"It took me by surprise as well when Ryan first brought him home. But I can assure you that he is nothing like that family."

Carrington nodded. "Can you find out something for me?"

"Sure, anything."

"Find out everything you can on that kid."

"Carri, why is this information about Frazier so important to you?"

"Charles, there are some things from my past I'm not proud of, but this is one thing I need to know for sure."

"What's that?"

"If he is my son." Carrington walked away, leaving Charles stunned.

After Carrington left, Charles reached into his pocket and made a call. "Joseph? I need you to find out everything you can on Dylan Michael Frazier. It seems our brother has been keeping a secret. Call me when you find something." He hung up.

*****

**Ryan**

Frazier and I hung out in my room, and I tossed him a can of pop and some chips. He sat on the floor with his back against the bed, and I sat down next to him.

"It's weird."

"What is?"

"There's something about your uncle that seemed familiar."

"Uncle Carrington is a lot different from the rest of them."

"What do you mean the rest of them?"

"Well, there is eight kids total."

"Eight?"

"Yeah. There's Mason. He's the oldest and more level-headed. He has a son named Cole, who's two years older than me. Next is Kate, who doesn't have any kids and runs a bakery. Then my dad, followed by Theresa, who has Dean. Dean is the same age as Cole. You have Joseph next. Then Christine, who has Sarah, who's gay, follows him."

Frazier raised his brows.

"Then Carrington and Elliot, and Carrington is the most laid back out of all of them."

"Damn, dude, you have a huge family."

"It's all right." I shrugged.

"So, any girl you like?"

"Nope. Most of them are ridiculous. They're always going on about something I have no interest in." I took a sip of pop. "What about you?"

"There was one girl, but it ended before I moved here. She had been my first for everything."

"Wait. Did you and the girl?"

"Yep."

"Wow. How old were you?"

"Fifteen." He beamed. "What about you?"

"What about me?"

"Have you ever?"

"No."

"You've never messed around with a girl?"

"Sure, I've messed around with girls but never all the way."

"You're a virgin?"

I grabbed his shirt. "Yeah, and if you tell anyone, I'll beat the shit out of you."

He put up his hands. "No worries there."

I released him and snatched the bag of chips.

"So out of curiosity, why not?"

"Because I want it to be special. It's dumb, but I want it to be with someone that sees me for me. Someone that looks past everything and loves me for me."

"Ryan, you're what they call a true romantic at heart."

"Never thought of it that way."

"There's nothing wrong with it. Trust me. It makes sex so much better when you love the girl." He grinned.

I shook my head. Most guys can't wait to get into a girl's pants, but I'm not one of those guys. I wanted it to mean something. Most girls dropped their panties if I glanced at them, but I didn't want a girl like that.

Call me weird, but I wanted the girl to be mine and only mine who had no guy before me. They're pure in every sense of the word, including her heart, and that would be the one that would capture my heart.

# CHAPTER 44

## SHAW

**Ryan**

Junior year started, and I drove over and picked up Frazier. He got in and rubbed his hands together. He had something planned because he always did.

"Do I want to know?"

"Nope." He grinned.

"Will this earn us detention?"

"Yep."

"Great."

I threw the car into gear and backed out of his driveway. The car roared along the road, and Frazier babbled on about something. I listened. I'm a man of few words, and Frazier talked enough for the both of us, so it's fitting.

We pulled into the school parking lot and got out of the car, making our way to hell. I hate this place. We walked up, and Mario ran his mouth, which better not be about my sister.

Then, before I got close to Mario, a guy walked up to him, hit him, and knocked him out in one punch. What the fuck?

The guy stepped over Mario and walked away.

"What happened?" Frazier asked me.

"I don't know."

We walked past Mario lying on the ground out cold and into school. As we made our way past the office, the guy who knocked out Mario sat there.

"Jordan Shaw! My office now!"

He stood up and walked into the back.

Then we heard screaming. "Who do you think you are? We don't tolerate fighting on the first day of school! Do you understand?"

"Go fuck yourself! I'm out of here!" He stormed out of the office and down the hall.

"Whoa, that boy has anger issues," Frazier said.

I glanced at Frazier, then down the hallway. The guy disappeared around the corner. Why will we meet?

The rest of the day had its mishaps with Frazier putting itching powder in the football teams' towels. I had to bail him out. We got detention. Fucking Frazier.

In my sixth hour, I sat in the back of the class. The guy from this morning strolled in and handed the teacher a note. The teacher pointed to an empty desk next to mine.

He walked down the aisle way to the empty desk, and drool fell from the girls' lips. He sat down next to me.

I turned to him.

"What?"

"Nothing." I turned my attention to the front.

We sat in class until the teacher called on him. "Mr. Shaw, what do you think?"

"I think about a lot of things. But the complexities of two characters who can't seem to figure it out makes them both inadequate emotionally."

I sat up. Who the hell was this kid?

"Elaborate," the teacher said.

"The girl understands that love is love but makes it harder than it needs to be. Then you have the guy who can't express himself, which makes him emotionally retarded."

"Um, excuse me, but that is so insensitive," a girl told him.

"What is?"

"Retarded. People don't like someone to call them that, and it's called mentally handicap."

He rolled his eyes, then rebutted. "If you paid attention, which you didn't, you would remember I said emotionally retarded, which is an adequate terminology for the topic. But you didn't since you're too busy working on your nails. Instead of correcting me on information and intelligence, which you lack, you should focus on class and learn something." He waved her off.

Everyone stared at him.

"What? Why must all you stare at me? Turn around and pay attention." He twirled his finger.

For the rest of the class, no one said a word. An intelligent person putting you in your place will make you shut the hell up.

After class, I made my way to detention and took a seat. The guy from the sixth hour walked in and took a seat, and Frazier bursts through the door as he always does. The other guy rolled his eyes as Frazier took a chair, and I sat there.

Frazier turned to the guy. "So, you're the guy that knocked out Mario."

"Who?" He asked.

"Mario is the douche that you punched out this morning."

"That's his name?"

"Wait. You didn't know Mario's name."

The guy shook his head.

"So, why did you punch him out?"

"Because he seemed like an asshole." He shrugged.

"I'm confused." Frazier sat back in his chair and turned to me. "He punched him out because he seemed like an asshole."

"Sounds like it."

"Who does that?" Frazier held out his hands.

"He does." I pointed to the guy. "Who are you?"

He sighed. "If I tell you my name, will you two shut the fuck up?" He tapped his fingertips against the top of the desk.

I looked at him.

He turned and looked at us. "Jordan Shaw. I'm new, and I fucking hate it here."

"Welcome to the club," Frazier said.

"What?"

"We all fucking hate it here," I replied.

Frazier turned to me. "Can he be our new bestie? Please, please, please, Ryan." Frazier bounced in his chair and clapped his hands.

Jordan stared at him. "Is he mental or something?"

"Who? Frazier?" I thumbed at Frazier.

"Yeah."

"No. Frazier isn't mental, but an idiot."

Jordan arched his eyebrow. "And you?"

"Ryan Jones. I hate this school and most people who go here except for my sister and Frazier." I pointed to Frazier.

"So, tell us about yourself, Jordan Shaw." Frazier pointed at Jordan while fangirling over him and making a fool out of himself.

I rolled my eyes.

"My dad moved here with my brother and me. My mom jetted years ago, and I hate my dad, my life, and this fucking place." Jordan frowned.

"You sure got some anger issues, don't you?" Frazier asked him.

Jordan yanked him out of his chair. I placed my palm on my face and ran my hand through my hair. Better save the idiot.

As Jordan let his fist fly, I caught it. "Hit him, and I'll drop you."

He dropped Frazier, then swung around, did a foot sweep, and knocked me off my feet. I landed on my back with a thud.

Jordan leaned over me. "What did you say about dropping me?"

I took a deep breath, swung around, dropped him on his back, and pinned him to the floor. "As I said, I'll drop you."

"Fine."

I got up and held my hand to him. He took it, and I helped him up.

"Where did you learn to fight?" I asked him.

"A guy named Hunter offered lessons, so I took them." He dusted himself off.

"Hunter Michaels?"

"Yeah. You know Hunter?"

"He worked for my uncle Mason and taught Frazier and me how to fight." I pointed at Frazier.

Frazier waved at him.

"Yeah, well, I wanted to learn how to defend myself, and he taught me how to hit."

"Why?"

"Because bullies are assholes."

"Well, Jordan, how would you like to be our friend?" I glanced at Frazier, who looked like he would pass out from excitement.

"You guys aren't assholes, are you?"

"Nope."

"Fine, whatever." He shrugged.

Then we heard a thud. We turned to find Frazier on the floor with his eyes closed and a smile on his face.

"What's the matter with him?"

"He thinks you 're neat."

He arched an eyebrow.

"Help me get the idiot up, will ya?"

He shook his head and helped me to get Frazier off the floor. We shoved him back into his seat and took our seats.

"Now what?"

I turned to Jordan. "Now we become the most feared boys of Saintwood."

With that, Cassen walked in.

Every group of bad boys must have three things. Brains, me. Humor, Frazier. And brawn, Jordan. Life at Saintwood would get interesting.

# CHAPTER 45

## THE MOST FEARED BOYS OF SAINTWOOD

**Ryan**

After detention, I offered Jordan to come over to my house with us, and he accepted. We climbed into my car, and I drove home. After I arrived home, we got out, and he let out a whistle.

"After a while, you get used to it." Frazier winked.

"You live here?" Jordan asked me.

"Yeah. It's my parents and sister."

"Twin sister and she's hot." Frazier grinned.

I shot Frazier a look. He shrugged.

Jordan wasn't sure what to make of us yet. We walked inside, and I sat down in a chair. Frazier jumped onto the couch and sprawled out. Jordan strode in with his hands shoved in his front jean pockets.

"Ryan! You'll piss off Dad when he finds out you got detention again!" Elena marched into the room past Jordan.

We argued.

Frazier got up and walked over to Jordan. "Hot, isn't she?"

"That's his sister?"

"Yep."

He stared at her.

She walked by him and stopped. "Who are you?"

"Jordan."

"And your friends with those idiots?"

"Y-yes."

"Sorry about your luck." She walked away.

He turned around and watched as she walked away.

"Dude, don't be staring at my sister's ass," I told him.

"I wasn't. I swear," Jordan said.

"Ignore Ryan. He knows not what he speaks of. His sister is hot, and he hates that, well, he's not." Frazier grinned like the village idiot.

"Okay. Do you mind if I get water?" Jordan asked.

I waved him off. "Kitchen is through there. Help yourself."

*****

### Jordan

I walked towards the kitchen, making my way inside to see Elena leaning over the counter and looking at her phone. I froze for a few minutes. She was gorgeous and had long, curly brown hair with beautiful chocolate eyes and a figure to die for.

She looked up from her phone. "Did you need something?"

"W-water."

"In the fridge." She pointed to the fridge behind me.

"Thanks."

She walked towards the doorway and stopped. "Mario told me that you punched him. Why?"

I stared at her. "Is Mario your boyfriend or something?"

"Yes." She looked at him. "Well?"

"He made some crude comments." I shrugged.

She rolled her eyes and walked away. Fuck. How the hell is she dating a douche like him?

*****

**Ryan**

Jordan returned, smacked Frazier for him to move, and sat down. "Ryan, is your sister dating that douche Mario?"

"Unfortunately." I sighed.

"Why?"

"Beats the hell out of me." I shrugged.

Jordan took a hasty sip from the water bottle, and he looked like he wanted to punch something or someone and seemed so tense. Meanwhile, Frazier became enthralled with this stupid movie called Mean Girls. Why must my best friend watch a film like that is beyond me?

While we hung out in the living room, Elena left to see Mario. She became so enamored by him that she didn't see him for the asshole he indeed was. Of course, it's easy when you put on a good show.

After a while, I took frick and frack home, and Frazier hopped out of the car. Then I drove Jordan home. We pulled up to a house around the same size as Frazier's, and he got out and walked inside as I drove off.

*****

**Jordan**

The minute I opened the door, my father met me. "Where the hell have you been?"

"I was busy." I clenched my fists.

"I got a call from the school today. Already fighting, aren't you?"

"Yeah, so?"

"So, how will you make the team if you get kicked out of school?"

"Because I'm not joining the team. I didn't even want to join the last one."

"Jordan, if you join the team, it's your ticket."

"No, Dad. It's yours." I walked to my bedroom and slammed the door shut. I hate being here, and my dad tried to relive his glory days through me.

On top of it, I have other issues, considering my cousin Bella was moving here. We're the same age, and I couldn't stand her. Most families should like each other, but I couldn't stand to be in the same room with her. Something rubbed me the wrong way about her.

I needed to get through the next two years. Then I'm out of this place, for good. At least, I met two guys I didn't hate but knew deep down they would change my life for the better. That thought terrified me.

*****

**Ryan**

After dropping off Jordan and Frazier, I strolled in and plopped in the chair. I'm not used to having people around me like Elena. That's how we differed.

She's more outgoing and opinionated than me, while I'm more reserved. Everything else about us was the same except for our personalities. She'll do the right thing while I don't give a shit. She stayed out of trouble as I got into trouble.

She's like a second mother to me when Mom's not here, and it's annoying. I love my sister, but damn, she needs to lay off.

She was dating Mario. I had no idea what she saw in that douche. He had a horrible reputation and disrespected women. It left a sour taste in my mouth.

I searched Dad's office for information about the Fraziers. I needed to look out for my sister, even if she didn't think the same way. I rummaged through his desk, finding files because I knew he had dealings with them.

Then I came across an unmarked file. What was this? I pulled it out and looked at it. It's some information on a family. As I read it, a picture fell out. I closed the file and picked up the image. Who the hell was this?

I studied the girl in the picture. She had light brown hair and steel-grey eyes. I looked for a name but couldn't find one. As I looked at her picture, all I could think of was she's beautiful, and I had to meet her.

I heard Dad come in, and I replaced the file in its spot. I shoved the girl's picture into my back pocket.

"Ryan? Why are you in my office?"

I held up a pencil. "I needed a pencil. Mine broke."

"Oh. How was school?"

"Fine. Met a friend today."

"What's his name?"

"Jordan Shaw."

"Oh."

"I'm going to bed now." I walked away from the desk and passed him, leaving him confused. I had the picture of the girl tucked in my back pocket. Whoever she was, I would find out her identity.

I entered my room and changed into a pair of sweats and nothing else. I picked up my jeans, pulled the picture out, and tossed the jeans aside then laid on my bed. I ran my finger over her face.

Who was she, and why did dad have her picture? Why was there a file with things blackened out?

As I studied the picture, I couldn't help but think that she's important, but also someone I had to meet. It's like this pull that I had never felt with any girl, and something was so innocent and pure about her.

Whoever it was, I would find her and make her mine.

# CHAPTER 46

## JUNIOR YEAR SUCKS, AND SO DO YOU

**Ryan**

Being a junior wouldn't suck, except I'm not a senior, and I'm still stuck here for two more years. The only plus side was meeting Frazier and Jordan, who hated this place as much as I did.

I picked them up and headed for school. As I drove, Frazier leaned forward on the back seat and rested his arms on the headrests between Jordan and me.

"What's on the agenda for today, boys?" He grinned like a fool.

"Stay out of detention," I said.

We laughed. Yeah, that wouldn't happen.

"So, you never told us why you hit Mario," Frazier said.

"Does it matter?" Jordan asked.

"Well, no, but I am curious about why you hit my cousin."

Jordan turned around and looked at him. "Wait. He's your cousin?"

"Unfortunately, yes." He let out a sigh. Frazier hates being related to Mario.

Mario had an annoying younger sister named Ashley, and she was always trying to go out with me.

"I heard things I didn't like."

"Well, okay, then."

I pulled up, and we got out of the car. Leaning against the car, Elena and Mario walked by, and I seethed because I fucking hated him. Then others walked past us until a girl with black hair and blue eyes walked up to us, resembling Jordan, except he had ice-blue eyes.

"Jordan?"

He let out a deep breath. "Bella."

"Dad said you're going here."

"Yeah, unfortunately."

"Well, well, well. Who is this?" Frazier grinned.

"This is my cousin, Bella. Bella, this is Frazier and Ryan," he said.

She eyed me up and down. She's cute, but nothing compared to the girl in the photo. "Well, it's nice to meet you." She smiled.

I nodded.

Frazier grabbed her hand and kissed it. "Ah, mon, Cherie. The pleasure is all mine."

She giggled as I rolled my eyes. Leave it to Frazier to use the worst French accent possible.

"Come on. We better go before we're late," I said.

"Dude, you're always late," Frazier said.

I shot him a look as he shrugged. Punctuality wasn't my thing.

We walked into school and headed to our lockers. Next year, I need lockers next to Frazier and Jordan. It sucked to be off on my own, and I will have Frazier fix that.

I tossed my stuff into the locker, grabbed my books, and slammed the locker door shut. Classes were boring as usual. I sat through most of them bored out of my mind until a girl behind

me leaned into my ear and whispered something. A smile curled upon my lips.

*****

Once class ended, I ended up in the janitor's closet with said girl. I didn't know her name and didn't care. All I cared about was what she wanted to do in said closet.

We went at it. Before I reacted, the girl dropped to her knees, undid my pants, and took me in her mouth. Her head bobbed up and down, and I leaned against the wall, enjoying her mouth around my manhood. It had been a while.

As soon as she deep throated me, that's when I felt the tightening. I let out a groan and released myself into her mouth. I kept her head there, so she swallowed every bit. When she finished, I released her head, and she wiped her mouth.

I pulled up my pants and redid them as she stood up. "Well, thanks for that."

"Any time. But if you want to go further, we can." She walked her fingers up my shirt.

"I'll think about it." I took her hand and removed it. That meant no way in hell was I having sex with you or anyone else. This right here was fine by me. If the girl were decent, I would return the favor. They had to be clean, which most girls weren't.

I opened the door and left. I made the girl wait until I was out of sight. I came walking down the hallway, meeting with Jordan and Frazier.

"Did you come out of a janitor's closet?" Jordan asked me.

"Yep."

"Why?"

"I was busy."

"He was getting a BJ from some random girl," Frazier said.

We looked at Frazier.

"Oh, like you're the only one."

"That must be some type of janitor's closet." Jordan let out a low whistle.

"Don't tell me you've done nothing in a Janitor closet."

"Oh, I've done more than receive a BJ in one. I have done nothing yet in these."

"Well, if you need to know who does what, ask us. The girls here drop their panties like nothing." Frazier smirked, putting out his hand.

"I'll keep that in mind. What about you, Ryan?"

"That topic is off-limits," I said.

Frazier might be keen on discussing his sexcapades, but I wasn't. The one thing I hated was anyone discussing my sex life, and that included girls. When I found out a girl talked to her friends about stuff we did, she wasn't talking anymore about it after I threatened to rip off her tits.

I respected a woman that deserved it. I don't respect women who run their mouths. It was a rule of mine. If you want to open your mouth, let me shove my dick in it. That way, you're doing something more productive than running your yap. Yeah, I could be a dick when I wanted to be one.

We walked to lunch and sat at a table, and Elena was with Mario and Jordan's cousin. That was quick.

Jordan turned, saw them, and released a disgusted breath.

"What?" I asked.

"Bella."

"What's wrong with Bella?" Frazier asked with a mouthful of food.

"Everywhere we go, she and her family follow. Then she inserts herself into my life, which is annoying."

"Don't you think you're a little hard on her?" I asked.

"I wish I was. There are things about Bella that rub me the wrong way. One time, I caught her tying a dog to a tree."

"Why?"

"I don't know. Bella wouldn't tell me. I untied the dog and noticed someone hurt it. She smirked. So, I took care of the dog and returned it to a neighborhood kid. That wasn't the only animal I caught her with, either. It was like she enjoyed torturing them."

I couldn't blame his disgust. That seemed messed up.

"Isn't that what psychopaths do before they move on to humans?" Frazier asked.

"Classic case," Jordan said.

Something told me to keep an eye on Bella. If she was getting close to Elena, I needed to keep her at bay.

"Well, if she hurts my sister, I won't hesitate to take her out," I said.

"If she does anything to your sister, you'll have to stand behind me."

I looked at Jordan. Something told me that Jordan had a thing for my sister. I wasn't sure if this was a good or terrible thing.

I wanted to drop the subject. The more we discussed Elena, the more I needed to beat the shit out of someone.

"Hey, Ryan."

I looked up to see Ashley and her two minions. "Ashley."

"Who are your friends?"

"Jordan. Frazier." I pointed to each of them.

"Well, my friends and I were wondering since there are three of you and there are three of us, we could all go out."

Frazier and Jordan looked at me, and I shrugged.

Her eyes lit up. "Great!"

I got up and looked at her. "I'll take your friend right here, and you two can decide between Jordan and Frazier." I took her friend's hand and led her away, leaving Ashley's mouth hanging open. We stopped once we were out of sight, and I turned to the girl. "I don't have any interest in you or them, so we're faking this. If you're a good girl, we might have some fun. But I have a rule, discuss nothing that happens between us. Got me?"

She nodded.

"What's your name?"

"Erika."

"Fine. I'll see you around, Erika." I walked away.

I had no interest in the girl but to piss off Ashley. The only girl I wanted was in the picture. Where are you?

# CHAPTER 47

## THE GIRL IN THE PICTURE

**Alex**

I came home from school and set my bag down. Another year, another year of bullying, and I hate it here because I have no friends.

Dad was on his twentieth job. We had to worry whether he would keep this one or not. My dad spent more time at the casinos than at home and constantly chasing after that next big payout.

I didn't talk, so people assumed something was wrong with me. But when you have perfect grades and social anxiety, it makes for rough teen years. Not to mention my classmates were complete assholes.

I pulled out Pride And Prejudice, my absolute favorite. I love Mr. Darcy and need a Mr. Darcy in my life. Someone that viewed me for me. Oh, how I yearned for someone like that, and I couldn't help it. The books I read were tragic romance stories, and I lost myself in them.

"Alex! Hunny! Can you come down here?"

I let out a sigh. Now what? I got off my bed and went downstairs until I reached the bottom step.

Mom was standing there. "How was school?"

I gave her a blank stare. Same, as always, I thought.

"Well, your father will be late again."

Translation: he was hanging out at the casino all night. I shook my head, turned around, and walked back upstairs.

Once inside my room, I closed the door and walked over to the window. It was only a matter of time before we would be moving. I let out a deep sigh.

New school, new assholes. I was lucky we stayed for as long as we did. I guess we will wait and see. Oh, Mr. Darcy, where are you?

*****

## Ryan

I would have preferred having fun other than agreeing to a triple date with Ashley and her minions. Frazier was with Vicky, and Jordan chose Ashley. I took the lesser of the three evils with Erika.

Time to have some fun.

We met them at the movies and picked one that disinterested me. That was fine. We'd sit in the back, away from everyone. I had plans of my own. Take me to a dull movie. I would have fun.

We sat in the back and waited for the lights to dim. Then I leaned over. "Did you bring it?"

She opened her purse and pulled out a bottle and a foil packet. "Yep. I've never done this. Are you sure I'll still be a virgin?"

"Trust me. You'll have nothing to worry about, but you need to relax, or it'll hurt."

She nodded.

I took the foil packet, undid my pants, and put it on. Then she handed me the bottle, and I made sure there was plenty on me. She removed her panties, and I shifted her onto my lap. Once I positioned her, I lowered her down, making sure I hit the second hole and not the first.

She tensed.

"Relax."

She nodded, and I lowered her slowly until I fully embedded myself inside of her. I gave her a moment to adjust and started moving her on me. I reached around to the front, moved my fingers inside of her, and let them roam.

She followed instructions and kept quiet with her bouncing up and down on me, which was a relief. I had done this with only a few girls. To me, it wasn't sex. Sex was full penetration, which was something I was saving for the right person. It was also a loophole.

Her muscles clenched me as she released a moan. I cupped my hand over her mouth and thrust into her hard. She let go as I found my release, and I leaned forward. "Good girl."

I lifted her off my lap, and she sat down next to me. I pulled off the protection, tied it, and tossed it, then fixed my jeans. This movie wasn't so bad after all.

After the movie, we got up. Erika tried to walk but was having trouble, and it didn't go unnoticed by the guys. We parted ways and walked to the car.

Once inside, Frazier asked, "How was it?"

"How was what?"

"The movie?"

"Not bad. What about you guys?"

"The movie was great, but Vicky was a dud. She didn't even want to do anything."

"Well, Ashley had no problem with her mouth." Jordan sighed.

I chuckled.

I dropped them off at home, made my way home, walked in, and went straight to my room. I pulled the picture out of my nightstand and laid down on my bed.

I imagined what it would be like to hold her. Kiss her lips. Hear her thoughts. No girl could be this beautiful and be real. Everything about her told me there was more to her than her beauty.

Those eyes. I could never get enough of those eyes. It's like the girl was hiding something behind those eyes. It seemed like there was an inert sadness to them.

The front door opened and closed, along with two voices, which meant Elena must be home. I opened my nightstand drawer and placed the picture in it, then closed it.

I got up and opened my door as she came upstairs with Bella.

"Where were you?" I crossed my arms.

"I was out with my friends." She glanced at me.

Bella stared at me.

"You're late."

"And you're not Dad, so back off."

"Whatever." I closed my door.

"What's up with your brother?" Bella asked her.

"He thinks because he's a couple of minutes older, that makes him king shit!"

"Fuck off, Elena!"

"Good thing I have a boyfriend," Bella said.

***** 

## Elena

Bella and I entered my room and sat down on my bed.

"So, how long have you and Mario been dating?"

"A couple of months."

"Have you two?"

"What? God, no. I am so not ready for that." I put out my hand.

"Are you sure? Because Mario doesn't seem like the type to wait."

"He knows I'm not ready. I'm only sixteen, for crying out loud. Plus, I'm not even sure if I love him, and I want my first time to be with someone I love."

"Elena, not all first times are about love."

"Well, mine is. I want my first time with my husband and not a high school boy that wants to get into my pants."

"Suit yourself." Bella shrugged.

"Enough about that. Are you going to the party this Friday?"

"I planned on it. What about your brother?"

"He doesn't do parties. I'm surprised he goes to school dances."

"What guy doesn't go to a party?"

"My brother. He hates parties and everything associated with them, and the dude doesn't drink or smoke, which is weird."

"Really?"

"Yeah. Ryan said he hates the smell of smoke and the taste of alcohol. My brother is the epitome of a bad boy but doesn't do everything a bad boy does. It's bizarre that he has these rules he follows."

"And what happens if a rule gets broken?"

"No one has ever broken a rule." I shrugged.

"That is interesting that a bad boy has rules."

We continued talking with Bella staying the night.

*****

**Ryan**

Jordan was right that there was something off about his cousin. Like they say, keep your friends close but keep your enemies closer.

# CHAPTER 48

## THE BAD BOY RULES

**Ryan**

Every bad boy has a set of rules. I have rules that I expect my friends and me to follow. Without rules, there is anarchy and chaos. It keeps us in check while it instills fear in the people that deserve it.

Rule 1: Loyalty. Loyalty is essential in any friendship, and it makes or breaks the friendship or relationships. Someone being loyal to you is significant because they have your back, and you have theirs.

If they're in a fight, you back them up. No questions asked.

This leads to rule 2. Fight fair. If you fight someone, you fight the person and not everyone else. It doesn't mean you and your buddies jump someone for the hell of it. You fight when needed if you need more than one of you to take on one person that makes you an asshole and bully, like Mario.

Rule 3: Honesty, whether it's in friendship or a relationship. Always be upfront with people and what you expect. It saves a lot of damn drama. When you're upfront, people understand what to expect from you. Yeah, I mess around with girls, but I always tell them what I expect, and we aren't exclusive. Some don't get it. I wish they would, but that's them, not me.

Rule 4: Don't make promises. Never make a promise you can't keep. The minute you do, it reverts to rule 3. Promise nothing to anyone. It's a given. Disappointment sucked for everyone.

Rule 5: Be your person. Don't be that stereotypical bad boy that has to drink, smoke, party, or anything else. That's complete bullshit, a waste of time, and gets you nowhere. If you want to drink, then drink, but not because people expected it.

Rule 6: Expect trouble. A bad boy comes with a reputation that is never good. It also means you get into trouble a lot. Especially if you have a best friend like Frazier, it's like trouble follows him. When trouble follows him, it follows us, and we end up in detention, often. Cassen has grown fond of us. The old man is growing on me.

Rule 7: The look. It isn't so much about clothing, but attitude. Make people fear you by one glance. When you do this, people leave you alone. I'm not saying go out and be a downright asshole. I'm saying make sure they understand you're not playing. Leave the weak alone.

Rule 8: Respect women, children, and animals. It brings us back to rule 7. Do not under any circumstance lay your hands on them. They might not be weaker, but they're innocent. Protect them. There's nothing wrong with a bad boy having a soft spot for these three. It doesn't make you a tough guy to disrespect women, children, or animals but an asshole, plain and simple.

I follow these rules, and so do my friends. I expect them to if they want to hang with me. I won't have anyone around if they don't. I don't need the bullshit.

***** 

We walked into detention to meet a new face. Mario. The three of us took a seat on the desk while he sat there. Wonder what he did.

Cassen walked in. "Really? Must you use my desk?"

"What can we say? It has more room," I said.

"Why is he here?" Frazier pointed to Mario.

"He's here because he was inappropriate with another student," Cassen said.

"Oh?" I climbed off the desk, walked over, and leaned on the desk with my palms. "Aren't you dating my sister, you piece of shit?"

"It was a misunderstanding," Mario said.

"Misunderstanding, my ass."

"Nothing happened. The girl is lying."

"Uh, huh. Don't fucking cheat on Elena, and I won't have to rip off your head. Don't hurt her, period."

"I would never hurt Elena. I love her."

"Good. Keep it that way." I stood up and walked away.

Lying piece of shit. I heard rumors about Mario. People love to gossip around here, but Elena didn't want to hear about it.

I walked back to the guys.

"Well?" Frazier asked.

"He claims he loves Elena." I shrugged.

"You believe him?"

"No. Mario's a lying piece of shit."

"Oh, he's a lying piece of shit, all right."

"How do we expose him?" Jordan asked us.

"We don't. Not yet, at least. I don't need Elena to get hurt and be angry at me." I let out a deep sigh. If it was anything I hated, it was Elena getting hurt, and Mario would hurt her.

While we sat in detention, Frazier blew spitballs at Mario and hit him every single time. Mario shot him a glare, and Frazier would send another one flying, smacking him right in the middle of the forehead. We laughed.

"Will you stop it?"

"No can do." Frazier spits another one.

Splat.

"Mr. Cassen, will you tell Dylan to stop?"

"Stop, Dylan." Cassen didn't glance up from his book.

Splat.

"Mr. Cassen!"

Cassen looked up from his book. "I told him to stop. Now quit whining because I'm at an important part with Mr. Darcy."

As Frazier kept shooting spitballs at Mario, I asked Cassen about his book. "What are you reading?"

"Pride And Prejudice by Jane Austen."

"What's it about?" I moved over and took a seat in front of his desk, causing Frazier to stop mid-spit and Jordan to glance at me.

"It's about how Elizabeth, the main character, is being forced into marriage, and she falls for Mr. Darcy, who lets his reserved nature threaten their relationship. It's a terrific book. Want to read it?" He held out the book to me.

I reached over and took it.

"Ryan, no one will fault you for reading a classic. Plus, you will find similarities between Mr. Darcy and yourself."

I couldn't help but wonder if he was right. I thought about it. Something told me I needed to read that book, so I did. I opened the book to hear the spine crack and started reading.

I got through a couple of chapters when Cassen said we could leave. As the others exited the room, I looked at Cassen. "Do you mind if I keep this for a while?"

He smiled. "You can return it after you finish."

"Thanks." I held onto the book and left the room.

*****

After dropping off frick and frack, I drove home and continued to read. I thought by reading this it would bore me, but it didn't. There were a lot of aspects to the story and characters.

Cassen was right. I noticed a lot of similarities between Mr. Darcy and myself. Where the hell was my Elizabeth Bennett?

I thought about the girl in the picture. Who was she? Was she, my Elizabeth Bennett? Was I her, Mr. Darcy?

The door opened, and Elena entered. She took a seat on the couch as I continued to read.

"Is my brother The Ryan Jones reading a book?"

"Looks that way." I didn't glance up from my book.

"So, why the sudden interest in reading an actual book? Did you get bored with your friend's stupid antics?"

"Did you get bored with that asswipe you call a boyfriend?"

She gave me an irritated expression. "I don't understand what your beef is with Mario since he's a sweet guy."

"If you say so."

"Give the guy a chance, Ryan."

"No."

"You're impossible." She threw her hands into the air and stormed out of the room.

What did she expect for Mario and me to become besties? No thanks. I had two best friends, and they weren't an asswipe like Mario. Although I wonder about Frazier with the shit, he pulled.

I continued reading until bed. Great, I get to do it all over tomorrow. Lucky me.

# CHAPTER 49

## TROUBLE

**Ryan**

I woke up in the middle of the night by my cell. I reached out from under the covers and answered it. "Hello?"

*Ryan?*

"Frazier?"

*Thank God.*

"What's going on?" I checked the time on my phone. "It's three in the morning."

*I need your help.* Frazier coughed, which didn't sound good.

"Hang tight. I'll grab Jordan, and we'll pick you up." I ended the call, jumped out of bed, and threw on a hoodie and sneakers. I called Jordan and told him I would be on my way to pick him up.

When I pulled up, he was waiting for me, and he climbed in and shut the door. "What's going on?"

"I don't know, but it didn't sound good." I pulled away from his house, drove us to the destination Frazier gave me and pulled into a playground. We got out of the car, walked around, and searched for him.

"Frazier!"

Then I heard coughing. We discovered Frazier leaning against a building while sitting on the ground. His face was bloody, and he was holding his side.

"Jesus," Jordan said.

I crouched in front of him. "Frazier?"

"Ryan, I tried to fight them off, but there were too many and a knife." Frazier raised his hand while holding his side with his other hand.

I pulled his hand away to discover that they stabbed him. I pulled off my hoodie and pressed it against the stab wound.

"Help me get him up."

Jordan helped me get Frazier to his feet. We walked him to the car as he stumbled. We put him in the backseat, and Jordan stayed with him. I got in and drove them to the ER.

After arriving at the hospital, we helped him inside, and nurses and a doctor took him from us.

"Who the hell did this?" Jordan asked me.

"I don't know, but whoever did will regret it." I pulled out my phone and called home. Elena answered. After bickering, she put Dad on, and I told him what happened.

Jordan and I waited as Dad showed up with Uncle Carrington. What the hell?

"Where is he?" Dad asked me.

"He's in the back. The doctors are trying to fix him up."

"What happened?" Carrington asked.

"He said people jumped him, and someone had a knife. He said nothing else." I looked at my dad. "Dad, they beat the shit out of him and stabbed him."

They looked at me, then at Jordan.

"Who are you?" Dad asked Jordan.

"Jordan Shaw," he replied.

Before they said anything else, in walked Frazier's parents. They spotted us.

His dad stormed over and punched Uncle Carrington. "Stay the hell away from my family!"

"Maurice, calm down," Dad said.

"Fuck off, Charles!"

I stepped in front of Dad, and Jordan joined me. "Get out."

"Who the hell do you think you are?"

Jordan hauled off and hit him with full force, knocking Maurice off balance.

"Ryan said get out."

He stood up and looked at Jordan. "You're Frank's kid. I should have known."

"Leave, Maurice," Dad said.

"Whatever. Let's go, Gloria."

"No." Her voice was quiet.

"What did you say? What did you say to me, you ungrateful bitch?"

"I said no. My boy is here."

"You mean your bastard child? Fine. Take care of the little bastard, you ungrateful whore!" He turned and stormed out.

Jordan and I glanced at each other. What the hell was that?

"I'm looking for the parents of Dylan Frazier," a nurse said.

Gloria walked by us and followed a nurse to the back.

"Boys, go back to the house." Dad and Carrington followed Frazier's mom.

We left the hospital and got into the car.

"What was that about?" Jordan asked.

"I don't know."

*****

The next day, Jordan and I skipped school to visit Frazier. Our best friend was more important than a place with a bunch of rejects. At least, I thought so.

We walked in, and the nurse directed us to his room. We walked in to find him yelling at the tv. "What? Don't go in there! Don't be dumb! That's where the killer is! No! Aw, I told you not to go in there, but you never listen to me." He was watching a horror parody movie.

"I take it you're feeling better," I said.

"I am. Her not so much since she's dead!" He screamed at the tv.

Jordan and I rolled our eyes.

"When are they springing you from the joint?" I asked.

"Tomorrow. The doctor wanted to make sure I don't tear my stitches." He lifted his gown to show us the majestic thing of gauze wrapped around his abdomen. He dropped his hospital gown. "Why aren't you in school?"

"We came to see you, you twit," Jordan said.

"Aww, I'm touched. You have a heart unlike the Tin Man from the Wizard of Oz."

"Unlike you who takes after the Scarecrow that has no brain."

"I have a brain." He stuck out his tongue.

"Really? Because if you did, you wouldn't have allowed yourself to get jumped in the middle of the night."

"Hey! I didn't ask for Mario and his goons to jump on me!"

I broke it up between them. "Mario? What do you mean, Mario?"

"I walked home from the store and cut through the playground. Mario and his cronies jumped me. I was doing great until the prick pulled a knife and stabbed me." He crossed his arms in frustration.

"Why did Mario jump you?"

"Cause he's an asshole. How should I know?"

Mario doesn't jump someone for no plain reason since he always has a reason, and I'll beat that reason out of him.

We hung out with Frazier a little longer, then left. After getting into my car, Jordan cracked his knuckles.

"Ready to pay Mario a visit?" I asked him.

"Yep."

We pulled out of the parking lot and made our way to school, then we waited. We sat off in the distance and waited. Jordan tapped his fingertips on the edge of the car door.

People came out of the school, signaling the end of the school day. I started the car and pulled into the parking lot. As soon as we saw him, we got out and walked towards him.

"Mario! You like to fight unfair! I'll show you unfair!" With that, my fist connected with his face. From there, I let my rage fly, beating the shit out of him. Jordan held back his cronies while I beat him until he was a bloody mess. People gathered to see the fight. Finally, I released him. "Touch him again, and I'll fucking kill you!" I wiped my hand on his shirt and nodded to Jordan, then we left.

Mess with mine, and you mess with me.

*****

**3rd person**

After Ryan and Jordan left, Mario's cronies helped him up. Ryan's beat down pissed him off.

"What now?" One guy asked.

"He thinks he can embarrass me, and now his worthless sister can pay the price." Mario spat blood from his mouth.

*****

**Ryan**

This chain of events would lead to devastating consequences for Elena. Things were intensifying between her and Mario, and she never said a word.

But all actions have reactions. If you have ever taken an introductory science class, they teach you that. When you create an action, in return, it creates a reaction. It's cause and effect and can have deadly outcomes, especially with the hatred between Mario and us.

What comes next would haunt me for a long time.

# CHAPTER 50

## CAUSE AND EFFECT

**Ryan**

They say everything has a cause and effect, and I believe that is true.

The hospital released Frazier, and I had him stay with us while he recuperated. After what I saw go down at the hospital, he didn't need to deal with that. Mom and Dad agreed.

While Jordan and I kept an eye on him and things at school, Elena had her troubles with Mario.

\*\*\*\*\*

**Elena**

Mario and I had another fight, but this time it became physical.

"I told you that I wasn't flirting with that guy!"

"Stop lying to me!" Mario slapped me.

The sound resonated through the empty hallway, and I grabbed my face.

He walked over and touched my arms. "Now, baby, I don't like to punish you, but you need to stop lying to me. Now be a good girl, and don't let me catch you talking to other guys." He leaned over and kissed me on top of the head. "Oh, and don't tell

anyone, or I'll make sure your brother has an accident. Understand?"

I nodded as he walked away. I stroked my face, still feeling the sting from the impact of his palm crashing across my cheek. Knowing Ryan would question it, I hurried to the bathroom and covered the forming bruise.

Every day, there were accusations and more hits. It got to where I started wearing long sleeves and extra makeup, along with hiding it from Ryan.

The times I was home, I locked myself away in my room.

Ryan knocked on my door. "Elena?"

"Ryan?"

"Are you okay?"

"I'm okay. It's that time of the month."

"Okay."

I pressed my hand against my door and sniffled, not realizing that Ryan was doing the same thing.

*****

**Ryan**

My heart ached. Elena was my twin, and we had a special bond. Her hiding from me or avoiding me was hurting us in a way that no one could imagine.

*****

Frazier and Jordan were sitting outside on top of a table at school as I paced back and forth.

"Ryan, talk to her," Frazier said.

I stopped and looked at him. "You don't think I tried that? She won't talk to me, and either hides in her room or avoids me."

"There has to be a reason that she's avoiding you," Jordan said.

"Thank you, Captain Obvious. Of course, there's a reason she's avoiding me. She won't tell me."

"Do you want me to ask Bella?"

"I guess." I sighed and ran my hands through my hand. My twin was in trouble. I knew it because I felt it.

*****

**Jordan**

Later, I found Bella at her locker. "Bella."

She looked at me, then put her stuff away. "Yes, Jordan?"

"Can I talk to you about Elena?"

She stopped. "What about her?"

"Is everything okay with her?"

She took a deep breath. "No."

I knitted my brows.

"She's in trouble."

"What kind of trouble?"

"The trouble that includes wearing long sleeve shirts and extra makeup, trouble."

"What?"

"Jordan, you can't tell Ryan."

"Bella, I can't keep this from him!"

"Jordan, you can't tell him. Elena swore me to secrecy because Ryan has a temper."

"But that's like breaking one of his rules. Always be honest."

"I don't give a flying fig what his rules are! You do not tell him!" She slammed her locker door closed.

Frazier walked up. "What was that about?"

"Trouble."

*****

### Ryan

Between Elena hiding from me and my friends avoiding things with me, things were getting out of hand. I hate secrets because they do nothing but sink people deeper into trouble.

If I said anything, Elena would avoid me even more. I wish she would talk to me. I never felt more alone than I did now.

I sat down and pulled the picture out of my nightstand. "I wish you were here. I need someone to talk to about my sister and twin, who is in trouble. I don't know what to do and feel like I will lose her."

Then it hit me. Stop sitting around and confront Elena. She might hate me, but I didn't care. I couldn't lose her because some asshole thought he could control her.

I threw the picture back into the drawer and slammed it shut. I walked to Elena's room and pounded on her door. "Elena! Open up!"

I twisted the door handle to discover she locked it. There's only one person I knew who could pick locks, so I called him.

Chello?

"Frazier, I need your help. I need you to pick Elena's lock."

And incur Elena's wrath? Um, no.

"Either pick the damn lock, or you tell what the hell you and Jordan know!"

Be right there.

Frazier arrived ten minutes later and walked over to her bedroom door. He pulled out a pick lockset.

"Where did you get that?"

"You never mind. You never saw this." He got to work picking her lock.

We heard a click.

"Wah-la."

I opened the door, and she wasn't there. I rummaged through her things to see if I could find anything.

"What are you looking for?"

"Anything to tell me what she isn't telling me." I searched her room until I found a key. I reached under the bed, pulled out a case, unlocked it, and lifted the lid. Inside were photos, letters, cards, and her diary. I pulled it out and skimmed through it until I found it.

"Dude, that is her diary, which hold her private thoughts. Anything in there about me?"

"Shush." I read. My brows furrowed at what I read. He was hitting her, calling her names, and threatening her. Why? I pulled out my phone and called Jordan.

*Yo.*

"Jordan, where is Bella?"

*She said something about her and Elena going to a party. Why?*

"Where is the party?"

*A house a few blocks away.*

"Get dressed. We're going to a party." I hung up.

I put her diary back, locked the case, shoved it back under the bed, and tossed the key back where I found it. We relocked the door and left.

We left my house and headed to Jordan's, then to that party.

He climbed into the back seat and sat forward. "Here is the address." Jordan handed me a piece of paper.

I took it from him and knew that address. I crumpled up the paper, tossed it out the window, and pulled out onto the street.

Ten minutes later, we arrived at the house. I walked towards the door with Jordan and Frazier behind me. I knocked on the door, and a guy answered it. "Ryan!"

"Where's my sister?"

"She's in the kitchen." He pointed in the kitchen's direction.

We entered and walked past people making our way to the kitchen.

I looked around and didn't see her, then turned to the guys. "Split up and find her."

We went our separate ways, checking every room in the house, but she wasn't there. We gathered into the living room.

I walked up to the guy. "You have three-seconds to tell me where my sister is. Or so help me, I'll start cracking heads."

"She's downstairs with Mario!"

We headed downstairs. When we reached the bottom, I saw Elena, and she was arguing with Mario, and he grabbed her, which was all it took.

I stormed over to him. "Get your damn hands off of my sister!"

"This is between her and me!"

I pulled her from him and pushed her behind me. "No, this is between you and me. You didn't think I would find out what you're doing to her." I glared at him.

"Fine. Take Elena, but until she tells me it's over, she still belongs to me." He raised his hands in defeat.

I got into his face. "Touch Elena again, and I will smash in your skull and enjoy hearing your bones crush."

He stared at me.

I turned to Elena and the guys. "Come on. We're out of here."

We walked out to the car.

"Ryan! You can't go around threatening people!"

I walked over to her. "I can, and I will! You're my sister and twin! I won't stand by and watch him hurt you anymore!"

"How did you find out? Did your idiot friends tell you? Because Bella told Jordan!"

I looked at Jordan and Frazier. "You knew?"

They looked at each other. I looked at Frazier and Jordan in disgust. I hated secrets, and they knew but kept them from me.

"No, they didn't tell me. I found your diary."

"You went through my stuff?"

"Hey, I told him not to," Frazier said.

We both gave him a look.

"You invaded my private, personal thoughts. You're no better than Mario, and you're as big of an asshole as he is!" She opened the car door in frustration, got in, and slammed it behind her.

They got in the back while I got into the driver's side.

That was one quiet and tense car ride home. I was so pissed at them. After dropping off the idiot brothers, I drove us home. When I stopped the car, she got out and stormed inside.

Things were about to change.

# CHAPTER 51

## SECRETS

**3rd person**

While Ryan dealt with Elena's wrath, Bella hid secrets of her own. What they entailed, no one knew.

Mario had Bella on the pool table, with her legs spread as he pushed into her. She had one arm around his neck and supported herself with her other hand.

As they both moaned, he thrust until they both found their release. He pulled out, and his crony walked over and dropped his pants. They continued while on the pool table. Next, the third guy took his turn with her. When he finished, she got off the table and lowered her skirt.

"Damn, you're a whore, aren't you?" Mario asked her.

"I suggest if you want to screw me, you shut your damn mouth! Unlike you're a precious virgin, I enjoy a good screw."

"It'll piss off Ryan when he finds out," one guy told Mario.

"Fuck him. I ain't afraid of him. His sister will get what's coming to her. Now turn around. I'm not finished with you."

Bella turned around. Mario hiked up her skirt and let out all his frustrations while pounding into her.

*****

**Elena**

The next day, Ryan and I didn't speak. We were both pissed at each other. I walked up to my locker and found Bella there. "Where were you? I tried calling you last night."

"Oh, Paul called me, and I ended up going to his house. Why?"

"My damn brother made a big ole scene at the party."

"Elena, he's worried about you." Bella smiled.

"I understand, but it doesn't help." I sighed.

"So, what happened?"

"He came in, saw Mario grabbing my arm, and flew off the handle like a damn nut."

"Oh?"

"Everything is so crazy right now. I got to get to class. I'll see you at lunch." I walked away.

Bella closed her locker and walked down the hallway, knowing she carried a secret, and smiled.

*****

**Ryan**

I parked in class, stewing. Not only was Elena and I not talking, but Frazier and Jordan pissed me off. All because they kept secrets, and I wanted to deck them.

As I remained there, I heard an announcement. "Will Mr. Ryan Jones come to room 254?" It was an old woman's voice, but not. "Mr. Jones, please don't be tardy since you're notoriously late." There was whispering as I moved forward. "And don't be an asshole. Thank you." Frazier.

The teacher looked at me as I got up. I swear I'll kill them. I wandered to room 254, opened the door, strolled in, and saw an empty classroom. The door slammed shut and locked, and I turned and pounded on the door. "Let me out, you idiots!"

"Nah, uh, not until you let us explain," Frazier said.

"What's there to explain? You knew what was happening with Elena and kept it from me!"

"Only because I didn't find out from Elena!" Jordan replied.

"Who gives a fuck? That's my sister!"

"And she's our friend like you are!" Frazier said.

I threw my body against the door. "You don't get it! She's my fucking sister! My twin!" I rammed the door, letting my frustration out until I couldn't hit it anymore. I dropped to the ground and cried. "She's my other half. If something happens to her, part of me dies, too!" I sobbed.

The lock clicked as the door opened. Jordan and Frazier knelt in front of me.

"Ryan, we didn't want to keep it from you," Jordan responded.

"But we also understand your temper, man," Frazier said.

I was on my knees with my head hung low. I hated the anger and frustration, which came out, and I became utterly broken.

"Ryan?"

I lifted my head with tears falling down my cheeks to see Elena standing behind them.

"What's wrong?"

I cried again.

She moved past them, dropped to her knees, and wrapped her arms around me. I held her tight.

"Shh, it's okay. I'm here. Your twin is here."

"Elena, I can't lose you."

"Hey, you won't lose me. Nothing will ever take me away from you."

I gripped her.

She let out a sigh. "It's time we talked."

I nodded, and she helped me up. The four of us stayed in the empty classroom and closed the door. From there, she told us everything.

*****

I sat there, trying to digest all the information she unloaded on us. It was a lot to take, but it made sense. Everything started after I beat the shit out of him for hurting Frazier and had become a vicious cycle.

I ran my hand through my hair as I leaned on the desk while she stood in front of us. I thought about everything she had told us.

"What will you do?" Frazier asked her.

"She'll break up with the asshole," Jordan said.

"Well, no shit, Sherlock!"

"You want to go, pretty boy!"

"Any time, any place. Bring it!"

I was trying to process everything. But the guys weren't helping with their bickering and were giving me a major

headache. "Enough! I can't think with you idiots babbling like apes!"

They shut up.

I looked at Elena. "You need to end things with him. Abuse doesn't stop but escalates with the abuser killing the victim."

"Ryan, I can't."

"Why not?"

"You don't understand." Her voice cracked.

"Explain it to me. Because all I want to do is leave this room and break every damn bone in Mario's body!"

"Because he threatened to kill you and others!"

I walked over to her.

She grabbed my shirt. "Ryan, I can't lose you!"

We stood there, shocked. Elena's weakness has always been me, as she was mine. It was a twin thing. I despised him for breaking her and shattering her by controlling her fear of losing me and using it against her. Not anymore.

"Hey, look at me."

She looked up at me, sniffling.

"Nothing will happen to me. I promise. If it means keeping Mario away from you, so be it. But as of right now, it's over between you and him."

She nodded, and I pulled her close to me. Mario was a dead man, and the first chance I got, I'd put a bullet in his head.

"Elena, we all have your back," Frazier said.

"Yeah, to get to you, he'll have to get through us," Jordan responded.

"It's over," I replied.

She relented, allowing us to do what we did best. And that was to protect her.

At that moment, we would forever become the most feared guys at Saintwood High. The gloves came off, and I was more than ready. I had two guys that backed me up, and their loyalty was like no other. For that, they had my respect.

# CHAPTER 52

## LOYALTY

*The following chapter will have disturbing content, and I recommend reader discretion.*

**Ryan**

After that day, we stuck to our word. One wrong look, and we beat the shit out of someone. To say it pissed us off was an understatement.

A classroom door burst open, and a guy flew into the hallway.

"It looks like Jordan's at it again," Frazier said.

Elena, Bella, and I looked on.

"Get over here." Jordan grabbed the guy by the leg and dragged him back inside the classroom. He closed the door behind him. There was a lot of banging and crashing.

I leaned against the locker and checked my watch. Two minutes later, we heard. "Shaw!" The door flung open, and the guy flew, landing at our feet.

"What? I'm busy!"

"Well, you have detention! My office now!" The principal said.

Jordan walked by us and smirked.

I glanced at the guy lying at my feet. "Aren't you one of Mario's cronies?"

The guy groaned.

"Give Mario our best."

We walked away. That was the start of it.

*****

Another day, Frazier was having his fun. He tossed a guy onto our table. We lifted our trays, so Frazier didn't wreck our lunch. He lifted the guy, grabbed Jordan's sandwich, took a bite out of it, and pissed off Jordan.

Then he beat the shit out of the guy.

Someone said, "Frazier!"

He delivered a swift kick to the guy's head and turned. "What?"

"Detention! And my office now!"

"Oh, fine." He walked by, taking someone's slice of pie.

"Hey! That's my pie!"

"And it's delicious!" He took a bite.

We couldn't help but laugh. As the lunch bell rang, we got up and stepped over the guy on the floor.

*****

The hallway doors burst open from Mario slamming into them after I punched him. People stood off to the side as I beat the shit out of him.

Jordan and Frazier watched as I picked him up and dragged him outside. I walked with him over to the dumpster, lifted the lid, tossed his ass inside, and dropped the cover.

"Well, got to hand it to you, that's a new one," Frazier said.

"I'm taking out the trash." I brushed my hands together.

The back door opened. "Jones! Detention!"

I rolled my eyes. That was nothing new there. If we didn't get expelled, it would be a miracle. Of course, it would piss off Dad. But that would never happen.

*****

We strolled into detention and took a seat.

"What did you do this time?" Cassen asked.

"What we always do. Beat up Mario and his stupid friends." Frazier grinned.

Cassen let out a chuckle.

"I have seen you here more than I ever have. And it's not even Halloween."

"What can we say? You're our favorite teacher." Jordan shrugged.

"I think you enjoy coming here to learn more about the classics," he said.

"Maybe, maybe not," I replied.

"Okay, so, why did Steinbeck set The Grapes of Wrath in the depression era?" Frazier asked him.

"He displayed the internal struggle of the main character," Cassen said.

We talked about the Grapes Of Wrath. Shocking, right?

Cassen was the biology teacher, but he read all the classics. When he handed me a copy of Pride and Prejudice, it piqued my

interest. From there, the others became interested. We would sit through detention talking about the classics.

That's what made him an excellent teacher. He loves to instruct kids, and they love to learn from him. We put aside our differences, and he turned out to be a cool dude. Plus, he understood us. No teacher did, but he did.

*****

With Halloween around the corner, we visited haunted houses, and we were too big to trick or treating. Plus, it wasn't our thing.

But that will come next week. Right now, we were busy beating up Mario and his crew and any other person that we met.

Elena kept her distance from him, and it was better that way. Bella didn't.

*****

**3rd person**

"Oh, God, Mario!"

Mario pounded into Bella while she sat on the dresser with her legs wrapped around his waist.

"Oh, yeah, baby! It's how I like it!" He worked her over until they both groaned. He drew out of her and did up his pants. "Damn, babe. That keeps getting better and better."

She jumped off his dresser and dragged down her skirt. "What can I say? I love how you screw." She smirked.

"So, have you heard anything?"

"Don't worry. I'm working on it." She walked up to him and ran her fingers up his shirt.

"Well, work harder. I want to make their life a living hell, especially that bitch. Ever since she opened her mouth, we can't catch a break."

"You'll get your revenge, and they won't realize what hit them."

"What's your role?"

"Trust me. I have plans of my own." She reached down and cupped him outside of his jeans. "Hmm, little man is ready to go again."

"He's always ready to go." He pulled her to him, spun her around, and pushed her on the bed. He dropped his jeans, hiked up her skirt, and slammed into her, going for round two. This time, it was rougher.

Whatever Bella had planned, she didn't tell him or anyone. No one knew, but Jordan was right with her not being all there.

She left Mario's and made her way to Jordan's house. She knocked on the door, and Frank answered it. She walked in, and he closed the door.

"Is Jordan or Josh here?"

"No. Jordan is at Ryan's, and Josh is at practice."

She turned around, started lifting her skirt, and teased him. He couldn't help but lick his lips and stare.

"You're a dirty old man."

"And you're a fucking tease."

She smirked. "I'm your niece, and you shouldn't be staring at me with lust in your eyes. What would Jordan do if he found out how you look at me?"

He pursed his lips into a thin line. Bella sauntered over and took a seat on the couch. She moved her arms across the back of the sofa and crossed her legs to give Frank a peek. He shifted in his place, trying to adjust from the bulge forming in his pants. "What do you want, Bella?"

"Help. You help me, and I'll help you. We both want something, and I need your help while you want to screw me. I see how you stare at me whenever I come over."

"You're my brother's daughter!"

"Oh, don't be such a Debbie downer, Uncle Frank." She rolled her eyes, reached down, and lifted her skirt. "Have a little fun." She uncrossed her legs and moved them apart. "You agree to help me, and you can have this. It's your choice." She raised an eyebrow.

He walked over and knelt in front of her. She leaned over and reached to the waist of his trousers.

"Let me help you." With that, she undid his trousers.

He was aching when she did that. His breathing increased, and he placed his hands on her legs, pulling her close.

She moved her legs apart so she was barely touching him. "Yes, or no?"

He stared at her as she brushed against him.

"Last chance. Yes, or no?"

"Oh, God, yes!" He pushed inside of her and thrust.

She wrapped her leg around his waist as he grabbed her hip and pounded inside of her. She moaned over and over.

"Shit! I've wanted this for so long!"

"I know, baby! I know!"

He continued until they both found their release. Bella fell back onto the couch as he knelt in front of her.

"Well, I guess with screwing, it doesn't matter if you're related or not."

His eyes bulged, and he knelt back on his legs. "What have I done?"

She leaned forward. "You became my bitch. Now get over here and screw me again, you dirty old man."

With that, he flipped her around and started again. He spent all evening screwing his ever-loving niece into oblivion.

It was one thing Jordan and Josh would never find out, and I doubt they could handle it if they did. Families have secrets. But with Bella, her secret would turn deadly. When? Ryan and the others didn't realize. That was the scary part.

# CHAPTER 53

## THUMP, THUMP, THUMP: A SAINTWOOD PREQUEL HALLOWEEN CHAPTER

**Ryan**

For Halloween, the five of us had gone to a haunted house, and it was a nice distraction from everything going on.

We were all joking around and laughing when Bella flirted with me. I didn't buy it. Something about her turned me off and brushed her off. Plus, she has a boyfriend. I'm not into messing around with other guys' girls and wouldn't want it done to me. I was also thinking about the girl in the picture. She never left my mind. Because of it, I couldn't even look at another girl.

We tried to make our way through the dark space when someone pinned me against a wall. A hand traveled to my manhood. "Hmm, someone is ready and willing."

That wasn't Elena since it would be gross. Bella.

I removed her hand. "I told you that I'm not interested, and don't touch me again." With that, I stomped away. There's nothing like getting groped in a haunted house. What is wrong with this girl?

As soon as I found the exit, I stormed out.

"What's up with you?" Jordan asked.

"Ask your cousin."

"What did Bella do?"

"She grabbed my junk for one. Jordan, deal with her, or I will." I stormed away.

*****

**Jordan**

The others came out of the house laughing.

"What the fuck? Was it necessary to grope my best friend?" I asked Bella.

Elena, Frazier, and Bella stared at me.

"What are you talking about?"

"Ryan said you grabbed him in the haunted house."

"He's lying. It was innocent flirting, and he misunderstood me. Why would I want him when I have a boyfriend?"

"I don't care what you were doing! Stay away from him!" I strode away.

*****

**Bella**

After Jordan stormed off, Elena turned to me. "What was that about?"

"It was a misunderstanding." I shook her head and smiled.

"Whatever it was, it got Jordan's panties in a bunch." Frazier chuckled and wandered away.

"Elena, you, believe me, right?"

"Of course. Ryan is on edge. Come on." Elena walked away.

I licked my lips, smirked, and followed them. Elena and Frazier were gullible, and Jordan was a thorn in my side. But Ryan was more challenging, and I'll have to scale back a bit, so he didn't get wise.

*****

**Ryan**

We headed to another haunted house, and I kept my distance from Bella. I didn't like her. What she did in the last haunted house irritated me. That's why I hate the girls that go to school here. They needed to use sex as the end all be all.

I made sure Jordan followed me, along with Frazier.

After our third one, Elena pulled me aside. "Ryan, what is wrong with you? You've been acting weird since the first haunted house."

"I'm fine." I shrugged.

"You are not fine. Jordan yelled at Bella for groping you in the haunted house. But Bella said you misinterpreted her flirting."

"When do you misconstrue someone grabbing you without your permission? Elena, I'm not into those things."

"Oh, because according to those two idiots, you're into a lot at the movies!"

"Whatever I do with a girl is my business."

"You're a fucking hypocrite."

"What are you talking about?"

"You have no issue using girls for your needs. But when a girl does the same, you have an issue. Seriously?"

"It's not the same thing, Elena!"

"Oh? So, explain to me how it differs." She stood with her arms crossed, tapping her foot. "You can't. Ryan, hooking up with a girl for a blowjob or anything else, is as bad as what Bella did. When you messed around with Erika, did you talk to her afterward?"

"Well, no."

"Of course not, because that's what you and other guys do. You don't think a girl has feelings. Brother, they do. Trust me. If you're hoping to find that special girl, I suggest you change your view of girls. Because when that one girl comes along, and she will, she won't mess around with a player."

"I'm not a player, and I've never gone all the way with the girl. What they see is what they get with me."

She shook her head. "It still makes you a player, but you're more honest about it." With that, she walked away.

I walked over and sat on top of a table and pondered it. Am I a player? I've always been upfront with girls. But they agreed because they figured they had a chance. I played on it. But I never promised them more. Then again, I made them think there would be more.

I sat there, trying to rationalize my actions.

"What is he doing?" Jordan asked.

"He looks like he's talking to his imaginary friends." Frazier smirked.

Jordan stared at Frazier.

"What? There is nothing wrong with imaginary friends, and it's healthy to have them."

"Yeah, when you're five."

"Okay, he's crazy." Frazier shrugged.

They walked over to me as I internalized everything.

"Is there a reason you're talking to yourself?" Jordan asked me.

"I think you 're nuts, but that's my opinion." Frazier grinned.

I rolled my eyes. "Elena and I argued."

"About?"

"The way I treat the girls."

Jordan took a seat next to me, as did Frazier. "Ryan, I hate to admit it, but she's right."

"But I'm honest. I tell the girls that I'm not looking for anything, and they know what they are getting into with me."

"It doesn't make it right," Frazier said.

We looked at him.

"Think about it. You like a girl, but she tells you she wants nothing and fools around with you, but you crave more. She was upfront, but it doesn't change your feelings." Frazier said.

"Elaborate," Jordan responded.

"Fine, I will. You meet a girl, and she's everything you crave. But she finds out your history of tossing other girls aside. Follow me?"

"Yeah," we said.

"She decides that if you do it to them, well, you'll do it to her. So, she casts you aside before you even get a chance. How would that make you feel?"

"Like shit," I replied.

"Exactly. Ryan, if you wish to meet a girl and settle down with her, realize that all women wish to be treated like they're the only one," Frazier said.

I got off the table and turned around. "That's why I've never had a girlfriend."

"Never?" They asked.

"No."

"Man, we've even had girlfriends." Jordan motioned between Frazier and himself.

"There hasn't been at least one girl?" Frazier asked.

"No. There's only one girl I crave. She doesn't even go to our school, and I don't even know her name." I didn't realize I let it slip until it was too late.

"What girl?" Jordan asked.

I pulled out the picture and showed it to them. "This girl."

"Who is she?" Frazier asked.

"That is the thing. There was no name in my dad's file," I said.

"She's cute, but I doubt you'd ever find her." Jordan handed the picture to me.

I tucked the picture into the back pocket of my jeans.

"What do you do when you see the girl you want but don't know who she is?"

They didn't have an answer for me.

*****

**Alex**

I sat in my room reading, wondering how my life became this messed up. My dad had lost another job, and people searched for him, but Mom always covered for him.

We were scraping by as it was. I closed my book, tossed it aside, got up, and looked out of the window. While people were enjoying Halloween fun, here I'm stuck at home with no friends and no options. I wondered if my dad would find another job, then lose it.

A sixteen-year-old shouldn't worry about surrendering their home. It's not right. I needed to get through school and get the hell out of here. My grades were excellent, so that scholarships would help. One thing was for sure. I refuse to turn out like my parents. I would make sure my children never worried about surrendering their homes to an addiction. No more.

# CHAPTER 54

## THE SH*T IS ABOUT TO HIT THE FAN

*This chapter will include mature and strong material. I recommend reader discretion.*

**Ryan**

After Halloween, I realized Elena and the guys were right. The way I was treating girls was wrong, and it needed to stop. I didn't want my girl to worry about my actions. I preferred to be different and required to be more. While I was looking at how to change, Elena had plans of her own.

*****

**Elena**

I was ending things with Mario once and for all. I showed up at his house. He opened the door, and we headed up to his room. When he closed that door, my life changed.

"What did you want to talk about?" He leaned against his dresser with crossed arms.

"I came here to tell you it's over."

"Oh?"

"Yes."

"Okay."

"I'm going to go." I started for the exit. When I opened the door, he shut it with one hand, and I looked at him. "Mario, let me go!"

"Not until we have our fun for one last time." He captured me, threw me onto the bed, and climbed on me.

"Get off of me!" I fought.

He seized my arms and pinned me down. "No! You think you'll walk away, you fucking tease! Now you'll give me what I want!" He struck my face, ripped at my top, and made his way down to my pants. Once he got them undone, he yanked them down while tearing my clothes. I cried.

"Shut up!" He undid his slacks as I whimpered. Before I knew it, he slammed inside of me. I screamed, and he slapped me again. "I told you to shut up, you whore!" I stayed quiet as he thrust inside of me. He took my virtue and innocence with it.

The pain was unbearable as he slammed into me over and over. It wasn't how I wanted my first time. My stomach erupted as I threw up.

After he finished, he got off and let me go. "Get out!"

I clutched my ripped clothes and ran out of that room, along with that hellish nightmare. I ran down the street with blood dripping from the corner of my mouth. I had smudged makeup. In my haste, I had left my coat at Mario's place. I fixed my shirt even though the buttons had popped off when he tore at it and tried to wipe my face.

I raced to a phone, knowing I had forgotten mine at home. It was a stupid mistake on my part. I banged the lever until the operator answered. "I need to call this number."

The operator dialed the number as I sniffled.

*Hello?*

"Jordan?"

*Elena?*

"Jordan, can you pick me up?"

*Yeah. Where are you?*

"I'm at the corner of Hayes and Montgomery."

*Isn't that over by Mario?*

"Yes. Please come get me and don't tell Ryan." I wiped my cheeks with my palm.

*Okay. I'll be right there.*

The line had gone dead, and I waited.

\*\*\*\*\*

**Jordan**

Ten minutes later, I arrived at the destination and lowered the window. Elena climbed in.

"Jesus!"

She turned to me with a vacant presence in her eyes. "Take me to this address."

I nodded and drove to it. Elena sat there in silence, not wanting to talk. If she spoke, she would break.

I drove around the back, and we entered through the rear entrance. We walked to an elevator. I glanced to see Elena with her arms wrapped around herself. She had smeared makeup, dry blood from the corner of her mouth, and torn clothes. We didn't speak a word.

Once we came to a room, she handed me a key, and I unlocked the door. We entered, and I closed it. I found the bathroom, started the shower, and exited the bathroom. She undressed, climbed in, and broke.

I opened the door, grabbed the clothes, placed them in a bag, and set them aside. I heard the sobs, then withdrew the bathroom.

I sat on the bed and waited for her to finish. The water turned off in the shower. Five minutes later, she appeared in a robe, and she walked over and sat down on the side of the bed.

I regarded her, not moving from my position, but she didn't face me. "Elena?"

"What?"

"Talk to me. I won't peek. I promise." I shifted, so my back faced her.

"Mario raped me," was all she could manage.

I couldn't press her for more information. "I need to call the guys."

Her head snapped in my direction. "No. Jordan, promise me you won't call them. I don't want anyone to know."

I angled my head and looked at her. My icy blue eyes met her chocolate brown eyes. "I'm sorry, but that is one promise I have to break."

"Please, Jordan."

I got up and knelt in front of her. "Elena, I can't promise you this. You might hate me, but Ryan would kill me. If something happened to my brother, I would prefer to know."

"Jordan, I need it to go away." She cried.

"I understand, but right now, they need to know. Trust me."

She nodded, and I pulled out my phone.

*Hello?*

"Ryan?"

*Jordan, it's late.*

"It's Elena."

*What's wrong with Elena?*

"Grab Frazier. We're at the Cascade Hotel, room 515."

*Wait. That is our suite. Why are you both there?*

"I'll explain when you get here. Trust me. It's not what you think." I hung up.

*****

**Ryan**

I tossed on a hoodie and sneakers and bolted out of my room. It better not be what I assume with my best friend and sister in our hotel suite. I'll rip off his head if he touches her. Yes, I'm a little overprotective.

I pulled up in front of Frazier's house. "Get in!"

He got in and didn't even have the door closed before I drove off. "Christ, Ryan! Could you let me close the door and put on my safety belt?"

My grip tightened around the steering wheel.

"Or not."

I sped until we reached the parking lot and drove to the back. Someone had parked a car behind the hotel, and I stopped and jumped out with Frazier hot on my heels. We took the elevator to

the floor of the suite, and I pounded on the door. "Jordan, open the damn door!"

The door opened. I pushed past Jordan to find Elena sitting on the foot of the bed in a robe with Jordan still clothed. I glanced at both and shuffled over to him. "What is this? Are you messing around with my sister?"

"What? No!"

"Then what is it?"

He leaned into my ear.

"What?"

He whispered again, and horror and shock filled my eyes. Jordan gave me a look as Frazier stood there.

I glanced at Elena. She lifted her head, revealing a void in her eyes. The happiness vanished, leaving nothing but emptiness.

I strolled over and knelt in front of her. I reached towards her, but she recoiled from my touch. I dropped my hand. "Elena?"

She stared at me. "Ryan."

"What happened?"

"Mario raped me."

My face drained of color as my blood ran cold. I was about to lose my shit when Frazier and Jordan stopped me.

Jordan shook his head. "Don't. She's already broken enough."

"He hurt her."

"She called me but didn't want me to call you guys. But Ryan, I couldn't keep this from you."

"Guys, she needs medical attention. I'm sure he used nothing," Frazier said.

Shit, he was right. Elena doesn't need an STD or bastard child from that bastard.

I called the one doctor I knew that would keep this quiet. I contacted Uncle Carrington's wife, Aunt Nikita.

She was in town and came right away. She entered the room, and I explained what had happened. She nodded and ordered us out.

*****

**Elena**

The door closed as Nikita looked at me.

"I need to examine you, and I'll give you something to prevent pregnancy and other medications. Okay?"

I nodded as Nikita started the examination, which took forty-five minutes until she finished. She handed me a pill, along with a glass of water, and I gulped it.

"Listen to me, Elena. Because of your age, I have to inform your parents."

"Aunt Nikita, please don't."

"Okay, I won't inform your father, but I advised that you file a police report and tell him. He should know."

"I can't."

"I understand, but please consider it."

"Thanks, Aunt Nikita."

"Any time."

*****

**Ryan**

Nikita opened the door, and she looked at Frazier. "You have your father's eyes." With that, she left. We shrugged. Yeah, okay. Frazier's dad doesn't even have green eyes.

That night, we all stayed in the hotel suite with Elena. She slept in the bed, and I laid next to her. She cuddled up to me like she did when she had a nightmare. It was the only time she felt safe. Jordan and Frazier camped out on the floor.

One thing was clear. Mario was a dead man.

# CHAPTER 55

## SURPRISE NIGHT VISITOR

**Ryan**

After that night, I wanted to break Mario into two. But I held off so I could take care of my twin. The guys also helped her with Frazier being his idiotic self, and Jordan staying with her at night. The first time I saw him sleeping next to her, I wanted to rip his head off but realized he was supplying security. If it was one guy that would let nothing happen to her, it was him.

We dealt with the aftermath of what happened to Elena.

*****

**3rd person**

Bella was becoming more and more unhinged.

Frank opened his door, and she walked in. He closed it. "What are you doing here, Bella?"

"Why, Frankie, we had a deal, didn't we?"

"It should have never happened." He walked away from her. "It was wrong."

"Was it wrong when you were screwing me all night long? Because I seem to recall that you enjoyed it. How long has it been since my dear old aunt, your wife, left?" She crept towards him and palmed his pants. "Hasn't it been years? I would leave

you, too, if I caught you checking out my niece's ass and tits."
She smirked.

He removed her hand. "This is wrong, and if Jordan ever
found out…."

"Jordan will never find out because I brought company."

"Company?"

She opened the door, and Mario walked in. Then she closed
the door.

"You've both been naughty, haven't you? You're a sexual
pervert who likes to screw young girls." She pointed at Frank,
then turned to Mario. "And you like to rape young girls, like
Ryan's sister. So, now that we cleared up, you both will do what I
say, or jail will look great for you. Now the both of you strip," she
told them.

They removed their clothes, as did she.

She walked over to them. "I prefer a bed, don't you?" She
grabbed their hands and led them to the bedroom.

From there, they did everything imaginable. Bella had them
both where she wanted them, and they would be her little
puppets, whether they liked it.

Frank had her bent over the bed while he went to town as she
made Mario watch. She had them switch until they collapsed
onto the bed together.

"My boys are good little boys. Get some rest because this will
continue all night long." Her eye held an evil glint as a wicked
smile formed upon her lips.

Bella was playing a dangerous game, and these two were her
pawn in said game.

                              *****

**Ryan**

Elena didn't return to school. She told my parents what
happened, and they conceded to allow her to stay home. She
told them part of what happened, but not who raped her. They
didn't press her but made her get help for it. They also hired a
private tutor, so she didn't fail.

Part of me became lost. Mario broke my twin, and there was
nothing I could do. I realized that I was heading down the same
path. So, that's when I changed. I didn't want a girl to fear me. I
wanted to protect them and take care of them.

I couldn't undo the damage with the girls at school, but I
could change for the next girl. I could become that guy she
needed, and that's what I intended to do. Elena showed me a
better path. For that, it made me forever grateful.


                              *****


I was putting my books away when Jordan and Frazier
walked up.

"Whatcha doing?" Frazier asked.

"Phineas and Ferb? Really?" Jordan asked.

"What? It's a funny show."

I shook my head as they bickered.

Bella walked up to us. "Hey, Ryan. How's Elena?"

I pulled out a book. "Elena's fine."

"Would it be okay if I visited her?"

"Another time. I've got to get to class." I closed my locker and walked away.

"What's wrong with him?"

"Oh, I don't know. Some asshole manhandled Ryan's twin." Jordan glared at Bella, then walked away.

"What did I say?"

"Leave it alone, Bella." Frazier followed suit.

Bella was becoming more annoying with each passing day. I was dealing with enough and didn't need her bullshit, either.

After school, the three of us stopped by the store, and I picked up some of Elena's favorite items.

"Was it necessary to buy a million assorted flavors of ice cream?" Frazier asked.

I pushed the shopping cart out to the car. "Yes."

"You're mad that he didn't buy your favorite." Jordan smirked.

"But I love Laffy Taffy ice cream," Frazier whined.

"That is gross." Jordan stuck out his tongue.

"No, it's awesome."

I loaded the bags into the trunk. "Are you ladies done arguing?"

"Yes," they said.

"Good. Now let's go back to my house before the ice cream melts."

"It's December and Michigan, and I doubt it'll melt that fast," Frazier said.

I glanced at him.

"Or it could."

I wouldn't stand here and freeze my balls off because Frazier pouts. I would like to have kids one day.

We got into the car and drove to my house. Once we pulled upfront, we unloaded the bags and carried them inside. I put the stuff in the freezer, then grabbed a container, along with other goodies, and brought them into the living room.

Elena was sitting on the couch.

"Here." I handed her a container of ice cream and a spoon.

She took it from me. "Thanks."

"How did therapy go today?"

"Like it always does. I sit there."

"Elena, you need to talk about it."

"Ryan, I can't. Not yet." She shoved a spoonful of ice cream in her mouth.

"Elena, it will help," Frazier said.

She snapped her head towards him. "Help?"

"Well, yeah. It has to help, right?"

She set the carton down and stood up. "How is it supposed to help? How is talking about Mario raping and hitting me supposed to help?" Then she exploded into a rage. "I hate him! I hate him so much! He took my self-respect! My trust! My dignity! He took everything from me!"

We all stood up.

She unleashed her anger. "Mario threw me onto his bed and tore my clothes! He hit me twice! He called me names! Then he fucking raped me! Why? Why me? What did I ever do? Why?"

Jordan placed his hands on her arms.

She pounded his chest. "Why? Why? Why? I hate him! I hate him! I hate him!" She looked up at Jordan. "Why, Jordan?" Then she broke.

He looked at her. "Because he's an evil person who wants to destroy people. Elena, you didn't deserve this. No one deserves this. What you deserve are kindness and gentleness and people that love and care about you. We all do." He pulled her close and wrapped his arms around her. "Right now, you deserve friends like us."

She buried her head into him and cuddled into him. She needed compassion. While Jordan could fight, he was also a compassionate person.

"I'm sorry for hitting you."

"No worries. I can take a hit, unlike little man over there who gets himself stabbed." He glanced at Frazier.

"Hey, I'm not little, and I almost had him!"

"Whatever makes you sleep at night."

Elena giggled. The three of us glimpsed at each other. That was the first time in weeks Elena laughed, making it the best sound ever.

I thought about it. Mario was mine, and I would beat the living shit out of him until he stopped breathing. That was a promise.

# CHAPTER 56

## INFORMATION

**3rd person**

Mason stopped by to talk to Charles about business while Charles's family was getting ready for the holidays. They closed the door to the office for privacy.

Mason sat in front of Charles. Charles pulled out a file in his desk drawer and handed it to Mason, and Mason opened it and read it. "Are you sure you want to do this, Charles?"

"I don't have a choice."

"We all have choices. Where's the picture?"

"It was there, then disappeared."

Mason frowned. "Pictures don't disappear, Charles. Only someone close enough to you has access to this room. If my guess is correct, you have a major problem on your hands."

"What will I do?"

"Let's see how it pans out. It might be nothing, but if it is, we'll make changes."

"How do we get them to agree?"

"Let me worry about that. I have Joseph working on the cover story and creating a backstory. But I'll tell you. It's not too far-fetched. The man can't stay away from gambling. We'll need a little extra help."

Charles rubbed his forehead.

"How's Elena doing?"

"She's not doing well. Elena won't tell me who did this."

"What about the boys? She seems close to them."

"They aren't talking. Ryan has this thing about loyalty."

"Ryan's a smart kid, and his friends are loyal to him. They would never go against him. You can thank Cole for that."

"That doesn't help me deal with the current situation."

"Charles, dreadful things happen to good people. Innocent people get caught in the crossfire, and there are casualties. Did you think your past actions wouldn't have repercussions?"

"Mason, that's my daughter. She didn't deserve this!"

"I didn't say she did, but seeing the full picture, I warned you years ago. Between you and Carrington, I've had to clean up more of your messes."

"Carrington? What does he have to do with anything?"

"Everything. Carrington's in as big a mess as you are. Between you not listening to me, him not keeping his pants on, Elliot's temper, and Joseph's cyber crimes, I'm surprised all of you haven't sunk this family into oblivion."

Charles drew a deep breath. Mason was right. Since he was the oldest and wisest of all the siblings, he took control and kept them in check. The girls were more intelligent than the boys and stayed out of things.

Mason took the file and walked out of Charles's office. As always, he would clean up Charles's mess.

*****

**Ryan**

We sat in the living room, and I heard, "Boys! I need to see you!"

We all looked at each other. Now what? The three of us got up and walked into Dad's office.

"Close the door and take a seat."

Frazier closed the door, and we took the seat.

He walked around to the front of his desk and sat on the edge. "I have a job for the three of you."

"What kind of job?" I asked him.

"A delicate package will arrive in a few months. I need you to intercept said package."

We looked at each other. Package?

"What kind of package, Charles?" Frazier asked. Leave it to Frazier to ask questions.

"It's a package. That's all you need to know," Dad said to him with a smile.

"Wait. So, you want us to intercept a 'delicate' package but won't tell us what the package is?" Jordan asked him.

"Precisely."

"You have to give us more information than that. A package could be anything."

"Or someone," I said, making them stop. The girl in the picture was what Dad meant. Frazier and Jordan didn't realize it, but I did.

Dad looked at me, and I looked at him, then I stood up. "Fine. We will intercept said package." With that, I walked away, with the two of them following me.

Whatever Dad had planned, those plans would change because this girl belongs to me.

We walked out of the house.

Frazier said, "Okay, so if this is a person, why are they so important?"

"I'm not sure. But it must be a huge problem for my dad if he wants us to handle it," I remarked from the car's roof.

"How are we going to recognize who it is?" Jordan asked me.

I pulled out the photo and handed it to him. "Her."

He and Frazier looked at it, then at me. "Wait. Are you telling us this picture you've been carrying around is the girl?" Jordan asked me.

I looked at them.

"Dude, she's hot," Frazier said.

"She's mine."

"But you don't even know who she is," Jordan said.

"Or if she is some psycho girl," Frazier said.

We looked at him.

"What? Hot girls are psychos."

"Says who?"

"Says every male species out there. It's a known fact that the hotter, the crazier."

"Elena's hot, and she's not a psycho," Jordan said.

"She's the exception," Frazier responded.

I looked at them both. "That's my sister, and she is not hot and off-limits."

"Ryan, Elena is hot."

"And I'm two-seconds from beating your ass. Now shut the hell up. I don't want to discuss whether my sister is hot."

I got into the car, and they followed suit. Jordan handed the picture back to me, and I took it. Whoever this girl was, she was important to my dad, but she was even more important to me. Who the hell was she?

*****

**Alex**

Christmas was almost here, and the snow fell to the ground, covering it like a blanket. There was pounding at the front door, and I opened my door and walked downstairs.

My parents were out, and it was only me. I opened the door to see two men standing there.

"Oh, hello."

I stared at them. The men wore nice suits and seemed like essential people.

"Hi." It was the only word I could mutter as I shifted from foot to foot.

"Don't be alarmed. We won't hurt you. They sent us to speak to your dad. Is he home?"

I shook my head.

The guy looked at the other guy. "Great. We got the kid but not the father."

"If we even take her, we'll be in trouble," the other guy replied.

"Why do we always get the stupid assignments?"

"Shh," the guy said, silencing him.

Great. More guys here to collect money from my dad. Well, this would be a crappy Christmas.

"You never saw us, and we were never here," the guy said.

"Okay."

They walked away, arguing. Those were two of the strangest guys that I had ever met. I don't think they need to worry about me talking since I barely say two words, anyway. I sighed and closed the door.

I returned to my room and read. One day, my life will be normal, and one can only hope.

# CHAPTER 57

## BLUE CHRISTMAS

**Ryan**

Right before Christmas break, I broke someone else, namely Mario. I looked all over the place and found him in a classroom with many people laughing and talking and didn't announce my presence before I charged him. From there, my vision became blinded with rage.

Frazier ran to find Jordan. "Jordan!"

Jordan looked up as Frazier waved for him, and he ran out of class, and they ran down the hall.

"Couldn't he have waited?" Jordan asked.

"It's Ryan! When does he ever wait?" Frazier asked.

They ran towards the classroom and inside to see me beating Mario into a bloody mess while other guys tried to intervene.

"You think you can rape my sister, you sonofabitch! I'm going to fucking kill you!"

Jordan took care of the guys while Frazier pulled me from Mario. "Stop, Ryan!"

I swung back and hit Frazier, not realizing who I hit.

"Ryan! Stop!" Jordan grabbed me.

"Let me go!"

"No! Not until we get you out of here!" Jordan dragged me out of there while I thrashed around, and Frazier grabbed his nose and followed us. We ended up in the bathroom.

I washed my hands while Jordan helped Frazier.

"Thanks. I always love getting clocked by my best friend," Frazier said.

"Hold still," Jordan said, trying to fix Frazier's nose.

"I already said I was sorry." I turned off the water and dried my hands.

I heard a crack, and Frazier said, "Sonofabitch!"

"Well, I put your nose back in place or let it heal crooked." Jordan shrugged. He turned to me. "How's your hand?"

"Hurts like a bitch," I said, holding it. I think I broke it when I slammed it into Mario's thick skull.

He walked over and checked it out. I hissed when he touched it a certain way.

"Yeah, you broke it. I'll teach you how to hit and not break your hand," Jordan said. Great. Just fucking great.

We went to the office. Of course, I got suspended, but they let us leave to get medical attention—me for my hand and Frazier for his nose.

In a few days, I would turn seventeen, along with having a cast on my hand. We got to the emergency room, and they took Frazier to one section, then me for an x-ray. Jordan called my dad.

While I was getting my hand checked out, Dad arrived. He wasn't happy to find out I was in another fight. Jordan followed him to the back, and as I sat there, while they cast my hand, then heard, "Ryan Matthew Jones!" Shit.

"What did you do?"

I shook my head and looked at him. "Got into a fight and broke my hand."

"Another fight?"

"Dad!"

"Don't!"

Then Frazier walked over with a band-aid over his nose with two black eyes forming.

Dad looked at Frazier. "What happened to you?"

"Ryan hit me," Frazier said.

He turned around. "What?"

"It was an accident! I didn't mean to!"

"Of course. Everything with you is an accident! Each fight is an accident! What happened this time? Some guy looked at you the wrong way?"

He hammered at me as I tried to speak.

Finally, I exploded. "No! I beat the hell out of Mario for raping Elena!" Shit.

He looked at me, stunned. "What?"

I turned away and couldn't look him in the eye. He looked at Frazier, who looked away, then at Jordan, who nodded.

He stepped back as his mouth hung open in shock. "Mario?"

"She went to break things off, and he raped her," Jordan said. "She called me the night it happened."

Dad looked like he was ready to be sick. He took a seat in a chair, still in shock.

"Charles, you can't tell Elena. She didn't want you to find out and knew you would kill him," Jordan said.

He rubbed his mouth and said, "I-I g-got to call your mother." He got up and walked out of the area we were in. I sat there, not saying a word.

*****

Once they released me, Jordan drove us back to my house. My hand was throbbing, and the meds were kicking in.

The minute we reached the door, we got barraged with questions, but I walked by them. All I wanted to do was sleep. I headed up to my room and walked to my bed. When I hit my bed, I was out.

*****

### Jordan

Frazier and I sat in the living room while Elena talked to her parents. It wasn't a joyous season in their house.

"This is a mess," Frazier mumbled.

"Tell me about it," I said, laying my head back on the back of the couch.

A few minutes later, Elena walked in, and we looked at her.

"You won't beat us, will you? Because Ryan already hit me once." Frazier winced.

She looked at him and rolled her eyes. "No, I won't beat you." She sat down in the chair.

"How did it go?" I asked.

"Well, Mom and Dad cried a lot."

"And you?"

"I'm relieved. To carry this secret around and not tell anyone, it's a big relief."

"Then it'll relieve you that Ryan announced to people at school that Mario raped you when he was bashing in his skull," Frazier said.

Her eyes widened. "Ryan did what?" She stood up.

I said, "Elena, he was raging, and it came out."

"Raging or no raging, I'm going to break his other hand," she said through gritted teeth as she stormed upstairs.

"Well, shit," Frazier said.

We got up and chased after her. We caught her as she entered Ryan's room and grabbed her. Ryan was out because of the medication, so he heard none of the commotion going on.

We tried to drag her out of my room. But she would get free only for us to capture her again. We argued and fought, trying to keep her from jumping on Ryan. Who knows, if he wouldn't have been in a semi-coma, what would have happened?

She ran into my room, and we chased her only for her to grab a pillow and hit us with it. Looks gave (*Frazier and me*) and fists thrown (*Elena*).

*****

## Ryan

At some point, I groaned, and they stopped. I rolled over, and the idiots crept over to me and leaned over me. I opened my eyes

to see three faces staring at me and yelled, causing them to scream as I fell off the bed and hit my broken hand.

"Sonofabitch!" I said, grabbing my hand.

"Looks like Ryan's awake," Frazier said.

I shot them a glare, and they bolted. What the actual fuck? I swear I'm going to hurt all three of them.

My hand throbbed inside the cast. The three of them poked their heads inside my room.

"Would now be a bad moment to tell you that Elena is furious with you for revealing her secret at school?" Jordan asked me.

I glared at them. "Do you think I care? No."

"Ryan's going to beat us with his cast," Frazier said.

"Who cares?" Elena asked.

"Well, he broke his hand while beating up Mario for you," Jordan told her.

"Well, in that case, we're even," she said.

For Christ's sake, they wake me up and cause me pain because of this bullshit? I need new family and friends.

I got up, walked over, and shut the door on them. Assholes.

"Are you mad, Ryan?" Frazier asked.

"What do you idiots think?"

"Yep, he's mad," Jordan said.

"Okay! We'll leave you to stew!" Frazier said.

I walked over and took a pain pill, then passed out.

*****

I opened my eyes and glanced at the clock that sat on my nightstand. Hell, how long was I out? I sat up and rubbed the sleep from my eyes. My hair was sticking up all over, and I felt like I got run over by a truck.

I grabbed my phone and looked at the time and day. December 25! What the hell? I was out for two days! I tossed my phone onto the bed and opened my door.

Jordan and Frazier stood there, grinning like the village idiots.

"What?"

"How much medication did you take?" Jordan asked me.

"I'm not sure, one, two, or three pills."

"Three!" They spoke.

"My hand hurt." I shrugged.

"Ryan, you have been out for two days straight," Frazier said.

"Thank you, Captain Obvious. I figured that out when I saw the date on my phone."

"Damn, you're cranky," Jordan mumbled.

"I'm tired, have a broken hand, and going back to bed after I take a piss," I said, turning around and making my way towards my bathroom. After relieving myself, I crawled back into bed and fell asleep.

Pretty pathetic, isn't it? Not only did I miss Christmas, but my seventeenth birthday as well. God, I hope next year doesn't suck as this one did.

# CHAPTER 58

## THINGS HAVE CHANGED

*This chapter will have disturbing content. I recommend reader discretion.*

**3rd person**

While Ryan nursed a broken hand, Bella was taking care of business. Bella paid a visit to Mario. He opened the door, and she strolled in. She looked at him and smirked. "Wow, you look like shit."

He looked at her. "What do you want?"

"I came to tell you that things have changed."

"What's that supposed to mean?"

"Exactly what it means." She walked up to him and looked him in the eye. "You're a liability to me, and I need to gain their trust. If they find out that I'm associating with you, it will ruin everything. Now, you're going to keep your mouth shut and not say a word. Okay?" She smiled a big smile, turned, and left his house, leaving him confused.

A little while later, she knocked on Jordan's door. Frank opened it, and she sauntered inside, and he grabbed her and pushed her against the wall.

"A little eager, aren't we?" She smirked.

He undid his pants, hiked up her skirt, and thrust into her with her back against the wall. "You like this? You like how I

screw you against the wall?" He said in between breaths as he thrust inside of her over and over.

"Oh, God, yes!" She wrapped her legs around his waist.

He thrust away until they both released, letting out a groan. "You're a little slut, aren't you?"

"But you like this little slut."

He released her and did up his pants. Then she pulled down her skirt.

"Well?"

"I told you I would take care of it, didn't I?"

"So, what's next?"

She walked up to him. "Next, I have to fake my way into their group. Jordan is a thorn in my side, but given time, he'll come around. Ryan was a tougher one. So, I'll act all sweet and innocent with him, and he changed his ways." She rolled her eyes.

"They will never buy it."

"Oh, they will. Those Frazier men are the biggest dumbasses to walk the face of the earth. So easy to play." She smirked.

He walked over to her and reached down, then turned her around. He leaned into her ear. "I want to bend you over the dresser and screw you from behind while watching your tits bounce." He slid a hand in between her legs, feeling her ready.

He moved her to the bedroom, tore off her clothes, spun her, and entered her as he slammed into her. She held onto the dresser, and he watched in the mirror as her chest moved back and forth, causing him to go faster. They both groaned with pleasure.

After they finished, he stood behind her and ran his hand over her body while kissing her. "Do you realize how long I wanted to screw this tight little body?"

"How long?"

"Ever since you developed. You would strut around in those tight little shorts and wiggle your ass."

"I was trying to get your attention."

He cupped her chest with his palm. "Well, you did. I would come home and jerk off because it was so fucking hot."

"You're such a pervert. An uncle checks out his teen niece, wanting to stick his dick into her and screw her into oblivion."

"Not as sick as you. What would my brother say if he found out his daughter had wanted to screw her uncle forever?"

"He'll never find out. Did you forget about that night in my room? When you snuck in and climbed into my bed? I was thirteen, and you took me."

He looked at her.

She turned to him. "That was my first time, and I enjoyed it. You were on top of me and inside of me. They say it's wrong, but you showed me how a man should be." She placed a kiss upon his lips.

"I couldn't help myself. You looked at me with affection, which I had lacked for so long. I wanted to have you."

"And you did. Then you wouldn't touch me after that. I was angry at you for not giving me what I wanted and have you all to myself, but you wouldn't touch me again. That wasn't pleasant." She placed a finger under his chin.

He picked her up, carried her to the bed, and laid her down. "How about we relive that night over and over?"

*****

**Flashback to three years ago when Frank visited his brother with Jordan and Josh.**

*"Boys, go play," Frank said as they came in.*

*The boys made their way outside.*

*"Hey, Uncle Frank," Bella said, bounding into the living room.*

*"Hi, Bella. How's my big girl doing?" He ruffled her hair.*

*"Better now that you're here." She wrapped her arms around his waist and hugged him.*

*"That is good. Have you been a good girl?"*

*"Oh, yes. The best." She smiled.*

*"Do you like surprises, Bella?"*

*"Of course, who doesn't?"*

*"Well, I have a massive surprise for you later. The boys and I are staying over, and there's something I want to give you."*

*"Really? What's that?"*

*"You'll see, but it's between you and me. Okay?"*

*"Okay. I'm going to see what Jordan and Josh are doing."*

*"You do that." He smiled.*

*Later, they had dinner together, and everyone talked. Then everyone settled in and watched a movie. The boys sat on the floor while Frank's brother- and sister-in-law sat on the couch, and Bella sat in Frank's lap.*

*"Would you like me to show you again?"*

*"Yes."*

*"I will show you as long as you want me to. Okay?"*

*"Okay."*

*He climbed off her, cleaned up, dressed, and left. She rolled over, laid there, and wanted him to show her again. She hoped that he would.*

*After that night, the minute she got a chance, she asked to stay over at Jordan's house. Then, when the boys were in bed, she would make her way to her loving Uncle Frank so he could show her love. It became their secret thing until he stopped. She didn't understand why since there was no reason. That was the day she would show the world how angry she had become.*

# CHAPTER 59

## OUTCOMES

**Ryan**

I was at my locker, setting my books in it, when the guys walked up, talking about something. I wasn't taking notice, lost in my thoughts.

Then Bella strolled over to me. "How is your hand, Ryan?"

"It's fine." After what happened on Halloween, I had nothing to say to her.

"Ryan, I want to apologize for that night. It was out of line."

I paused and shifted to Bella while Jordan and Frazier peered around me. That drew our attention.

"After giving it consideration, I recognized you're not that kind of guy, and it was flippant."

"What kind of game are you playing?" Jordan asked her.

"I'm not playing a game."

"Guys, I think she's genuine," Frazier said. "Why don't we offer her a chance?"

I thought about it. People make mistakes, and the three of us have made our fair share.

"Friends?" She held out her hand.

I shook her hand. "Friends." Unbeknownst to me, I shook hands with the devil herself. "That's all we are, Bella." I removed my hand.

"That is fine. Being friends is cool with me," she said with a smile. "I've got to get to class and tell Elena that I'll drop by to see how she is doing."

"Okay."

With that, she sauntered away.

"I don't trust her," Jordan said.

"Neither do I. But you know what people say. Keep your friends close, but keep your enemies closer," I said.

"So, what are we going to do?" Frazier asked.

"We'll play this close to our chest. Keep an eye on things. If she's lying, I will put a slug in her head," I told them.

"What about the girl?" Jordan asked.

"She's mine. She hasn't realized it yet, but she will."

"When is she arriving?" Frazier asked.

"I'm not sure. No one can't pin the girl dad down since he continues to run and never stays in the same place for long."

"He can't be that slick. If they have been capable of discovering him," Jordan said.

"The minute they detect him, he changes homes. It's the same story that he lost work and found a new job." I shrugged.

"It's time he got offered a new job which sustains him from fleeing," Frazier suggested.

Jordan and I studied him.

"What?"

"Frazier, you might be an idiot, but you're a smart idiot," I said.

"Gee, thanks," he said.

With that, I shut my locker, and we headed to class. Frazier had a point, and my dad had to give this guy something so remarkable that he wouldn't run.

*****

**3rd person**

Once the boys were out of sight, Bella walked out of the school and over to her car. She got in, took off, and headed to Frank's place. She tapped on the door.

He answered it. "Shouldn't you be in school?"

"Shouldn't you be at work?"

Then a smile spread on their faces as he yanked her inside and closed the door. They didn't realize Josh had come home early because he was under the weather.

Josh walked in to hear moaning coming from his dad's room. He knocked on the door, and it ceased. "Dad?"

"Josh?"

"What's going on?" Josh twisted the knob, but Frank had latched the door.

"Nothing, son."

"Are you certain? Because I heard a noise coming from your bedroom?"

"Positive, son. I'm under the weather."

"Must be something in the air. The school sent me home because I'm not feeling well."

"Head to bed, and I'll check on you."

"Okay." Josh stepped away.

When the door closed, they started back up, but this time staying silent.

He had her leg over his shoulder as he plunged into her, submerging his head into her breast. "Shit, Bella, I love being inside of you."

"Shut up and screw me, you perv."

That's what he did. When they finished, he got up and washed up. He tugged on a pair of pajama bottoms and a tee-shirt and checked on Josh.

She laid in bed nude when she received a text from someone. She opened it and responded:

*Be there soon. Must gratify the old man.*

She closed her phone, got up, and dressed.

He wandered back into the room. "Where are you going?"

"I have to leave. The school will call my parents if they find out I'm skipping. Then my parents will demand to learn where I'm at, and I doubt you wish to explain to your brother about how you're screwing his daughter, now would you?"

"But you showed up here so we could be together."

"And I did. Don't fret. Shoot me a text when the boys aren't here. Then we'll have more time together."

He strode over and draped his arms around her. "But I love you, Bella."

"I love you, too, Frank." She placed a slight kiss on his lips. "Now I have to run." She drew aside, snatched her purse and phone, slipped out of the bedroom and the house, making her way to her car.

Men always assume they're in love when they screw someone. She rolled her eyes at the notion. Sex to her wasn't about love. That had disappeared a few years ago when Frank stopped offering her love, and he halted them from being together and supplied no reason.

Betrayal was the term she learned best and had became most familiar to her. Everyone betrayed her in her life. The men that you expect to protect you hurt you the most.

Hurt was all she received through her life. All the men in her life had punished her. First, Frank took away his love from her, and next, her dad did the same thing. She relived the day that happened. It shouldn't have happened. But she awakened to notice her father in bed with her, like Frank. Then it ceased. That's when the depravity set in for her.

She grasped the steering wheel as she drove. She pulled into the driveway and got out. She opened the door as her father greeted her.

He pinned her against the wall. "What did I tell you?"

"Are you envious?"

"I told you to stay away from him."

"I need him."

"Does that include screwing him as well?"

"Him, others. A dick is a dick, and I hop on."

He leaned into her. "You've been a terrible girl, Bella. You've been sharing what belongs to me. Frank shouldn't have been your first, but me. He beat me to the punch."

"Does it make you feel like a man to screw your daughter? Knowing your wife could stroll through that door and catch you

with me on the dresser and my legs spread. You go to town as you moan my name and not hers. Knowing her daughter satisfies her husband the way she can never satisfy? Well?"

"For that, I'll punish you."

"I like when you punish me."

"Good. Now get your ass upstairs and strip. I want you ready for me." He released her.

She sashayed up the stairs and became ready for him. A few minutes afterward, he strode in, loosened his belt, and discarded it.

She was naked on her bed on all fours as he drew the strap and gave her three good whacks. Tears formed, but if she wept, he would continue to discipline her, and that was it.

He released the strap and stripped. He got onto the bed and caressed Bella's ass. "I hate hurting you, baby."

"Yes."

"I don't like to discipline you. But the way you were speaking to me was contemptuous. I can't have you disrespect me, now, can I?"

"No."

"Good, now I'll reward you." He spread her and slammed into her over and over, causing her to groan each time. A part of it was from the pain, and a portion was from the pleasure he delivered. Then they both erupted, and he released himself inside of her. He pulled out and flipped her around onto her back. "I love that sight of seeing my essence spill out of you. Your mother won't oblige me. She's scared she'll get pregnant."

"You can't get pregnant when you already are."

"What?"

She sat up. "Well, it could be anyone's. Yours, Frank's, Mario's, or others."

He got off the bed. "Get rid of it!"

She got up. "Relax. I'm not fucking pregnant. I would never have one of your bastard children or anyone else's." She rolled her eyes at him. She opened the side drawer, plucked out a pack of smokes, and lit one. She blew smoke into the air. "Do you think I would be that reckless? In the beginning, I didn't know any better. After my first time, a baby wasn't in the cards for me."

"You were pregnant?"

"Don't sound surprised. It's not like Frank used any protection when he took my virginity, and it's not like you pulled out, either. But we took care of it, not letting anyone discover that our love produced in a bastard child."

"That's why you disappeared that weekend." He sat down on the bed.

"When you decided you wanted a turn, I had Frank help me take care of it. After that, I was sick of that shit. So, I made certain it would never happen again." She pulled another drag from her cigarette. "Plus, I have bigger plans, and it doesn't involve no damn kid." She snuffed out the cigarette, walked over, and placed herself on his lap. Then she lowered herself onto him. "Now, shut the fuck up and screw me. Oh, and if you ever hit me with your belt again, I will cut off your dick."

He stared at her with fear in his eyes. That was when he became petrified of his daughter. Her eyes were vacant and filled with a void. He found himself in a precarious situation.

# CHAPTER 60

## FAKING IT

**Jordan**

I strolled up and found Bella at her locker. "Bella."

She peeked at me. "Yes, cousin?"

"I'd like a word with you."

"About?"

"About this change of attitude."

"I have no idea what you're talking about?"

I seized her and jerked her to face me. While gripping her arm, I said, "Don't fucking play me."

Her eyes expanded. "I'm not playing anything."

"I'm warning you. You do anything that reveals this is an act. You and me," I gestured between us, "will go a couple of rounds."

"I swear! I'm not playing!" She withered in my grasp.

I shoved her. "You had better not." Then I walked away.

"Don't fret, dear, cuz. You will be the first I deal with, you ass," Bella murmured.

*****

**Ryan**

I sat in class, and Jordan walked in and picked a spot next to me. "What's up your ass?"

"Who else? Bella."

"Now what?"

"I don't trust her."

I let out a sharp breath. "Relax, Jordan. If Bella is planning anything, we'll sense it. Keep an eye on her."

The teacher walked in a few minutes later. "Welcome to Psychology, everyone. This semester we will jump into the human mind and distinct psychological afflictions."

Yep, they required us to take a psychology course in high school. Pbbbt.

The teacher lectured about basic human emotions and their psychological condition. I had no interest in it, but Jordan did. He basked in the material. I don't get him. He'll beat the shit out of anyone without a second glance but will speak intelligently. He was a walking contradiction if I ever met one.

After class, we strolled out, and Frazier walked up. "How was psychology?"

"Interesting," Jordan said.

"Boring," I replied.

"Learn anything?"

"Yeah, you're an idiot," Jordan said.

"I am not! I like to have fun." Frazier grinned.

Jordan gave him a glimpse, and I rolled my eyes. Great. Jordan will analyze the village idiot.

We strolled to lunch and talked. Bella was chatting with other people, which was fine by me. Jordan was already tense as it was, and whenever she was around us, it only made him more anxious.

Suppose Elena hung out with her, fine. But I was good with the yahoos I had as friends.

After school, we went back to my house and hung out. We all sat around and watched movies. Frazier and Jordan sat on the couch with Elena while I sat in the chair.

"So, when are you coming back to school, sweet cheeks?" Frazier asked her, fluttering his eyelashes.

She rolled her eyes. "In a couple of months."

"Really?" Jordan asked.

"Yeah. My therapy is going well, and the medication is helping. Dad still wants to string Mario up and torture him. But I want it to go away. The more we make a big deal out of, the longer it takes for me to move forward." She sighed, playing with her fingers.

Jordan reached over and touched her hand to stop her from fidgeting. "Elena, you have all of us. Mario won't get near you."

"I know." She gave him a soft smile.

"Elena, has Bella been by to see you?" I asked, interrupting their moment.

"Yeah, she has. She's been a great friend to me, and it's been nice. Why?"

"I was wondering," I said.

Frazier leaned over, laid his head in her lap, and threw his legs over the arm of the couch. She stroked his head. Frazier jokes with her a lot, making all these weird comments, but there wasn't anything going on between them.

Now Jordan may be more of a concern, but I guess time will tell. As for Elena, it will be a long time before she will even look

at a guy in that way. Mario took more from her than any of us realized. Seeing her that night made me cringe, and I hated walking into that room and seeing the brokenness.

Elena has always been feisty, but she also has values and morals. She told me she was saving herself for marriage, and it was one thing only her husband deserved. I couldn't disagree with her and found it honorable. Then one night, Mario ripped it from her.

One act destroyed everything. When I saw that, I didn't want to be that guy. A guy uses girls and discards them or forces a girl into something she doesn't want to do.

I look back on the things I did with those girls, not caring how they felt afterward. Their faces and names ran through my mind. The more I thought about it, the more it made me sick, and I got up and shot out of the living room.

I ran into the bathroom and held onto the toilet, heaving. Each face, each name, made me heave even more. They ran after me, finding me emptying the contents of my stomach into the toilet.

"Ryan?" Elena asked.

I finished, closed the lid, and flushed the toilet. I sat with my back against the wall next to the toilet. Elena walked over, grabbed a washcloth, and wet it. She knelt in front of me and cleaned me. "What's wrong?"

"All those girls, faces, and the things I made them do because they had a thing for me. Elena, I didn't care about them. To me, they were nothing but a little fun. But seeing you that night made me realize I was as bad as Mario, if not worse."

"Guilt," Jordan said.

We looked at him. "Huh?"

He leaned against the doorway and crossed his arms. "It's a classic case of guilt. Knowing that you're doing something wrong but still doing it and feeling bad later."

"How do I get rid of it? Because it sucks." I sighed.

"You treat the next girl you meet with kindness and understanding," Elena said. "Ryan, we're young and make mistakes, but we learn from those mistakes. Trust me, when you meet that one girl, she will make you see things way differently. She will frustrate you but will make you so happy at the same time. She will have a thing about her that endears you to her but also makes you crazy. But more than anything, when she looks at you, she will be in love with you, and you will feel the same way." She smiled.

Elena was a true romantic at heart, and Mario didn't take that away from her. It made me glad that he didn't.

"Remember what I told you in the bedroom, Ryan? Sex was so much better when you're in love," Frazier said.

"You had sex?" Jordan asked.

"Yes, does that surprise you?"

"I'm surprised a girl would even let you touch her, let alone have sex with her."

"I'm quite desirable."

"Yeah, for a rock."

"Okay, tough guy. What about you?"

"What about me?"

"Did you get your cherry popped?"

"Yeah, when I was twelve."

"Twelve!" We spoke.

He shrugged. "The woman was older and hot."

"Wait. How many girls have you been with?" Frazier asked.

"Enough. That's all you need to know."

"As much as I enjoy hearing about your sexual conquests, I'm good," I said, getting up.

Let's see. Jordan had casual sex, Frazier had relationship sex, but I wanted something more. I wanted to be with one girl and one girl only. I wanted the girl in the picture, and something told me there was more to her than meets the eye.

# CHAPTER 61

## ANGER

**Ryan**

At some point in our life, we all have anger. Whether it's over something that happened or someone, we can't keep it hidden forever no matter what we do. It's like a pressure cooker that blows, and that's what happened to Frazier.

Frazier is the most laid-back guy you will ever meet. Throughout our friendship, he became my best friend, and I would do anything for him.

Life hasn't been easy for him while growing up. People kept secrets from him, and he lived in a house with an abusive drunk that would send anyone reeling, not Frazier. He kept his easy-going personality no matter what happened until his drunken father pushed him too far.

\*\*\*\*\*

**Frazier**

I headed home and cleaned up as I usually did when my sperm donor stumbled in drunk.

"Why isn't this place cleaned up yet, boy?"

"Because I got home a few minutes ago." I shoved more cans into a bag.

My dad walked over to me and shoved me. "I'm sick and tired of you disrespecting me! Now you're going to learn to respect me!" With that, he yanked off his belt and attacked me.

People told me never to strike my parents, and I took it until my mom got in the way. When my father hit her, all hell broke loose.

My day lunged at me, but I slammed my fist into him.

"I'm sick and tired of you!" *Crack!* "You want to hit someone! Hit me!" *Bam!* "I hate you, you drunken piece of shit!" *Pow!*

Punch after punch, I unleashed hell onto my father, letting my rage overtake me.

Mom ran to the kitchen and called Ryan.

*****

### Ryan

I didn't need an explanation. I called Jordan, picked him up, and sped over to Frazier's house.

We pulled up and ran inside to see Dylan unleashing his anger on Maurice. I grabbed him and yanked him off.

Jordan checked Maurice. "Call 911!"

Dylan struggled, and I tightened my hold on him until he calmed down, then he broke. "He wouldn't stop. He kept hitting and hitting. Then he hit my mom." He sobbed.

I held him as he sobbed, and Jordan looked at us. When Dylan's mom got hit, it broke him.

We got him out there before the ambulance showed up. His mom covered for him while I took him back to my house. Once

inside, I helped him to my room, had him sit on the bed, and removed his shirt.

"Jesus," Jordan said.

Frazier's body had welts, bruises, and faded marks from the pain his dad inflicted on him. He said nothing but sat there, and I cleaned him up and put ointment on him.

He stared at the wall in shock. Shock is what you experience when you suffer a traumatic event, and it's how your body and mind copes.

"Jordan, get Elena," I said, standing there and looking at Dylan.

Jordan left the room and returned with Elena. She walked in, sat down next to him, wrapped her arm around him, and whispered, "It's okay. I got you."

He buried his head into her, gripped her sleeve, and cried. She held him while he cried.

He needed comfort only Elena could offer. Having been through her own horrific experience, she knew how he was hurting. Jordan and I sat down and hugged them both.

*****

I walked over and handed Dylan a glass of water.

Dylan leaned with his back on the couch. "Thanks." He took the glass from me.

I sat down on the coffee table in front of him. "Why didn't you call me?"

"Ryan, all I did was clean up his mess. Everything happened so fast." He sighed.

"Dylan, you almost killed him."

"I know." His voice cracked.

"Dylan, you're not a murderer," Jordan said, taking a seat next to me.

"It was the blind rage that hit me, and I couldn't stop if I wanted to," Frazier said.

"Now you understand how I was with Mario," I said.

"I guess I do." He looked at Jordan. "How come you don't lose your shit?"

"Because someone taught me control." Jordan shrugged.

We looked at him.

"What?"

"That's it? Control?" I asked Jordan.

"Trust me. If I didn't have control, I could kill someone."

"So, if I did this, you won't do anything?" I gave him a push.

He sighed. "No."

"How about this?" I gave him another push.

"No."

"How about now?" I kept pushing and taunting him until he lost "control" and lunged at me. It turned into a full-blown war in my living room. His anger came out in full force, and stuff was getting destroyed.

Frazier got up and tried to separate us, only to get mixed up in the fight. It turned into a full-fledged brawl and wasn't pretty.

*****

The three of us sat on the couch holding ice packs to our heads as Elena stood in front of us, tapping her foot on the floor. It took a five-foot-five girl to subdue us by grabbing our earlobes, which hurt like a bitch.

Dad and Mom walked in to see the mass destruction of our living room. "What in the hell happened here?" Dad asked.

"These three idiots thought it would be a great idea to beat the shit out of each other!" Elena said.

"They did. I tried to stop it," Frazier thumbed at Jordan and me. "Then Jordan hit me, and I hit him. Good times."

"You're not helping, you idiot," I grumbled.

"Who started this?" Mom crossed her arms.

"He did!" Jordan and Frazier pointed at me.

I looked at both. There's nothing like getting thrown under the bus.

"I have no words." She shook her head and walked away.

"Ryan and Jordan, clean up this damn mess! Dylan, come with me," Dad said.

"Great. I didn't even do anything, and I got the lecture," Frazier got up and followed my dad into his office.

Jordan and I cleaned up the living room while Elena supervised us.

\*\*\*\*\*

**Frazier**

In Charles's office, I walked in and closed the door behind me. I took a seat in a chair in front of Charles's desk.

Charles walked around and took a seat behind his desk. "Dylan, I received a call today about someone breaking into your house and putting your father in the hospital."

"Really? Huh. That is quite shocking."

"Uh-huh."

I acted casual.

"So, you have no idea what happened or who did this?"

"Ah, nope."

"The boys will tell me since your mom called Ryan." He got up, walked to the door, opened the door, and yelled for Ryan and Jordan.

*****

**Ryan**

We walked to Dad's office, and he waved us in.

He shut the door. "This afternoon, someone beat Maurice and put him in the hospital. Police are searching for the assailant. Now Gloria called you." He pointed at me. "What happened?"

I looked at Jordan, and he looked at me. "She asked if Frazier was with us, and I told her yes."

He looked at Jordan. "Is Ryan telling me the truth?"

"What do you think?" Jordan asked him.

"Boys, I won't hand you over to the police. If I need to clean up a mess, I need the truth."

"Fine." Frazier sighed. "It was me."

"Why?"

"Because he was beating me with his belt, then he hit my mom." He shrugged.

"I see. Okay, you boys can go."

Frazier got up and walked towards us.

As we were about to leave, Dad said, "Dylan, say the word, and your dad will never be a problem again."

Frazier looked at me as I shrugged. Then he left. Frazier didn't know what to say, but the offer remained. It's when he cashed in on it.

Anger turns into fury, and fury turns into rage. Rage can destroy a person faster than anyone, and we were prime examples of it. It was time to get it under control or end up in jail. Although ending up in jail wouldn't be because of our anger, but Frazier's antics, which happens towards the end of the school year.

# CHAPTER 62

## TRAINING

**Ryan**

After the antics at my house, Dad wanted us to control our anger and put it to beneficial use. So, he made a call. Someone dragged me out of bed at four am on a Saturday.

"Get moving," a guy ordered.

I walked out in a pair of sweats and nothing else. I walked down the stairs to meet Hunter.

He handed me shoes and a coat. "Throw this on and follow me."

I pulled on the hoodie and sneakers, following him out of the house towards a car. I climbed in and noticed Uncle Elliot.

"Hello, Ryan."

"Uncle Elliot."

Hunter climbed in, and Elliot ordered him to drive. It took a while, but we pulled up to a building and got out.

"Where are we?" I asked.

"No questions." Elliot waved for me to follow him.

Two other cars pulled up, and they shoved Frazier and Jordan out of them.

"Hands off the merchandise, bub." Frazier yanked down his hoodie.

"Man, I'm freezing my dick off," Jordan said through chattering teeth.

They opened the door and shoved us inside. Once the door closed, it was total darkness. Then the lights flicked on. I looked around to find a boxing ring, punching bags, mats, and other things.

"Welcome to the training facility, boys!" A voice said.

We stood there as Mason appeared, along with Cole. Mason walked over to us. "Dylan Frazier and Jordan Shaw, my name is Mason Jones, and this is my son Cole Jones. He, along with Hunter and a few others, will train you. Get Dean, Cole."

Cole nodded and walked to the back.

Frazier leaned over and whispered. "Ryan, what's going on?"

I sighed. "We're about to get our asses kicked."

Cole returned with Dean.

"Now, from what Charles has told us, you three need to have a little refinement. Anger can destroy you." He looked at Frazier. "It can cause you to lose everything," he told me. "And it can make you destructive." He glanced at Jordan. "So, Hunter, Cole, and Dean will teach you how to control your anger. Elliot will teach you how to use knives and guns."

"Guns?" Frazier and Jordan asked.

"Yes, guns. You won't always fight people with fists. And I will teach you techniques," he said. "Now, we have a lot of work to do." He walked away.

My gut told me that we would suffer a lot of pain.

*****

We rose at four am every weekend, worked before the sun came up, and long after the sun had gone down. As a well-trained fighter, your body requires physical conditioning, including stamina and endurance, which is a necessity. So, they took us on five-mile runs.

Frazier stopped, trying to catch his breath. "Go on. I'm going to lie down and die." He fell to the ground.

Jordan puked.

"Well, that's gross," Frazier said.

We ran past Jordan.

"He shouldn't have eaten that breakfast." I shrugged, then tripped and rolled down a hill. I heard laughter and noticed Frazier and Jordan laughing their asses off. Some friends they are.

Besides running and weightlifting, we had to consume excess protein, which included chicken and fish. I hated chicken and fish and needed a steak.

The guys and I crawled to the facility and the beds, then collapsed.

"My body is killing me," Jordan mumbled.

"My hair hurts," Frazier whined.

"Zzzzzzzz."

They noticed me snoring, and they groaned.

*****

It didn't take long for us to become conditioned. Next, we moved on to fighting. We had a lot to learn.

We crawled to the room again, this time covered in bruises and dry blood. Even Jordan had gotten banged up, and that says a lot about him.

Once our fighting improved, we took our opponents down quickly as they timed us. The quicker we were, the better.

*****

Weapon training came next. Elliot showed us how to hold a knife and throw it. Jordan and I were quick learners, but Frazier, not so much.

Frazier pulled his arm back and snapped it, but the knife didn't fly forward at the target, and it flew backward at the wall, landing next to Cole's head. He turned and looked at Frazier.

"Oops," Frazier said.

Jordan rolled his eyes. I gave Frazier a look and shook my head. I swear the only way he would hit a target is by throwing the knife behind him.

It took a long time for Frazier to get the hang of it. The dude is not the most graceful person and landed the knife in Hunter's boot. I thought Hunter would kill him at one point.

He landed a knife between Dean's legs, almost castrating him. Dean almost beat the shit out of him.

He almost took off Mason's head. You get the point.

Finally, we learned about firearms. Hunter showed us how to disarm and arm a gun, take it apart, put it back together, and then aim and shoot.

While Jordan and I were practicing, Frazier picked up a gun. He shrugged, aimed, and pulled the trigger several times.

We stopped and watched him. He put the gun down after emptying it and walked away.

Hunter pulled the target to him. "He hit dead center at twenty feet."

There was a big hole in the target. We looked at it, at Frazier, then back at the target.

The village idiot takes forever to learn how to throw a knife. But then he takes out a target like that. Will wonders never cease to amaze me?

Later, we asked him how.

His response was, "He pictured the target as his sperm donor." Figures.

We trained when we weren't in school, and they worked us hard. We increased our muscle mass, along with our size.

It caused us to become closer, creating a brother bond. I never imagined that I would meet two guys who would become my brothers. When you spend as much time together as we have, it's bound to happen.

We were working on moves when Mason walked over to us.

"Boys, I have some excellent news." He smacked his hands together and rubbed his palms.

We stopped and looked at him.

"For spring break, you will stay with me and put your skills to use."

We looked at each other and smirked. That ought to be good.

# CHAPTER 63

## COMPLICATIONS

*This chapter contains disturbing content, and I recommend reader discretion.*

**3rd person**

While the boys were busy training and getting their asses kicked, Bella was worming her way into Elena's good gracious. She visited Ryan's sister and asked many questions, only to stop when suspicions arose.

Elena and Bella were hanging out in the living room.

"Where are the guys?" Bella asked.

Elena didn't take her eyes off the tv. "They're busy."

"Doing what?"

"Guy stuff." She shrugged.

"It must be important."

Elena turned to look at her. "Why?"

"There's no reason except the guys are always around." She smiled.

Elena gave her an odd look. "You don't have a thing for my brother, do you?"

"What? No!"

Bella's outburst caused Elena to raise her eyebrow.

"I mean, Ryan isn't my type. Plus, I have Paul."

"That reminds me. You talk about Paul, but you have never brought him around. I wonder if he even exists." She giggled.

"Oh, Elena, trust me, he does. Why would I make that up?"

"Trust me. I've seen people make things up." She turned her attention back to the tv.

Eventually, Bella exited Elena's house and walked to her car. She made her way to Frank's house. She knew Jordan wouldn't be there, and Josh would be at practice.

She knocked on the door, and he opened it, pulling her inside, only to place kisses on her but have her pushed him away.

"What the fuck, Bella?"

"Not now! I have bigger problems!"

He walked over and wrapped his arms around her. "What's wrong, baby?"

She pulled away. "I need a fake boyfriend, like now. Elena keeps asking about him."

"So, find a fake boyfriend."

"It's not that easy, you dolt. I need someone that doesn't go to my school, or the others have met."

"Well, what do you want me to do?"

"Find me a fake boyfriend, or you can kiss me goodbye."

"Fine. But you can't mess around with the guy."

"Oh, Frankie, you can't tell me what to do." She strolled over to the couch, sat down, lifted her skirt, and opened her legs slightly. "Now, get over here and take care of business, you disgusting freak."

He walked over and knelt in front of her. He lowered his head, and she wrapped her legs around his shoulders as he

kissed and sucked, making her moan in pleasure. It had become a ritual between them. She waited for the boys to leave, then showed up and made Frank agree to anything she wanted.

He would become her bitch without realizing how low he would sink. They say if a person is good, that the good always wins over evil. What happens when evil looks you dead in the eyes and controls you?

Bella knew Frank's weakness, along with her father's, and she played on it. Both brothers had a thing for young girls, and she enjoyed watching them withered because of it.

Thinking back to how it started with her father, a smile crept upon her face.

*Flashback to two years prior.*

*Someone knocked on Bella's bedroom door.*

*"Come in!"*

*The door opened, and her father stepped in and closed the door. He walked over and sat at the foot of her bed as she laid there flipping through the magazine.*

*"Bella, is there something wrong?"*

*"No, why?"*

*"You've been acting distant."*

*She looked up from her magazine, got up, and sat next to her father. "I'm fine. Really."*

*"Is it because you stopped going over to your uncle's house? You two have always been close."* .

*"No."*

He placed a strand of hair behind her ear. "I'm always here for you." His hand rested on her thigh, then stroked it.

She looked down and moved her legs apart. Her dad glanced down to see what he wanted. He knew it was wrong, but something drew him to her. She inched closer to his hand. She lifted her head slowly. "You're always here for me, Daddy."

"Yes, I am." He inched his hand up further and rubbed outside of her panties. "Hmm, someone is a little...." He stopped before he finished what he would say.

She took his hand and moved it under her panties. "You mean this?" She looked at him.

He placed one finger inside of her, then removed it.

"What's wrong?"

He stood up. "Who took it? I can tell you have been with someone. So, who took it?"

She rose from the bed and looked at him. "You know who." She smirked. "Does it bother you that he came into my room one night and made me touch him? That he touched me and took the one thing that you've wanted."

He stared at her.

"I notice how you both look at me. It's not a secret. How would my mother feel to learn that her husband is a dirty man who wants her daughter?" She turned her back to him, tapped her finger upon her lips, and then turned back to him. "But she doesn't have to find out. You give me what I want, and I'll give you what you want." She shrugged.

"What's that?"

*"I won't tell her about your dirty little secret and let you do whatever you want if you don't question me about anything. And I can do anything I want."*

*That was the thing about secrets. Once you make a deal with the devil, there is no going back. Bella was the devil herself, but no one knew it. How can people suspect when you appear sweet and innocent?*

*Her father was a weak man and succumbed to her the minute she made that deal, taking her. He knew it was wrong, but lust won out, and he fell into her trap. It was a game, and he would lose in the long run.*

*He sat there in his boxers and held his head in his hands. She crawled behind him and wrapped her arms around him.*

*"You got what you wanted, and now, I get what I want." She kissed his cheek, then let go and walked out of the room naked.*

**Present-day**

It thrilled her to remember that day and excited her that she had two people where she wanted them. An evil smirk grew upon her lips as Frank was on top of her, thrusting in and out.

The day would come when she would put her little plan into action. Like most people, she needed someone to take the fall and had a person in mind.

Besides what she had planned, she set her sights on a bigger prize. However, she would never obtain the reward she wanted.

# CHAPTER 64

## SPRING BREAK SURPRISES

**Ryan**

Do you know how most high schoolers go somewhere fun on spring break? Well, not us. They took us to Uncle Mason's place to put our training to use. But they had someone help them.

Once we arrived, we got settled. Of course, Jordan and Frazier got lost several times but found me, though.

"Dude, we need a map here," Frazier said.

He and Jordan walked up to me.

"Or at least a GPS," Jordan added.

"You get used to it after a while." I shrugged.

"Yeah, but you have been here several times, and it's our first time," Frazier whined.

I rolled my eyes at him. "Come on. Uncle Mason is waiting for us." They followed me downstairs to the kitchen and outside. Mason was waiting, along with Cole. We stepped out, and they explained what would happen. An assailant or foe would hunt us, and we had to take them down. Our training started when he finished.

We headed into the training facility and had to work together. Rely on each other's strengths and take down our adversary. They warned us about not sticking together since we were stronger together than separated. We made our way around until

someone dressed in black jumped us. The person wasn't huge, but stealthy and fought each of us.

They did flips and fight moves. Twisting and turning, we remembered what they taught us and fought them. Then a few others appeared. Jordan took one person, while Frazier took another, and I took the quicker one. They threw a kick and punch at me, but I blocked each one. It looked like a ballet with our fluid movements.

Mason watched from a distance, as did Dad. We worked as a team, switching and fighting them.

"They've come a long way," Dad said.

"You have no idea, Charles. They have worked hard, and it paid off. Their size has increased, they're quicker, and their stamina and endurance have increased tenfold."

Frazier and Jordan took down their opponents as I took down mine, causing them to hit the ground with an "oomph." That wasn't a guy. I walked over and yanked the mask only to become shocked. Elena?

"Hey, brother." Elena smiled and waved at me.

I helped her up. "Where did you learn to fight?"

"You didn't think I sat home and studied, did you? Dad sent me to learn how to fight." She smiled.

"I have to admit, you were tough." I rubbed the back of my neck.

"I figured I needed to be tough since I can't stay hidden forever. Plus, I refuse to have Mario take my senior year from me."

I noticed Elena was returning to her old self. Nothing like what I had discovered that night. That night broke my heart, but today had filled my heart with hope.

"Lunch!" Mason said.

We walked towards the house and had lunch. Aunt Luci made a big meal for us. We sat around the table and talked.

"Are you excited about senior year?" Cole asked me.

"As excited as one can be." I took a bite of my sandwich.

"What about you two?" He asked Jordan and Frazier.

"What's not to be excited about? It's senior year. One more year, and we're out of that hellhole." Frazier grinned.

"You got me detention for blowing up the toilet in the boy's bathroom with a cherry bomb," I told Frazier.

"What can I say? I like to explode onto a scene." He grinned.

I chuckled.

"Wait. You blew up a toilet on your first day at Saintwood?" Jordan asked him.

"Yep, sure did. Then at lunch, I took two jocks down and punched one in the dick." He smirked.

Jordan raised his eyebrows.

"Frazier, you're a nut," Cole said.

"You have no idea," Frazier said.

After lunch, Cole and I took a walk. It had been a while since it was the two of us.

"So, who is she?" He asked me.

"Who?"

"The girl."

"What girl?"

"Ryan, you have no interest in most girls because they tend to be superficial, but I can tell that there is a girl. So, who is she?"

I pulled out the picture and handed it to him.

He glanced at the picture and handed it to me. "Does your dad know?"

"Probably."

"Ryan, be careful. I heard there's more to it than any of us realize."

"Something about this girl intrigues me."

"I also heard there's a new girl in town. Any chance of things happening there?"

"Who? Bella?"

"Yeah."

"Oh, hell no."

"Why not? At least, she's there."

I sighed. "There's something off about Bella. I can't place my finger on it, but Jordan doesn't trust her, and I trust Jordan."

He rubbed his chin like he did when he was thinking. "I'll tell you what. Let me do some digging. If your instincts are telling you that this girl is trouble, chances are, she is."

"That is the thing. Bella's trouble, but how do I prove it?"

He stopped. "You find Bella's weakness. Everyone has a weakness, and I'm guessing hers is personal. Most people think they have fooled people, but they don't. There is always something they let slip, and you see the cracks. Trust me."

It's true. Everyone has a weakness, and no matter who the person is, they have one. I gave it a thought and decided I would

enlist the boys to help me. For Elena's safety, I needed her to stay out of it.

*****

"Are you sure about this?" Jordan asked me.

"Jordan, you said it yourself. There has always been something off about Bella," I reasoned.

"But she seems so.... nice," Frazier said.

I looked at him. "So does a barracuda. Do you see me cuddling with one?"

"Well.... no."

"Exactly. All I'm saying is that we keep an eye on her."

They glanced at each other.

"Fine by me. My dad has been acting weird lately, and it's like he couldn't wait for me to leave the house," Jordan said.

"What about your brother?" Frazier asked.

"He's wrapped up in football, trying to fulfill Dad's dream. When he isn't at practice, he's at his buddy's house," Jordan answered.

"We play this close to our chest and say nothing, especially to Elena."

They looked at me and agreed. At that moment, we decided to keep an eye on Bella. At some point, she would crack, but it was a matter of when.

*****

## Jordan

While Frazier and Ryan got ready for bed, I grabbed a snack. The only problem was I got lost again but ran into Elena, and she showed me to the kitchen.

"I will never get used to this house," I said, causing her to laugh.

"Don't feel bad. We used to get lost a lot as kids. But we found our way around." She pulled out stuff for sandwiches and something to drink. She fixed us something to eat.

We sat down and talked.

"Thanks," she said.

"For what?"

"For that night and the other nights after that."

"It's no big deal." I shrugged. I helped people who I care about but hated when people made a big production made of it.

We finished our food and cleaned up. Once we put everything away, I turned to leave only to come face to face with Elena. Without thinking, I leaned down and pressed my lips to hers, surprising her, and she kissed me back.

I pulled back, realizing what I had done. "Uh, sorry." I spun and walked away, leaving her confused. I found my way to our room and climbed into bed. Frazier and Ryan glanced at each other.

"What's the matter with you?" Frazier asked me.

"Nothing. Go to sleep." I turned my back on them.

"It must be that time of the month," Frazier whispered to Ryan.

"Yep." Ryan turned off the light and laid down.

As Frazier and Ryan drifted off to sleep, I thought about what happened in the kitchen. As much as I liked Elena, she wasn't ready. Plus, Ryan would beat the shit out of me.

That's when I backed off and decided not to think about it, but Elena consumed my thoughts.

\*\*\*\*\*

### Ryan

We worked as a team for the rest of spring break and put our knowledge and skills to use. When the week ended, we were ready. Uncle Mason helped to refine our skills. Because of that, we were a force of nature. We had become the most feared guys of Saintwood.

# CHAPTER 65

## FAKE BOYFRIEND

**3rd person**

Bella sat on the couch and studied the guy that Frank had found. She stood, walked over to the guy, and ran her pointer finger over every inch of him. "He's cute."

"Cute? Do you have any idea what I had to do to get him to come here?" Frank asked.

She raised an eyebrow at Frank, then looked at the guy. "So, you'll be my fake boyfriend."

"That's what the guy told me," the guy said.

"I'll call you, Paul."

"My name is Patrick."

"Yeah, yeah, whatever. I need you to be Paul."

"Fine. But what do I get out of it?"

"What do you mean? I paid you!" Frank said.

"It'll take more than cash to keep me quiet." Fake Paul shot Frank a glance.

Bella said, "Fine. But you'll help me convince everyone that we're a couple and in love. When the time is right, we'll break up."

"Whatever."

She grabbed his hand and led him outside. They got into his car.

"Drive."

He started the car and drove to a secluded area. Then she climbed onto his lap. He didn't need someone to tell him twice what was happening. He undid his pants and pulled up her skirt. He slid into her as she sat on his lap, facing forward. She bounced up and down on him as he groaned.

As their breathing increased, their movements became faster until they both groaned, releasing together. Bella got off the guy and sat down in the seat next to him.

"Damn, babe. No one told me that you're a little slut."

"Well, everyone has their specialties. Mine is this." She smirked.

He turned to face her. "You're the type that likes to have her legs in the air, aren't you?"

She pulled out a cigarette and lit it. She inhaled and exhaled, letting the smoke waft in the air. "When you get screwed enough, sex means nothing. The man who paid you is my uncle. He screwed me when I was thirteen and still screwed me. My daddy, well, he likes to have his turn. Then there's Mario and his friends and anyone else that comes along, except one." She took a drag from her cigarette.

"Your dad and uncle?" He cringed.

"They like young girls and also like to knock me up, too."

"Jesus."

"But I got rid of those bastard children. I always got rid of them since they're only good for is not to bleed."

"It doesn't bother you?"

"No. Because in the end, there is no love, no emotions, and no feelings but screwing. That is it."

"So, that's all you want? Is someone to screw you?"

"Isn't that what everyone wants? Now, if you don't mind, I need you to drop me off somewhere."

"Okay." He started the car and drove her to a house. He left, and she knocked on the door, it opened, she stepped inside, and the door shut.

She leaned over the dresser. A man slammed into her, making her groan. When he finished, he pulled out and did up his pants.

"You've been a naughty girl, Isabella." The guy ran his hand up and down on her.

She turned to face him. "You taught me well."

"Yes, I have. I enjoy fucking you."

"And this doesn't bother your wife?"

"She keeps her mouth shut." He shrugged.

There was a knock at the door, and another man walked in.

"I'll leave you both to it." He walked by the man and whispered, "Enjoy her brother. I understand how rough you can be."

"I'm going to tear her up and down." He smiled.

The man left, closing the door. The other guy walked over to her, grabbed her, tossed her onto the bed, and then undid his belt. "I hope you enjoy it rough because I do." He flipped her onto her stomach and slammed into her, making her scream. He grabbed her hair as he pounded into her, gripping her wrists. "Whores like you need to be fucked properly."

She screamed.

When he finished, she whimpered. He did up his pants. "Why are you crying? Whores don't cry."

"I-I'm not a whore."

"But you are. You play with dirty old men and boys. Why would he ever want you?"

She glared at him.

"Oh, don't give me that look because it's true. You come here wanting to fuck us, hoping to make a deal. Did you figure we would be gentle? I'm not like the others. I don't care. I will fuck a woman hard, and she will scream as you did. Get some rest because I'll be back." He left the room.

She laid there and whimpered while waiting. She knew better than to disobey the man and had made the wrong choice before, suffering the consequences for it. But like everything, it was her own doing.

He returned later with the other man and tied her up. As one took her from one end, the other took her from the other. Once they had finished with her, they untied her and let her get dressed.

One guy said, "Now let's discuss business."

She said, "You know what I want. You do your part, and I'll do mine."

"Fine. You can leave, and we'll discuss it further." He dismissed her while gesturing to the other guy.

She turned and walked away. As she walked away, she heard them speak Spanish, not understanding what they were saying.

Once she was out of the house, one guy asked the other, "Well?"

"Let her sink. If she doesn't do what she intends to do, it's her problem, not ours."

"But this could be a terrific opportunity to take them out once and for all."

"You're asking for a full-fledged war by doing that. The Jones family knows many people."

"Who cares? They mean nothing to me." The one guy shrugged.

"You're playing with fire, brother. It will piss off Luis when he finds out."

"Luis is getting soft in his old age. He agreed to that deal, not us." He walked away.

The guy rubbed his forehead. A war would start between their family and Ryan's, but they had to play this smart. He picked up the phone and made a call.

"It's me. Meet me. We have a business to discuss." He hung up and walked out of the room. Being as young as he was, he had seen enough and had to handle this with discretion. No one could trace anything to them.

# CHAPTER 66

## SH*T HIT THE FAN

**Ryan**

After we returned from Uncle Mason's house for spring break, Jordan acted weirder than usual. I'm not sure what had happened, but something did. As for Bella, she was getting stranger by the minute. It was that, or she had a weird hormonal imbalance. I'll never understand girls.

I didn't know who the ringleader was between them, but both got on my fucking nerves.

"Dude, what the hell is wrong with you? Are you on your period or something?" Frazier asked Jordan.

Jordan glanced at Frazier as I searched my locker for something.

Then someone walked up and placed their hands over my eyes. "Guess who?"

"I don't have to guess." I removed their hands.

"Oh, don't be such a grumpy Gus, Ryan." Bella jutted out her bottom lip.

I rubbed my forehead, turned around, and leaned against the lockers. "Bella, you seem like a great girl, but I'm not interested."

"Ryan, it's called innocent flirting." She smiled.

"Whatever it's called, I'm still not interested. So, please stop."

Jordan and Frazier watched us.

"Oh, please." She rolled her eyes. "Who says I'm interested in you? I'm sorry that you expect all girls to want you. But I have a boyfriend." *Crack number one.*

"Oh? So, he would be good with his girl flirting with other guys. Because if it were my girl, I wouldn't be okay with it."

"Well, not every guy is jealous and possessive, now, are they?" *Crack number two.*

I stood up straight, took a step towards her, and looked her dead in the eyes. "Only the good ones are."

Then I saw it. Bella might have had a smile, but her eyes told a different story. They were dark and cold. *Crack number three.*

"Well," she stepped back, "I have to meet Elena." She turned and walked away.

"What was that?" Frazier asked.

"That was someone thinking they figured things out," I said.

"Huh?"

"Don't worry about it." I shut my locker door and walked to class.

They shrugged and walked with me. I knew what I was doing, and the boys never questioned my motives.

Around lunchtime, Jordan disappeared. Where the hell did he go?

*****

**Jordan**

*Click.* The light turned on in the janitor's closet, and Elena and I stood there.

"Elena, what are you doing?"

"Jordan, we need to talk about what happened at Uncle Mason's."

"No, we don't!"

"Yes, we do!"

I sighed. "It happened. Can we move past it?"

"You want to move past the weird sexual tension between us?"

"No, but with everything that happened, I can't. Then your brother will cut off my balls if he finds out."

"My brother is a pansy."

"It doesn't matter." I took a seat on a crate and looked up at her. "Elena, I'm not someone who takes advantage of a person after something traumatic happens."

She walked over and took a seat in front of me. She reached over and grabbed my hand. "Jordan, I understand. Trust me, I do."

I pulled my hand back. "I want to say that I feel nothing for you, but that's a lie. It isn't the time, Elena. I like you. A lot. But I want to make sure you're okay and your brother doesn't rip my head off."

She sighed. "I guess you're right. I'll make you a deal. When I'm ready, and you're not dating anyone, then we can see where things stand between us."

"What about your brother?"

"Ryan can kiss off because he doesn't decide who I do or don't date. Plus, if he gets a girlfriend, he'll be busy with her and not pay attention to my love life or lack of."

I hugged her, and she hugged me back. I lingered, then pulled back before I kissed her again. As much as I wanted to kiss her, it was better to wait.

We snuck out of the janitor's closet, making sure no one saw us. We didn't need anyone spreading rumors about us, mainly tales that weren't true.

\*\*\*\*\*

**Ryan**

Frazier and I found Jordan after lunch.

"Where were you?" I asked Jordan.

"Oh, I ran into Elena."

Frazier and I glanced at each other.

"What was my sister doing here?"

"She's planning to return to school sooner than expected." He shrugged.

"Do you realize that you're a terrible liar?"

"Fine. Elena wanted to talk to me in private about something."

"Such as?"

"Ryan, it was private. If she wants you to find out, she'll tell you."

"Something happened between you two, and that would be your first mistake. Or it has something to do with Elena returning to school. If it's the latter, we don't have a problem. Now, do we?"

He looked at me with a serious expression. Things were about to get ugly.

"Okay, I confess. Jordan talked to Elena about this thing we have going on. And we didn't want you to find out because it's so sordid," Frazier said.

We turned our heads to look at him.

"What? Don't you believe me? I'm offended."

"Frazier," I said.

He put his hand up. "No, no. You assume that I'm a terrible person, and I see how it is." Frazier walked away.

"I swear he isn't wrapped too tight."

"Oh, I know he isn't wrapped too tight."

"Answer one thing."

"What?"

"Is what you and she talked about will cause me to hit you?"

"You realize that I can knock your ass out, right?"

"Yeah, but I get one good punch."

"Fine. You get one punch, but only if I deserve it, then I get to hit you." He walked away.

"You can't hit me when you deserve the punch!"

"Wanna bet?"

Yep, something happened between him and my sister. When the time comes, I will deal with it. It's not that Jordan would be a terrible person for my sister to date, and he would treat her well, but it's what she experienced. Realizing a guy will do that much damage scared the shit out of me.

I knew one thing for sure. When it came time for me to meet that girl in the picture, I would do nothing like that.

# CHAPTER 67

## CRAZY DOESN'T EVEN EXPLAIN IT

**Ryan**

Have you ever wondered how Frazier and I remained friends? Yeah, I do, too.

I knew the guy was nuts, but I never expected him to land us in flipping jail! It started when he wanted to have a little fun with Mario. A little? I meant a lot.

"Frazier, what are we doing here?" I asked.

"Shh, or you'll blow our cover." He shushed me.

"Fine, but can you tell us why we have to wear these ridiculous outfits?" Jordan asked.

We glanced at our black clothes.

"Because we're ninjas, duh. We're stealthy and quick, like rabbits. Or when I use Ryan's toothbrush to scrub certain areas of my body."

"What? When have you used my toothbrush?"

"Never mind. You don't need to know." He gestured at me.

"Dude, get a new toothbrush," Jordan said.

I'm throwing out my toothbrush when I get home.

"Now come on before someone finds out," Frazier whispered.

From there, we started teepeeing Mario's house. Then Frazier threw eggs at it. As he got started, we heard sirens and turned to see three cop cars pull up with flashing lights.

Some old guy came out of his house and yelled at us.

"Frazier! I thought we were at Mario's house!" I spoke.

"Uh, well, I might have mistaken this house for his house." Frazier winced.

"Good going, you idiot!" Jordan smacked Frazier upside the back of his head.

We ended up in jail. That was arrest number 1.

**Arrest number 2**

This time, we found Mario's house, but Frazier did a little redecorating with his car, namely with a baseball bat. We joined in and got caught.

Here we go, again.

**Arrest number 3**

We got caught at Mario's buddy's house. Let's say it wasn't pretty. A fight broke out, and here comes the police again.

We were making good with our jail time. Every time we ended up there, Dad came and bailed us out. If Frazier weren't my best friend, I would beat the shit out of him.

**Arrest number 4**

This time Elena got involved, but we got busted for breaking into the school.

"Dad will kill us if we get arrested," she said.

"Well, he won't if you quit yapping and let me do what I'm supposed to do." Frazier picked a lock.

"Wait. Where did you learn that?" Jordan asked.

"It's one of my many talents." Click. "Wah la and away we go." He opened the door.

We made our way into the principal's office. He turned on a flashlight and shined it around the office.

Then he found a file cabinet, opened it, and thumbed through the files, finding the one he wanted. He pulled it out.

Then we heard, "Freeze! Put your hands in the air!"

The four of us raised our hands. I looked at Elena, who was none too happy, then looked at Jordan, who looked like he was praying. Frazier, well, he whistled.

Yep, our arrest would piss Dad off.

*****

We sat in the jail cell and heard footsteps coming our way. Dad walked up and looked at the four of us, and we looked at him while sitting on the bench. The officer opened the door, and the four of us got up and walked out of the cell.

Dad said nothing. Once we got home, Dad had plenty to say. After he finished tearing us a new one, he left the room.

"If this was so you didn't get caught in the girl's locker room, I'll beat your ass," I told Frazier.

He rolled his eyes. "The ladies love me. So, no problem there."

Jordan raised an eyebrow. "Only because you're a lady. You're in denial."

"Really? Because you're in more denial than I am!"

"Will you two ladies knock it off?" I was in no mood for their bullshit.

Then Frazier lifted his shirt and yanked out a file. "It's a good thing that I'm quick."

"What the hell?" Jordan asked.

"How did you get that file past the cops?" I asked him.

"Ancient Chinese Secret?" He smirked.

"What is that?" Elena asked.

"See for yourself." Frazier handed the file to her.

She took it and opened it. Reading through it, she asked, "Who is Alexandra Hartley?"

I got up and snatched the file from her. "Let me see that." I thumbed through it, then looked at Frazier. "Why did you pick this file?"

"Why not?" He shrugged.

"Do we even go to school with Alexandra Hartley?" Jordan asked.

"No, but she's a new student scheduled to transfer to our school next year."

"So, what does it say?" Jordan asked.

"It's basic information besides, whoa." I looked at a paper.

They walked over, and Frazier let out a low whistle.

"Is that even possible?" Jordan asked.

"It has to be some mistake. No one has an IQ like this." That wasn't true. The only one I knew that had an IQ that high was me. But they didn't need to know that, and not even Elena knew that.

"Oh, my God. Check out her test scores," Elena said. "Perfect scores? No wonder Saintwood High wants her."

"Is there a picture?" Frazier asked.

"No, but whoever Alexandra is, she's brilliant," I said, looking at the information.

Alexandra Hartley must be the nerdy type who studies all the time. She's the girl who wears big glasses and dresses like it. It didn't matter, though. I was at the top of my class. Even if I got suspended, I was still number one. I intended for it to stay that way.

I sat down in the chair and skimmed through the file, which held information about Alexandra's academics. I tossed the file onto the coffee table and sat there, contemplating.

"Ooh, someone is in deep reflection," Frazier said.

I rubbed my chin with my hand. Why did this information bother me so much? Why was I so concerned with that file?

"If it worries you about her taking your spot, you should be."

I stopped and snapped my head in Elena's direction.

"Whoever this girl is, she has to be important."

I couldn't help but wonder if she was right. But then again, we could all be off base with this. We're friends with Frazier if that tells you anything.

I picked up the file and took it up to my room. I opened my dresser drawer and tossed it in, closing it behind me.

"Ryan, there is a reason I pulled that file," a voice said.

I turned to see Frazier leaning against the doorframe. "I thought you didn't have a reason."

"I always have a reason." He smirked. "You'll understand better when you put that picture you've been carrying around with that file." He turned and walked away.

Frazier left. I pulled out the picture, opened the drawer, then the file. I looked at the empty doorway. What the fuck?

# CHAPTER 68

## THE VILLAGE IDIOT STRIKES AGAIN

**Ryan**

We were sitting in class when we heard a big boom, the sprinkler system sprayed, and the fire alarm sounded. We ran out of the classroom, slipping and sliding in the hallway.

Jordan and I ran towards the chemistry room.

"Frazier?" Jordan asked me.

"Who else?"

When we reached the classroom, we had gotten soaked, and Frazier walked out of the classroom, fanning smoke from him while coughing. Stuff covered him, and his hair was sticking up.

"It's not good to mix water and concentrated acid." He coughed.

"Frazier, you're an idiot." I chuckled.

"At least, we get out of school for the day." Jordan smirked.

The three of us ran down the hallway towards the doors and left. We headed to my house so that Frazier could shower and Jordan and I could put on some dry clothes.

I walked out of my room only to have Bella stop me.

"Hey, Ryan." She smiled.

"Bella."

"That was an interesting thing that happened at school, wasn't it?"

"Typical Frazier." I shrugged.

Frazier came out of the bathroom and stopped.

"God, he is such an imbecile. I don't understand how you and Jordan can be friends with him since he could have injured you."

I glanced to see the hurt flooding Frazier's face. "Frazier isn't an imbecile but my best friend. Yeah, he does idiotic things, but I wouldn't trade him for the world."

I walked past her and went downstairs. Frazier was sitting on the couch, not saying anything.

"Frazier?"

"What?" Frazier snapped at me.

I walked over to him and sat down. "Ignore Bella."

"I don't understand, Ryan. I have been nothing but nice to that girl, and she bashes me."

"Because she doesn't know what she's talking about."

"Whatever." He got up and strolled into the kitchen. Frazier cooked when something upset him because cooking calmed him.

Jordan walked in. "What crawled up Frazier's ass?"

"Bella."

"Oh, for fuck's sake, what did she do now?"

"Bashed Frazier."

"That girl doesn't keep her mouth shut." He shook his head.

While we were in the living room, Frazier was making food.

\*\*\*\*\*

**Frazier**

"I didn't know you knew how to cook," a voice said.

I glanced at Bella. "Yeah, and there are many things that you don't know about me."

"Frazier, people would like you more if you weren't such an idiot." She smirked.

I turned off the stove and glimpsed at her. "Huh."

"What?"

"Nothing."

"No. What is it?"

"For the life of me, I couldn't figure out what I did to make you not like me. But I realized that you don't care whether we're friends. I figured the guys were a little too hard on you, then discovered Ryan doesn't want you."

"No offense, but I have a boyfriend." She scoffed.

"Uh-huh. You keep telling yourself that. See," I jabbed my food with a fork and took a bite, "most guys fall at your feet, but not Ryan. He has rejected you each time you try to get his attention, and it must suck to get denied the one thing you want." I smirked.

She glared at me.

"Oh, and this imbecile has a high IQ, so don't even try to pull stupid shit on me." I continued eating, dismissing her with a wave.

She turned and marched out of the kitchen. *Crack number four.* Never assume you're brighter than others because you may find out they can beat you at your own game.

\*\*\*\*\*

**Ryan**

After Frazier finished eating, he came into the living room and sat down, pleased with himself.

"Why are you so cheerful?" I asked him.

"Let's say I'm feeling a lot better." He grinned.

That could only mean two things when Frazier grinned. Either he had something planned, or he had something planned.

"We won't get arrested again, will we?" Jordan asked him.

"Nope."

"Good, because I don't want to deal with my old man or Ryan's again." He sighed.

"I take it that our arrest pissed off your dad?"

"Pissed? Oh, no, no, no. He was way beyond that. I listened to him bitch about how I will never amount to anything if I have a record and hung out with you guys. And I can't play sports because of it," he said, mocking his dad.

"Is your dad still on you about sports?"

"The dude won't let up. Like, it's the end all be all. Been there, done that. Last year I played football, but the guys were assholes. I spent more time getting into fights than anything. They kicked me off the team."

"So much for being a team player," Frazier said.

"I can't be on a team that prefers to be assholes to people."

I can't say that I disagree with him. Even with my reputation, I stayed away from picking on people, especially when they had done nothing to me. I call it human decency, which people our age lack.

As for Mario and his idiot friends, they got what they deserved, especially Mario.

Jordan eventually left, but Frazier stuck around. He didn't feel like going home, and I couldn't blame him.

"Is your dad still being an ass?" I asked him.

"No. Ever since the hospital, he's been attending AA and not drinking. If he stays away from the sauce, he's fine. It doesn't mean I forgive him, though, not after what my mom and I endured." He placed his hand on the side of his head.

"Yeah, I wouldn't either."

"Can we watch a movie? All this heavy talk is bringing me down."

"Yeah."

He got up to pop in a movie.

"Anything but Mean Girls."

"Aw, come on! I love Mean Girls!"

"Fraze, it's a chick flick."

"It's funny!"

"It's stupid."

"You, sir, have no sense of humor." He held out his hand to me.

"I must have since I'm friends with you."

"But I make life interesting." He raised his pointer finger.

"You tried to blow up the school today." I arched an eyebrow.

"I did not! Trust me. If I blew up the school, it would have been a bigger explosion."

"That reminds me. What on earth possessed you to mix two incompatible chemicals?"

"I was testing a theory, and I was right."

"That you're an idiot?"

"No. By the amount I used." He pulled at his lips.

"Wait. You did that on purpose?"

"Of course. Dude, I'm not that stupid to do it on accident. Trust me. I knew what I was doing but forgot that I needed an accessible area and not to stand too close." He waved a finger.

"Okay, genius. What was your point?"

"To create a big enough chemical explosion to take out a building."

"A bomb?"

"A chemical bomb."

Now, why the hell would Frazier create a chemical bomb? I don't want to know, but he had a reason for what he was doing. Yeah, he may do things that made him seem like an idiot, but he had a reason for doing them.

Frazier's mind works differently than most. There was always a logic behind his actions, even if we didn't understand it, but I understood it better than most. You're don't fit in because you're not considered acceptable in the eyes of other people. Then, depending on your appearance, is what makes people accept you or not.

My mind drifted to that picture and file. Before I put the two together, I assumed things about the girl but knew nothing about her. I was as bad as everyone else.

Frazier popped in a movie, but it wasn't Mean Girls. Thank God. He stretched out on the couch.

"Hey, Fraze. How did you know that picture of that girl and that file were the same person?"

"Oh, that? I overheard them talking in the office about a new student. I put two and two together." He shrugged. "Think about it. Your dad had a file on a girl, and we're collecting a package. There are transcripts on a new student. Coincidence? I think not."

Interesting. Out of everyone, Frazier's the one that figured things out before the rest of us did.

We didn't realize someone was listening to our conversation the entire time. Good thing we never mentioned the girl's name. With Bella hanging around, we couldn't speak freely with our discussion.

Jordan didn't trust her, and Frazier hated her while I tolerated her. Eventually, it would all come to a head.

# CHAPTER 69

## NOT MY FATHER'S SON

**Jordan**

While Frazier and Ryan hung out, I checked on Josh. I wanted to make sure he was okay. I walked in, and Dad was sitting in a chair.

"I noticed you came home."

"I always come home." I ignored my dad's tone.

"We need to talk about these so-called friends of yours."

"What about them?"

Dad got up from his chair and walked over to me. "They're ruining your future."

"My future? When have you ever given a damn about my future?"

"I always gave a damn, but you're too damn stubborn to understand what's best."

"What's best? A team with a bunch of people who treat other people like shit is not what's best!"

"Don't raise your voice to me. I'm your father, and you'll treat me with respect!"

"Or what? Newsflash, I'm not my father's son!"

With those words, Dad hauled off and struck me. I snapped back and stared at him. In a quiet voice, I said, "Touch me again, and I'll beat the shit out of you." I walked away, leaving Dad speechless.

I walked to Josh's room and opened the door, and I closed it and sat on the side of his bed. Josh was sitting at his desk and working on homework.

He turned and noticed the mark on the side of my face. He furrowed his brows. "Dad?"

"Yeah." I sighed.

"I overheard you two arguing."

"Sorry, you had to hear that."

"It's fine. I get it. Dad's busting your chops." Josh shook his head.

"I wish Mom was here." I looked at my lap, twiddling my thumbs.

Josh got up, walked over to me, and sat down next to me on the bed. "I miss her, too, Jordan. It was better when she was here."

"Yeah, it was."

"So, what are you going to do?"

"I'm not sure. But you need to stay away from here every chance you get. You got me?"

"Why?"

"Please do this for me, Josh."

"Okay, Jay."

I wrapped my arm around Josh's neck, pulled him into a hug, and kissed the top of his head. I got up and walked out of the room, closing the door behind me.

Dad met me in the hallway. "Listen, Jordan. I'm sorry."

"Save it." I shot Dad a glare, stepped towards him, and looked him straight in the eyes. "I don't care what is going on with you.

But if you lay one hand on Josh, I'll beat the hell out of you. Don't ever fucking touch Josh."

Dad furrowed his brows. "I would never touch your brother."

"Yeah, well, you said you would never touch me either, but here we are."

"Jordan, you're changing because of those boys."

"I'm not changing. You refuse to see me for who I am. I'm not you. I won't be that golden boy that you were in school. As for my friends, they're loyal, and they got my back. Believe what you want, but nothing you can say or do will ever change that fact." With that, I walked away and slammed my bedroom door.

I didn't understand. My dad never laid a hand on Josh or me. My dad begged me to play sports. When my mom was around, we were happy. One day, she left. No note, and no phone call. No, nothing. She left.

When I questioned my dad, all he said was that she was unhappy. Unhappy with what? Unhappy with her family? Her sons? Were we not good enough? I didn't understand. All I wanted was my mom. Josh and I needed her, but we couldn't find her.

Tears welled in my eyes, and I wiped them away. I hated crying because it made me feel weak. I picked up the phone and made a call.

*Hello?*

"Um."

*Jordan?*

"Yeah."

*What's wrong?*

I couldn't even form words. Sobs wracked my chest as I threw the phone across the room, breaking it. I fell to the floor and cried. The little boy inside cried, wanting nothing more than his mom.

Ten minutes later, shouting came from the other side of my door. My door flung open. I looked up as my ice-blue eyes met emerald-green eyes and chocolate-brown eyes.

"Jordan," the voice said in a soothing tone.

"I miss her." My voice cracked.

"Who?"

"My mom." I broke.

\*\*\*\*\*

**Ryan**

I've never seen Jordan so lost or broken. He wears a poker face, but not this time. This time, he was vulnerable, and every emotion he had buried broke through.

Frazier and I held and comforted him. We let him cry. Frazier, with all his jokes, understands what it's like to be broken. If anyone knows, it's him.

When Jordan calmed down, Frazier asked, "What happened? Something must have happened."

"My dad hit me," Jordan whispered. "He has never hit me, and tonight was the first and the last time. I threatened to kill him if he ever laid another hand on Josh or me."

I looked at Frazier, who let out a deep breath and shrugged. He knew how far someone could push you because it happened to him, and he almost killed his dad.

"Listen, Jordan. No one will hurt you, Frazier, or Josh. You have my word," I said.

"Thanks, man." Jordan bumped fists with Frazier and me.

We stayed with Jordan. He told us about his mom, along with everything else. It was cathartic for him to talk about it, and I don't think he has been able to speak to anyone about it.

Josh joined us. He was funny and had that happy-go-lucky personality. The only problem was there was more going on with Josh than anyone knew, but we wouldn't find out until later what that was.

Overall, Frazier and I hung out with Jordan all night. The last thing he needed was to be alone.

As for Frank, when we came in and argued, he refused us entry until I made it known we weren't going anywhere. He threw a punch. Wrong move because I caught his hand and cracked him right in the nose with my fist. Yeah, never tell me that I can't visit my best friend.

There's no love lost between Frank Shaw and me. Of course, Frazier had to make a stupid joke like, how was your trip? See you next fall. He always says inappropriate things.

Thanks to that night, Frank wanted my head on a silver platter. Game on.

# CHAPTER 70

## LET'S MAKE A DEAL

**3rd person**

Frank opened the door.

Bella walked in. "What was so important that it couldn't wait until later?"

He closed the door and walked over to her. "If you want my help, you need to give me something in return."

She rolled her eyes. "What? Isn't sex enough?"

"Oh, no. You'll still please me, but you'll also cough up some dough." He sat down on the couch and stretched out his arms.

She laughed. "Yeah, okay. In your dreams."

"Fine. I will have no issues going to the cops." He shrugged.

"You won't go to the cops because you would have to admit that you screwed your thirteen-year-old niece."

"Yeah, I will tell them all about your little plan. Or better yet, I'll go to some other people. It would interest the Frazier and Jones families with what I have to say."

She glared at him. "Fine."

"Oh, and one more thing. You keep Jordan and Joshua out of your twisted plan. If you go after either of them, I won't hesitate to break your fucking neck."

"Fine. I won't touch your sons, but I want him."

"Good luck because he doesn't want you." He scoffed.

"He will."

"And why would he?" He got up and walked over to her. "Why would he want a damaged whore like you? Huh? You forgot one thing. When you play with the big dogs, you better get prepared for the outcome."

"Is that so?"

"Yeah, that is so. You've been pulling the strings long enough, and now it's my turn." He backed her against the door, spun her, and pinned her. He undid his pants and forced himself into her. "You want to play. We'll play, and you'll enjoy it." With that, he thrust into her until he released himself into her.

He pulled out and did up his pants. Bella faced the door, shocked at what had happened. He leaned into her ear and whispered, "You're nothing but a sociopathic whore. You pretend to be something you're not, like this good person. But deep down, you're damaged goods. Who lets their father and uncle fuck them and spreads their legs for any random person? You think that's how you will get what you want."

"I'm not a whore."

"Whatever you say, sweetheart."

She turned around and slapped him across the face. "I'm not a whore!"

He rubbed his face. "You keep telling yourself that."

She backed away, yanked open the door, and ran out of the house.

Frank picked up the phone and made a call. "Yeah, it's me. Yeah, don't worry. She won't open her mouth." He hung up.

If Bella knew what was good for her, she would keep her mouth shut. She raced home. Once inside, Bella ran to her room,

slammed her door shut, and screamed as she threw things around her room.

Someone knocked on her door. "Bella, Hunny, it's Daddy. Open up."

She walked over, opened the door, and threw her arms around him.

He wrapped his arms around her. "Shh, it's okay. Daddy has you."

"Oh, Daddy. I don't know what to do." She sniffled.

"It'll be okay, baby. Let Daddy make you feel better."

She nodded. Henry carried her to the bed and laid her down. He undid his pants and climbed on top of her.

Henry made his way in between her legs and placed a soft kiss on her lips, then slid into her. He started thrusting inside of her over and over as he whispered, "You're such a good little whore, giving your daddy what he needs."

She looked at him with furrowed brows. Before she screamed, he covered her mouth as he went faster and rougher.

He whispered into her ear, "I'm going to fuck you until you can't walk because you're such a dirty little slut. You want to fuck men, and I'll show you what happens when you're bad."

From there, he kept his word. He screwed Bella over and over until she couldn't move. When he finished, he got up and redid his pants as she laid there on her stomach, whimpering.

He walked over and knelt next to her bed. "Now, this is what will happen. You'll give me and my brother turns because we like to share our toys. You'll pay us the amount Frank asked for and do what we say. Since Charles took something from us, we'll take

something from him. Now be a good little girl and rest up. I'll be back later with company."

"B-but Mom will be here."

"No, your mom is out of town visiting family. Oh, and Bella, if you mention one word about this, you will be sorry." He got up, patted her head, and left.

Bella didn't realize that her dad and uncle were more screwed up than her. If she was a sociopath, they were far worse. She knew the only way to keep them at bay was to get her hands on a large amount of cash. One person had that type of money - Ryan.

That's when she formulated a plan in her head. She didn't realize the obstacle that would stand in her way. It would be the new girl that was coming to Saintwood in the fall. No one knew what would happen, but they knew, whoever she was, she was important.

# CHAPTER 71

## CHANGES

**Alex**

I was sitting in class when I got called down to the office. I didn't understand why. I had kept my head down and did my work.

Kids would pick on me, but I would always stay to myself. It was a lonely existence that I had become accustomed to.

I walked into the office, and the principal and a man stood there.

"Follow me, Alex." The principal gestured to me.

I followed them to his office, and he closed the door. The man stood there, stoic, and I looked at both.

"Alexandra, we have decided that starting next year, you will attend Saintwood High."

Saintwood High? What the hell? That was on the other side of the state! My parents hadn't told me anything about this. To say it confused me was an understatement.

"The transfer must confuse you," the man spoke.

Confused? Confused doesn't even explain half of it, buddy.

"Well, I will clear up the confusion for you. I have decided that Saintwood would be a better fit for you overall."

I stared at him.

"Of course, you will finish your junior year here. Come fall, you will start at Saintwood High School."

I didn't know what to say. I was in absolute shock. What about my parents? My home? Friends? Well, friends didn't matter because I didn't have any.

"You can return to class now," the principal said, dismissing me.

Oh, yeah. I got up and flipped the principal off as I stormed out of the office.

The guy looked at the principal. "Did she flip you off?"

"Yes. Alexandra doesn't speak."

"Is there something wrong with her?"

"No. We evaluated Alex, and no one knows why she doesn't talk, but she doesn't, and it's unnerving."

"I see."

*****

I sat in class and couldn't believe that I was attending a new school next year. It must be a mistake. My parents would have told me if we were moving, but they said nothing.

I went through the rest of the day in utter confusion. I didn't understand. Was I so horrible that they were kicking me out of school and sending me to another school? Did I do something wrong? I didn't cause trouble. Hell, I didn't even talk.

After school, I walked home with my shoulders slumped. Wasn't it bad enough that my classmates hated me? Now the school was rejecting me. This sucked.

I walked inside my house to discover my parents talking to a man. I walked into the living room, and they looked at me.

"Hi, Hunny," Mom said, smiling.

I stood there.

"We have some exciting news! We're moving!"

My eyes widened, and my jaw slacked.

My dad got up and walked over to me. "This gentleman has offered me an excellent job." He gestured to the guy in the chair.

The man stood and walked over to me. "Alexandra, you'll find it's a better opportunity for you and your parents."

I swallowed as I looked at him.

"We have everything set for your family and you. There is a house waiting for you, and school is all set."

"Saintwood High," I whispered.

"Yes."

"Hunny, this is what we've wanted. Now we can get our life back with a second chance," Mom said.

I closed my mouth and took a deep breath, then said, "Okay." I turned and walked upstairs to my room.

*****

3rd person

"That went well," the man said.

"Alex doesn't talk much." Greg sighed.

"Most teens would throw a fit."

"Not Alex. We're lucky if she does anything."

The man turned and extended his hand. "Mr. and Mrs. Hartley, you will find everything in order. I will send movers to pack your house and move you. Everything is waiting for you. If

you have questions, please call this number." The man handed them a card.

Greg took it, and the man left.

The man walked out to a car and got into the back seat.

"Well?" Someone asked.

"They're all set."

"And the girl?"

"She didn't fight it." He shrugged.

"Good. This should be a smooth transition."

"Mr. Jones, how will you keep her safe?"

"I have three boys that will do the job. My nephew and his two friends will keep her safe."

"And what if one gets involved with her?"

He looked at him with his blue eyes. "I'm counting on it. If my theory is correct, and it usually is, he will protect the girl with his life. His loyalty is like no other." He turned to the driver. "Head to the airport. I have business."

The driver nodded and pulled out, driving to the airport. They pulled up, and he got out, buttoning his suit coat. The other man climbed out and followed him as they boarded a plane and took a seat.

"Hunter, take us home."

"Yes, Mason." Hunter walked into the cockpit and gave the orders to the pilot. With that, they took off and headed home.

Once they landed, a car was waiting for them. Mason climbed in with his assistant, and they made their way home, with Hunter at the wheel. Mason made calls and eventually hung up

as they pulled up in front of his house. He got out as his wife greeted him.

"How did it go?" She asked.

"Well, Greg and his wife agreed."

"Mason, why are you doing this?"

"Because a child is not a pawn. She doesn't deserve it for the sake of the past, and it would be the same way if it were Cole. It's one time I can't stand by and do nothing."

"And what if one of them gets involved with her?"

"Then so be it. No one should decide who someone falls in love with, which should be their own doing. Charles thought he was so smart. Not only did he mess up and do the wrong thing, but he thought he had everything figured out. Little did he realize that someone else changed things."

"Who?"

"His son." He walked away from her and walked inside only to be met by Joseph. "Now what?"

"Mason, we have a problem."

"What kind of problem?"

Joseph handed him a file, and Mason opened it.

He read it and looked at Joseph. "Are you fucking kidding me?"

"No. I had the tests run three times by different people."

He closed the file. "Call little brother and tell him I would like a word and tell him that I'm not happy!" He walked to the kitchen, opened the fridge, and pulled out items to make a sandwich. The trip famished him, and he needed a full stomach, especially if he planned on yelling at his brother.

It was another mess to clean up. Why couldn't Mason's brothers stay out of trouble?

His phone rang. "What?" He listened to the person on the other end. "Tell Hector that if his psychotic brothers do anything, I will put a bullet in their heads." He ended the call and tossed his phone onto the counter. He continued eating his sandwich as his phone rang again. He picked it up. "Yes?"

The person on the other end spoke.

He listened. "That's a shame, but I warned you and told you not to touch them. Yeah? We'll see about that." He ended the call and made a call.

*Hello?*

"It's Mason. I'm coming to visit you."

*Do I want to know why?*

"No, but we have a problem. I'll be there in an hour."

*Fine.*

He hung up the phone and finished his sandwich. He set the dishes in the sink and walked out of the kitchen and past Joseph.

"Where are you going?" Joseph asked.

"To take care of a problem. Tell Carrington to wait. I'll be back later." Mason walked out of the house and got into the back of a black explorer, and Hunter got into the front and drove off.

Someone created a mess. That figures.

# CHAPTER 72

## A MEETING

**3rd person**

Hunter pulled up in front of a house, and Mason exited the explorer. He walked up to a door and knocked as someone answered, and he stepped inside with the door closing behind him.

"It's been a long time, Mason," the man said.

Mason looked at him. "This isn't a social visit. If you want a social visit, call Charles. I'm here to discuss business."

"You're quick and to the point."

The door opened and closed as three rowdy boys came barreling through the house. The man looked at them, as did Mason.

"Sorry, Dad," one boy said.

He gave them a look and walked to his office, with Mason following him.

"I'm sorry about my son and his friends. They're young."

"I'm used to it, and I have a boy of my own and nephews." Mason took a seat.

"So, what's the problem?"

"Ramon and Carlos have been causing problems, from what I understand."

"Have you talked to Hector?"

"Yes. Hector tried to assure me that his brothers weren't messing with my family, but they were planning something. Ever since Charles pulled the stunt he did, I've had to clean up mess after mess after mess." He sighed.

"I warned him it was bad, but he didn't listen."

"That's why I took care of things on our end. We have pulled that family's ass out of trouble countless times, and now they're messing with mine."

"Mason, your father made a deal with that family years ago. When the head died, the oldest boy took over. He doesn't care. If you get in his way, he won't hesitate to eliminate you."

Mason rubbed his chin, thinking. "Fine. Deliver a message from me."

"What's that?"

"You tell Luis if he fucks with my family, I will not hesitate to take his out one by one, and I won't be nice about it."

"I'll visit them and will assure you, Mason. If they try anything, I will have my crew take them out. Fucking cartels are always causing trouble," he mumbled.

"Brian, they always do when they get messed up with drugs and guns."

"So, what's with Charles making a deal with the devil?"

"Yeah, it's another bad judgment from my brother. The only difference is he wasn't counting on his son getting involved."

"Ryan, right?"

"Yes."

"I've met him a few times. He's a good kid with a good head on his shoulders. Ace hit it off with him."

"Ryan is different. He has this way about him and two friends that are loyal to him. I've never seen someone that commands loyalty as he does, and it's quite unusual."

"Because he's a natural-born leader. Mason, that kid is like Ace, and they command loyalty because it's who they are."

"That's why I stepped in and made some changes. I refuse to allow my younger brother to make decisions for someone with no idea of his bad dealings because it's not fair or right."

"So, who is it?"

"It's a girl. From what I gather, she's different."

"How so?"

"She doesn't talk."

"Is she deaf?"

"No."

"Mute?"

"No."

"What's the deal?"

"That is the thing. No one knows, and not even the girl's parents. The girl says one or two words at the most. Other than that, she does not talk."

He scratched his head. "She needs the right people to bring her out of her shell."

Mason thought about it. "She's shy."

"That would be my guess."

"Interesting. I have to get back." He stood up as Brian stood. "I must deal with a different mess with Carrington."

"Good luck." He chuckled.

Mason shook his hand and walked out.

Brian picked up the phone and made a call. "Luis? It's Brian Morgan. You and I have a problem."

*What's the problem?*

"Your family has breached the deal that our families made years ago. So, this is how it will work. If they do anything to the Jones family, my guys will visit you."

*You have my word that we will not touch them.*

"Good, because I would hate it to come down to that. You might head a cartel, Luis. But I'm a boss. Don't fuck with me because I don't like it."

There was a sigh on the other end. *You have my word.*

"Yeah, well, your word doesn't mean shit to me. It's your only warning, Luis." Brian ended the call and sat down. A boss had its advantages but also came with problems and headaches.

The Jones family was powerful and ruthless. They weren't into illegal activities but could be dangerous, and that's why he kept them on his good side, especially Mason.

You didn't mess with Mason because he wouldn't hesitate to take out someone in a blink of an eye. It didn't matter who you were. If Mason was coming to him, it was in good faith.

*****

Mason climbed into the explorer.

Hunter turned to him. "Is everything good, Mason?"

"Let's hope so. Hunter, get a team together when we return. I have a job for you."

"Yes, Mason."

With that, Hunter pulled out, heading to Mason's house.

*****

"Bring Ramon and Carlos to me, Hector." Luis sat in a chair.

"Yes, brother," he said, leaving the room, only to return a few minutes later with the two younger men.

"You wanted us?" Ramon asked.

"Sit." He ordered them.

Both sat down.

"What's this about?" Carlos asked.

"It's about your extracurricular activities of late. Since you're both young and stupid, I will tell you. Whatever you're planning, don't."

"We don't know what you're talking about, brother," Ramon said.

Luis gave him a stern look. "I'm not fucking stupid. You want to fuck around on your wife, fine. But I recognize the girl that has been coming here. I'm warning you both. Whore or no whore, I do not want a war."

"We're having some fun," Carlos said.

"Fun?" He stood up and looked at both. "When a boss calls me because another family called him, that isn't fun. That is trouble. I'm warning you both. I know what you both have been doing, and I want it to stop." It was an order. When the head of the family spoke, you listened. Or you got a bullet in your head.

"Fine." Carlos got up and walked away.

Luis looked at Ramon. "I mean it."

"Whatever you say, Luis." Ramon got up and walked away.

"Well, that had gone well," Hector said.

"Don't count on it. I want you to watch our brothers. Carlos is young, and Ramon influences him too much. No one is to touch the Jones family unless I say so," Luis said, walking away.

The Santiagos were young but dangerous. The boys wouldn't learn the full extent of it until later. It was a deal, which Ryan would regret later.

# CHAPTER 73

## ALL HELL BREAKS LOOSE

**Ryan**

We stood at my locker when we heard a scream. The three of us glanced at each other and took off in the scream's direction. We stopped to see Mario and his goons surrounding Elena.

Oh, hell no. Elena can take one, but not all three.

The three of us rushed them. Before Mario and his goons realized what had happened, we yanked them from her and shielded Elena.

"Oh, it's the big bad boys coming to protect the little girl," Mario said.

I looked at Jordan and Frazier as they looked at me. We started cracking our knuckles and smiling. It would be a suitable time for them to run away, which they didn't—big mistake.

They got tossed through the air without pants and bloody lips and noses. Jordan thought beating the shit out of them was enough, and Frazier preferred to pant them.

They ran past everyone as people laughed. We held up their pants.

I tossed a pair aside and turned to Elena. "What are you doing here?"

"I came to get things situated for next year, and they ended up cornering me," she said.

"Does that mean you're not coming back until next year?" Jordan asked her.

"Yeah. I have the grades that I don't need to return until my senior year."

"Well, at least you're coming back," Frazier said.

"True. Weirdly, I've missed school," Elena said, looking around.

"Man, you are weird to miss this place," I said with a look, causing us to laugh.

I missed having Elena at school. Even though Elena is a pain in the ass, I still miss her.

As we stood there and talked, Bella walked up. We turned and looked at her, and she looked like hell.

"What's a matter with chu?" Frazier mustered the worst possible Italian accent.

"I had a rough night, okay?" She snapped at him.

"Bella, what's wrong?" Elena asked.

Then she started crying. "It's Paul, and we had this horrible fight, and he might break up with me." She became so upset that she hyperventilated.

Elena hugged her. "It's okay. I'm sure it has been a bad night, and everything will blow over." She rubbed her back, comforting her.

"What will I do if we break up? I love him so much."

"How about you and I have a girl's day and pamper ourselves?"

"Okay." She sniffled.

They walked out of the school.

Frazier asked, "What the hell was that?"

"Got me." I shrugged.

The rest of the day was fine. Then we got detention because of what we did to Mario and his cronies. When you pant someone, the school frowns upon it. Well, so is beating the shit out of them, but here we are.

I sat in detention on top of one desk. Jordan threw a tennis ball at the wall, sitting at the desk with his feet propped on it. Cassen walked in, stopped, gave Frazier a glimpse, and shook his head.

"Really, Dylan?"

"What can I say? You have the comfiest chair that my butt has ever graced." He grinned.

Cassen walked over and leaned against the front of his desk. "What did you boys do this time?"

"Oh, a little of this. A little of that," I said.

"Beat the shit out of Mario and his stupid friends." Jordan threw the ball against the wall and caught it as it bounced back.

"Did we mention we pants them as well?" Frazier asked him. He raised his eyebrows and chuckled.

As we sat there talking, Josh burst into the room. "Jordan!"

Jordan stopped and looked at him as his brows furrowed. We got up and walked over to him.

"What happened, Josh?" Jordan asked.

"I came out of the locker room and got jumped." Josh had a bloody nose, and his clothes were a mess.

"By whom?" I asked.

"A guy with dark hair and two of his buddies." Josh tried to get the words out.

Then Jordan hauled off, threw the ball, slammed it into the wall, and got it stuck. He stormed out of the room.

We looked at it.

Frazier said, "I would say Jordan's pissed."

We raced out of there and after him. He had a head start and was faster. We chased him, and he took on Mario and his buddies.

He dropped one while he slammed his fist into another, followed by him tossing another. When Jordan got pissed, no one could take him. He beat the shit out of all three of them.

He would have killed them if Frazier didn't jump on his back. I have no idea what possessed him to do that. Sometimes, Frazier doesn't think things all the way through.

I shook my head and let out a sigh. Better help the yahoo before Jordan kills him.

I jumped on them, taking them down and causing us to crash on the floor.

Of course, Jordan struggled. "Get off of me!"

"No can do, you lovable lunatic. We let you up, you kill them, and we lose you to prison. Orange isn't your color," Frazier said.

"They hurt Josh!"

"And you hurt them," I said.

"Let me go!"

"On one condition," Frazier said.

He stopped struggling and looked at him. "What's that?"

"That you let me give you a big wet kiss." He puckered his lips.

"Oh, hell no, you freak!" He pushed us off and stood up.

We both stood up.

"Frazier, you even think about kissing me. I swear to god, I will beat the shit out of you!"

"Aww, come on, Jordy. Kiss Frazier." Frazier walked towards Jordan with his hands out, smacking his lips. Jordan took off as Frazier laughed.

"Was that necessary?" I asked.

"Nope, but it was funny." He chuckled.

"Is there something you want to tell me?" I arched an eyebrow at him.

"Dude, I'm not gay, and I have no issue with gay people, but it gets under Jordan's skin." He smirked.

"I wonder about you sometimes, Frazier." I shook my head and walked away.

He followed suit. We stepped over the crumpled mess of Mario and his cronies.

"Can we watch Mean Girls tonight?"

"No."

"Aw, come on! It's funny!" He chased after me.

Sometimes, I wonder about my friends. They're nuts, but I can't imagine my life without them.

# CHAPTER 74

## END OF THE SCHOOL YEAR

**Ryan**

The end of Junior year came quickly. Between everything that happened and beating up Mario and company, I looked forward to downtime this summer.

With Jordan and Frazier around, summer wouldn't be dull. As for Bella, she worked things out with Paul, and she even introduced him to us. He's decent.

I might have misjudged her, but then again, I'm the tooth fairy, too. I still had my reservations about her. Frazier had an issue with her but never elaborated. He's polite, but he forced it.

Jordan still didn't trust her and had his reasons, and I trusted him. She and Elena became closer, so she came around more.

One evening we talked like two people do, and she leaned over.

I pulled back. "What are you doing?"

"Oh. I thought…."

"What? Because we talked, you thought it gave you the green light to kiss you?" I ran my hand through my hair. "It was a conversation, but I'm not interested. Plus, you have a boyfriend."

She inched closer to me. "And if I didn't have a boyfriend?"

I got off the couch. "It wouldn't matter, Bella. I'm not interested in you in that way. So, please stop." I walked away. This girl didn't take a hint. The only girl I wanted wasn't here

because she hadn't arrived yet. I'm not sure what to expect when she comes. I had little to go on except she was intelligent and beyond beautiful.

She had beautiful light brown hair and the prettiest grey eyes I had ever seen. Something about her drew me to her, and I didn't know what it was. When we came face to face, things would get interesting, and something in my gut told me it would.

*****

**Alex**

It's the last day of school where I would ever have to deal with these people with the mocking, the jokes, the name-calling. All I ever wanted was to fit in, but I never did.

My shyness overtook me, and it became hard to speak to people. If I even tried to open my mouth, people would already reject me. I walked home, appearing like the biggest reject ever. Not one person offered to become my friend or talk to me. Not one person.

I sat home during every dance. No homecoming, junior prom, or dance because no one had asked me. I clenched my books to my chest in hopes a guy would ask me, but they never did.

In grade school, kids would get a Valentine while my little pocket stayed empty. The kids got excited as I sat in the back with my head down. Why did no one like me? Am I so terrible? I didn't understand.

Middle school was worse. I sat alone at lunch and by myself at school functions, so I dove into books. Books became my only

friend and salvation and helped to develop my love for reading. The library became my haven. The librarian was kind to me, often allowing me to sit in her office, so I read or worked on homework.

High school was the same, so I gave up ever wanting friends. It's easier that way. It didn't matter, though, because they always made me feel like shit.

I entered the house and headed to my room. We had to pack since the movers would be here tomorrow to take us to our new home. Come this fall, I will start my senior year at Saintwood High, but I wasn't sure whether it should excite or scare me.

How are the students? Would they be nice, or would they be the same as the others? Would things be different? I packed my stuff, then took a shower and changed for bed.

I laid in bed and stared out of the window. As I looked at the stars, I wondered what waited for me.

*****

**Ryan**

I came out of the bathroom in a pair of sweats, strolled over to my window, and peered into the night sky. The stars were brighter than usual, and I had to wonder if she looked at the same stars as me.

What was she like? Was she friendly, funny, or snobby? God, I hope she's not pretentious.

Was her skin soft? Her lips? Why did I think about these things? She might not even like me.

My mind drifted to her. I had to meet her and learn everything about her. The thought of her drove me nuts since I only had that stupid file and picture. Other than that, I knew nothing about her.

I wasn't even sure when she would start school, but this summer couldn't end fast enough. Whatever happened, I would make Alexandra Hartley mine.

# CHAPTER 75

## SUMMER BREAK

**Alex**

I dressed, walked out of the house, got into the car, and didn't look back. No one wouldn't miss me, and I wouldn't miss them.

Dad pulled out of the driveway, as did the movers. We drove towards Saintwood. While Dad and Mom talked in the front seat, I sat in the back and read. It was a three-hour trip, which gave me time to read.

Before I knew it, we pulled up into a driveway, and a man waited for us. We got out of the car, and I looked up at the house, which was nice.

I glanced around, and it's your typical cul-de-sac type of neighborhood. I closed the car door and followed my parents.

We walked up to the man, and he opened the file. "I need you to sign these papers, Mr. Hartley."

Dad took them and asked, "What are they?"

"It's paperwork regarding the house and your new job."

Dad signed the documents and handed them back to him.

The guy handed him the keys. "Enjoy your new home, Mr. Hartley." He walked away.

Dad opened the door, and we walked inside. They had already furnished the house and even decorated the walls. What in the world?

I walked upstairs and opened the door to find my room. I walked inside, and it seemed interesting. I noticed an envelope on the desk, opened it, and read the contents.

*Alexandra,*

*I hope you find everything to your liking. I took extra precautions to make sure things were to your specifications.*

*You'll find that everything is waiting for you. On September 5, you'll start your senior year at Saintwood High, and they're expecting you.*

*Trust me. You will find this is the best decision for all.*

*M*

Who the heck is M, and who's expecting me? This situation is beyond weird.

*\*\*\*\*\**

**Ryan**

"Will you boys sit around all summer in the house?" Elena asked us.

"Why not?" I asked with a shrug.

"Because it's summer before our senior year." She smiled.

"You make it sound like it's supposed to be a big deal."

"Because it is," Bella said.

"Summer is about being lazy and lounging around the house as lazy asses." Frazier stretched out on the couch.

"Say you."

He shrugged.

"Summer blows." Jordan tossed a ball in the air while lying on the couch.

"Since you three idiots are moping around the house, we're hitting the beach," Elena said.

"Have fun," we said.

She shrugged and left with Bella.

I had no intention of going to the beach and didn't need Bella trying to put the moves on me again. Her trying to kiss me still made me uneasy. The less time I'm alone with her, the better.

"So, when are we supposed to get the package?" Frazier asked me.

"Dad said she would arrive this summer and start at Saintwood in the fall. We need to keep our eyes open for her," I replied.

"Is there anything we should know about her?" Jordan asked me.

"The day she starts at Saintwood High. Other than that, Dad said nothing else."

"So, let me get this straight. All we have is a picture, and the girl's super smart, but we know nothing other than that about her. Fanfuckingtastic," Frazier said.

"I guess we will find out soon enough," I said.

Yep, this situation screwed us.

*****

The summer flew by. Thank God. Jordan and Frazier got on my fucking nerves. If I hear Frazier recite Mean Girls one more time, I will knock his teeth out.

On top of that, I had to deal with Bella and her stupid flirting. It got to where I barked at her. Some girls didn't get it through their fucking heads. Not every guy is interested in them. She's one of those girls, and I'm one of those guys.

School would be a welcome distraction for once because she would be there. Thank God. God I, hope she is everything I imagined.

*****

**Alex**

I came out of the bathroom, turned off the light, and climbed into bed. Tomorrow's the first day of school and the first day of senior year. The first day in a new school, with meeting new people that would ignore me. Great.

"Saintwood?" Saying the name out loud sounded foreign to me but any time I spoke seemed foreign to me. It's a weird concept.

I laid in bed and rolled over. Dad would drive me tomorrow to learn where I'm going when I'm on my own. That's fine. I'm used to being alone and have become accustomed to it.

I didn't realize my life would change tomorrow. I hope people leave me alone so I get through my senior year with minor bumps.

Something deep down told me that would never happen. My life would get flipped upside down, and it would be because of the three most feared boys.

# CHAPTER 76

## HERE WE GO

**Ryan**

I got up early, got ready, and had to pick up frick and frack for school. I swear, sometimes I'm like a damn chauffeur. I came downstairs and grabbed a bite on my way out the door.

Elena rode with Bella to school. Thank God. I didn't need to deal with her bullshit. Not today of all days.

I started the car, pulled out of the driveway, and let the engine roar. I picked up Frazier and Jordan from their houses.

Jordan and Frazier fought on the way to school like they usually do. It's Frazier's fault because he torments Jordan, and Jordan smacks him, followed by me having to separate them. It's a vicious cycle.

We pulled into the parking lot and got out. The three of us walked up to the school.

"Senior year," Frazier said, letting out a low whistle.

"It's about damn time. I hate this fucking place," Jordan said.

I rolled my eyes as we walked inside. This year we had lockers next to each other, thanks to Frazier. You got to love his computer skills. I tossed my stuff into my locker and closed it.

We all went our separate ways. I headed to the boy's bathroom since nature calls.

*****

**Jordan**

I found myself in a fight in class. Of course, the teacher tried to break it up and got an elbow to the nose. Leave it to me to land in the principal's office on my first day.

As I walked to the office, I turned to walk inside when someone bumped into me, causing them to drop their stuff. I crouched and helped the person pick up their things when our eyes met.

We stood up, but I said nothing. The girl scooted around me and walked away, not saying a word.

*****

**Ryan**

I heard the bell. Shit. I'm late on my first day. Even if I try to be on time, it always falls through. Well, if I'm going to be late, I'll make my entrance dramatic.

I flung the door open, letting it crash against the wall and alerting everyone to my presence.

The teacher glanced at me. "Ah, Mr. Jones, nice of you to join us."

I mumbled, "Yeah." I waved him off, strolled to an empty desk, took a seat, and turned my head to see a girl. She turned her head and faced me as my chocolate brown eyes met her steel-grey eyes. She averted her eyes.

I sat there, staring at her. It's her. The girl in the picture was sitting next to me, and she was breathtaking. I kept staring at

her. Throughout the class, I glanced at her because I couldn't help it. She was here in the flesh.

When class ended, she got up and took off. Shit. I needed to talk to her.

Each class, I waited to see if she was in my other classes, but she was only in my first hour. Damn it.

I was at my locker when Jordan walked up and rambled on about a girl he met twice, saying how beautiful she was. She couldn't be any more beautiful than Alexandra, who's stunning, quiet, and didn't ramble about frivolous things like most girls did.

Then Frazier walked up on cloud nine. He bragged about how he got this girl to talk to him. What else is new?

Then I added how I met the best girl ever but never told them that it was her. I didn't need them getting the wrong idea. No way would I let them get a shot, and not this time. She's mine.

As we talked, a locker closed next to us. We all turned around to see Alexandra, and she looked hella confused. None of us said a word, and not even Frazier, which surprised Jordan and me. The idiot always has some stupid thing to say.

We stood there.

She took a deep breath, held out her hand, and said, "Hi, I'm Alexandra Hartley."

An intoxicated voice spoke four words. Alexandra's voice was soft, warm, and beautiful, like her.

We all shook her hand and introduced ourselves to her. She gave us a smile, turned, and walked away. We watched her leave. As she turned the corner, she stopped, glanced back, and smiled.

I stood there. At that moment, I realized one thing. I'm in love and deep shit.

We left school and headed to my house. We walked in and sat down in the living room. As Frazier and Jordan yammered on about her, I rubbed my chin with my finger, thinking.

She's nothing like I expected, but more. I also knew that I would have to handle this delicately. Something told me that she's nothing like any girl I had ever met. I didn't know whether that was good or bad, but I would make her mine, and that was a promise.

Made in the USA
Monee, IL
19 December 2023

49820038R00247